THEN AND US

THEN AND US

KEN CHAMPION

First published March 2022

ISBN 978-1-913144-30-2

Cover drawing by the author

PENNILESS PRESS PUBLICATIONS
Website :www.pennilesspress.co.uk/books

Keefie

'This is a splendid novel of the London Blitz that captures life mostly through the eyes of a bright and creative working class boy whose knowledge of what is happening is limited, but whose experience leads us deep into a time and place – and the lives of ordinary people – with more power than any history book can convey.'

Meredith Sue Willis, Books For Readers, USA

Noir

'A book of great depth, tightly written and with a surprise - and so much life - on almost every page. It's an unusual, gripping book.'

Meredith Sue Willis, Books For Readers, USA

Thrust

'In this expansive novel, at times angry, funny, touching and tender, the author confidently strides the world's stage posing huge questions that need to be answered. It is a compelling read.'

Chris Connelley, Hastings Independent

The Politicos

'A seasoned portraitist of a changing London, Champion captures 'the shifting landscape and language of the city he so clearly loves, embracing the personal as well as the political in an epic novel.'

Chris Connelley, Hastings Independent

Future Tense

'Ken Champion's Future Tense is a novel of ideas brought to life by a cast of characters struggling in a new world order where Equality under a neo-liberal regime has been codified to an authoritarian extreme in an Orwellian dystopia. Meanwhile, the true master - internationally conglomerate capitalism - has the puppets tangle their own strings. Champion leaves room for doubt and a semblance of redemption even if the better times of childhood may be more false dawns. With a strong, contemporary premise tackling head-on the prominent controversies of today, this book ought to come with some kind of health warning.'

Phillip Ruthen, Waterloo Press

1

He had first heard of the place when sitting on a tram and listening to two elderly women talking about it.

'Ooh yeh, it's going to be lots of big 'ouses with gardens and trees, gonna have shops and things, too.'

It had been mostly fields when he had first come here almost two years before.

Now, there were piles of scaffolding, and you could tell there were houses behind them because of the empty shapes in the brickwork for the windows to go. Apparently, the houses weren't going to be represented as numbers on plots but be given names; if his own home had a name it would be 'Measly', or 'Squashed', something like that.

It was going to be a Garden City, he liked this term. He had a sudden picture of himself as a boy with some toy wooden houses he'd set out on the small, ragged lawn at home and tried to make a street with them but didn't have enough. He didn't really want to think about that time anyway, and if he lived here he wouldn't have to.

But at the moment it was nearly all countryside; alright to visit for a few days, but to live so near trees and streams and a horizon he could see as he looked across the estuary… well, that was different. There was such a lot of space, it was so flat, it would be lonely, wouldn't it?

He had been here with his parents as a child; it had been a farm then. He had a photo of himself when he was about ten in his school team's football shirt trying to milk a cow. The place had smelt of horse dung and mud; every time he smelt the latter a part of him was at the farm again. But it wasn't called a farm any more; it was now the land bought by Richard Colls, the builder, to create his city in a garden.

He would like to have had the money to buy a house here, 'though it would be a while before they were finished, of course. He looked at the scaffolds again, turned and began making his way across the fields in the direction of those few homes he'd been told were almost finished, he'd heard that one or two roads had been made up, too.

After walking through fields, he came to a stream with a large, recently-laid pipe crossing it, no doubt to do with the building works, but he still felt he was in the middle of the country. From where he was, he couldn't see any buildings at all. Builders, he mused, were our unsung heroes, without them the world would be all mountains, forests, jungles, icecaps and deserts.

Making his way across the stream by walking along the pipe he continued down a path leading to a small, barn-like shed. There was a display of flowers in tubs around it, the upper half of its typical Essex black obscured by yellow paint on which was a sign saying, 'Richard Colls Limited', and above it a larger one reading, 'Ash Park Estate Office'. He remembered then that the farm had been called Ash Farm. It seemed like a good marketing ploy, to let potential home buyers know that they really would be living on ex-farmland, a country estate, or rather, an estate in the country.

He went to the door and used its ornate knocker. It opened, and a smiling, rather chubby man in a waistcoat beckoned him in. The walls were covered with sketches and watercolour prints of houses in a similar style to railway posters. Among some flat-roofed ones were gabled semi-detacheds with large front gardens and wide, flower-lined paths, one showing a car at its side and a female figure in a red coat and hat about to enter a front door.

'Yes, that's what they'll look like,' said the man. 'And here,' he turned to the opposite wall, 'are the other types. One I particularly like, though I shouldn't state a preference, is this suntrap one,' he pointed to another water colour. 'Pretty modern, eh? Sort of glitzy. They've got names.' He pointed to the prints. 'That's 'Rosewood', that one's 'Vilette', and that there is 'Arcadia''.

His listener liked the last one best, it had a certain ring to it; he wasn't sure what it meant but it sounded like some sort of utopia to him. Bending forward, he peered at its curved Critall window.

'I can just about imagine the Tudorbethan ones, but hard to believe that the... what do they call them? - the Moderne, will exist around here though.'

'They will,' said the man. 'Very stylish. Americanish. Are you interested in purchasing a house, Mister... ?'

'Woods, George Woods.'

'Want a cup of tea?'

'Tea as well?'

'Yes, we aim to please.'

There was a gas cooker behind the makeshift counter and some cups on a tray.

'We also have some slices of lemon cake, on the house, forgive the pun.'

'Are all estate offices like this?'

The man chuckled. 'I shouldn't think so. This is a big project that's being developed here and we want it to be community-centred.'

George asked him how big it was going to be.

'Almost two farms worth: seven thousand homes on six hundred acres with two churches, four shopping areas and a cinema. And lots more.'

'Going to take a time.'

'Sooner than you think, young man, and before then we'll run special buses from the East End to here. The station's almost completed, so we'll probably pay for free travel for potential buyers and then we'll have salesmen pick them up and take them around the estate. Incidentally, this,' he flicked his hand, 'is only a temporary office, the proper one'll be at the a junction of The Avenue and Timmins Lane.'

He gave his visitor his tea and cake and gestured behind him to a small table and two chairs. George sat down.

'A quarter of a mile away are some homes almost finished.'

'They'll be quite something if they're as good as your pictures.'

'Go and see for yourself.'

George finished his repast while the agent busied himself with some papers, thanked the man and left, heading in the direction indicated.

It wasn't long before he saw them, behind a copse of trees, a row of them, they looked like the gabled variety, he'd forgotten their name. He walked over a narrow railway track and saw a hopper truck filled with sand and cement, and another close behind piled with bricks and pieces of timber. He supposed this was the builder's way of getting material around the site, at least until more roads were laid. Then, moving around a tree, he saw the crane, he hadn't noticed it before; it was the biggest he'd ever seen. It was scooping up buckets of ballast which it took up towards the top and somehow crushed it then fed it down in a huge pipe to a large cement mixer at the bottom of the crane. He guessed it would be taken to the hoppers by the rail line.

As he got nearer the homes, noticing there were more workmen on this part of the site, he could see their gables standing generous and proud. The road was still being worked on, they seemed to be doing it in two halves; the half nearest the houses was finished as was the pavement. He walked along it. He liked the sunray front gates, and the coloured yachts and sailing ships in the leaded glass of the doors and the ample front gardens with set-back garages.

He walked some more until he came to what looked like an end-of-row house. A builder was on the scaffold spreading render on the bricks below the green, metal frame windows, moving his trowel smoothly across the cement. It would probably be painted white as would the chimney stack.

It was different from the others; its long windows were curved at their ends and had more glass in its door. The man was right: 'Americanish', there was even a recently planted palm tree in the front. He went closer to look in the window at the newly plastered walls and ceilings.

He could imagine Dietrich inside, maybe talking with Gable and smoking a Lucky Strike cigarette, tossing her hair back as she blew out the smoke. Maybe Joan Crawford or Cagney would come in and join them. It was so different, this place, as different from the house and the street he had been raised in as if they were on a different planet. He was filled with the images of both, and what went with them.

They were Victorian and his, or rather, his mother's, was one of many in a long, packed, treeless terrace: slate roofs, cluttered chimneys, small, narrow windows above a mean bay window next to a skinny, porch-less front door.

He had a memory of h imself as a boy of climbing on a heap of coal in the cellar, standing and stretching his neck to peer out through the narrow grill beneath the front doorstep and watching out for Bill the coalman and getting out of the cellar before the latter emptied the sack from his shoulder and deposited its contents into the manhole in the paving stone in front of the door.

He thought of the outdoor toilet, the aluminium bath hanging from the fence for its Friday night use, the black stove, the cast-iron fireplace bars, the smell of Brasso, the stair rods and patterned carpets…. He knew every square inch of the place: the slightly loose panel in the cellar door, the floorboard that had creaked outside the parlour, his mother's mahogany wardrobe… he could have gone on.

Then there was the tree-climbing over the park, playing cowboys and Indians - he liked being shot, he'd been the best at pretending to die - playing knock-down-ginger, odds and evens, Tin-Can Tommy, cricket down the middle of the street and footie under the lamppost outside the Brown's house.

There was little to remember about the war, he knew little of it, he'd been too young; except, of course, that his father had died in it, in Flanders, inside of a tank. He'd found out later that a shell fired from a British Mark IV tank captured by the Germans had pierced the side and ricocheted around inside, reducing its occupants to a pink spawn.

Then another memory. As a child, he'd been taken to see an aunt, his father's sister who he'd heard described as 'posh,' on the other side of London. Her home had a wood-panelled hall, rooms with picture rails and friezes, but the house opposite had white stucco and long lines of sparkling glass; it would probably have chrome taps as well, he thought. He'd never seen one like this before, he knew only of dark, grimy brick ones.

He'd had a book at home called 'The Pink Cloud,' with illustrations of an aeroplane flying low over white houses then ascending until it was swallowed up by a cloud and enveloped in a world of huge plateaus, jungles, vast rivers and dinosaur-like creatures.

It was the drawings of the airport's control tower and the horizontal lines of the main building that had captured his attention as well as the houses. He had wanted to be in that aeroplane in the cloud looking down on the trees and cliffs, not in the room where he was then sitting: in a corner of a gas-lit, dark-distempered space with brass ornaments on the mantle shelf over a black range stove, and an oak table with table mats and a leftover serviette.

He looked up at the builder, who smiled at him.

'Don't get too near; don't wanna get cement all over yer.'

George hardly heard what he said. He turned and began hurrying back to the estate office, marching purposely over the fields and across the little railway line. It was nothing to do with logic, even rationality, he was aware of that; just… something he had to do.

He knocked on the door of the shed. The man opened it again.

'Ah, it's you. Come in. Interested now are you?'

George took a deep breath.

'I am. It's going to be quite something, isn't it.'

'It certainly is. Do you know the price of the houses? Have you chosen a particular type?'

'Er, yes.' Pointing to one of the pictures on the wall, he said, 'That one.'

'Good choice. It's good value, too. The price, Mister Woods, is five hundred and sixty pounds; a mortgage may be obtained from the Hartford and Co-operative Building Society.'

It sounded like a fortune. For him it was. But, he was in regular, well, almost regular employment, and he was doing okay; at least compared with some of the boys he'd been to school with and who he'd seen recently. Things weren't looking good generally, of course, but seemed to be a little better lately; phrases like 'The Great Depression' weren't quite so prevalent at the moment, and mum was still working at the toy factory where she'd been for quite while now; she'd be okay, though he'd help her out with her rent, of course.

'The deposit is one pound,' the man was saying.

He could afford that, if he didn't have it with him there was enough, and more, in his tin at home.

He reached into his pocket. He had a pound and a few pennies.

'Before I take this,' said the agent, 'I'll show you the map of the estate and you can see the locations of the house-type you've chosen.'

He reached under his counter, produced a map, rolled it out, briefly scrutinised it and pointed to three different locations.

'These,' he said, indicating with his finger, 'will be a row of six and nearer the shops - they'll be called The Broadway - then the ones here and here which will be in the middle of rather long streets.'

'The first one,' his listener replied.

'Fine. I'll take the deposit; give you a document which we'll sign and also a form for the building society. You can actually begin paying before the house is built if you so wish,' the man said with a smile.

He had never been involved with so much money before. He'd done some pretty expensive jobs for the decorating and signwriting firm he worked for, West End places and stuff which he knew his governor had charged a lot for, but nothing in the hundreds he didn't think.

The agent signed a piece of paper, took another sheet which he neatly folded and gave them to his customer who put them in his jacket pocket to look at later before committing himself. But he knew he would.

And, now, he didn't have to think about his childhood, or his little book, or any other reasons why he'd wanted to live here. The estate was almost finished, and he was moving in. Indeed, at this very moment he was sitting on the tailboard of a removal van, swinging his legs as the narrow, cobbled streets and cramped houses receded and he entered a place of broad roads and bright homes with bushes in front gardens and newly-planted pavement trees.

'It's just along here,' he shouted, as if the driver or his boy could hear him anyway, but he liked saying it.

The vehicle slowed and stopped. He reached behind him, took two cases and gave one to the lad who had jumped out of the cab and come around the rear. He then grabbed a chair and carried it towards the garden gate which the driver and his helper, having deposited inside the porch the figured walnut dressing table its owner had managed to get cheap, were holding open for him.

The cloud-back armchair he'd recently bought while working on a shop front in Kensington, he carried himself along the path to the front door, placing it on the step, by the side of which he noticed United Dairies had left a complimentary box of milk, eggs and butter. The driver put a case with some rolls of cartridge paper and drawing materials by its side, returning to the van for a bed headboard and a Valmier rug while the house's new owner proudly got the key out of his pocket, which the day before he'd picked up from the salesman who'd sold the house to him, and opened its door.

He looked at the light, cream-coloured hall, the wide, solid-sided staircase, the single-panelled doors and the parquet floor. He forgot for an instant where he was. He shook his head; the excitement came back as he remembered.

'Excuse me, sir.'

It was the driver, carrying some more of the van's contents, trying to get by him. George liked the 'sir', he'd rarely been addressed thus. It didn't take long between them to get the rest of his belongings in. He should, he supposed, have made them cups of tea, instead, wanting the place to himself, gave the driver and his mate small tips and closed the door behind them.

He sat in the cloud-back chair and looked at its curves; probably the blokes at work would have laughed at it, called it 'fancy,' 'silly,' but then they were probably happy with brass stair rods, floral carpets and cabbage rose wallpaper. He'd seen the inside of most of the house some time before when the site agent had let him wander about, as long as he didn't get in the way of any workmen. The kitchen was still being built and not all the windows were in place, but the shape of the rooms, of all of it really, was... right.

He looked at the floorboards, they were as bare as they had been then, of course; he would use yacht varnish on them and lay his rug. He got up and opened the folding glass-paned doors that partitioned the through-lounge and looked out of the French window at the back of it. There was some eighty feet of new, fenced lawn and, beyond, another garden and the back of what he knew was one on a road of smaller houses.

He returned to the chair. It wouldn't take him long to sort out his belongings and place them in their allocated spots. He should, he knew, have been enthusiastically doing that now, but he wasn't and he was aware of what, and who, was stopping him. It was her. It was Doris. He hadn't told her that he was buying a house, or even that he was actually now moving into it and away from where he'd lived all of his life.

He thought briefly of his mother. She'd wished to meet him here or even come with him, but he'd wanted to do it on his own, he was a big boy, twenty-five soon. He was leaving the nest. He'd only told her a week ago what he was about to do, and she'd been surprised. 'You're too young to buy your own house,' she'd said, but he'd felt, hoped, that there had been some pride there, too. She was also rather hurt, especially when he asked her not to tell Doris. He'd insisted, without really giving her any explanation.

But he would have to tell the girl. He found it hard to explain to himself why he hadn't. He had known her for nearly six months; she was his regular girlfriend; going to the flicks together, the occasional clumsy dances at the town hall, the heavy petting, and more when she let him, though rarely. Once, when his mother had gone to bed, he'd asked her to relieve him and had exposed himself. She'd told him to 'put it away' and that it was 'disgusting.' On one occasion when her parents were away, he'd stayed the night at her home, but didn't tell his mother that her mum and dad weren't there.

It wasn't as if she could live here with him; they couldn't live in sin. They had to be married to live together. That's what you did. What else? But she would expect to be told by him what he was doing, and at least to have a say in choosing furniture, curtains, all sorts of things. She would be so hurt. But he wanted this place for him, didn't want anyone else here, or rather, he realised, with sickening apprehension as he briefly leaned forward in the chair then straightened again; didn't want her.

2

'Yes sir, no sir, three bags full, sir,' Rupert said under his breath as he left his father's study after its owner had again insisted his son read something worthwhile at Oxford like maths or history, not a pointless subject like philosophy.

'If you can do philosophy you can do anything,' Rupert murmured, continuing talking to himself.

As he left the house and made for the park, he wondered whether his father sometimes, just sometimes, thought he was still on the Western Front being a Major and ordering his subalterns about, he was occasionally like it at home and more so in the office. But then, he'd always, as long as his son could remember, had this martinet quality. His father before him had been a colonel in the First Boer War and that was probably why his offspring would persuade and sometimes almost force Rupert to play 'soldiers' as an infant and, later, to play the real thing and enlist. He hadn't.

He should, of course, have worked harder to matriculate six years previously, but instead, he had been lazy he now realised, taking it for granted that it would be easy for him; It hadn't been.

Thus, he'd spent his time between having a good one, involving a fair bit of imbibing with his pals, especially with Andrew, and in his father's office and, more enjoyably, spending time with his mother and helping her rehearse her scripts for the occasional stage roles she was asked to play. He even stayed with her for a few nights in an Aldershot boarding house when she was on tour with a rep company.

As much as she liked her son being with her and occasionally helping her, she told him that he couldn't do this for ever, nor should he continue working for his father, at least not in menial office work. He needed to discover what he wanted to do himself. A start, she suggested, would be to get to Oxford. After two years of evening classes, he had.

He left the house. A milk cart was being pushed along the road in front of him by the ever-reliable milkman, Rupert not seeing it like that; reliability just... was, as it should be. Sometimes the man used a horse and larger cart at weekends when he delivered milk and cream, though not quite the type of nag his father placed wagers on who, more often than not, seemed to win.

He'd been taken by him in his teens to a race meeting at Epsom where, for some reason, they'd taken a position on the rails at Tattenham Corner, and seeing these supposedly elegant animals in full flight and catching glimpses only of their receding arses, any interest in his parent's favourite sport had been nullified.

It wasn't just quadrupeds that defined their difference in interests; Rupert felt at times that they inhabited different symbolic universes. His parent's rigid view of the world, a place for those born to lead and those destined to obey and of 'good' and 'bad' people', meaning the British ruling class and their allies, and the Huns; of 'real' men, validated by his military days, of those who went 'over the top' and fought with guts and bayonets in intimate combat, was not akin to his.

He at times appeared such a stereotype, Rupert wondered if he used to wax his moustache when on duty. His parent didn't seem to like anything 'modern.' He was still suspicious of the wireless, especially when his son listened to dance music. The BBC would, from time to time, play swing jazz and boogie, which he thought were not 'proper' tunes, songs were too sentimental and the lyrics too 'American.' The flounces and frills of women's dresses were too 'fussy' and the beret too 'cheeky'. He still called films 'talkies' he didn't think Groucho Marx was funny and thought 42nd Street and Dietrich in The Blue Angel 'too sexual.' The only sartorial exception he made to modernity seemed to be the tweed suit he wore.

Rupert didn't like the manner in which he treated his mother either, he appeared to order her about at times as if she were his batman, although he could, on occasions, be generous towards her, buying her expensive clothes and jewellery, possibly, Rupert thought, he'd done so mainly to show her off at the functions they went to, like his old regiment's get-togethers and the occasional Freemasons' grand balls.

He appeared ambivalent about her choice of career, a wavering between pride in her talent and whether she was in a trade meant for harlots.

Rupert needed to get his things packed for university: some text books which would probably be rather redundant at this level and some clothes - he wasn't sure whether he was supposed to always look smart or whether, under the gowns, casual wear would be acceptable. He hoped he didn't have to wear a mortar board, he thought they looked rather silly, especially the tassels. Exeter college sounded... he wasn't sure whether 'exciting' was the word, but he was looking forward to it a great deal.

The previous evening he had taken his father for a drink at the local hostelry. He had forced himself to do so, he hadn't done it before. It had been quite crowded so they'd sat at a table with others. The conversation was stilted, the elder talking of his new housing development outside east London, which Rupert had worked on in the office in its initial stages, and the latter trying to interest his father in the part his mother had in her latest play. He was interested in neither the role nor the story. 'As long as it makes her happy, son,' he'd said, which Rupert had translated as 'As long as she's occupied and makes little demand on my time and returns to continue her domestic obeisance.' Perhaps he was being unfair, he wasn't sure.

Halfway through the conversation his parent, gesturing at his son, had suddenly said to a man close by, 'My son's going up to Oxford.' 'I bet you're proud of him, aren't you?' said the man. 'Would have been if he'd gone at eighteen,' was the reply.

Rupert had had little to say in the context of what his father had said, and there was little need for any elaboration. Rupert could have said that he hadn't exactly been encouraged to go into higher education, but then, he knew that, at least for his father's colleagues, it was possibly the norm that he would go. There was little need for encouragement, or incentives, one just went. They'd left soon after this.

He was now halfway across the park, at the end of which was his destination, a six-bedroom Georgian house where Rupert's friend, the owner's son, was waiting for him. It was on a road opposite the park entrance. Rupert climbed the steps, used the boot scraper and lifted the heavy knocker. As it thudded down the door opened.

'Hello, Roop.' It was Andrew.

'Hello Andy, are you going to stand there or let me in?'

'I could do both, you could crawl between my legs.'

'Indeed I could,'

He did so.

Andrew turned and sat on his friend's back.

'Take me to the ante-room. Giddy up.'

Rupert crawled through an open doorway on his left, taking his pal's weight, and into the large, high-ceiling room. He halted in front of a chaise longue which, after dismounting, his pal laid upon, while his mount stood then sat on the armchair opposite.

'I shall miss these little rides,' said Andrew.

'I promise I will not let anyone use me as a horse for at least the next three years.'

'Wish I were going with you.'

'I know you do. Perhaps one day you'll go,'

'That depends,' said Andrew, sitting upright, 'on whether father will allow me.'

'Of course, you're becoming more essential to him now, aren't you.'

'It would seem so, and capital must be accrued.'

'Perhaps someone else will climb the golden ladder and take over from you.'

'Could be, though I doubt it, but in time I hope they do. In the meantime, I shall have to live vicariously through you. When are you off?'

'Tomorrow, I want to get up early and see my mother, she's in a thing, 'The Apple Cart' I think, at The Festival in Worcester, she's doing rep. It can be tiring and you can get some pretty rough places to stay, but, she'll enjoy it.'

'Gets her away from the old man, eh?'

'Something like that.'

'Incidentally, father's not here, Bank Holiday and he's still working. Fancy a drink somewhere?'

'I do, but I still have packing to do and will be up at the crack of.'

'I'll get us something.'

Andrew left the room while his friend laid back and admired his surroundings: the elaborate hearth with the miniature Doric-style columns, two larger Greek ones on either side of the door frame, an Adam-style ceiling rose, cornices, Roman swags and high, moulded skirting boards. There was a carved plaster dolphin on a corner table with large vases on either side of it. The place had been mostly kept in period. His friend's father loved the 'grand', perhaps befitting a successful merchant banker whose father, and his father before him, had been equally, if not more, successful.

He stood and went across to the window and looked out on the park with its bandstand, neatly-kept flower gardens and an avenue of sycamores, upon which were two riders on their cantering mares.

His friend returned with their drinks.

'It's a cocktail, apparently all the rage in New York at the mo. Tally-ho.'

'Cheers. Mmm..., it's good. Things still tough in the financial world?'

'For some, in fact for many, but we're just about riding the storm.'

'Who was it said that, 'A bank is something more than men. It's a monster.''

'Can't do without them, integral part of life.'

'The life of capitalism.'

'Let's not get into the heavy stuff at the mo, enjoy your drink, I won't be seeing you for a while. And how's your, or rather your father's, business?'

'The big one's proceeding well; he seems to think about little else. The whole devekopment's being officially opened soon.'

'I assume your mother will be there looking as gorgeous as ever in a Hollywood gown or something, or maybe she could go as Cleopatra to your father's Caesar.'

'Caesar: 'When I heard of her fame, I straightaway laid claim, ahead of my legions, I invaded her regions, I saw, I conquered, I came.''

'Who d'you think you are, 'Jimmy Durante? You still reading philosophy?'

'Indeed.'

'The study of general and fundamental questions about existence, knowledge, values, reason and language.'

'Who's a clever boy then?'

'Thought you'd have read literature or something; maybe politics.'

'I could do the latter with economics, but I'm not interested in numbers. If *you* were going, what would you do?

'Economics, I reckon.'

'You've got the background for it.'

'S'pose so. Want something to eat with that drink?'

'Thanks, but no, I'm going to have to say *au revoir* soon.'

'I'll miss you, little baby.'

'Me too. I'll write to you, you lanky sod.'

'Better still, telephone me.'

'I shall endeavour to discover a telephonic transmitting and receiving apparatus I can utilise at my future alma mater.'

Rupert swigged the last of his drink, placed the glass next to a vase, looked at his friend with a rueful grin and held out his hand.

'I'll give you a quick cuddle instead, you Oxonian, you,' Andrew said, and hugged his pal, who went into the hall and opened the heavy front door. He turned on the step.

'Cheerio again, you old bugger.'

Giving a little backward wave, Rupert went down the steps and towards the park entrance, leaving his friend leaning against the door and watching him walk into the park.

His father was at home when he reached it. Other than two framed theatre programmes and a poster on the bedroom wall showing his wife in dramatic profile playing Countess Maria in 'Damask Rose', it was very much his father's house. There was a regimental sword hanging on the wood panelling above the fireplace in the lounge, a map of the Battle of Albert, photographs showing charging soldiers at the second Battle of the Somme and one of him being presented with a military medal adorning the walls of the parlour. There was also an oil painting of the Forest of Dean.

His demeanour was as if it was just another evening and not one which would mark a significant event in his only child's life; he would retire to his study or, if his wife was present, would spend a little time with her, but usually merely nodding in recognition at Rupert. He did the same now, although did show some interest by asking whether he had packed his bags for his journey, using the word 'son' again, a term so ubiquitous in his father's vocabulary that Rupert would, half- seriously, wonder whether he actually remembered his name.

In his room, the soon-to-be student put a few more clothes in a second suitcase, added some more books and a sweater and went downstairs again to concoct a meal. When he'd finished eating it he had a bath, walked towards his room on the landing, hesitating before knocking gently on the study door and saying, 'Good-night father, if I don't see you in the morning, I shall talk to you on the telephone soon.'

There was no sound from the other side of the door. He turned away to his room then heard, as the study door opened. 'Well, all the best then, son, work hard. Good night.'

He saw the door closing. He returned to his room and tried to sleep.

He didn't see his parent in the morning. He left the house where a pre-arranged cab took him to Paddington Station.

On the train journey, his excitement seeming to increase the enjoyment of his mackerel, scones and jam in the buffet car, he mused on what it would actually be like at Exeter College. There would, he knew, be few, if any, females here, their number had been limited to a quarter of that of males. Perhaps, as the classical influence on subjects, especially, he suspected, on philosophy, waned, there would be some sort of feeling of dissent, of opposition to dominant avademoc ideologies, as there had been in the country generally, manifested of course in the recent hunger marches.

Surely these things would infiltrate the sensibilities of the upper and middle classes? The rich and the richer were, to an extent, suffering also, but their belief in the system of course remained, as it did in the idea that eventually all would be as it should be again, at least for them.

He had been there, in Hyde Park, when the marchers had arrived from places such as the Welsh Valleys, Scotland and the
north. There were an estimated hundred thousand present, and he
recalled the almost blanket condemnation of what appeared to be
seen as a as a threat to public order, mostly drummed up by the
more hysterical parts of the conservative press. He hadn't seen
much, as, arriving late, he'd been on the periphery of the mass,
standing with his back pressed against one of the metal columns
holding the main gates.

He'd expected mostly working class people, men especially;
people who understood, through experience, some of what most
of the marchers had suffered and were therefore in support of
them. But this was a less experienced, less sympathetic crowd
than the marchers long treks had warranted. He'd even heard
shouts of 'Get back up north', and 'We don't want you lot in
London.' He hadn't liked the feeling of it. He'd looked around
him; there were less flat caps visible than trilbies, there was a
smattering of bowler hats. He'd been rather disappointed and left
soon after he'd got there.

He had been with Andrew a few times before this to Speakers'
Corner to listen to the likes of Donald Soper, would-be politicians and religious, and non-religious, advocates, but the significance of these sorts of soapbox protests had been swamped by
the footsore, often poverty-stricken and hungry marchers; the Li-
do and Serpentine seeming like symbols of some indulgent and
unnecessary privilege.

As Andrew had been lukewarm about accompanying him this
time, feeling that somehow his father would get wind of it, Rupert had gone on his own. To this day, he hadn't told his own father; something he was now feeling rather ashamed of.

He now stepped off the train at Malvern Link and, refusing a
porter's assistance, moved as fast as his heavy cases would allow
him to the ticket barrier but, as expected, his mother wasn't there.
She'd said there would almost certainly be a further rehearsal that
afternoon to, as she would have put it, 'tighten things up' for the
evening's performance. She had told him he should go to the
Theatre and they'd let him in.

He caught a taxi to the venue where, after knocking rather a long time on its main door, was ushered through by a uniformed attendant. Leaving his luggage in the foyer, he went quietly to the rear of the front rows, sat and began watching the action on the stage.

For a while he didn't notice her, then she stepped forward; she was wearing her usual day clothes, none of the cast seemed to have changed into their character's apparel as yet. It was Orinthia's monologue, and as far as he could tell she delivered it faultlessly; the 'It's what I am, not what I do, that you must worship in me,' seemed somehow appropriate. The director called for a rest after this and as he did so his mother saw him and came elegantly down the steps at the side of the stage and hurried towards him.

She sat next to him and kissed his cheek.

'Hello, my lovely,' she said, how was your journey?'

'Slow, I wanted to be with you.'

'You are now.'

'How's the show?'

'Going well.'

'Good, loved the way you delivered your piece, you got it just right.'

'I think so too, this thing is merely a warm-up. Excited about where you are going?'

He looked at his watch.

'Yes, apparently, the latest time I can arrive is midnight. I can't be with you long.'

'I'm just glad you could come.'

One of the actors gave a wave from the stage and silently mouthed Rupert's name.

He smiled back at him.

'That's David Tripp, you've met him, He's playing King Magnus, took over from Martens, who's unwell, last week. He's doing very well. How's your father?'

'The same, of course.'

'Indeed. 'I've heard him referred to as, 'The man who's building a new city,'

'Hardly a city, but it's pretty large.'

'Are you still happy with the subject you've chosen?'

'I think so.'

'If you don't know what to do, do philosophy, eh?'

'Maybe, but I'm looking forward to it.'

'And the same with the social life?'

'Of course.'

'Don't get into trouble, darling. Enjoy it, but work hard.'

'I shall.'

'There's Frank, our director, looking at me, I'm going to have to go back. I'm sorry, my love. Telephone me, write to me; miss me.'

'I will. All of those things.'

They hugged each other. His mother then made her way to the aisle and toward the stage, her son turning away towards the front of the theatre, collecting his luggage and requesting the attendant to acquire a cab. It was time for him to return to the station, but this time going the other way. Towards Oxford.

3

He was looking around him at shops, houses, and people walking by on the High Road and occasionally at the backs of Doris and his mother arm-in-arm ten yards in front of him with his parent occasionally nodding in that rather predictable, wise way she had. He may as well have not been there. If he had stopped and just let them walk on they would have continued on their self-absorbed path until they were out of sight; it could well have been ten minutes before one of them had remembered he was supposed to have been with them and turned around to see where he was.

The day before, he had worked fast until lunchtime and gone home to help his mother and the neighbours with trestles and tables, and carry out cakes and buns, apples, oranges, jellies and sandwiches into a street that had been transformed into a kind of red, white and blue carnival, with strings of flags criss-crossing the street from every bedroom window and bunting wrapped around the lampposts, even the old sewer wall at the end of the street had been painted red, white and blue.

It was the silver jubilee, and even miserable old Jenkins had carefully arranged in the window of his corner shop, a large gold frame with a portrait of the king and queen. There was a clown with baggy trousers, huge red nose and large, floppy boots he inevitably kept tripping over. The piano, which George had helped push from the Paynter's house into the toad, had been played, with people dancing around it and there'd been loud cheers when Mrs. Nixon had come out of the shop carrying the largest cake he'd ever seen.

He had mostly sat next to his mother and not far from people he had lived near all his life. A few of the lads he'd played street games with, had had adventures over the park and caught tiddlers in the stream after tram rides to Wanstead Flats with, had come over to him and shared memories.

''member when you threw that cricket ball a that bloke and it missed 'im and went though Mrs. Green's parlour window?' And when we went into Nixon's and you kept 'im talkin' about sumfink while I pinched some ciggies?' 'What about when...' And so it had gone on. They were still living in nearby streets, two working at the gas works at Becton, three humping sacks of sugar about at Tate & Lyle. He told them what he was doing for a living but not where he had moved to. It had been good to wander back to those days, but he was now out of it. He wouldn't have to live here again.

He had gone back to stay a second night in the house, telling his mother that he was with a friend, Reg or Jimmy, he couldn't remember now which one he'd used. He'd wanted to get the place looking 'respectable', as she was wont to say, to surprise her with it, to please her. He'd managed to purchase a diomede light for the sideboard mirror and some Bakelite set-back photo frames awaiting his choice of photos; he wasn't sure whether he wanted those his father had taken of him many years ago with his black Kodak and accompanied by the inevitable 'Watch the birdie.' He'd slept well on both nights but it had been strange and so pleasing to wake up and see a world of green from the bedroom's curved side window.

She'd been surprised by the place and pleased for him when he had bought her to see it. 'Almost as good as Gwen's up west,' he could almost hear her thinking as she'd looked around with a delighted gleam in her eyes. But he could feel her realisation that he had, indeed, left home, and concerned when, in answer to her immediate question, he'd told her that he still hadn't told Doris. He'd had to virtually promise her that he would the next day.

He'd been painting a sign in letters with fishtail serifs on a butcher's shop in Shoreditch and wasn't sure, as he'd told the owner in his blue-and-white striped apron, that this style was appropriate for his shop. The man, however, was determined that's what he would have. George may not have liked it but he would have painted the letters upside down if he'd been asked to; he wasn't working for his governor on this one, it was private. He'd picked it up on a recommendation from a nearby greengrocer who he'd done a job for. As long as his boss didn't find out, it was okay. He'd finished it early, went to a phone box and told

Doris he'd see her at her workplace. It was where he had first met her.

The place she'd worked in and still was - he'd been writing stuff like 'Way Out,' 'Deliveries,' and other notices on its rear doors - was a furniture store in Tottenham Court Road where she operated the switchboard. He was just finishing the 't' in 'Exit' on the inside of a door using his chisel-edged brush, when he'd heard a voice behind him.

'How d'you get it so straight?'

He turned briefly and saw a girl of average height, about his age with fair hair, pale-green eyes and something a little different about her nose.

'You mean 'horizontal',' he said.

He laid down his brush and mahl stick, got a lump of chalk from his apron, rubbed it along a length of string with a looped knot at its centre, held both ends and, spreading his arms across the door so that the string was taut, bent his head forward, gripping the loop in his teeth, pulled back then let it go, leaving a fine white line on the paintwork.

'I do that again a little higher of course to get the height of the letters,' he explained.

'That's clever.'

'Not really, I should think it's been around for hundreds of years.'

He looked at her. He liked the clothes she was wearing. She must have noticed the glance.

'Do you like this?' she pointed to her jacket.

'Yeah.'

'It's a bolero.'

'Isn't that a dance?'

'Think so, but this is a jacket.'

'It's a nice one.'

She smiled at him again and turned to go.

'Er, what do you do here?'

'A lot of hard work on the switchboard.'

He wasn't used to this, speaking to women. He took a breath and asked her name.

She told him, adding, 'And what's yours?'

After he'd informed her she said, 'Perhaps I'll see you again.'

He took another breath.

'What about tonight then, or whenever? We could go to the pictures, there's that new place at Stratford, the Rex. I dunno what's on, but… '

'Don't think I've ever been to Stratford.'

He asked her where she was from.

'Islington.'

'You'll come, though?'

She thought for a while.

'Okay then, we can arrange something later; I have to get back to work now.'

He asked her what time she finished.

'Five o'clock.'

'Shall I come to your switchboard then?'

'I'll see you here, where we are now. Bye.'

She went quickly up the stairs.

He mused a while. He was a little surprised at himself, he'd only had one relationship with a woman. Other than his mother, a couple of aunts, a cousin he used to see on visits with his parent, and walking over the local park a few times with the girl who lived opposite him when he was a kid, there had only been Shirley, and that hadn't lasted long.

He thought of when they'd been sitting in the back row of the local flicks and he'd put his hand inside her bra. She'd seemed to like it, but he didn't enjoy it as much as the thought he would, she'd had a rather ample bosom. They had been seeing each other for a couple of weeks when this occurred. Neither of them had contacted the other after it. He hadn't minded at all, it. hadn't mattered.

He finished his work, he had a small sign to write on the side of the premises which he would do, or at least begin, next day. After quenching his thirst with tea and getting tactile pleasure peeling the wrapping off a roll of ice cream in a nearby Lyons Corner House, he returned to where he'd first seen her. She came down the stairs again soon afterwards.

'Hello, then,' she said, putting something into her bag and placing the strap around her shoulder. 'Do you know what we're going to see yet?'

'No, afraid I don't.'

'It's alright, I do, it's supposed to be good. Shall we go,' she asked, raising an eyebrow and turning from him towards the road. They walked to the station, travelled east on the Central London Line to Liverpool Street, she telling him as they stood, he holding a strap, she a pole, that she'd phoned her mother to let her know she would be late.

He told her that he didn't have a phone at home, and knew few people who did. She seemed a little surprised.

'My dad would be angry if I hadn't rung,' she said. 'He'd be even more so if I got home after midnight.'

'That's political,' he said.

'Why?'

'Because politics,' he said, 'isn't just about elections, assassinations and coups and things like that, it's about any individual or group that has power, or potential power, over other individuals or groups.'

'I suppose you're right', she replied with a shrug of her shoulders.

They took a steam train the rest of the way

They didn't speak much on the journey, he contributing more to the conversation than she, talking of films and getting her to play the 'favourite films' game, and though trying, she didn't have that much to say on the subject. When they got to the cinema, they saw that the picture starred George Raft and Carole Lombard.

'My jacket's the same name as the film' she informed him. He paid for them both and mentioned it would be a change to see Raft playing a dancer and not his usual gangster.

It wasn't the back row but two seats at the side; the place was full. They didn't speak during the showing and on the way out she told him that she must hurry back.

'Or else?' he said.

'Something like that.'

He went back to Liverpool Street with her. Sitting opposite each other in the carriage, she looked out of the window occasionally, but mostly glancing expressionlessly at him while he tried to think of something to say to her that wouldn't bother their fellow, and equally quiet, passengers.

Leaning forward and beckoning her to do the same, he said, 'Let's try an alternative definition or two, eh?' Okay, overdue - chief rabbi. Get it? Bath salts - attractive women from the west country.'

She frowned.

'That's what we call girls, 'sorts.' Well, me and my mates do. Get it?'

She smiled.

'Try and think of some.'

She couldn't.

At the station she told him she would get a bus.

He walked with her a little way to the stop and waited. Neither spoke. The bus came quite quickly.

'Goodnight then. See you tomorrow, I suppose. And thank you.'

'Goodnight,' he said with a wave, and watched the vehicle and its lights disappear northwards.

He didn't really know what to feel. It had been - for him - an unusual evening, but as he went back to the station knew it had been rather an unexciting one, as if he'd had lots of relationships with women and it had been, as a man of the world, just a night out with another one. Nothing had happened. He had seen a film, had enjoyed it; had quite enjoyed the company, but only quite. She and the evening had been... ordinary.

Somehow, the word seemed reluctantly applicable to what they did over the next few months. They saw more films together, went for walks, meeting mostly in her local neighbourhood, though not being invited to meet her parents. He would point out to her various architectural features of the houses they passed: the proportion of the windows, especially Georgian, their relationship with the London bricks, he occasionally directing her attention to chimneys, trees, gardens, and what he felt when seeing them; she gradually stopping her feigning of being interested and becoming, it would appear, genuinely so, once telling him that he 'drew people into his world.'

He liked that, he'd never considered it before, but it was one of the few good feelings he'd gained from her, except perhaps from the way she dressed, though in a too neat-and-tidy manner, a way that seemed over-conforming, too conventional. She took to wearing cloche hats. One of them she called her 'madcap' hat. He secretly wished her temperament would occasionally suit its name.

But, sometimes, she had a sort of authority that made him feel apprehensive, though he would never admit it to his friends, especially when she was with his mother, the two of them seeming to be a kind of force that, If he'd let himself, could be subjugated by.

He began to realise that the dulled child in him was too prevalent; and making him too accepting, weak. It was just a partial recognition, aware of it only in reluctant glimpses. The rest of the time he just went to work and saw his mates, mostly at football matches at the Boleyn ground where his father had taken him when he was six and he had been indoctrinated into a psychological ownership of the club. He'd played the game himself at school and at tech college; or the 'School of Building' as people called it.

He liked being with them, it was different from being with her. They hadn't met her; he didn't really care about them doing so. With her, it seemed a different way of being and nothing to do with them. He assumed it was fairly natural to be occasionally irritated by a woman, it never seemed to happen when with his friends, but it was more prevalent when she was with his mother. They seemed to talk about the most mundane things, 'woman's talk' he thought he remembered his father saying, referring to women gathering; 'gossips' was another term he'd used. He felt left out, perhaps all men did when women were together, but Doris seemed to be more at ease, more herself when with his parent.

Sometimes, he got quite an enjoyment being with her: when she listened to his observations on people's accents, on a book he was reading, a rare art gallery visit, on a newspaper article, his attempted analysis of a painting, or a film. But there was, all too often, a kind of jaded feeling, an unsatisfied space.

Now, here he was, ready to inform her that he'd moved into a house; his own one. He still didn't want to tell her. They were in the West End, not going any place in particular..

'Let's not go anywhere yet,' he said to her as they crossed a road, 'let's have a tea.'

They went to Lyons, and while they had scones, she talked of a settee in the store sale that she was thinking of getting her parents then interrupted herself.

'I haven't seen you for a while, where have you been?'

'Working, a bit of overtime.'

'S'pose it's about time you met them, eh?'

She said it with a smile that seemed to anticipate a positive reply from him.

'Er, yes I guess so.'

'That doesn't sound very enthusiastic, I've met your mum, surely you want to meet mine, and my dad.'

'Yes, sure, but … there's something I want to tell you.'

He looked around him. They were at a corner table and there weren't many other diners.

'Sounds mysterious.'

'Look, I've done something I suppose I've been wanting to do for a while, a long while, really.'

'What is it?'

'I've… bought a house.'

She looked mystified.

'You've what?'

'Bought a house. I got a mortgage'

'But how can you afford… Are you,' he saw her eye becoming bright, 'asking me to live with you? In a house? Where is it?'

'No. I wasn't going to ask you that. Just that… I've bought it and I'm living in it.'

"Living in it." What do you mean?'

'I moved in a few days ago.'

'You've already moved in?'

'Yes.'

'Where is it?'

'Near Hornchurch.'

'Never been there.'

She was silent, frowning at him.

'How could you just do that without telling me? Who else knows? Your mum?'

'Yes, don't blame her, I told her not to tell you.'

'Why? Have you told anyone else?'

'I told a couple of friends.'

'But not me.'

'No, because... '

'Because what? You didn't know how I'd take it?'

'Partly, I suppose.'

'What's the other part? You don't want me to live there with you?'

'We can't.'

'No?'

'We can't live in sin.'

She looked angry. He'd never seen her like this.

'If you loved me it wouldn't be sin, would it.'

'But - '

'Haven't the courage? Or just don't want to?'

'We can still see each other, can't we? You can stay some-times.'

'Oh, thanks, that's considerate.'

'I've not known you be sarcastic before.'

'Well, you have now.'

Out of the corner of his eye he saw a nippy stop serving for a moment to look across at them.

'Lower your voice,' he told her.

'Why?' Her face was becoming almost distorted. 'Do you want me or not?'

He hesitated. She broke the silence by suddenly standing and looking down at him.

'If you don't want me, say so.'

She bent forward, her face almost touching his, he, noticing in a moment of pointless irrelevance that the tiny twist in her nose seemed more pronounced. She said quietly and, almost in slow

36

motion, 'I'm going to kill myself then, see how you feel. It's your choice.'

Unable to move, he watched her hurry out of the teashop, almost scurrying; her hat hanging down one side of her face.

She'd said it with such finality that he couldn't seem to move, he felt he was stuck in a kind of vacuum, hemmed in by fear.

He looked around at the diners, a couple at a table near the counter were looking at him then looked down quickly as he caught their eyes. He didn't move for a while then forced himself to stand, the legs of his chair making a sharp, screeching that sounded, to him, like a scream. He forced himself to go to the till, paid and went out. He didn't think of chasing after her. He didn't think. He caught a train. After a while he got out and began walking.

It was north of Romford somewhere, anywhere would have done, knowing you couldn't really get lost so close to London, it didn't matter, there were always people, a station, a bus stop. He was trying not to think of what had just happened. A part of him wasn't sure that it had. After a while, he asked a woman coming towards him if he was going in the right direction for Ash Park Station.

'Almost,' she said, 'but it would be easier if you took the first-right then left and carried straight on from there past the market.' He thanked her and continued walking. He liked her smile.

Suddenly, he was a ten-year-old again walking back from the sewers - he thought it was called the Northern Outfall or something - and he had gone towards West Ham along the path atop the grassy slopes covering the huge pipe, and then turned back. He knew his mother would shout at him for coming home late again, past nine o'clock, at least. She'd be angry and may even have smacked him with those red, raw-boned hands.

A few streets from his home a woman had come towards him e and enquired if he was alright, and that he was out late and looked a little lost. He'd shyly told her that he was okay. 'That's alright then,' she'd said. 'Goodbye to you.' She had such a lovely voice, a 'posh' one, his parents would have called it. But, to him, it was gentle and soft, and somehow... loving.

Walking along the main road he'd felt awful, he'd wanted to....
he didn't know, but he didn't want to be where he was, he'd
wanted to run away to somewhere, to, he couldn't quite formulate it, to a proper mother, a *real* one, someone who had loved
him properly - though not knowing what he meant by it - someone who'd spoken nicely, who was interested in what he was saying, what he wanted to talk about, art and drawing and stories and
words.

But, the guilt. How could he leave his mother? Where would
he run to? Just keep on running, just running for ever perhaps,
until he ran into a lady who would smile and maybe pick him up
and hold him and be beautiful and speak nicely; another mum,
the right one. No. He had to go home. He remembered standing
there, people walking by him, some looking at him questioningly.
He was ten. What could he do?

He realised there was a similar conflict now, perhaps that was
why he'd thought of his childhood self. It was the sudden, corro-
sive guilt. But, this time, he didn't want to run away, but home-
wards, to his new home, one he was going to make into a 'glitter-
ing citadel' as he'd named it to himself. It was an ambition and
he'd begun the foundation for achieving it, but what if she... No.
He couldn't let her.

He halted and looked around, Two street corners away he
could see a phone box. He had coppers; he always carried them,
anyway, in case he wanted to, or had to make a call. He hurried
to it. He hoped she was at home; he wanted to tell her that she
could live with him; that was all; that she could. He went into the
phone box and hurriedly took some coins from his pocket.

4

The college looked almost castle-like from the taxi as it neared its destination in Turl Street.

'Floreat Exon,' Rupert murmured. It was the college motto. 'Let Exeter flourish' it meant, or so he had been told. So this was it. He was here. Paying the driver and leaving the cab with a case in each hand, he walked towards the main entrance. It was now dark and getting late; he hoped they hadn't shut. He saw what looked like a porters' lodge at the side of the front entrance and, as if on cue, its uniformed occupant emerged.

''Evening, Sir. And your name?'

Rupert told him.

'Welcome to the college. I'm afraid student rooms haven't been allocated as yet. Unless you've arranged alternative accommodation, temporary accommodation will have to suffice for this night. Is that alright, sir?'

His listener wasn't really sure what he'd expected, so told the man that it would be fine.

'I'll have your bags, sir.'

Rupert let him carry one while he followed him along the length of the six hundred-year old building's exterior and, entering a door at its end, walked into a dormitory of some twenty beds, four of them with sitting occupants he guessed were younger than himself. He wondered why there weren't more. As if aware of what his charge was thinking, the porter said, 'I expect most new entrants have arranged accommodation away from the university, at least for this night. I have a feeling that not all were informed in time about the delay in the study bedrooms being ready.'

'I wasn't,' was Rupert's reply, 'but no matter.'

The man smiled. 'I can assure you, sir, that the college is very efficient in all other ways.'

'I'm sure it is. I hope so, anyway.'

'Select what bed you wish. And, goodnight, Sir.'

The porter left and the newcomer returned the gazes of those he assumed were his fellow students. One, a tall, handsome man, came forward with outstretched hand.

'Hello, I'm Eric, and these bounders are Edward, Alec and Thomas.'

Rupert returned the greeting and shook hands with them.

'Not a very auspicious start is it, this dorm,' asked Eric. 'Ne'er mind, we'll have our rooms by tomorrow. Why'd'you choose Exeter, old man?'

'Not sure, really, but someone told me they were competent in my subject, so here I am.'

'Which is?' asked Alec, a rather short, broad, fair-haired boy. Philosophy.'

'Ah, Aristotle, Plato, et cetera.'

'I rather hope not. I trust that that influence is waning.'

'I wouldn't know. What's in its place then?'

'Logical positivism.'

'What's that?'

'That only statements verifiable through direct observation or logical proof are meaningful. And you?'

'Architecture.'

'Ah, the Seventeenth-Century dining hall, Radcliffe Square and, of course, the neo-Gothic chapel,' said Eric.

'They interest me of course,' said Rupert, 'but one hopes that the syllabus is appreciably wider than that.'

'Edward, here,' said Eric, pointing to a solidly built, dark-haired boy, 'is doing History.'

'William de Stapleton, Bishop of this town, founded the place as a school to educate clergymen. It was popular initially with the sons of Devonshire clergy,' said Edward with a smile.

Rupert asked Eric what he intended to read.

'Literature and a bit of art. Sounds as if we're all trying to impress each other, though Thomas hasn't said anything yet.'

'Maths, if anyone's interested,' said a rather slim, sad-eyed young man.

'Well,' said Eric, 'that's pleasantly eclectic, but I'm sure we all have other interests. What of yours, Rupert?'

'Well… politics and, though like Alec, am interested in architecture, the chapel for example, I'm not that interested in its contents and persuasions. I - '

'You're not an atheist are you?' asked Alec.

'I am. We can't prove God; only infer his or its existence.'

'Oh Lord, sacrilege. Should have expected it from someone of your philosophical bent, but - '

'Let's not argue,' said Eric.

'It could be called a debate,' said Rupert.

'Doesn't sound like one. What I mean by 'interests' were… well, let's start with women, eh?'

'That may be a bit too stimulating at the mo,' interjected Edward. 'Time's getting on. I'm tired, expect you lot are, too. Anyone hungry? I am, I've got some goodies mater gave me. Let's finish them off and get some shuteye, eh?'

As the others spoke, or at least grunted positively, he began sharing out some cheese-and-cress sandwiches, two doughnuts which he cut in five pieces and, picking up cups from stools at the side of the beds, poured the contents of a large vacuum flask into them. The scanty but welcome snack was consumed quickly, but not before Eric asked where they were all from. He then changed this to, 'Or, rather, let me guess. You, Rupert,' he said, pointing at him, ''though you haven't the London 'f', which is the domain of the lower classes anyway, are from our capital city, as is Alec. Edward, I note, has a Novocastrian accent, Thomas I'm not sure about; sort of Essex, perhaps.'

He looked at them encouragingly. 'Well, am I correct?'

'County Durham, but you're not far away,' said Edward. Both Rupert and Alec said, in concert, 'Yes, correct,' while Thomas said, 'Essex-Sussex border, really.'

'Well done, matey,' said Alec, 'We've got to guess you now, eh?'

'Yer canna be an ahtist and wearkin' cluss, mun, yer canna,' said Eric.

'Not bad,' said Edward. 'And you're a home counties wallah, correct?'

'Indeed. Surrey, no less.'

'The golf courses there take up more acreage than the towns,' said Alec.

'Golf; the interruption of a pleasant walk,' remarked Edward.

'Do I detect a smidgen of jealousy here?' asked Eric.

'Look,' interjected, Alec, 'are we *really* tired?'

'Why d'you ask,' enquired Rupert.

'Because I have here,' said Alec, as he walked to the side of a bed, opened a case, removed a cardboard box, and from it took out a record player. 'You may have noticed the power points by the side of the beds, thus I shall plug my contraption in.'

He did so, watched with interest by the others. He put a record on, 'Dancing in the Dark.'

'Are we supposed to move sensuously to this?' asked Eric.

'Certainly not with any of you, I trust,' said Edward, moving himself into the rhythm of the music.

'Let's try this,' said Alec removing the record and replacing it.

"Cheek to Cheek,' eh?' Said Eric, 'Anyone care to?' he asked, holding his arms out with a simpering look and pursing his lips.

'Thanks all the same,' replied both Rupert and Alec.

They laughed, then the latter put on some more songs while they all, except Eric and Edward, sat on the edge of their beds, listening.

'Tell you what; to energise us, let's imbibe,' said Eric, walking over and, after a little rummaging in his case, extracted two bottles, one larger than the other.

'Obtain your cups, gentlemen, and bring them here forthwith,' he ordered.

Edward walked quickly to the stools, grabbed some cups and shared them out with the others, Eric then pouring some of the bottles' contents into each.

'I am, of course, assuming that we all enjoy gin-and-it. Cheers.'

He raised his cup, the other four doing the same with theirs, and swigged it down. He poured himself a little more then continued moving in time with the music.

'I've got a jive here,' said Alec, beginning to play another record.

'Do it with me,' said Eric, moving towards him. 'You can be the girly.'

'I'll try, my master,' said Alec, holding his partner's hand and spinning around.

'Let's talk literature,' shouted Eric, holding Alec's hand high and exaggerating the last word. 'We can move and talk at the same time, can't we?'

'Glad you didn't call it 'dancing,'' said Edward, standing still, watching the two of them.

'Read Lawrence?' asked Rupert, tapping his feet.

'Ah, Lady Chatterley's Lover. Bet you haven't read it.'

'No, heard about it though.'

'I have a copy.'

'Didn't think it was published here.'

'It isn't, but a friend bought me a copy back from Paris. But let's talk of better stuff; of intellect, of intellectualizing.'

'Of sodomizing,' said Alec, awkwardly attempting to follow his partner's steps.

'Have you not read Huxley's 'Brave New World''? Rupert asked.

'Where we're all kept happy with Soma?'

'Prefer alcohol, old chap,' said Eric, trying to jive on his own as Alec pulled away from him.

'Isn't it about some sort of future where the social hierarchy is based on intellectual ability?'

'And what's wrong with that?' asked Edward.

'It akready is,' replied Rupert.

'Survival of the fittest and all that,' said Alec.

'That's a tautology,' said Rupert. 'We're told of the survival of the fittest, yet when asked, 'How do you know they're the fittest,' the answer is "Cos they've survived.'

'What do you mean, 'It aleady is'?'

'Depends on what, or rather who, defines what counts as ability,' replied Rupert. 'You could argue that the values of the ruling class - '

'Are we that?' asked Edward.

'I don't really know your backgrounds, but I should think you're getting there. Their, your, values are embedded in our educational system.'

'And?' queried Eric, stopping moving and facing Rupert. 'There's got to be somebody's... some criteria for what counts as intelligence and ability, there's no absolute is there?'

'Quite, but it's about power. Look, let's say that our values, our family's values are those that permeate higher education. We have, in essence, been taught to have these abilities, brought up with them, internalized them. The elite, if you like, have defined what counts as higher abilities, those deemed more important than others, that is those of the working classes. That's why we're *here*.'

'What, in this dorm,' asked Thomas.

'In this university.'

'What d'you suggest happens then?' Eric asked. 'Could, say, mending roads, or laying bricks, or spreading plaster over walls and mixing cement be taught here at Oxford? And, perhaps, writing a thesis or reading Classics or PPE be the province of any old secondary modern school somewhere?'

'Put it this way, replied Rupert, 'middle class values are nearer to those of the ruling class than those of the working classes, thus the latter have little chance in education.'

The music had stopped. Alec didn't put on another record.

'In the end, most definitions are power definitions. One class has the power to define another class as somehow 'lower'.'

'But surely,' said Alec, you can't... I dunno, say that mending a ball valve or cleaning houses or laying slates on a roof is as skilled, say, as a barrister or a brain surgeon.'

'Bet you're only saying that 'cos your father's a lawyer, said Edward.

'Actually, he is, but the point still stands.'

Rupert continued. 'But manual workers are just as functionally important, are they not?'

'Lord, what sort of philosophy are you doing?' said Eric, looking skyward. 'Leave the lower orders alone, let 'em be, with their speedway, billiards and soccer.'

'A game for gentlemen played by hooligans,' commented Alec.

'And their pubs and darts,' said Edward.'

'Darts: middle class archery,'

'Don't know where your views will get you in this place,' Edward said in a lightly warning tone.

'I'm hoping that my subject is about what *is* and how we know it's so, more than views.'

'Children,' said Eric, tapping Alec's knife on the empty gin bottle, 'let us have a sing-song or something before bed.' He looked around. 'Shall we not?'

'I'm glad I'm doing something as clear-cut and straightforward as architecture,' stated Alec, ignoring him.

"Clear-cut'?' Rupert replied, 'When does an architectural style, era, age, begin? When precisely does it end? What happens if you're building a house or something, say Georgian, influenced by classical Greek, et cetera, and suddenly it's 1811 and it's the Regency period. What does the boss chappie say? 'Hold up, men, they've invented curved glass now so we'll have to change these flat windows and stick in some bow ones, and that hip roof and dormers have got to go, they're old-fashioned now. "

'Alright, so you know a little about architecture, but the subject you've chosen to do, well… the first law of philosophy is that for every philosopher there is an opposite one. The second law is they're both wrong.'

'Not bad,' mumbled Thomas.

'You're so ignorant you think ethics is a county in the southeast of England,' said Rupert, smiling.

'Even better,' said Thomas.

'He speaks,' said Alec.

'Desist,' said Eric, 'Alec's going to put some more music on.' He looked at him. 'Aren't you? Let's have a sing-song. Come on. Watcha gonna put on, Alec?'

The latter took some more discs out of a paper bag and said, 'How about this one? I've got a Velvet Tone version.'

The sound of 'Happy Days Are Here Again' came out of the record player.

They all joined in, even Thomas, though still sitting on his bed.

45

'Happy days are here again, the skies above are clear again, so let's sing a song of cheer again, Happy days are here… '

Their loosely synchronised chorus petered out as they heard, 'Excuse me, sirs,' from the porter. They hadn't heard him enter.

I'm sorry to disturb you, but your music can, I'm afraid, be heard in the college. The study bedrooms are more soundproof, but I must ask you to be quieter. What time do you wish to have your breakfast? You could, of course, go to the refectory, but I could bring it to you earlier if you wish.'

They looked at each other questioningly.

'Indeed,' said Eric, 'we will stop now. Although,' he looked at the others, 'I was about to request a Cab Calloway number so I could do the Lindy Hop.'

'You'd have to do it alone,' said Alec.

'Half-past eight will do, I suppose.' Eric gave a brief look around him. 'I think there's a consensus.'

'And a goodnight to you, young sirs,' the porter said, giving an inkling of a bow before leaving them.

'Let's fall in, chaps, we'll be in class tomorrow, or at least attend a lecture or two,' Eric suggested.

'And we'll be given our rooms,' said Edward.

'Of course.'

Eric opened his case, took some things out, laid them on his bed and announced that he was going to the bathroom.

'Don't be long,' said Edward, taking out a bar of soap, a flannel, towel and pyjamas from his luggage and, sitting on a bed, placed them on his lap and patiently looked towards the bathroom. The others also organised some of the contents of their luggage for the night.

Whilst watching the others go to the bathroom or organise their toiletries and sleeping apparel, Rupert thought about the next day. And the next three years. Tired now, but excited, he thought also of Andrew. He would ring him tomorrow. He hadn't noticed a phone box near the college, but there would be one somewhere.

5

He had just washed his brushes with turpentine after finishing the eighth of the nine illustrations in an Egyptian wall tableaux he was painting in his through-lounge - it had folding dividing doors so it may officially have been a living room - which had taken him almost three months to do. There were pharaohs, queens, soldiers, servants and workers. He didn't really care what the names of the royals were or whether the depictions were histori-cally accurate; he liked the look of them and knew that since the big discovery of tombs in Egypt ten years previously, they some-how went with the period his house was built in; he'd noticed Egyptian-style prints on dresses and also seen the entrance to Abney Park Cemetery in north London.

For some of the work, especially the outlines of tiny animals and various zig zag patterns, he'd used a brush with only six bris-tles. He'd copied what he was doing from black-and-white sketches in a library book.

He liked copying other people's work; segments of Hollar's long view of London were among his favourites and which he'd use a mapping quill for, but he would also copy photos, especial-ly of racehorses, in watercolours. He recalled when he was at col-lege and he'd acted as runner for a bully boy who'd set himself up as an unofficial bookmaker. George would occasionally turn losing bets into winning ones for his fifteen-year old mates, mak-ing a ha'penny or two for himself. He'd always liked drawing anyway; it was and always had been a kind of escape, though he hadn't really been aware of it. He knew now what he was escap-ing.

He couldn't remember the last time he'd touched her. Some-times when she looked at him, he was aware that she couldn't either. He hadn't wanted to. What he wanted was to decorate his house, to build a garden; *his* garden. He wasn't sure why he had decided on the garden first, he wasn't that interested in plants and flowers, but, as he liked looking at them, he thought he would build a pond and a rockery, plant a conifer - there were already an apple and a damson tree which he'd guessed was part of the original farm orchard - lay a lawn and, feeling ambitious, buy a small fountain and somehow make it play.

He had worked on it until one in the morning sometimes, occasionally popping into the kitchen to warm himself by the paraffin heater. He hadn't really built things before, let alone a pond, which he did by digging out the earth, using it for the rockery, utilising thin plywood sheets with wedges of wood pushing them out from the sides and pouring cement into the space created. He'd dug a further, square hole, two feet away for a pump from which he attached pipes into the pond, the fountain and the waterfall he'd built with broken-up paving stones. He'd made steps into the rockery and laid marble tiles on them and also on the short L-shaped section which went behind the waterfall. He'd surprised himself, he'd just visualised it and done it.

She had hardly commented on what he'd been doing. He would come home from work; hurriedly and silently eat a meal she'd cooked, then into the garden. If he briefly looked into the French windows while he was working, he would see her sitting at the table holding a cup of tea to her mouth and staring into space. They had lived together for some months now..

It had felt strange when she'd arrived in the house. He'd met her at her local station; somehow he couldn't bring himself to go to her home. Her father had helped her with her luggage on the bus journey. He was a small, grey-haired, quiet man, who had spoken little on the only other occasion George had seen him, so he couldn't really tell what he was thinking about his daughter's departure from her home. He shook hands with the man she was going to live with, gave Doris a kiss on the cheek and left the station.

They hadn't spoken much on the journey to Ash Park, though she seemed quite unusually animated and would occasionally squeeze his hand. They'd walked from the station and as he turned the key in the lock and ushered her in he wasn't sure what he felt, it was as if his feelings were in abeyance, as if he was waiting for them to appear so he could learn something about what he was doing.

It was she who had suggested, some time after he had moved in and before she had actually done so, that they have a honeymoon. The word bothered him. He made the point, though not as strongly as he wanted; that people had to be married for that to happen.

'We can still go somewhere,' she'd said. 'You know what I mean, have a holiday some place. Your mum was talking about your Aunt Gwen having a caravan at Clacton, perhaps we could use it.'

Whilst he liked his mother's sister - apparently he was her favourite nephew - he didn't really want to spend his time in her caravan, it was too confining, it would be him and Doris. There wasn't enough space.

He knew he shouldn't have felt like this; other people went on a honeymoon, a real one, full of anticipation, excitement, that was the stereotype anyway, but… he would have been keener if his mates had been around. Reg had a girl friend now, Doris could have spent time with her, and he with his mate, 'though they couldn't have gone to Upton Park, could perhaps have attended a lower league game not too far away, at least they could have had a kick-around with each other or found some lads on the caravan site to play with. Maybe they could have had a walk around Clacton; it had been a while since he'd visited.

Doris didn't really like walking, and these days she no longer seemed to be as interested as she had been in his descriptions of the walks which he sometimes went on around the streets near where he'd been working, when he'd gone without lunch and finished early. But his mates weren't coming, and he wouldn't have dared suggest to her that they should. She was determined only they do it.

They arrived at St. Osyth Beach caravan park by train and bus and after unsuccessfully searching then asking caravan owners where their particular one was - his aunt and uncle had named it 'Gwenbert' after their names - they found it. It was pale cream inside with brown velvet curtains, two single beds and beyond, a small table, four chairs, and further on a tiny kitchen with oven, cupboards and sink.

At home, his bedroom was large, as was the bed, here the feel of the space was too intimate, he felt apprehensive, he didn't want to cuddle tightly, didn't want to sleep in a space not much wider than himself, 'though of course he knew she would want to push the beds together. He didn't want that either. They unpacked, he sat and lit a cigarette; she looked at him with a quick frown. He knew she didn't like him smoking, but if he gave in to her here, it would set a precedent for her to outlaw it in his own home when she came to live with him when this holiday was over.

He went outside with his fag and began walking around looking at the other caravans, most were similar to his relations' one, though there were a couple of larger, brightly-painted models. He could see a small shop at the corner of the site. He went to it and bought some beers and as an afterthought, a bottle of wine. He took them back.

'Where you been?' she asked. 'I knew you wouldn't be swimming, it's too chilly. What's the sea like?'

'Didn't really notice it.'

'You got some drink then. Good. Pour me some of that wine then, it'll be dark soon. We'll have an early night, shall we?'

He poured their drinks.

She drank hers quickly. 'Go on, get it down you, and I'd like you to sit in here for a while. I'll call you when you can come to the bedroom.'

This was the first time they'd been really alone, in a separate dwelling with no one entitled to come bursting in on them; his mother, her parents, or passers-by when they'd indulged in some heavy petting in a shop doorway the previous night before she'd pushed him away. He wondered what would happen. Whatever it was he'd have to get used to it. She was going to share his home with him.

'You can come in now,' she called from behind the partition. It was as if she was making her voice a little hoarse for some reason. He opened the door. She was wearing a black negligee which he'd never seen on her before, with high-heeled shoes higher than she usually wore. He wasn't sure whether she was simpering or whether it was a shy smile she was giving him, but it seemed almost embarrassingly false. She sat on one of the beds she'd pushed together.

'Going to join me then?' It was almost a whisper.

He sat next to her.

'Aren't you going to take your clothes off?'

He stood up and did so.

He felt shy. But she pushed him back on the beds, leaned over him and kissed him. He couldn't remember her acting like this before. He put the tip of his tongue in her mouth then gently touched her nipples. They were erect. He rolled her onto her back and lay on her.

It was the first time they had gone all the way. Neither spoke until she got up and said she'd make a meal for them and disappeared into the tiny kitchen. He lay there; again, he couldn't describe to himself how he felt. If he had tried to articulate it he would probably have described it as a cross between a kind of healthy, momentary exhaustion and an almost emotional impoverishment. He dressed, went into the kitchen and offered to help. She refused it. He could tell nothing from her expression as to whether she had enjoyed the experience, had been satisfied.

They stayed five days, he trying to feel comfortable holding her in his arms at night, but couldn't for long, she didn't feel… precious enough.. They repeated their first-night's activity twice more, he enjoying the experiences only a little more, though again she had given no clue as to what she felt. During the days they wandered around the beach, paddled in the sea a little and went into town to eat ice cream and candy floss and, on one occasion, going to the cinema to watch 'King Kong' again.

They returned to Liverpool Street station then parted, she to her parents' home, he to his. On the train back to it he felt that when he reached it he should somehow put his arms around it, grasp it tightly, hold it to him as if it was a super dolls house, knowing that in two days time it wouldn't really be his anymore. She would be there.

She had, of course, cooked for them both in the evenings after they'd returned from work. In the mornings he would hurriedly make a boiled egg and toast before leaving the house an hour earlier than she and occasionally, but not often, did the washing-up before they listened to the BBC in the evenings.

He soon tired of this and wished for time to himself. He decorated the entire interior of the house, working most evenings and weekends, though they would go to the cinema together on a Friday or Saturday. When this was done he'd work on his mural, while she would sit listening to the wireless in the front part of the lounge. There had been very little conversation, 'though she would sometimes stand behind him silently watching him work. After painting a small Japanese black-and-white illustration on a toilet wall, he'd begun the garden.

Whatever time he had to get up for work, he would invariably get to bed after her He would enter it gently, quietly, her back always to him, not wanting to disturb her, always with that slight sense of apprehension about doing so. This would happen even if he had to get up extra early because he was working miles away, like a job in Wimbledon painting sign boards around new blocks of flats and some work at the nearby council offices; he'd also managed to get a bit of private work writing a greengrocer's fascia.

He also, around this time, was sent to Simpson's-In-The-Strand next to the Savoy Hotel and while writing the name on its curved fascia board someone called him down from his trestles and scaffold boards to ask him to do a job for him. It was the owner of a barbers in a side street opposite who, impressed with his work, asked him to write 'Gentlemen's Hairdressers' on the glass panel of the shop door.

He'd wanted it in gold leaf with a black outline. George had informed him that it would be less expensive if he were to use gold radiator paint, a little of which he had at home. The thought had also crossed his mind that he could pretend it was gold leaf and charge him more, but he'd quickly dismissed it.

It wasn't just his honesty that prevented him, but the deterrent of a family tale of a distant decorator uncle who, soon after the Depression had begun, had painted a shop front whose owner had wanted its fascia grained and varnished. Whilst his uncle was quite adept at the former, he had no money to buy the shellac. He had, apparently, used the contents of a Tate & Lyle tin of treacle.

Unfortunately, it had been a hot summer's day and an increasing number of flies had become stuck. It seemed that he'd spent the night in a police cell.

He began to go out for walks on Saturdays when she was shopping; he rarely accompanied her. He took an underground train to Epping, but instead of boarding the push-and-pull one to Ongar he decided to walk there as near as he could to the railway line, whether it would be on suburban roads or through fields. Most of it seemed to be farms and barley. The grass was long and tangled at the side of the crops so he had to walk through them away from the railway.

He'd fallen into a ditch; he hadn't noticed it was one because of the thick foliage growing out of it. It was a pleasantly warm day so, laying on his back looking at the sky, he thought, when he got home, he would, make a sketch of himself lying there, maybe turn it into a watercolour, it would be a change from copying something. He looked forward to doing it. He raised himself and managed, keeping the tracks in sight, to find his destination.

As he approached the station it occurred to him that although he should perhaps have been looking forward to seeing her, to spending the evening, and the night, with her, his drawing would be yet another escape. While she was sitting at one end of the long room reading Woman's Own or Barbara Cartland, rarely wanting to listen to Flanagan and Allen or Sid Field on the wireless, and the risque Max Miller she thought 'disgusting', he would be sitting at the other end using his pencil and, maybe, his Indian ink pen and brushes and immersing himself into the world of his drawing.

It wouldn't matter what it was of. He was almost denying she was there. He didn't really want to believe that this was a large part of the reason for his murals and the work in the garden. It was as if only he should be there. He'd done his duty by going to the caravan. He should be here on his own, in *his* home.

He remembered, on her arrival, that she had put her case and bags down on the bare floorboards, looked around her and said, 'You've got to get a carpet for us.' She looked up the stairs. 'And a runner for up there.'

'No, not a runner; fitted. This isn't a Victorian house, is it.'

'Well, everybody has runners whatever the house, don't they? Where's the wardrobe then?'

'Upstairs, of course.'

He took another bag from her and went to the main bedroom holding two of her cases.

'Ooh, this is a nice room, isn't it big.'

She went to its long, metal window. 'Lot of space and trees,' she murmured. 'Can I have the other cases with my clothes in, please?'

He placed them on the bed. She took out some shoulder-padded jackets, flared skirts, a couple of hats, gloves and slingback shoes. Pushing his clothes to one side of the wafrdrobe, she put hers in. They took up more room than his. He felt for a second as if *he* were being pushed out of the wardrobe, the room, the house.

'I want to see the rest of it,' she declared, and walked in and around the smaller bedroom and box room.

'We could have people stay here couldn't we,' she said with enthusiasm.

'Such as?' he asked.

'I dunno. My friend Beatrice, or Sheila.'

He'd never thought of anyone staying here, except, perhaps, one of his mates, but then he'd have to pretend that Doris was staying just for the night and that it was something she rarely did. His mother had said that she wouldn't come to see him while he lived with a woman. It was living in sin.

6

It was a respectful knock, though not too gentle, and enough to wake him and Eric; the others seemed to b still asleep.

'Do come in, my man,' Eric called.

The door opened, the porter entering with a wooden trolley in which were bowls of corn flakes, plates of toast and marmalade, a bottle of milk and two large teapots. He trundled his contraption into the middle of the dorm, placed the cups at the sides of the beds; gave the cereal to them individually - the others now being awake -followed by the plates of toast.

They dressed and consumed their meal without speaking much. Then, before taking it in turns to visit the bathroom, Eric got them to put their plates and bowls back in the trolley, turned to Rupert and asked, 'What now then?'

As if on cue, the porter returned and said, 'If you'll follow me, gentlemen, we'll go to the head porter's office where you will be allocated your study bedrooms.'

They hurriedly repacked their luggage and did as requested.

In the office behind the porter's room, they were given their room numbers by a red-faced, corpulent man who looked as if he was in the middle of rehearsals for the role of Falstaff in the University Drama Society.

'I'm afraid, gentlemen,' he said, after giving them the required information, 'you'll have to delay your unpacking, I believe the bursar is expecting you.'

He looked out of the narrow window.

'Across the Front Quadrangle there,' he said, pointing to a window with bright red curtains.

They went in the direction indicated; found an office wherein another large, florid-complexioned man briefly confirmed the details of their fees and grants.

'Enjoy your stay here, gentlemen, I trust your learning goes well. Talking of which, I've been informed that a lecture will be starting at half past ten. There's a notice board across the Quad near your rooms that gives your subjects and times, and of course, where they will be.'

After a quick look at the information boards, they made their way to their rooms in the undergraduate and fellows' lodgings. Eric's was next-but-one to Rupert's, while the others appeared rather widely dispersed. Rupert's was a small one with a bed, desk, bookshelves, a rather Baroque fireplace, a small table, some chairs and a settee. He had a lecture in a short while so didn't spend much time after unpacking in arranging his belongings.

He wasn't sure where the lecture theatre was, but as he left his room, promising himself that in the evening he would try to relax and congratulate himself on being here, he saw some other undergrads leaving their rooms and walking in the same direction along the corridor. Among them was Eric.

'Hello, I assume you're going to the lecture, I'm surprised; it's not your subject,' Rupert said to him.

'Your assumption is correct, dear boy, but I thought I'd go anyway. And I'm assuming that you've probably forgotten we have to see tutors and also get our gowns and things.'

'Oh, yes, that's not till this afternoon, is it not? That's what the college letter said.'

'You're correct. Okay if I sit with you, Plato?'

'I'm hoping there will be little of him to read.'

The corridor led them into the Quadrangle and some fifty yards along its side path they entered their destination. It wasn't as large as Rupert expected and dwarfed by the nearby Chapel, which Rupert, atheist or hot, wished to discover.

As they both sat, near the front, a tall man in a dark gown came from the side of the low stage, walked to the empty lectern, looked at his audience without saying anything until they became a little restless then said, 'The difference between Oxford students and Cambridge ones is that when the latter's lecturers say 'Good morning,' they write it down.'

After a ripple of appreciative laughter, during which Eric whispered to his companion, 'I bet he says that at the beginning of every academic year,' he continued.

'Philosophy, from the Greek 'philosophia', meaning 'love of wisdom', Is the study of fundamental and general questions about existence, knowledge values, reason, mind and language.' He briefly paused. 'Talking of which, we will not be delving into the two biggest mysteries, which are the existence of human consciousness and how the universe got here. Philosophical methods include questioning, critical discussion, rational argument, et cetera.'

He paused again and looked mock-sternly at his audience.

'There will not be a great deal of emphasis on Classical philosophical questions such as, is there a best way to live? - which depends of course on who or what defines 'best', Do humans have free will? The answer to that, incidentally, is almost certainly 'no'. One that is of interest, however, is, Is it possible to know anything and to prove it? The question we should of course ask is, What does it mean to 'know?'

Rupert looked around him; the hall was now almost full.

'Historically, philosophy encompassed any body of knowledge from the time of Aristotle to the Nineteenth century. Natural philosophy encompassed astronomy, medicine and physics. For example, Newton's Mathematical Principles of Natural Philosophy later became classified as a book of physics. In the modern era some investigations that were traditionally part of philosophy became separate academic disciplines, including psychology, sociology, linguistics, and economics.'

He looked around the hall, encompassing all of them.

'Do stay with me. I'll cut it down to the basics then you can go to the library and do some reading. So,' he continued, 'investigations closely related to art, science, politics or other pursuits remained part of philosophy. For example, is beauty objective or subjective? Are there many scientific methods or just one? Subfields of philosophy include metaphysics, concerned, of course, with the fundamental nature of reality and being, and epistemology, about the nature and grounds of knowledge, its limits and validity.'

He halted briefly before saying, 'Right then, young minds, think on these things, and as short as this was, you can depart now to books and things; the things being to see your tutors and such. Do settle quickly and I shall see you here at this time next week.'

He turned and walked off the stage.

'That was interesting,' Eric said as, walking behind the others, he and Rupert moved slowly to the exit.

'You know, it occurred to me when he talked ab0ut knowledge, that it can only come from the way we see he world, really.'

'To the manor born,' said Rupert. 'I believe it's called the ultimate tautology, the epistemological-ontological one. That is, what is in the world is determined by how we know what is in the world and - '

'And how we know what is in the world is determined by what is in the world. Is that it?'

'Correct. We'll make a philosopher of you yet.'

'Hope not. When have you to see your tutor?'

'At two, I think.'

'Mine's about then, too. We have some time; don't fancy going to my room yet, I'm a lazy bugger, domestically. Let's have a drink.'

'Where?'

'The common room, I suppose. It's near our lodgings I think.'

They left the lecture theatre and turned towards their rooms then through an entrance door and into a spacious room with an archway at its centre, a high ceiling and an almost pew-like arrangement of seating. There were a few others there, none of them drinking.

'Perhaps we're not supposed to imbibe here,' said Rupert.

'I've got a little flask of whisky with me, I tend to carry it around with me in case of emergencies.'

'This isn't one.'

'Depends how you define 'emergency.' Let's have a couple of sips.'

They sat away from the others and Rupert was offered the flask. His father was quite a whisky man, but not him, nevertheless he took a small sip and handed it back, its owner taking a couple of large ones before smiling and saying, 'I say, I haven't really introduced myself have I. Pullis.' He held his hand out. Rupert shook it and told him his surname.

'Good to meet you, Rupert Colls. I feel we're a little older than most of the other chaps here, am I right?'

Rupert told him his age.

'Me too. My father needed me, finance, banking and all that. What about you?'

'Rather lazy I suppose, worked for father, didn't qualify; took evening classes then did the entrance exam. Don't tell anyone.'

You surprise me. Your secret's safe with me, old chap. What did you think of the lecture anyway?'

'Liked the lecturer, there seems to be some changes afoot. Think I'm gonna like it.'

'Expect it'll be the same old, same old in Literature: Shakespeare, Milton, Jane Austen, Tolstoy… '

'At least you'll study a woman's work, possibly the only bit of femininity we'll get here.'

'I believe some universities are allowing women to do degrees.'

'Well, thee certainly won't be many here.'

'Have you a girlfriend, old chap?'

'Nay. You?'

'Ah yes, Fiona. She's my darling, known her for absolute yonks.'

'What's she like?'

'Oh, what to say? Slim and pretty and gorgeous.'

'I wonder how subjective beauty is. Do we learn what counts as beauty in women or is there a general beauty independent of the race or class of the beholder?'

'We tend to like blondes in the Western world methinks,' said Eric. '

'And Africans think African women are beautiful.'

'Especially if they are corpulent.'

'*We* may think they are, but it seems the more rotund the better for African men. Some of their women go to fatting farms to increase their amount of flesh.'

'Doesn't sound very pleasing.'

'Because, as said, we're Western. I did hear, though, that researchers showed photos of women from all nationalities that were considered beautiful by their compatriots, to people of all walks and races, and a smiling Indian woman won hands down.'

'Perhaps it was the smile and that erotic, dusky skin eh?'

'Did you know that not so long ago African women with their sticking-out buttocks were put in freak shows?'

'How awful.'

'I wonder if the labia is just as pink on the black girls, eh?'

'What a lovely contrast.'

There were now more students entering the room, among them was Thomas looking just as sad and skinny as when Rupert had first seen him.

'Hello you two,' he said with his slight country blur. 'Where are your rooms?'

Eric informed him that he and Rupert were housed on the gound floor.

'Have you been to a lecture yet? He asked.

'We both have,' answered Eric. 'What a bout you?'

'No, but I've been to the library and got a book or two.'

Rupert asked him what they were.

'Hardy's A course of Pure Mathematics, and, for fun, Euclid's Elements of Geometry.'

'Doesn't sound fun to me,' said Eric.

'All that's after the equal sign is merely another way of saying that which in front of it,' said Rupert,' shaking his finger in mock scolding.

'Yes, we know. I'm getting off to my room. I shall see you around the place I suppose. Bye.'

'Are monsters good at maths?' asked Rupert.

'Yes, if you Count Dracula,' said Thomas walking away with a backward wave.

'What a ray of sunshine he is,' said Eric. 'Anyway, I need some things from my room then I'm seeing my tutor. There's an Eng Lit lecture afterwards. Are you coming?' asked Eric.

'I noticed it on the board. I'll see you there, perhaps, after I've seen my man.'

'We'll have lunch afterwards,' suggested Eric, as they made their way back to their rooms.

Rupert organised things in his, then went up ancient stairs to the top floor and to the other end of a corridor where there was a half-open door. After looking at his watch to make sure he wasn't too early, he tapped his knuckles on a panel.

'Come.' ordered a voice from the room.

The man, who could have been Rupert's age or ten years older, wasn't wearing a gown, just a simple tie and rather worn cardigan. He leant over the desk he was sitting at and shook Rupert's hand.

'Mister Colls, I assume. Do sit.'

He gestured to a chair a little away from a corner of his desk. Rupert sat.

'I won't keep you long. Welcome to Exeter. I trust that you will work hard and succeed. You're a little older than most of the undergrads here aren't you, but that may help in the subject you're studying. You'll obviously need to let your relatively youthful spirit out at times, though, and there's the drinking club of course. Do not, however,' he said, looking over his spectacles, 'indulge in that place too much. I say this for your own good. If there is anything that really bothers you about your work or, indeed, your social life, et cetera, do come to see me.'

He stood.

'Sorry this has been so short, but I have other pupils to see and other things to do.'

He rose and offered his hand again. Rupert shook it.

'Goodbye then, Mister Colls.'

Rupert went out of the room towards the lecture theatre again where he intended to wait for Eric, hoping the lecture would interest him.

This time he didn't sit near the front, but towards the higher area at the back. It filled pretty rapidly. He saw Eric come in then walk up to join him.

'See tutor man?'

'Yes, pretty nondescript but seemed a kind soul. Yours?'

'Looked and sounded like someone out of Shakespeare. I thought he was going to call me Yorrocks. Very classical man I think. Questioned me on what I'd read. I remembered the pretend list I'd made, it seemed to satisfy him. I hope the lecturers aren't like him.'

'Perhaps he's one of them.'

'Heaven forbid.'

'Here comes one now.'

A grinning Figure emerged from the side of the low stage as if he was in a West End theatre and had swept from the wings to face an ecstatic audience.

'Welcome to Exeter College,' he greeted it in a loud voice, spreading his arms expansively.

He stopped in front of the lectern, picked it up, turned and placed it behind him.

He scanned the new entrants and said, 'The subject is English Literature, though during your time here we will be looking at the works of Hugo, Tolstoy and Dostoevsky, as well as Dickens, Austen and of course the great bard. We may also,' he said with a teasing smile, 'take some notice of Mister Scott Fitzgerald.'

'This is more like it,' Eric whispered.

The speaker looked around him again.

'The study of English literature, of course, focuses mainly on analysis, debate and critical theorising about a large number of published works, be they novels, poems, plays or other literary works.

'What do we teach when we teach Literature then? That's a rhetorical question of course. It involves, dear students, more than knowing about a list of texts, it teaches ways of thinking and approaching material, habits of mind, if you like. It could be argued then that it teaches an identity, a way to be. Maths teaches students to be mathematicians, history teaches them to be historians: indeed, so pronounced is this that one could describe disciplinary identities as 'tribes'. But what do we teach our students in English to be when we teach them literature?' He grinned. 'Possibly not 'Englishers', as a student once replied enthusiastically when I asked him what he was learning to be.'

He began pacing the stage.

'I'm not sure that being uncertain about our tribal denomination should be taken as a sign of weakness or confusion - indeed, it could be argued that a discipline is healthy when it's thinking hard about what it is and what it is for. I would say that we teach our students in the seminar room to be literary critics. As said, in a broader, more active sense, it's an identity, and much more than simply 'knowing about' a text or period, it's part of 'knowing how to be' a critic; a literary critic.

He had stopped pacing.

'I want you, us, to have a clear-eyed view of our recent intellectual, cultural and social history, at least in relation to literature. Of course, claiming the term 'literary critic' will not, in itself, meet the range of intellectual challenges the discipline faces from other disciplines, especially from sociology.' He grinned. 'One of the tutors asked a sociology student recently what he was having most difficulty with. 'The bourgeoisie,' he said, 'they own the means of production.'

It seemed obvious that he expected the appreciative laughter and perhaps the rather superior nodding of a few heads and, still deadpan said, 'Economists don't like us either, apparently. Three people, a chemist, engineer, and an economist are shipwrecked on a desert island with just a tin of beans for company. 'Best way to open it,' says the engineer, is to make a fulcrum with these stones and bend the tin till it splits.' 'Simply leave it in the sun,' said he chemist. The heated sauce will form a gas and eventually he tin will explode.' The economist said, 'Assuming we have a tin opener… '

More laughter.

'Though, of course,' he added, 'If there was a philosopher there he'd undoubtedly say, '*What* tine of beans?'

Rupert felt Eric nudging hm.

'However, that I'm afraid is going to be all for now. This is supposed to be merely an introductory talk, but do think on what I've said and I shall see you all soon.'

He gave a rather buccaneering wave and left the stage to some quite enthusiastic clapping.

'What d'you think then?' asked Rupert.

Eric smiled. Sounds pretty good, especially the Fitzgerald bit, The Great Gatsby, Tender is he Night, et al. Hope I'm in his seminar group.'

'I didn't think the bourgeoisie bit very funny though.'

'You don't have a sense of humour.'

'Au contraire, I didn't laugh because I *do* have a sense of humour. They do own everything.'

'Am I of the bourgeoisie?'

'I would say so.'

'And you?'

'A little bit, I suppose.'

'Well, forget that; let us celebrate the beginning of the next three years by having some food.'

They left the lecture hall and made their way across the Quad to the dining hall.

'I didn't think we were allowed to eat here,' mused Eric, 'it's used for events, but apparently we can have lunch and supper here if we choose.'

'Well, *we're* here, that's an event.'

'Indeed.'

It was a long, high space with curved wooden beams delineating the apex ceiling, tall windows, a dark wooden dado with a chequered, tiled floor and paintings of, Rupert guessed, some of the college's illuminati. There were four long tables with lit lamps on them very few feet. There were about forty or so other people there. They sat at the end of one of the tables where a waiter immediately approached them and offered a menu.

'What you going to have, old boy?' asked Eric. 'I'm paying.'

'If you insist. Think ill have the hachis parmentier.'

'I shall be a trifle more adventurous and have the poulet chasseur.'

Eric beckoned the waiter, ordered and glanced around him.

'None of the makeshift dorm lads are here, I see.'

'Perhaps they have their noses stuck in books.'

'I doubt it.'

'He looked at Rupert.

'What's this 'no girlfriend' business then?'

'Just that.'

''tis a pity. Perhaps Fiona could fix you up with one of her pals.'

'She's special, isn't she.'

'Indeed. Have a snap of her here.'

He took out his wallet, removed a small photo from it and showed it to Rupert.

'She looks like a young Harlow; that fair hair, those eyes, and there's something about her mouth. I can see why she's special. What does Freud say love is, 'An 'overestimation of the sex object'?'

'Why so cynical?'

'I can be even more so. Women, like ourselves one could say, are just stimulus-response mechanisms, they, we, have intestines, sternums, livers, blood, lungs et cetera. They - '

'You're objectifying them aren't you. why?'

'A leading question.'

'Your apparent detachment serves a purpose, doesn't it.'

'Er… maybe.'

'Are you,' asked his companion quietly, 'afraid of the opposite sex then? Be honest. You can with me.'

Rupert sat upright then shifted around on his chair.

'You could just be right,' he said casually. 'Ah, the waiter doth arrive.'

Their meals were placed in front of them.

They hardly spoke during their savoury, concentrating on satisfying their appetites.

Eric finished first.

'Hurry up old man, our creme brulee awaits.'

'Mmm, yes.'

'What does papa do then?' Eric asked, scoffing his dessert.

'Construction and development.'

'Suffered in the slump, dd he?'

'Actually, no.. Doing far better, of course, than the nearly four million unemployed.'

'Constructing anything at the moment?'

'A new town to the east of the capital.'

'A whole new town? Well done. He'd require quite a bit of funding for that enberprise mehinks.'

'Yes. He got it of course. Perhaps some of it from your old chap, eh?'

'Doubt it, but money works in complex ways. Makes the world go around and all that.'

'Whoever invented douible-entry bookkeeping has a lot to an-swer for.'

'Yes, *tabulae rationum*. But what could replace cash as a means of exchange? Would you want a bartering system or something?'

'Too late for that, the world's too big. Incidentally, referring to a previous conversation, why d'you think the idea of the fittest's survival is so widely believed?'

'Cos it's true?'

'Because a rulinng class have put their weight behind it.'

'Why?'

'What section of society is seen as *the* fittest then?'

Eric thought for a while.

'Yes, got your point. And why not? 'Aren't they, we, the fittest then?'

The waiter interrupted them.

'I'm afraid the dining hall closes in ten minutes, sirs, I do hope you enjoyed your meals.'

'We did indeed,' said Eric, paying the man.

On the way back to their rooms Rupert thanked him for the meal.

'Don't mention it,' said Eric, dismissively waving his hand.

As they stopped outside the former's room. Eric shook his companion's hand.

'Good to meet you, you know. See you tomorrow.'

'Yes, goodnight.'

Once inside his room, Rupert finished arranging his things then almost fell on the bed, feeling tired but also a pleasurable feeling of anticipation.

He reached up to move the curtain aside and looked out into the dusk at the Quad and its grass, shrubs, its few trees, and the centuries-old stone of the buildings.

How many times, he wondered, had the words 'analytic', 'a priori', 'synthetic', 'a posteriori', 'metaphysics' quietly echoed off these walls over the ages? How many bits of learned tomes had been written on warm summer days by long-legged masters relaxing on the student-free grass, or student despairs at receiving the news of their poor Thirds or even Fails? He was determined to be in neither of those categories.

He knew he should have read more on his subject before coming here. Yes, he had been rather lazy. He wouldn't be from now on. He changed into his pyjamas, switched off the light and lay on his bed again. He still hadn't telephoned Andrew.

He was walking along his old street, visiting his mother; he hadn't seen her for a while.

'I don't like what you're doing son', she'd said when he'd last been with her. 'You'll always be welcome here, you know that, I'm your mother, this is my home; it was yours, too.'

Before he had decided to see her he'd been shopping in the Co-op in The Broadway - Doris saying she didn't want to perform her weekly ritual this time, preferring to stay indoors - watching money in metal tubes whizzing across the ceiling in all directions to and from the cashier's booth as he'd waited for his change to be returned to him. He'd also bought some groceries for his parent and had walked from the local station.

As he turned into the street he saw the lamppost outside the corner house and recalled the evening tennis ball kickabouts of his childhood under its light. it didn't feel that long ago that he was knocking on people's doors and hiding behind a horse and cart, or a rare motorised vehicle, to watch someone come out, look perplexed then annoyed that no one was about who appeared to have been responsible for knocking on their door.

He passed the house where Pam Hill had lived and who'd seemed forever to be playing hopscotch on the pavement with her sister or, wearing ineptly applied lipstick and their mother's high-heeled shoes, they would often pretend to ballroom- dance, with Pam taking the man's part and bending her sibling backwards until her head was almost touching the road.

He thought he could remember a party in the parlour when he was very young. They'd all kick their legs out sideways and sing, 'Oh, 'okey cokey, cokey,' and 'put yer left leg in, yer right leg out, in-out, in-out, and shake it all about,' and the floorboards would bounce and the noise wake him up. He would come out of his bedroom into the passage and stand at the doorway and watch. His aunts and uncles would rub his hair and say 'Aah,' and give him a farthing or ha'penny or two.

The parties he'd liked best were the New Year ones, where dad would rub soot from the grate on his face and they would all go out into the street together in a line and put their hands on the hips of the person in front of them, stick their legs out to the right and left and sing, 'Ay ay ay ay conga, ay ay ay ya conga, lala la la, lala la la.' Other lines of people would come out of the houses and into their line; he felt like he was part of a dancing snake. He rarely thought of his father, but it was good to remember him again with the few memories he did have of him.

It occurred to him that Doris seemed increasingly to be keeping at home - though when he used 'at home' the image was of the house, not of her, nor of them. It suited him in a way; he occasionally got out to see Reg or his other pals, and he was pretty absorbed, anyway, in painting a series of butterflies on foot-square pieces of painted plywood which he would eventually put up in the hall and staircase.

Trying not to think of this part of his existence, he looked at the houses. They'd hardly changed.

Front doors, with the length of a brick separating each pair, were painted in different colours: maroon, black, dark blue and an occasional faded red, they seemed like striped deckchairs in grey tundra. There were a group of women on the opposite pavement wearing headscarves tied under their chins, talking, one of them absentmindedly working the heel of a foot in and out of a shoe, alternately stretching and crushing the leather and, with her eyes pointedly open and pursing her lips, emitted long, surprised, 'Oohs', while another placed an arm loosely across her breasts and the tip of a finger into the comforting grip of teeth as she looked eagerly at the others in anticipation of another neighbourhood exposé.

He was aware that he was becoming involved with details, of behaviour, movement, as indeed he was in his art work, and that he could get lost in them. But that was what he needed.

Had he been a child again he would, standing astride the gutter, have played marbles or, by the side of an end-house, take turns with other boys to throw a bald tennis ball at a coin or two dropped on a paving stone and catch it as it curved back to them. Sometimes, somebody would achieve the object of the game and knock a coin out of the square, the ball flying off towards the thrower having to dive with outstretched hands to hold it. He and his mates called this activity 'odds and ends'.

There were times when, out of a shrill boredom, they would run about pulling ridiculously grotesque faces and screaming for screaming's sake and then noisily fight each other, rolling over and over down the camber of the road.

The homes were all rented. Virtually every house on one side of the street and a few on the other belonged to one landlord, who still visited every place he owned once a week to collect the rent.

They all had outside lavatories, often with doors peeling paint, cisterns with string taking the place of chains and, not far away, hanging on the tall fences that prevented neighbours peering into each other's dining rooms, tin baths.

Sometimes, on a Saturday, he'd watched men sitting a outside on their window sills, their slowly swinging heels clicking the bricks while they checked the racing results or idly talked to a neighbour, looking around now and then to see if any of their mates were coming back from the pub where, amongst the beer and obscenities, they would discuss work, horse racing and their sexual adventures which, by the time they left for home, they may, he thought, have believed.

His mother answered his knock almost immediately, and embraced him. It was good to see her, though not really wanting to be in the house.

He suggested they go over the park; there was a new café place that had opened where they could have a cuppa.

'That'll be nice, son.'

She went to the tiny passageway, took a coat off a hook and said, 'Come on then, move yourself.'

They went to the top of the street, through the park's entrance, with its black Corporation of London name board showing a map with a 'You are here' pointer.

'How do they *know* we're here?' she asked in mock seriousness, and laughed.

It was nice to hear her laugh.

He saw the bandstand and reminded her of when she used to tell him, when he told her he was going to play in the sandpit next to it, not to because he could get nits.

'You're a big boy now and I don't, or shouldn't, have to tell you what to do.' She looked at him with a frown. 'Though you know how I feel about what you've done.'

'Here's the café, mum, come on.'

They went over to it and looked at its offerings. They chose jam scones and cream and a pot of tea.

'Well then', said his mother as they sat,' 'How's life in the country then?'

'Hardly country is it,'though from parts of the estate you can see right across the estuary, it's nice.'

'Well, it's certainly not like around here.'

'No, you can say that again.'

'I think of you a lot.'

'I do you, too, mum.'

'And I feel very uneasy about it all.'

'I know you do. I expect someone who kept telling me to say my prayers every night till I was eighteen to feel like that, but there it is.'

'I got on well with her, but… are you happy, son?'

He couldn't simply say 'No', it would cause her pain, but he knew his silence was virtually answering her question.

'It's… difficult to say.'

'Say it.' She leaned forward. 'Say it, George. Be honest.'

It was difficult to be honest, to face a truth which he hadn't quite formulated to himself yet, let alone to his mother.

'I can't, mum.'

'Why ?'

'I'm supposed to be a big boy now; I'm buying my own place.'

'And very nice it is, too. Maybe one day I'll be able to see what you've done to it.'

'I want you to. I've done the - '

'Don't tell me now. I asked you why.'

For a moment he put his elbows on the table and rested his head in his hands.

'You're frightened of her aren't you, men can be like that. It comes from baby, probably. 'The hand that rocks the cradle rules the world'. Isn't that the saying?'

'But man has the **magic wand** that rules the world. **Christ!** I shouldn't have said that.'

'It's alright, I think it's funny, but don't blaspheme.'

'I don't know how to answer the question.'

'Do you see her much? That seems silly, but do you spend time together that's good? Share things?'

'**No**, not really.'

'I've always thought you were a bit different from each other.'

''Cos we're different sexes?'

'Silly. You know what I mean.'

'We don't have shared interests?'

'Yes. This may sound like your father here, but are you doing your duty?'

'In what way?'

'You know what I mean. In bed.'

'I don't want to talk about it.'

'Well, talk about it with someone else then. It's not going well there is it?'

'Can we talk about something else?'

'When you've told me, yes.'

'I can't. I'm sorry.'

'So am I.'

'Come on, you've finished your grub, let's walk a bit more, or go shopping or something.'

'You used to dislike going shopping with me when you were a kid. D'you go with her much?'

'Not if I can help it. Come on then.'

They got up and walked round the bandstand and into the flower garden.

'Expect you wish you were still playing football with Frankie Benn and Terry, eh?'

He smiled at the mention of his childhood friends.

'We played till it was dark once, and got locked in.'

'You never told me. How did you get out then?'

'Forced a hole in the railings somehow.'

'I s'pose you got up to a lot of things you didn't tell me about.'

'Probably mum, it's what boys do.'

He asked her how his **relatives** were, which formed the basis of their conversation until they were in the street again.

'I won't stay for a cuppa.'

'Haven't asked you yet.'

At the front door he gave her a hug. She kissed him.

As he moved away from her, she said, 'Talk to somebody, even if it's Reg. I don't suppose you've told him anything.'

'No, not really. Don't worry about me. Keep well.'

He gave her a quick wave and began walking back to the station.

He went into the High road, glancing into a grocer's shop where a man behind the counter was cutting cheese with a wire, then passed the Jew shop where Aunt Gwen had sometimes worked when he was young, slipping him the occasional packet of Trebor Fruit Salad or a stick of Spanish wood to suck - he hadn't known it was liquorice root - when Ikey wasn't looking. He wasn't sure if that was his real name, his father had called all Jews 'Ikeys' or 'yids' or 'four-be-twos.'

Thinking of his father, a memory came of sitting next to him in a café while he ate a pie with lots of tomato sauce on which had made him feel sick just watching him. It had made him feel queasy when his parent used vinegar with the cockles and whelks he and brother-in-law had outside the pub, ripping them with his teeth and spitting bits out. He had very few memories of his fathe that made him feel something positive. His mother didn't speak of him much; today's comment was her first reference to him for quite a while.

He didn't have to see Frankie's old house to recall the things they'd got up to. Once, they'd played a game where they would go to the phone box in the main road, look in the directory to find the numbers of shops that did domestic repairs such as mending electrical goods and ask them to come to an address in their street of someone neither of them liked. Frankie had paid for the calls and did the talking while George searched through the directory. There had been a neighbour that was always scowling at them and telling them off. George, using the phone, had arranged for someone to come to her house to fix her typewriter. Sitting on a garden wall opposite her house they almost fell off it laughing when a van stopped and she, looking bewildered then angry, had argued with the driver. The boys doubted whether she even had a typewriter.

Another memory came as he saw the dentists. His mother had taken him there and, as its entrance had been at the side of a shop selling musical instruments, had pretended they were going into it because she didn't want him to be frightened. He had asked her why she'd said it was a music shop when it was a dentist's.

'Oh, you know where we are do yer? Didn't know you knew yer alphabet,' she'd said.

It wasn't as if he'd been away from her for long, it was only a few weeks, but it felt as if it was far longer. Perhaps it was the walking over the park with her that had rekindled the child in him.

Then, looking down the familiar road, he saw his old Elementary school. He'd seen it a thousand times since he had been a pupil there, but the images, memories, seemed to become clearer, stronger now.

It was a large, Victorian building with tall windows, and clusters of chimney pots on its slate roof. He would like to have seen an aerial photo of it showing it rising from the maze of terraced houses huddled into each other.

At twenty past nine every Monday to Friday morning he, along with three hundred other children, straggled through its tied-back iron gates, crossed the narrowest point of the playground - an asphalt square with several grimy trees standing brittle and solid in their narrow circles of earth - to the main entrance, climb a flight of stairs and shuffle into the big hall for morning assembly. This was a long, lofty space with wooden arches curving into the highest points of the flaking ceiling, its windows having dusty panes of distorted glass, while brown-painted girders formed the lintels above classroom doors.

The Lord's Prayer was ritually shouted by the grim-mouthed Headmaster against a backdrop of shuffling feet, girlish giggles and boys muffled protests as elbows dug into ribs, or toes trodden on either playfully or seriously depending upon being delivered by friend or foe.

Those who were interested enough learned the basic rudiments of maths - though he wasn't sure he had actually learned these - the English language, a primitive science in an ill-equipped class-room-cum-laboratory, handicrafts in a long asbestos-roofed workshop just inside the school railings, and music from a fat, chubby-fingered man who, as he played his records, leaned back in his chair until he was almost lying against the blackboard and, with closed eyes and without embarrassment, wave an imaginary baton and lived in the lilts of sound flowing from the classical composers. He attracted ridicule and often riotous disrespect and, from the more sensitive, pity.

History was a jumbled confusion of places and dates taught from a faded book and read aloud with an obvious reluctance in a flat, toneless voice by a weary, pinched man who looked as if he would rustle like papyrus if he moved.

The majority of the boys formed gangs and in the lunch hour, either in the playground or on the pavements and gutters outside, engaged in sweaty, knee-grazing battle, inspired occasionally by girls shouting encouragement to whatever group they held sym-pathy with or to their favourite hero.

Some of the boys learned, in quickly snatched unofficial les-sons in the high-walled outside toilet and with stinging eyes and much coughing and spluttering, how to smoke. Any enjoyment derived was almost accidental. As long as cigarettes, sometimes bought singly from a friendly tobacconist, could be lit inside un-necessary and exaggeratedly cupped hands and held tightly be-tween lips, this was what really mattered.

He hadn't indulged in this but, In the stirrings of puberty, he experienced, though just the once, along with some of the other lads, the tense, wonderfully strange experience of running a hand up and down a girl's leg when, sitting next to them in class, the teacher was turned away from his pupils as he chalked on the board.

He was, at the time, unaware that he craved attention but he now knew that it had manifested itself in several ways, one being to court acceptance by defying authority and causing trouble, though 'mischief' was a more appropriate word.

Once, he crept quietly from the back of the classroom to place a lighted firework next to the shoe of their Irish science teacher while he wrote on the board; the sharp explosion startling him. He felt suddenly sorry for this ineffectual man with flaring nostrils and an accent the young East Enders could barely understand, when, after asking them what was going on then turning back to the board, he frowned and said, 'Dere's sometin' scorchin'.' It was the bottom of his trousers.

He'd picked a fight with a long-legged boy from the next street to where he lived, this particular road his mother decreeing out of bounds because 'rough' people lived in it, and one he had only looked along, not been in.

They'd been in different classes and both had waited impatiently for the bell signalling the end of a lesson so they could hurry out the rooms to hunt each other, punching and pulling each other's hair as often as the limited time period allowed. He remembered hurrying from an art class and grappling with the boy, stinking of chemicals from the science lab, and not knowing how it had started, or what it was about.

Fighting had been expected. When he had first come to Pretoria Road School he'd been picked on by the class bully and knew intuitively that he had to hit back or be at his, and others, mercy for the rest of his time there.

Around this time he remembered joining a group of boys headed by a West Indian lad who insisted they call him 'Sambo'. They smashed the windows of the local public bath house one night and, later, when he asked the others involved why they had done it, they'd said they thought that each of the others had wanted to and had gone along with them. It was a comedy of errors.

He winced now at how self-conscious he had felt. He was small, skinny and rather anaemic-looking and although occasionally given sarcastic advice by other pupils to make him taller, such as putting weights on his feet when in bed to stretch him or putting horse dung in his boots, he had gained some status by playing football for the school, though the team was invariably bottom of the local schools league. Although the smallest member of the team, he played in goal but preferred to be the tricky inside forward he felt he was.

He practised over the park and in the school playground, diving around between two stools set up against the school building. One of the maths teachers had played centre forward as an amateur for England and, while in the playground watching him inadvertently building up scar tissue on his elbows, said in his posh, public school voice, 'You are a very brave boy, Woods.' This pleased him. He didn't know how a man like this came to be at his school.

Although he went his own way in art lessons, preferring to draw and paint what he wanted, not what he was told, the teacher informed him that he had been chosen to go to Art School. As an insecure thirteen-year-old, George asked if any of his friends were going. When told peremptorily that it was only he who had been selected and, having no guidance, encouragement, nor another word from the teacher, had said 'no'. He had never mentioned this to his mother, he felt there was little point, she wouldn't have understood.

He had no idea what he wanted to do after he'd left his school, except perhaps something to do with art. At the end of one summer term he and other boys and girls in his class were sent one by one into the Headmaster's room, with its oriole window looking down on the hall. Those who weren't leaving to work at the local leather cloth works or in the leather cloth factory, or Tate & Lyle, were to be told what school they would be going to in the furtherance of their education. This meant a tertiary school.

When his turn had come he had timidly knocked on the Head's door, entered when told to and walked towards the massive desk, standing with his hands fidgeting behind his back. The Headmaster had been looking through some papers, turning them slowly and carefully and, without looking up, had asked disinterestedly if George knew what he wanted to do when he left school.

'I'd like to, er, study art; drawing and painting,' had been the hoarsely-whispered reply.

He remembered it clearly. The Headmaster had stopped what he'd been doing for a few seconds and mumbled that George would be going to the 'School of Building,' and had continued with his work. The silence had held a heavy air of finality and George had quietly closed the door the door behind him wondering anxiously if anybody else he knew would be going there. The Head had not looked at him once. Art as a means of earning a living wasn't really in keeping with the ethos of Pretoria Road School.

But, though not doing what he thought he had wanted to do, he had learned things at the college; not only some rudimentary knowledge of bricklaying and carpentry - it was in the latter class that he'd met Reg - but to grain, marble and, above all, to signwrite.

Although it hadn't been a very gratifying experience, a part of him now wanted to be back there, wished that he was, once again, too young to be living with a girl, to be considered responsible enough to be in a mature relationship, to be part of a convention where he was supposed to make someone happy, to consider their needs, their desires. He wasn't sure of hers. He felt briefly ashamed when he admitted to himself that he didn't really want to know what they were. He wasn't sure of anything about her, really.

He had reached the station and went through its ancient entrance, down stairs and onto a platform. He looked along the track and felt suddenly lost as if his surroundings had become alien, hostile. Not knowing what to do, for a second he felt paralysed. Then, just before a train halted in front of him, he visibly shook his head as if attempting to hurl unwanted things out of it.

He stepped into a carriage, sat down and gazed out of its widows, watching the grimed bricks, slate roofs, old lamp posts and grey streets gradually turn into painted fender, large panes of glass, red and, sometimes, green-tiled roofs, glimpses of wide roads and, above all, trees. At least, he had this, his home was in this place; a little further along and he'd be there. He didn't want to think who he was sharing it with.

8

'So, I'm going to branch out a little into sociology, most of you have heard of it, I'm sure. It is the study of society, patterns of social relationships, social interaction and the culture of everyday life. It's a way of looking at the world. 'Society' is an abstract noun that we reify; that is, we *feel* it as something real and tangible, just like love and loyalty. Incidentally, children naturally reify, how would they learn the concepts that control them if they didn't? How many,' he asked, standing behind an empty lectern and looking meaningfully around him, 'died through abstractions like 'patriotism' and 'duty' during the last war?'

It was the same man who had given the introductory lecture Rupert had attended. It had already begun when, having woken from a satisfying sleep rather late and eating a hurried breakfast in the common room, almost on his own as it emptied quickly as the various lectures started, he'd arrived.

'It is a social science that uses various methods of empirical investigation and critical analysis to develop a body of knowledge about social order, acceptance, and change, or social evolution, if you will.

'It touches upon moral philosophy, but let us not go into that byzantine maelstrom of the genesis of morality, Aristotle Socrates, et cetera. Morals are,' he raised his voice a little, 'culturally determined, full stop, or as the Americans are wont to say, 'period'. Saint-Simon published La physiologie sociale in eighteen thirteen and devoted much of his time to the prospect that human society could be steered toward progress if scientists could distract groups from war and strife by focusing their attention to generally improving their societies' living conditions. As well-intentioned as that may sound, 'progress' is a value judgement; one man's so-called progress may be another's disaster. Again, the war: explosives, guns, shells… 'Progress'?'

Rupert looked briefly about to see if Eric was here and spotted him at the front.

'Society, then,' continued the lecturer, whose name Rupert still didn't know, 'means order, behaviour removed from the randomness of chance, and sociology is a perspective on that behaviour. And yes, it's a generalising enterprise, but let's not apologise for it, if we don't deal in generalisations then we couldn't attempt a social science. Psychology is full of them; the Oedipal, manic-depressive, paranoia, et cetera. Talking of which, we're getting close to natural explanations of behaviour. But how are they manifested? Alright, does anyone want to ask a question?'

Someone in the front row put a hand up, but was cut short before he could speak.

'Do you all think,' continued the speaker, pointing downwards, 'that it is 'natural' for him to put up his hand to denote he intends asking a question? Or, is it *learned* behaviour?' He paused. 'When do we first do it? That's a rhetorical question by the way; I have a tendency to ask them. It was at school, wasn't it.'

About half of the gathering nodded their heads and smiled.

'I was going to say, 'Say no more,' but of course I shall. These are two of the prerequisite statements of the subject then. We internalize the social world, its norms, and values - we do in fact do so from birth; baby girls are put in pink, boys in blue - they get inside us, form us. Secondly, *Man* makes society, not the other way around.

'This is not to say that we are merely stimulus-response mechanisms; we have creativity and the like. Alright, we are doing philosophy, so there's a philosophical point to make, is there not. Anyone?'

He looked around the theatre.

The student who had previously raised his hand to ask a question, said, 'Isn't that a circular argument between the psychological and the sociological? Man makes society, society makes man?'

Rupert realised it was Eric who had spoken.

'Indeed; yet another tautology in the world of theory and knowledge. Good.'

The speaker looked down at Eric and asked him to ask the question he was about to pose earlier.

'I was going to ask that if humans are considered part of nature then wouldn't everything they do be 'natural'?'

The lecturer threw his hands in the air then began twisting about and whirling around as if imitating the proverbial dervish, while uttering distorted, animal-like sounds, all the while with a twisted mouth and eyes almost bulging. He stopped.

'You would argue that that is natural then?' he asked the questioner.

'I could do.'

'Of course, anything goes, a carte blanche, we are part of nature, yes, but my behaviour then went against our current social norms and thus, would, perhaps, be considered 'unnatural.''

'A kind of nature versus nurture thing, then,' said Eric.

'It doesn't have to be one or the other of course, and it depends on context, we'll come to that when we discuss deviance - and you'll find that all of you have been offenders in one way or another - but as implied here and as I've said, our norms, our behaviour, are largely *socially* determined. Keep hold of that idea, think on it. In fact, I would like you to see it almost as a truism. Any more questions?'

There were two more; one on what strands of philosophical thought economics had emanated from, and another relating to Socrates, which got a long but disinterested answer. Then, after the lecturer had given a rather abrasive answer to a query on metaphysics, the lecture finished.

Eric was looking back for Rupert when the latter hurried down to him. They went out into the Quad.

Rupert suggested they go to the Fellows' garden which he knew was nearby. They went out to it through a passage and found a bench to sprawl on.

'Well, here am I,' said Rupert, 'thinking you were all, 'Romeo, Romeo...' and 'Is that a knife I see before - '

''Dagger''.

'And here you are, a regular rationalist, a logician, you've kidded me.'

'That's an Americanism. My lecture starts later than yours; that's why I dropped in and had a taste.'

'And it had a taste of you.'

'Did you like the taste?'

'Of course. Come over to my side, the king of subjects; the empire of thought.'

'That your own phrase? Think I prefer Will's 'majesties and dominions'. He's an engaging chap, your philosophy man, isn't he, d'you know whether he's your seminar leader?'

'I hope he is.'

'I believe the English bloke we heard is going to be mine.'

He looked around him and pointed to some stone steps at the end of the Garden.

'I say, let's walk up there, I think it's called The Mound. See what we can see.'

They walked to the end of the garden and climbed the steps, there weren't that many of them and the top seemed a lot higher than it should have been. They could see buildings in a rather large, cobbled square.

'That's Radcliffe Square,' said Eric, and pointing to an imposing circular building in its centre, told his listener that it was the Radcliffe Camera.

'It's a library, and the main building there is the Bodleian. Apparently there's an underground railway that transports books between them.'

'You sound like a guide.'

'I've merely done my homework, that's all. That's Brasenose College to the west and opposite is All Souls, they have only fellows there, I suppose it's mostly dedicated to research. Oh, and the tall spire there is **The Church** of Saint Mary's.'

'Are you going to charge me for this stationary tour?'

'I'll let you off. It's grand though, isn't it?'

'Just to be here is; and to be a part of it.'

'Wonder how Alec et al are faring.' asked Eric.

'Trying to settle down, as we are.'

'Let's go down and lie on the grass.'

'Soak up the last of the **autumnal** sun,' said Rupert.'

'You sound poetic. You know, I wonder if your lecturer man is positing a sort of tabula rasa.'

'A blank slate upon which experience has yet to write?'

'Yes, that we are, somehow, infinitely malleable and educable.'

'And?' asked Rupert.

'Well, when we feel something strongly - '

'You don't think that it can come from outside of us?'

'The cause can, but the emotions are ours', replied Eric.

'Of course, but maybe you wouldn't have those feelings, those reactions to the same things if you were brought up in a different culture.'

'Alright, but - '

'Psychology provides rock-bottom explanations? I think that's what you're getting near to.'

'A tempting view.'

'Are you going back to birth experience?' The womb?' asked Rupert. 'I believe there's a school of thought that posits the influence of the latter.'

'Freud?'

'Don't think he goes back that far. Don't forget, the womb experience can be a result of the outside world. Let's say, in this recession we're going through, it affects Joe Bloggs - it's put three and a half million out of work up till now - and he's depressed and arguing continuously with his pregnant wife.'

'And it affects the embryo, I understand that. Oh dear, life is hard then you die. Lord, my lecture!'

Eric looked at his watch, and stood.

'I've got five minutes.'

'Thought fob watches weren't de rigueur.'

'They aren't. Continue laying in the sun, young man.'

'Must ring my friend Andrew, I haven't yet. Need to find a phone box.'

'Oh, there's a phone box opposite our rooms, it's almost hidden inside an alcove across the Quad.'

'You seem to know everything.'

'Well, things worth knowing. I rang my Fiona earlier, she's pretty excited about this whole thing, really, despite that sweet, calm manner, and missing me. I shall see you anon.'

He touched an imaginary forelock and hurried away.

Rupert, wanting to decipher his hastily-taken lecture notes, went back to his room. It still felt strange despite having his clothes on display, some in the open wardrobe, the rest flung over chairs and a bed, and a photo on the desk of his mother in her first major part in rep playing Juliet.

He also had a picture of her laying a protective hand on his shoulder in a smile-for-the-camera snap his father had taken just before he went to boarding school in Eltham, He'd been thirteen. He certainly wouldn't have kept a photo of just himself, with or without other pupils or masters. Nothing had been said in his hearing at the time, but he knew that she hadn't wanted him to go. Again it was his father ruling the roost.

He had insisted on accompanying Rupert to the new school despite his protests, for not only did he constantly embarrass his son when out with him by telling him to pull his shoulders back and to breathe deeply - a leftover from his army days - but seeming to wait purposely until they were in earshot of a dozen people. He remembered his mother appealing to her husband not to wear his uniform that day.

It had been arranged that he go with a boy whose father was a friend of the family and who lived quite near them. They had previously been to different schools, but when Rupert had learned that he, too, was bound for the same institution for the next five years he purposely saw more of him than he had done in the past, and towards the end of the summer holidays they had sworn eternal friendship, a type of relationship that is started by a sympathy of feeling towards a common situation and which is, often, bound by only that.

As they'd neared their destination, an hour's drive from home in his father's Ford de Luxe coupe, isolated groups of fathers and sons, occasionally mothers, stood, in the silence of newness, outside a Georgian manor house on a wide, sloping forecourt. Rupert's friend leaned against a nearby wall, his father next to him. The latter had walked across to Richard Colls, shook his hand and said, 'Got here then, old chap,' and, bending his face forward to look down at Rupert, said, 'Well, young man, ready for the off? You and Edwin will do well here, I'm sure.'

His son had smiled nervously at Rupert, who felt tense, as he often was when with his father, and willed both the grown-ups to return home.

Richard Colls had looked around with a self-satisfied air and rocked slowly backwards and forwards on his heels with hands held loosely behind him. He repeatedly pushed his shoulders back, vigorously sniffing and nodding his head in approval as if in the middle of the countryside admiring the scenic beauty spread before him.

'Yes, it looks a nice school, son. They seem to be decent boys. I think you'll be tickety-boo here.' He'd said it quietly, but it seemed to bellow out, echoing around the forecourt. The sound of a bell had come from within and parents and progeny had moved towards the entrance.

'You'll be alright then, son?'

Rupert remembered gritting his teeth and momentarily closing his eyes, He'd felt like an eight-year-old.

'Yes, dad.'

His father had looked uncomfortable and said hesitantly, 'Well, cheerio, son.' and walked away, Edwin's father following him.

Almost immediately the boys were herded together by masters wearing gowns, and ushered into a hall. It seemed vast; Rupert had recently seen a photo of an aircraft hangar, it appeared just as large, though the hangar didn't have oil paintings covered in heavy varnish, of elderly men with town hall faces, smug eyes, snug waistcoats, mayoral chains and, some, mortar boards.

The Principal of the school, a preparatory one his father had assured him was amongst the best in England, had welcomed them. He was rather squat and wide of girth with a deep voice which, echoing around the space, informed them that they would be educated to the highest standard and made ready for their entrance into academia and the good things of life.

Rupert had never slept in a room with other boys before. He had once been camping with the scouts, but it was in a small bell tent and there were only half-a-dozen of them in it, here there were sixty. He'd felt shy about undressing in front of the other boys. He wanted to cry and wished his mother was with him, but knew that both the want and the wish were pointless. He had lain under his sheet and blanket, sniffed a few tears away and mentally squared his shoulders. He was a big boy now and, apparently, according to his father, a brave soldier.

In the morning, after removing their pyjamas and dressing quickly, they had been ushered by a master into the refectory for a breakfast of corn flakes, toast and boiled eggs then once more hurried into the hall for the Principal's speech. He was already standing at the front of its stage and had impatiently waited for his young audience to settle.

'Welcome to Eltham', he'd rasped. 'You will be taught many things: maths, science, history, geography, literature, foreign languages and drama. You will also learn independence, resourcefulness, to live with others, to adapt and....' he paused for effect, 'to be careful who you trust. Above all, you will learn to respect yourselves. Your masters will put you into you separate classes. Off you go.'

He'd gestured with arms and hands as if urging them to go away.

They had, indeed, learnt the specified subjects: English language being the one Rupert was most enthusiastic about. In compositions, or essays as they were sometimes called, he would relentlessly use all the adjectives he could think of, appropriate or otherwise, to create the scenes he imagined, and wrote until he had to stop to rest himself from the colours and words spinning inside him.

He would look up in class to see the few boys that were left after the bell crowding around the classroom door to get out. At times like this he'd felt elated and excited and ran along the hall, passing his classmates, then turn back to them, babbling in a high-pitched voice and laughing and feeling that he could fly. He'd cried when his English teacher had left.

There had been a few extra-curricular activities not mentioned that would lighten the classroom rituals. One such had been created by a geography teacher who had decided to teach his young charges, in the main hall and after hurriedly scoffed meals in the lunch hour, ballroom dancing. Attendance had been voluntary, though there had been gentle pressure from most of the other masters to go along.

The boys would dance with each other, those having to play the woman's role gritting their teeth in the midst of playfully sarcastic comments. One boy, a particularly small lad, had been made to stand on the teacher's shoes and was whirled around as a teaching aid, like a puppet at a seaside fairground.

And, of course, there was the game. He recalled his father, who had played scrum half for his regiment, standing on the side of the pitch at a Saturday morning game on a rare visit to his son, shouting, as opposing backs thumped towards his offspring, 'Stop them, son. Hold them, hold them.' To Rupert, their legs had seemed like giant slugs.

He had shown some ability for boxing, but his interest ceased when he'd knocked a boy's front tooth out when sparring.

During Christmas, a rare weekend at home for him, his father had bought a pair of sawdust-filled boxing gloves and at a party had told him to come into the dining room where he had tied them on him and challenged his son to hit him. Rupert had feinted with his left then hit him hard with his right. The recipient had looked astonished and, wiping the blood from his nose, had called proudly to some relatives and neighbours gathered in the front room to come and look at what his offspring had done. Never did Rupert see him so enthusiastically proud again.

Something in him had told him to try not to adopt the ways of the school. He saw, though could not quite articulate, the attitudes the boys were forming; there was something superior about them, even to each other they tried to show that they were. Edwin, though Rupert hadn't known him that well, had changed; he felt sometimes that he was looking down on him because his father was richer than his own.

Recalling that time now, he could detach and view it dispassionately. Or try to. He saw his old school, amongst other, similar, schools, in essence as a centre of socialization for the next generation of the political upper class and which virtually reproduced the class system. Looking back at his encounters with members of the boys' families, he could see now that they valued power and hierarchy as the main concepts to be internalized by their male children. He suspected that they shared a virtually unthought sense of entitlement, which was reinforced by the boys living and mingling with others of a similar hierarchy; an 'old boy' network' as his father would say.

At some boarding schools, elite ones - he was unsure whether Eltham was in that league - students were, he was sure, brought up with the assumption that they were meant to control society and that significant numbers of them would enter the political class or join the financial elite. He thought that perhaps Eric was in the latter group.

He could now see how important the idea of hierarchy was to their education, especially in the refectory where cliques had formed on the basis of wealth and social background; and from there a pervasive form of explicit and implicit bullying came, with excessive competition between the cliques. He had never been really sure where to sit, who to sit next to.

Looking back, he could see that he and the others had been living in a world almost completely dissociated from home life. They had a different vocabulary, even different voices. He recalled talking to one boy after he had returned from being at home for a few weeks who had told him that, when first arriving home, he had referred to his mother as 'matron' and had addressed male relatives and friends of his family as 'sir', as if they were masters. It was as if school life had become the reality, and home life the illusion.

But, maybe, it had all helped him to 'toughen up' - one of this father's favourite terms - for the competitiveness of university, though he didn't want to compete with anyone, didn't want to beat other students at his subject, and had little desire to be 'the best' for the sake of it. He wished to learn his subject, to use it in debate, argument, in seminars, in his essays, and if he did well in these, that would do him.

A part of him missed his mother. He wondered how her play was doing. He sat at the small desk and began writing a letter to her. He would ring Andrew later.

9

It was happening again. It made him gape and stretch his lips. It was a similar feeling to when he urinated after holding it in for a long while, something affecting his throat and neck. But this wasn't merely physical; it was what he felt emotionally. He couldn't really describe it, but knew where it came from.

He'd just glanced at an estate house as he passed it while walking home after work and purposely taking the long way around. It was almost identical to the 'posh aunt' one, or one nearby he had seen as a young child, and he was immediately there again in time and place. It could, though, have been a house in a book illustration, on a station poster, or in a film where a man in a trilby hat and a woman in a smart dress came out of their home, perhaps to greet him in their well-spoken middle class accents. Or it could have been a dream of any of all of them, or even a dream of a dream. But it was strong. He sat down for a few seconds on someone's front wall then continued walking. He knew it was significant, and was, he was convinced, an early refusal to accept his parents.

He may have been little more than a baby when it happened, he didn't know. But he hadn't wanted to live with them, especially dad. The house that now filled his head somehow represented different, compensatory parents, and more than substitutes; ones he *should* have had. He felt the sensation in his throat again and stretched his mouth.

He'd wanted another mum, a different one, someone gentle and sweet and… He halted again and another emotion overtook him, it was the same feeling he'd had then; one of guilt. It had inhabited him. No, he could not have accepted another mother, couldn't have left his own, couldn't have run out of his father's house and found the nearest well-dressed couple and told them he wanted them as his parents. He was glad his mother was alive; the child in him would otherwise have had to bear its guilt for ever.

He became aware of why he was doing so much with the house, it was a sort of fake self, not the real one that he should have developed from an early acceptance of his parents. He had little knowledge of psychology but knew this was so. He wanted to tell someone; knowing that he wouldn't. Doris had got to it without him saying anything to her when, watching him briefly and with disinterest painting his final butterfly, she had said, 'This house is more real to you than I am.'

But was it solely a function of him? Would he be different, would he, perhaps, be more grown up with someone else? She would have to be more physically attractive, not have that rather annoying little bend in her nose that Doris had, and have fuller lips. Doris had been his first real girl friend, other than Pauline Parker who had lived opposite him as a child and who he'd had a crush on. He remembered walking over the park with her; and his mum passing by them with a neighbour and saying, 'What are you up to then? Enjoying yourself are you?' He'd felt shy and, somehow, a little ashamed and hadn't gone for a walk with her again.

He'd liked going to dances with Doris, she had nice legs and when they'd been jitterbugging at the Hammersmith Palais and she'd spun around, they, along with her knickers, had showed in their entirety. But these things, he knew, shouldn't have led him to where he was now.

When he got home she was listening to The BBC Dance Orchestra, it had a distinctive sound, one he rather enjoyed, though he would have preferred it if she had not been in, he liked the moments on his own when coming in from using his brush in the West End or the City or wherever.

She turned off the radio as he entered the room

'Why d'you do that? You know I like it.'

'There's lots of things you like, doesn't mean you can have them though,' she said as she got up from her chair and went into the kitchen.

'Don't understand. You gonna make a cuppa then?'

'If you want one I suppose. You going to paint your butterfly again this evening?'

'I want to finish it.'

'What are you going to do after that then? Paint a picture of New York at night on the bedroom ceiling? Or do a mural with Myrna Loy in it? Or perhaps dig up the garden and redo it with three fountains this time?'

He sighed. 'What is it this time? I've just got in, just a bit of… peace would do.'

She came out of the kitchen holding a plate.

'This is yours, I've had mine.'

It was an undercooked and lukewarm sausage with mashed potatoes. He took it from her, told her he would re-warm it and returned the meal to the oven.

'Please yourself,' she said and sat in front of the radio and turned it on then off again.

He came back into the room, took a deep breath and started singing, loudly and out of tune, 'We are the West Ham boys, we are the West Ham boys, we know our manners, we spend our tanners, we are respected wherever we go. When we walk along the Barking Road doors and windows open wide, when we see a bobby come, it's up with the ball and away we run, we are the West Ham boys.'

She looked at him, frowning.

'What d'you want to sing that for? I'm fed up.'

'I know.'

'Well, why don't you do something about it?'

'Such as?'

'You just … spend all your time doing things that are nothing to do with me, really.'

'You mean the house?'

'Yes. We don't do anything together. When was the last time we went out to see a film or something? We used to go dancing, but not any more.'

She looked down at herself.

'And why am I wearing this bloody pinny?'

She pulled it off.

'I don't want to cook any more. Why don't you do some of it? Your mum's always done the cooking so you expect me to.'

'I thought you liked cooking.'

'Well, I don't. And when's your mum coming here again? Ever?'

'You know why she doesn't.'

'She could invite me over to hers, couldn't she?'

She threw the apron down.

'I'm lonely, George,' She said defiantly.

'Well… you've got your friends.'

'I had one friend and she won't come to see me. It's too far, she says.'

'Sounds like an excuse.'

'Oh, thanks, that's cheered me up.'

She was silent for a while.

'You've never cheered me up, really, have you. You don't know how to. Well, not these days, anyway.'

He didn't want any of this. She was sweet in some ways, but he wanted to be on his own.

'You think more of this house than you do me.'

She said it quietly, but there seemed a tone of finality about it, as if something absolute had been said.

'That's not fair,' he said, knowing that the words held some truth, but he didn't know what else to say.

'D'you remember what you said when you thought Arthur was after me?'

'Arthur?'

'Arthur Biggs, the order clerk in the office; you said you thought he fancied me. You met him once.'

'Don't remember.'

'I do, he's a **work friend,** we get on well, he's funny. I wondered if you were jealous.'

'Like I say, I - '

'It would have been alright if you *had* been jealous, it would have meant that I meant something to you. I don't think you're capable of jealousy, not about me, anyway. If you **had** been it would be because you'd considered me your property, and you certainly don't. The only property that interests you is the one we're living in, if you can call it living.'

'What's brought all this on?'

'Is that all you can say? You're so corny at times.'

'How do you want me to phrase it then? 'Oh darling, why are you so seething with rage?'

'Actually, I'd like you just to go. Go and see Reg or someone, just leave me alone.'

'I'm not touching you.'

She took a step towards him.

'When was the last time you did? What's the point of sleeping with me? It's not as if you're affectionate anyway, as if you cuddle me or- '

'Whisper sweet nothings?'

'That would be better than just silence wouldn't it.'

'Silence is golden.'

'Yours is tarnished.'

'Oh, we are witty aren't we.'

'Sarcasm, the lowest form of wit.'

'Humour.'

'I don't care what it is, George, you're just being awkward. You're not taking me seriously.'

He felt as if immersed in an alienating vacuum. He wanted to break out of it but didn't quite know how, or where to go when he had.

'I don't want to argue, just… ' He felt too weary to finish what he was going to say, whatever it was.

'And you don't want me here to argue with, do you,' she said, her face pinched and bloodless.

He took a deep breath.

'Look, if you've had a rotten day at work, then… I don't know, listen to the **wireless** or something; make a cuppa.'

'You sound like your mum.'

'You said that with a sneer. Why?'

'I don't want my thirst satisfied, and the appetite I do have you won't'. She hesitated. 'Or, perhaps, can't satisfy, not these days, anyway. But that's secondary; a real relationship would be nice.'

'I don't think I've known you be quite so sarcastic like this.'

'There's a lot you don't know about me. It's because you don't really care. In fact, I don't think I want you to know me now.'

She turned and went into the kitchen. He could hear cupboard doors being noisily opened and shut then the lid of the waste bin clanging open and a second afterwards the kitchen door swinging against the fence. He heard rubbish being put in the dustbin.

'Nice garden,' she called, 'just like a landed estate in minia- ture. Is that what you had in mind? Ooh, look at the rockery with its lovely white stones and flowers and pampas grass between them, and some marble here too, and that tree. Did you plant it? That'll look lovely in a few years.'

He went inside and looked through the window above the sink. She was walking determinedly towards the pond.

'Oh, what a lovely fountain, it's so sweet,' she shrilled, 'I think I'll take a look.'

She took a step to the edge of the pond, drew back her leg and kicked at the fountain.

It was her bare, outstretched leg that momentarily filled his mind rather than the falling stone cherub holding its cornet- shaped shell and, with a splash, sinking below the water. He knew he should be angry, but it was as if as if his emotions had been rationed and he'd used them up.

She walked back to the kitchen, went straight past him and up the stairs, her feet making more noise than her weight suggested. It seemed deliberate. He could hear the wardrobe door opening, and some ruffling sounds.

'I don't want you sleeping with me again, George. You've got that new fancy bed you bought for the other bedroom, you can sleep on that, you'll probably prefer an empty one.' She was al- most shouting. 'You **bought it,** you use it.'

The bedroom door slammed shut.

It took a while for him to realise what she'd said. He was un- sure whether she had **said,** 'again' or 'tonight.' He felt a hollow- ness which then filled with apprehension. He wasn't sure how to react. He was split, and knew it was the child in him that was frightened. He remembered Reg talking about a psychology book he'd read which stated that, to the child in each of us, every man you met was your father, every woman, your mother. Doris was, perhaps, his mother rejecting him, telling him she didn't want him any more. But he had a mother; he'd seen her recently and had told her some jokes, her face, as always, lighting up when he told them, even if they were corny. 'You silly sod,' she'd say affectionately.

He went out to the garden, knelt by the pool, immersed his hands in the water, pulled the statue up, with water pipe still attached, and placed it back on the top of its mound of stones. He would cement it later. He sat on the sofa. The sound of the slamming door still seemed to be reverberating in the silence.

He liked the bed, 'though she'd thought it too 'showy,' but would he feel more alone in it than he did when sharing a bed with her? He wondered what other men would do in his situation. Perhaps they would march up the stars and confront their partner, either angrily or, in a conciliatory manner, talk it though with them, vow that they would behave differently, would change. He couldn't do that, perhaps wasn't mature enough; maybe didn't want to. He would sleep in the other bedroom, like a lodger. But he wasn't. It was his house.

Still feeling unsure of what he should do, how he should feel, he went out. He would, he decided, go to the phone box in The Broadway and ring Reg, and if he was in suggest the Park men's club and have a drink and maybe play billiards. He passed a baker's electric barrow on the way being pushed by a whistling man and with 'use your loaf' written on one side of it and 'get your crumpets here' on the other. The words still mildly amused him. He hadn't thought of saying anything to Reg, though thinking of his mother's advice; thought that perhaps he should.

It occurred to him that the estate was being officially opened at the weekend. He thought it already had been and was surprised when told it hadn't. He would ask a mate or two to go with him, but he'd be quite happy go on his own. He wouldn't want her with him; it was he that was buying his own place. It was *his* celebration.

10

'It's been a while, what?'

'Not that long.'

'I say. Are you still in the club?'

'Of course, I'm a town member.'

'Oh, I'm a country member.'

'Yes. I remember.'

They both laughed.

'You can't beat the old ones can you,' said Andrew.

'The old ones are the old ones.'

Using the phone box in the alcove, Rupert was speaking with his friend.

'Should have rung you earlier, of course.'

'How's things?'

'Pretty good, will be attending my first seminar in a little while.'

'Accommodation?'

'Small but satisfactory.'

'I asked about your room, not your penis. How are the other people, or rather, undergrads?'

'I've got a bit friendly with one chap, rather moneyed, I think.'

'Nouveau?'

'No, old money, probably.'

'Money talks'

'All mine seems to say is goodbye.'

'You're doing okay.'

'Father seems to be.'

'The lectures?'

'Pretty good.'

'Any women?'

'Not at oxford.'

'What sort of people are you studying? What are they famous for?'

'Oh, you know… 'To be is to do', Descartes. 'To do is to be', Marx. 'Be do be do be do', Sinatra.'

'Not bad, for you. How's your mother?'

'Wrote a note to her wishing her luck with her play.'

'Shouldn't think she'll need it. I trust you are adhering to the values of the elite social class which you have sprung from, or at least are aspiring to be part of.'

'If I hadn't left prep when I did I'd have *become t*hose values. Boarding schools not only control their students' physical lives but their emotional ones as well. You know this, anyway.'

'Not through personal experience, fortunately.'

'The firm holding up?'

'Yes, considering everything, we're doing alright really. Dad's pretty astute. This slump's a bad thing. I admire your dad, he took a chance with his development, but it's come off.'

'Yes. Catastrophic for some, though. What caused it all?'

'Many reasons. Credit interest rates not high enough, war debts, Farms in the States going bankrupt and not able to pay back loans, banks going under.'

'Unequal distribution of wealth?'

'Yep. Plus high tariffs, over-production in industry and agriculture, especially in America. It apparently started with a bank run in Nashville, Tennessee, which kicked off a wave of similar incidents throughout the country, too many depositors losing confidence in their bank all at once. Deflation meant too little income for loans and debts to be repaid, bankruptcies and defaults increased. It's still happening. You okay with this?' Not using too much jargon for your relatively untrained ears? Though it's not as gobbledegook as your philosophy.'

'They're both kinds of restricted codes, based on the assumption of shared experience.'

'Some codes would have more status than others, yes?' Andrew asked.

'Interesting. Doubt whether, say, poetry would have more status than the financial code, though.'

'It'd have more status than the codes of the so-called great unwashed, I'm sure.'

'Such as?'

'Their football pools, dog racing, billiards and their 'alf o' pint and winkles down at the pub.

'It 's good to hear you, you know,' said Rupert.

'Ditto.'

'What have you been doing with yourself?'

'The flicks; saw 'Born to be Bad', then yesterday went to the Dominion to see 'Mutiny on the Bounty.' Just a minute.'

There was a short silence partly filled by the tapping of typewriters.

'Dad calling me, some stocks in trouble again, must go. Ring me again, Roop. Jeers.'

He had time before his seminar to get to the library and see what books from his reading list he could find and walked to nearby Tirl street, recalling a description he'd read of it. 'A masterly composition with fenestration and carved detail, the arcade articulating the quatrefoil windows which admit a diffuse light to the reading room.' He wasn't sure why he'd remembered it.

It was like entering a church. Amidst its restfulness, he had a familiar feeling of disquiet which was made all the more relevant as he made his way to the philosophy section and passed tomes on religion illuminated by the sunlight coming through the stained glass window at the end of the aisle. He moved further down it, ignoring treatises on morality, until he found copies of Descarte's, Principles of Philosophy, Hobbes, Leviathan and, pleasingly, the first volume of Marx's, Das Kapital.

He had intended to return to his room to read, especially as the cloistered pseudo- religiosity of the place suppressed his spirit a little, then, with a smile, he took confidence in his holding the book of a man who, in agreement with its soon-to-be reader, saw religion as the mass's opiate, and took a seat at an empty table. He read and took notes, wondering why he hadn't bothered to read the book before, for almost an hour then decided to get some refreshments. He glanced around him, something he hadn't done since beginning his reading.

There weren't many students there, 'noses stuck in books' as his father would have remarked, but a few feet behind him, standing on a wooden pair of steps replacing a book on the top shelf, was a tall, flaxen-haired girl with full lips, pale blue eyes and a rather purposeful expression. It felt for a moment as if he was in an academicized place of worship and she was the chief angel in charge of it. He hadn't seen a woman in the college since he'd been there, he didn't think they were allowed.

He must have stared at her for an unacceptably long time for, looking down at him, she said quietly but clearly, 'Is it because I am on a pair of steps, or because I'm a woman or, perhaps, because I am looking down on you? something you may not be used to.'

He wasn't sure how to react; she seemed so... solid, so instantly inflexible. Then he saw the slight glint of humour in her eyes.

'Er... all of them, in that order,' he replied.

'And, of course, because you don't expect to see women here.'

'That, too. Alright, it was the main one.'

He watched her replace several more books before she came down the steps, went to a small trolley at their base, took some more publications from it and climbed up again. He looked at her legs; long slim and clad in dark blue stockings.

'Are you looking at my stockings?' she asked, peering at the spine of a book.

'Yes, why?'

'Why am I asking or, why am I wearing them?'

'The latter.'

'I like the colour.'

'It's more than that. It's an Eighteenth Century thing isn't it?'

'If you mean that it originated then, yes. It symbolised an informal women's social and educational movement emphasising education and mutual co-operation,' she said, replacing more books.

'You've done your homework.'

'Llet's hope you are doing yours.'

'Are you wearing them as some sort of statement?'

'If you like.'

'What is the statement? That you are a modern woman who wants to be seen as intellectually equal to men?'

She stopped what she was doing and, looking down at him again said, 'At the very least, and also desiring, as of right, to have equal chances educationally.'

'I was going to ask what else you wanted, you've already got the vote.'

'Some have.'

'What many women want is to be allowed to study at Cambridge, and, particularly for me, to study here.

'Why here?'

'Because I work here, yet cannot study here.'

'But you can go to another university. You can get a degree.'

'I'm aware of that. What I mean is that... I'm not in a position to study for one.'

'There's Girton College, maybe one day that will be part of Cambridge.'

'One day, perhaps. You don't understand. I can't study, there's an obstacle. My mother is an invald, I can't leave her for long periods.'

He suddenly wanted to know more about her.

'What does your father do?'

'The classic question to discover someone's class background. It doesn't matter. He left mother some time ago.'

She came down the steps and continued gathering books and putting them on shelves.

He didn't really want to leave, so went back to his book. He read for a few minutes until interrupted by her asking him what he was reading, her voice just a little louder for this time she had moved further along the shelves away from him. He told her.

'Is that not a foundational text in material economics and politics by Karl Marx?' she asked.

'The way you asked it you know it is.'

'Do you like what he says?' she asked, engaged in her work and not looking at him.

'I don't know that much about him, but I like what I do know.'

'Which is?'

'That the wealth of the bourgeoisie depends on the work of the proletariat. That capitalism *needs* an exploited underclass.'

'To state the obvious.'

'I think you could also say he argues that the way we see the world, our consciousness, identity, our reality even, our political, cultural and economic systems are determined by the ways in which we technologically transmute the physical world.'

'I suppose he is.'

'You've read him then.'

'I have, as well as Barbara Cartland if that makes you feel more comfortable?'

'Why should it?'

'You can fit me into an easier stereotype. Though I do read Virginia, of course.'

'Woolf?'

'Yes.'

'I can't imagine you being a stereotype. You're - '

'Different?'

'Indeed.'

She asked him what he was studying. He told her.

'A route of many roads leading from nowhere to nothing,' she said.

'I think you can do better.'

'Why do Marxists,' she asked, 'drink only horrible tea?'

'Don't know.'

'Because all proper tea is theft. Better?'

'Perhaps.'

He watched her stretching to the top shelf, her official-looking white coat now lifted above her knees and her calves taut inside her worsted stockings. He wanted to help her.

'It's okay,' she said, 'I can manage.'

'Are you clairvoyant?'

'I think you're suggesting I have extrasensory perception. But, no, it's just the sort of thing a gentleman would suggest; to assist a woman although she is quite capable of doing what she's do-ing.'

She climbed down again, leant on her trolley and turned to him.

'If this scene was in a play, I would slip on the steps and you would rush forward to save me from falling and we would begin a relationship of dazzling charm, humour and sadness and, eventually, triumph.'

'I think I'd like to be in it.'

'Perhaps I could find you a small part.'

'Kind of you.'

'Think nothing of it.'

'I don't.'

He watched her pick up more books.

Look… Er, I feel strangely rather shy now, but my name's Rupert.'

She smiled.

'Mine's Constance, though I don't actually like it, to be honest, to be constant is rather boring.'

'Can be a good thing; honest and true and all that.'

'I haven't seen you here before. Just arrived?'

'Yep.'

'You look a little old for a First year.'

'Age is relative.

'To say it's all relative is to deny an absolute, yet the statement that it's all relative is itself an absolute. It can't claim privileged exemption.'

'I didn't say 'all.''

'No, but….' She looked to her side for a few seconds.

'I think I can see the librarian looking at me. I should get back to work.'

She gathered a few more books, moved the steps along the shelves and climbed again.

At the top she turned towards him and said, 'You're still looking at me. Haven't you work to do?'

He glanced up at the library clock.

'I have a seminar.'

He picked up his books and said, 'Incidentally, I do like your name.'

'Thanks.'

'But it kind of surprises me. It's too… innocent, girlish, if you like.'

'I am a girl. What d'you think it should be?'

'Maybe Zelda, or Ingrid, perhaps.'

'Not Greta then? Marta? Sadie?'

He smiled at her, told her he had to go, waved, and left the building.

Hurrying to his seminar, he realised that it wasn't just that she was a woman in an Oxford library that was the chief reason he'd stared at her, it was because she was such an attractive one.

He entered the classroom a second after Pym; who looked even taller from behind. There were a dozen or so students present. Rupert sat down on the nearest chair. Pym, who seated himself at one end of the long table, removed his gown and causally let it fall on the floor behind him. He leant forward and began.

'Okay then, I assume, and hope, that you have at least begun reading the books introducing the philosophical discipline of sociology which I wish to pursue and which lends itself to the criticisms emanating from the generic discipline which you are here to study and which were mentioned in my lecture, which I'm sure you all attended.

'As said, it's a way, one in which there is not one body of general theory that is widely validated and accepted. That, as philosophy students, you should see as a good thing and should, one hopes, provide for some academic cut and thrust amongst you. I did mention in the aforesaid lecture that our behaviour is largely determined by the social world around us, it gets into us from birth, it's called socialization. It's the process of internalizing the norms and ideologies of society and thus the means by which both the social and cultural is attained.

'It's part of the psychological development of children. In short, what we often feel is natural behaviour is learned through this process. I will come back to this occasionally during your time with me.' H e looked around at them briefly and rather casually and said, 'You probably feel it's perfectly natural that you come to university, I would guess that for most of you it would be this particular one. It comes of course from your upbringing - note I didn't say 'breeding' - where your parents 'automatically' as hey say, expect you to go into higher education. This 'taken-for-grantedness' is learned.'

'That wouldn't be so for sons of manual workers though, would it.'

It was Rupert.

'I don't suppose it would,' sad Pym almost disinterestedly before c saying, 'We feel it perfectly natural to shake hands when introduced to someone, do we not? The French feel the same when kissing somebody on both cheeks, and the Japanese bow, et cetera. Okay then, to business. Let''s look very briefly at a functionalist theory. I call it that but only came across it recently when I did some teaching the USA and met a Mister Parsons. He uses an organic analogy of society whereby the main organs - major social institutions - of the body function together for the good of the whole.'

He leaned back in his chair and looked around him.

'Anyone?'

Rupert put up his hand and lowered it quickly.

'Sorry.'

'You did come to my talk for beginners then.'

'They don't,' said Rupert, 'operate for the good of the whole. If they did, there wouldn't be the inequality that there is.'

'Indeed,' said Pym, 'it's biggest weakness I think. There are others which some of you can allude to when you do the essays I'll set you.'

He stood, went to the board behind him and wrote some essay titles on it.

'One of these, you'll notice, is on Karl Marx, who, somewhat obviously, would not have been a fan of Parsons. I want to keep this short because you'll be better served when you've done more reading. Any questions?'

A student sitting opposite Rupert asked whether the theory mentioned had the effect preceding the cause in that the institutions were already there and then explained why they were.

'Yes, it has little capacity for prediction.'

Another questioner asked how long their essays should be and when they were required, and another wanted to know when the next seminar would be.

Rupert, rather reluctantly, left wanting more, but with his interest in reading the required texts increased.

He went to the common room where, amongst a dozen other students, Eric was half-sitting, half-lying in a chair reading. Rupert went silently to him.

'Ah, Horton's Guide to Eng' Lit. I would have thought you'd have your own opinions on the subject, as huge as it is.'

'I have, but haven't lived for the amount of years required to have read everything considered worth reading.'

'I suppose it's difficult to get a consensus on what constitutes 'great' works. After all, 'though we know what we have to presuppose to settle an empirical matter, we don't know what we have to presuppose to settle an aesthetic one.'

'Christ. Your subject kills everything. Been to a lecture or something?'

'A seminar.'

'The tall man?'

'Yep. Went to the library afterwards, there was a girl in there.'

'In the library? At Oxford? Perhaps your subconscious is hallucinating in order to service your wish-fulfilment. A woman may only go to the library, apparently, if she is accompanied by a tutor or has a letter of introduction

'She works there, she was rather nice.'

'So is my Fiona. It's time I rang her, I shall do so post haste if not sooner if the queue for the phone's not too long. I shall knock on your door before the weekend and we'll do something. Bye.'

He dragged himself off his chair and left.

There was a letter awaiting Rupert when returned to his room. It was from his father reminding him that the official opening ceremony for the estate was due to take place on the coming Saturday. He had forgotten. He remembered that it was to have taken place eight months previously but his father had purchased a piece of land adjoining what used to be Ash Farm and had built some more homes. He would ring his mother to tell her that he would drop in to see her on his way to the event.

There was only one person in front of him for the alcove phone and his mother was in the theatre when he called her landlady's number. He rang again later and she suggested he could stay with her; there was a spare room next to hers. He then, on a sudden impulse, went to the library. It had just closed.

Three days later, after two lectures, one with a different lecturer and the other attended with Eric, and two more visits to the library but with no sightings of the girl, he was with his mother in her lodgings helping her rehearse her part in 'Private Lives', the next play she was to perform. It was for the same company and had the same director as the play she was currently in and he'd suggested that his actors playing leading parts should begin learning them.

'So, you're Amanda then,' Rupert asked her.

'I'm too old for the part really, but as, apparently, I look young for my age, they said it would be fine,'

'It will be. Now, Victor, is it?' asked Rupert. 'He's on the balcony of a hotel in Paris and you're inside and he calls you.'

"Mandy.''

"What?' 'Shouldn't that be 'pardon?''

'No, the script says, 'What?''

Rupert continued.

"Come outside, the view is wonderful.' He lights a cigarette. You come out onto the terrace now. It says here, 'She is quite exquisite.' And you are, mother.'

'Thank you.'

'You're also wearing a negligee. Amanda then says, 'I shall catch pneumonia, that's what I shall catch.''

'I know,' his mother said.

'I'm Victor again now. 'God''

"I beg your pardon.''

"You look wonderful.''

"Thank you, darling.''

'You're perfect for the part, mother,' said Rupert.

'I trust that line's not in the script.'

'Then he says, 'Like a beautiful advertisement for something.''

'And I say, 'Nothing peculiar, I hope.''

"I can hardly believe it's true. You and me, here alone together, married.''

'That would be incest, my boy.'

'That's Victor.'

'Really?

'You're supposed to be taking this seriously.'

'I am.'

'You then rub your face on his shoulder and say...?'

"That stuff's very rough.''

"Don't you like it?''

"A bit heatty isn't it?''

"Do you love me?'''

'Of course, that's why I'm here.'

"More than…?"

"Now then, none of that."

"But do you love me more than you loved Elyot?"

"I don't remember, it's such a long time ago."

"Not so very long"

'Now, I fling out my arms and say, 'All my life ago.''

' And I, or rather Victor, says, 'I'd like to break his damned neck."

"Why?'"

"For making you unhappy."

'I enjoy this, mother, but you know this part like the back of your hand, like you usually do all of your parts. You don't need this.'

'Don't you want to do it then?'

'Of course I do, but you have a matinee tomorrow and I have to get up early to get to the estate.'

'I think your father's rather displeased that I shan't be there.'

'He likes showing you off, you know that, but you can't just drop out of a performance. He knows that, too. Anyway, let's carry on for a little bit, it's Amanda again.'

''It was mutual.''

"Rubbish! It was his fault, you know it was."

"Yes, it was, now I come to think about it."

"Swine!"

"Don't be so vehement, darling."

'I'll never treat you like that.'

"That's right."

'I love you so much."

"So did he."

"Fine sort of love that is. He struck you once, didn't he."

"More than once."

"Where."

"Several places."

'What a cad."

"I struck him too. Once I broke four gramophone records over his head. It was very satisfying."

'I bet it was. Mother, I think you should rest. I really want to see you in this part.'

'Well, let's hope it'll be a while yet, I'd like the one I'm in to have a run. 'Do you wish to go bye-byes now then?'

'I think I'll turn in, as they say.'

He kissed her cheek and said, 'I hope I shan't disturb you in the morning and I shall tell you all about the ceremony soon. Goodnight.'

He was correct in his assumption that he wouldn't disturb her in the morning; it was she who disturbed him by purposely waking him. After she had got up and dressed she had passed his room and heard a noise from inside. It was her son, snoring. She rapped on the door, opened it and entered. It seemed obvious his alarm cock had failed. He dressed quickly and refused to stay for breakfast, saying he would get something at the station.

'Lordy, your father's not gong to like this.'

'I know. Well, goodbye again, mother,' he said as he kissed her and hurriedly left the house.

To add to his lateness, his train was delayed and it was some hours afterwards that he arrived at Ash Park station, seeing, as the train slowed, a large marquee at one side of the station where little had been built. As he went towards it he saw a crowd of people milling around the front of it. He felt that he'd let his parent down, not just in arriving when he had, but not having interested himself more in the plans for this ceremony, for it was a recognition of his father's work and foresight.

The local paper, he knew, had claimed that the estate had been built at a cost of three-and-a-half million pounds and would become the largest single private housing estate in England, eventually housing thirty five thousand people. It was, as he was aware, slightly exaggerating the cost and the number of potential homes, but it was, indeed, the largest of its type in the country.

As he went towards the tent, he spotted someone he'd met before and was employed by his father. He went to him.

'It 's Nicholls, isn't it? The surveyor?'

'Young Rupert. Hello.'

They shook hands.

'Have you seen father? Afraid I'm rather late.'

'It's all over, really. Your father's in The Anchor, and that's only just officially opened as you probably know. He's with the dignitaries'.

Rupert thanked him and went back past the station and down the incline known as The Broadway and to the pub at the side of the roundabout. It was a largish place, rather like one of the road houses being built on the new roads around London, and there were quite few people christening their new drinking house, especially in the public bar. In the lounge he bought himself an 'Ash Park cocktail,' whatever that was supposed to be, and not seeing his parent there, asked a barmaid if the function room was being used. It was.

'It's upstairs, it's for the people who opened the estate,' she said, 'It's the local mayor and the East Ham one I think, dunno who the others are.'

He was easing his way through to the stairs when, passing the snug's frosted glass window, he heard his father's voice. There were other voices also, but, as ever, his parent's was the loudest. He knocked on the door.

'What d'you want?' someone asked.

'Father, it's me; Rupert.'

'Come in then, boy,' was the gruff response.

Inside, sitting opposite his father, who was in full military uniform, was a large man who Rupert recognised as the current Minister of Health. There was a woman seated next to him.

'You're rate,' said his father. 'How d 'you find me here?'

'Guessed. I do apologise. It actually wasn't my fault.'

'Never mind,' was the response, though clearly not meant. 'Let me introduce you to Sir Hatton Phelps and his wife, Katherine.'

Rupert said hello to them, the woman asking him to sit at the table.

'You're at Oxford then,' began the minister.

'Yes, just begun. Rather exciting.'

'Was there myself, young man. Damn good place to be. What you studying?'

'Philosophy,' said the Major. 'What's the difference between a park bench and a philosophy degree? A park bench can support a family.'

'Indeed,' said the Cabinet man, 'although there are countries that would want the State to support everyone.'

'Not politics again, darling,' said his wife, squeezing her husband's arm.

'I wonder.' Said the latter, what would be built around here, if anything at all, if we were in a Socialist state.'

'Rows of rigid, characterless, brutal concrete structures occupied by the proles wearing regulation uniforms, I suspect, and all eating their meals at a given time, too,' replied Richard Colls, 'and perhaps all going to the lavatory at the same time as well.'

He turned to the woman, saying, 'I do apologise. Lady Katherine,' and bowed his head.

'Like damn robots,' said the Health Minister. 'There'd be no economic growth, less entrepeneurial opportunity, your estate just wouldn't be built, as simple as that, there'd be no competition, no incentives to get things done, and a lack of motivation all round.'

'And too many damn layers of bureaucracy.'

The Knight continued. 'The smooth running of an economy is too complex to be directed by central planners.

'You don't have to have central planning,' Said Rupert, 'and look what's happening now to the - '

The minister interrupted him by announcing that as much as he had enjoyed the day and talking to the new city's developer, he should be leaving.

'It's a bit of a drive to Bucks, and although I'm sure my chauffer is enjoying himself in the public bar, he needs to drive us back.'

He looked at his wife. They both stood and shook hands with the Major and his son.

'Again, congratulations, old chap. Bloody marvellous show. It'll fulfil the aspirations of the hoi polloi.'

'And then they'll all vote for your party, darling,' said his wife with a knowing smile.

Rupert's father stepped to the door with them then sat down at the table again.

'Seen your mother?'

'Stayed with her last night.'

'Supppse I should make time to see her in her play.'

'She'll be great, as ever.'

He looked restlessly around him.

'I need to go back to the office now, son. You may come with me if you wish. Up to you.'

Rupert didn't wish to, he would sooner look around the estate which he had done little of, his experience of it being a vicarious one working on stages of its planning and its finances in the office. He didn't particularly want to be with his parent. He told him what he would do and that he would probably see him before half- term.

His father briefly shook his hand.

'Yes, see what the figures have added up to, look around you. I find it rather satisfying, Invigorating almost. See you then, my boy. Work hard,' he said as he left the room.

Rupert sat there for a while, conscious that his father hadn't asked him how he was getting on at university. At least he'd enquired about his mother. Thinking of what both the men he'd sat with had said moments before, he felt like rushing to Marx's Highgate Cemetery grave and thrusting a large red flag into the earth beside it.

Deciding that he wouldn't stray with his mother on the way back that evening, he left for his walk. He would leave her to rest while he returned to Oxford and continued his education.

11

The little man with an almost ridiculously small face and pointed ears sticking out from the sides of his peaked cap and walking firmly around the station platform in circles, kicking imaginary footballs, darting his little head up and shouting as if he were selling newspapers, 'District train, Ealin' train. G'mornin' guv, get your District train 'ere,' and then repeating himself and still kicking his footballs, turned his back on the incoming train and stared at the sky.

George took a seat next to two young lads with long hair parted in the centre and buzzed very short at the back. He didn't particularly like this style, though he did occasionally pomade his which showed off a natural wave. In between pulls on cigarettes they were talking animatedly about the party they had been to the previous evening.

He watched their every mimicked gesture and expression, wondering what grown-ups they were attempting to emulate and if it was worth the effort, anyway. By the time he'd reached Ash Park Station he'd noticed that they'd described how four different people had 'turned round and said ...' He had an image of people walking backwards, coming to an abrupt halt as they reached the one they had chosen to talk to and then spinning around to face him as if the whole process was an obscure religious ritual.

The platform was crowded with people waiting, he supposed, for the dignitaries to arrive. The event was supposed to begin at one pm. He had a little while to wait, so stepped off and joined the throng. His mates happened to be working, and Doris was more interested in going to the shops in Rumford. He hadn't asked her to come with him, anyway. The wait wasn't long. The crowd, looking along the tracks, began murmuring, 'Here it comes,' as the train approached.

It was a tank engine decorated with bunting, the front of it bearing the legend, 'The Ash Park Special.' It had two coaches. Some well-dressed people alighted; women in padded shoulders and puffed sleeves, a few wearing hats and gloves, and amidst the flared skirts, George spotted a fur jacket. Two constables gently eased people away to allow them room so they could walk past a line of young girls dressed in frilly frocks and white ankle socks, and boys in blazers and shorts all standing politely to attention with hands behind their backs. The dignitaries, led by a man who George presumed was the stationmaster, and followed by the people from the platform, made their way up the bunting-bedecked ramp of the station towards the exit.

George found himself near the front of the crowd and could see a man in a dark suit and tie being given a large silver key by the stationmaster to open the barrier gates, which, accompanied by cheers from the onlookers, he did. Once through the gates, the party erupted on to the road. There were no shops this side of the station, but poles had been erected along the roadside and hung with streamers. There was large marquee at the end.

Directly outside the station was a band of local girl pipers waiting for them who, he knew, were quite famous, he'd heard them on the wireless. The smart-suited and be-frocked people were led by them down the almost finished Broadway to Ash Park Avenue, the first main thoroughfare to be completed. George was feeling quite excited.

As they reached the bottom of the hill, the pipers led off to each side to allow the leading group to come forward and pass under a large ornamental arch which proclaimed 'Welcome to Ash Park.' He had noticed this being built over the last week but had not known what it was for. As the party went under it a blizzard of coloured paper poured down from it and people cheered again.

The leading figure stopped to cut a tape stretching across the road then climbed a wooden platform with loudspeakers at the side of the arch and began to make a speech to the large crowd, many standing on the grass in the centre of the nearby roundabout.

'On this auspicious day I wish to thank all those involved in this grand enterprise, all the agencies, the architects, local authorities, the government for giving the go-ahead for this grand scheme, the bricklayers, carpenters the roofers and all of those who built this fresh and open place.'

He looked up from his notes and said, as if meaning it, 'It gives me great pleasure to see so many happy and cheerful faces and to feel everyone's pleasure at the re-housing of so many families on such a beautiful and healthy site under the best modern conditions, and certainly in comparison to the old homes, especially those in the slums.'

'We certainly had to work for it,' murmured George under his breath as the crowd cheered again. But this important man, whoever he was, seemed to be telling him that he, too, was important, was part of a community living in a new, bright place with wide roads, trees and fields.

'This project is not finished yet,' continued the speaker, 'and will one day house more of you.'

He paused and looked down as a woman held up a little girl towards him.

'Ah yes, Mrs Jeffrey with her daughter, Sylvia I think it is, from, I believe, Durban Drive, the first baby to be born in Ash Park.'

There was more cheering.

'Now, last but certainly not least, the developer and also builder of this grand place, Mister, and ex-Major, Richard Colls.'

Amidst the cheering, the uniformed figure climbed onto the platform and stood next to the speaker.

'Thank you, Sir Hutton and all of you who have come here today. This has been an enterprise that has taken over two-and-a-half years from its beginnings to what you see now and, as you've been told, it is not over. I do want to mention that the whole project is local, many of the building materials have come from this area, including the bricks and windows. I hope you are all happy here and will continue to be so.'

He handed the microphone back to Sir Hutton, and after the applause had ceased, climbed down to the road again.

The main speaker continued.

'Before I go; I am told that outside the marquee there will be the pipers, the Legion of Frontiersmen band and some trick equestrian riding. There will also be, in the marquee, cookery and other demonstrations, and afternoon tea will be served. Thank you.'

114

There was one last cheer and the crowd gradually dispersed, most making their way up the incline again and heading towards the giant tent. George, feeling thirsty, went towards the new pub. It was getting pretty crowded. He eased his way to the bar, treated himself to a glass of brown ale and looked for somewhere to sit. The few tables were occupied so he stood at the end of the bar. He looked around him, feeling a sense of something like belonging. It was to the area, to the people in the other houses, those in his street, a shared experience, though he had never met them and had hardly said a word to his next-door neighbours or the people who lived opposite.

He decided to walk around for a bit. As he lived north of the station, he'd probably only been once along the west part of the Avenue. He finished his drink and was about to go through the exit when the main party began to enter; at the rear of which was Sir Hutton and the developer man. There was a woman with them. He held the door back for them. There were a few 'Thank-yous' before most of them headed towards the stairs.

The feeling of goodwill suddenly seemed strong enough to pull him back and after having to almost push his way through the crowd, he ordered the same as before and stood at the end of the bar.

His thoughts turned to his partner. He didn't want them to, they took up too much of his life, too much of his energy. He would like to have gone home, laid on the grass beside his little pool, look up at the sky, whether it was sunny or snowing, and go back into an empty house, one with a deco lamp, a ziggurat wardrobe and bed, butterflies, Egyptians and... peace.

He went towards the toilet; it wasn't in use so he used the one in the lounge. Returning past what he assumed was the snug - he had never been in one, the public bar was his domain - he heard some rather posh voices which immediately reminded him of the people he had just heard giving speeches. One seemed to be criticising socialism, another mentioned robots, and a younger voice appeared to disagree about something.

He left and began his walk, passing some front gardens with newly-planted bushes and burgeoning trees. The houses were mostly 'Rosewood' and 'Vilette' - he remembered their names -

and a couple of chalet houses, but none of his own type, which he felt somewhat pleased about, liking the idea that his was somehow special.

The evening sun broke through, illuminating top windows and chimneys, and creating a desire in him to go to the nearby fields and sit under some autumn leaves.

He went northwards towards the fields. The grass was pretty high but a rudimentary path led under some trees and towards a ramshackle bridge over a stream. Nearing the latter he saw a man sitting on a rustic bench under a willow. As he neared him the figure murmured a lazy 'Hello' then said with a smile, 'Didn't expect to find a bench on farmland.'

'I heard they're going to turn it into a park, perhaps it's a practice one.'

'It's nice around here, makes you think that, as unusual as this place seems, everything, in the beginning, is built in the country.'

He looked around him, leaned back, gazed up at the tree and asked his listener if he lived locally.

'Yes, I live on the estate.'

'I was going to walk around it then thought I'd like to sit in the evening sun.'

'You're not a local, then?'

'Oh no, just wanted to see, after all the work inside, what it would be like on the outside. Haven't been here since the start of it, really.'

'The 'inside'?'

'Yes, I worked in the firm's office. It planned, developed and built the place, is still building it.'

He moved to the one end of the bench.

'Do you wish to sit down?'

George accepted the offer.

'I'm Rupert.' He held his hand out for George to shake.

The voice seemed recently familiar to the latter.

'Was it… was it you in the pub just now, sort of arguing with someone?' he asked.

'In the snug?' I didn't get much of a word in, did I.'

'Someone with a posh voice was moaning about socialism.'

'Posher than mine?'

116

'A little bit, but you're okay, I think you were going against him.'

'He was opinionated but uninformed. You're bit of a left-winger, eh? Good.'

He looked a briefly but rather intently at his companion.

'I'd say you were a skilled artisan.'

'I'm a signwriter.'

'There is, apparently, a marked division between 'rough' and 'respectable' working class… Sorry, too much social science reading. Forget it.'

'No, it's okay, reminds me of my mother telling me not to play or be friends with anyone in the street next to ours 'cos they were 'rough'. I expect you didn't have that.'

'No, no roads like that near us. Incidentally, I'm trying to be objective,I'm making no value judgements, really.'

'Or trying not to.'

'No, I really - '

'I'm kidding.'

'Have you always done what you're doing?'

'Yes.'

'Didn't want to do anything else?'

'Art school. Never mind, the money's not bad.'

'What decided your politics? Your work experience?'

'Partly, but dad was a socialist, the Daily Mirror and that.'

'Ah yes, Jane et al.'

'And don't forget Belinda and 'Great Jehosophat!''

'The fourth king of Judah.'

'You seem to know lots of things.'

'Not really, just a retentive memory.'

'Don't you work in the office now?'

'No, At Oxford.'

'The University?'

'Yes.'

'What's it like there?'

'I say, d'you fancy a walk around the lake before I have to go?'

'Alright.'

They eased themselves off the bench and began heading towards it.

'Where to begin? said Rupert. 'Only just started. Am enjoying it, it's going to be hard work. I don't think my politics are going to help much.'

'Where'd they come from?'

'I suppose it's a reaction against my father. Also my boarding school. The whole thing, really.'

'Very Tory is he?'

'You could say that.'

'The Times, Telegraph?'

'Certainly not The New Worker.'

They were quiet for a while, looking at the lake and watching some paddling ducks and geese.

'Wonder why people like lakes so much,' mused George.

'Perhaps it's because it's a change from our salient frame of reference, which is the earth.'

'It wouldn't be for sailors.'

'That's why they're so pleased to see land.'

'For a while.'

'D'you like your job?' asked Rupert.

'It's what I do. I'm pretty good at it I suppose, though I'd like to do more creative work. It's mostly knowing the typefaces.'

'Such as?'

'Roman, Gill Sans, that sort of thing.'

'What does your father do, if you don't mind me asking?'

'Died in the war.'

'Sorry. My father was a Major in it. Your mother?'

'Just a cleaner. Cleans City offices.'

'Does she refer to the offices as 'hers'?'

'Suppose so.'

'Theory is that as the working class own little, they have a kind of psychological ownership of their job.'

'And of their football team.'

'You too?'

'The Hammers. Guess you're a cricket bloke.'

'Surrey.'

'Saw a game at The Oval once. Bit boring. You've mentioned 'class' before.'

'As a category. As Durkheim says, 'Treat social facts as things.'

'Shouldn't think *your* mother cleaned offices,' George said with a smile, looking across at Rupert as they went around the lake.

'She doesn't, she's an actress.'

'Would I have heard of her?'

'Only if you go to the theatre.'

'I don't. Pantos and that. Perhaps I should, but it's films for me.'

This started both of them talking about films and they still were as they completed the perimeter of the lake and found themselves again at the park entrance. Rupert asked his companion where he actually lived.

'Towards the station, third on the left.'

'Look, I've enjoyed our little chat. Maybe we'll meet again. It could be around here if I come again, or, perhaps, even on a protest or demo somewhere. Keep the red flag flying, eh?'

'I'll walk to the station with you. I assume you're going there.'

'Indeed, got to get to Padders then off to my seat of learning.'

They walked in silence for a while.

On a whim George said, I'll give you my address for what it's worth,' and scribbled it down along with his name on a piece of tissue he took from his pocket.

'Jolly good,' said Rupert, taking it and, handing him a business card, said, 'That's the office address.'

George took it and thanked him.

'Look, I'm going to run up this little hill, The Broadway is it? Don't want to miss the train.'

He turned to George and they shook hands. The latter then watched him run to the station.

He made his way towards home. It had been an unusual experience. An unusual day. He was going past the pub then decided that he didn't want to return home. He went in and, for the sake of it, to the lounge bar. He couldn't remember the last time he'd been in one. The place was less crowded now. He bought a lemonade and sat by a window.

He took the card from his pocket and looked at it. The bloke had the same name as the developer. 'I bet you're his son', he said almost aloud. 'Bloody Hell.'

He'd never met anyone from this sort of family before. He felt, somehow, as if he belonged here that little bit more. He knew it was silly to think that, but there it was. It was kind of planned for him. He hoped he would meet Mister Colls junior again, wherever it was.

12

'I am aware that I'm repeating myself, but functionalism sees social structure, society's organisation, as more important than the individual. Some anthropologists argue that in some so-called primitive societies, the society is more real to the individual than they themselves.'

'Reification to the nth degree,' a student pointed out to Pym.

'I find it difficult to believe, also,' said the latter. 'However, it views society as a system, and any social system has four basic functional prerequisites: adaptation, goal attainment, integration and pattern maintenance.'

Perhaps, Rupert thought, he'd mention the anthropological view to Constance, then wondered why he'd thought it. He hadn't seen her again despite two more library trips.

This was his second seminar and was taking place soon after another Pym lecture on structural theory in the social sciences.

'So, Parsons wants to establish action theory to integrate the study of social order with the structural view. That is, the necessity of the subjective dimension of human action in sociological theorizing, but trying to maintain the scientific rigour of positivism.'

'We seem,' said Rupert, 'to be going into the round-and-round bit of whether man makes society or - '

'Yes, we know this, but if we don't have the man-creates bit then we have, arguably, man as a responsive robot view,' replied Pym.

'We keep saying 'man,'' said Rupert, 'why don't we use 'humankind' and include women?'

There was a little silence.

'Well, because men do make society,' said a member of the group.

Another said wearily, 'No, the other way round.'

'Yes, the action bit, the interaction of people. You've spotted the logical difficulty here, as,' Pym looked briefly around, 'you should do as philosophy students. My lecture was on this theory, so let us now look at the next one, another structural thesis, but this time not a consensual, but a conflict theory. Let's look at Marx's overarching view, another meta-narrative, you could say.'

'Society must be seen in terms of power and conflict and how the interests of the few are better served. Each class normally pursues its own interests which brings it into conflict with other classes, in this case the bourgeoisie and the proletariat. In all societies there are two major classes, one is more powerful than the other and the relationship is exploitative.'

Someone - Rupert hadn't learnt most of the others names yet - asked how class was defined.

'It's a social status determined by an individual's location in, and relationship to, the means of production,' said Pym. 'I'll personalise this with examples. I assume that most of you, if not all, have parents that own and control some of these means. What does your father do?' he asked a rather fat and bespectacled boy who Rupert hadn't as yet heard say a word.

'He's in the steel business,' was the answer.

'At what level? On the factory floor?' asked Pym.

The student frowned.

'Of course not. He and his partners own a firm of steel makers.'

'Of course they do,' said Pym, with what Rupert felt was a slight hint of sarcasm.

'And what of yours?' he enquired of a student sitting at the end of the table.

'He owns an import and export business, deals with all sorts of things.'

'Quite. But it's not as simple as that; there are gradations, of course. In the end, it's head knowledge over hand knowledge.' He asked what occupations could be divided in this way.

Answers were readily forthcoming from around the table, though the question from Rupert was *why* one form of knowledge was considered superior to another. Pym, admitting they could be arbitrary, answered that those in power had the knowledge to transmit this view as virtually an absolute.

Rupert thought of the ceremony he had witnessed three days before and the taken-for-granted privilege and unquestioned right by Sir Phelps to be looked upon by the crowd as somehow superior. He had an image of his father standing next to him and seemingly portraying a similar attitude. He knew that in terms of his schooling, especially if he had stayed on, and of course his background, he should have carried the same attitudes within him. However, fortunately for him he thought, an 'is' cannot be derived from an 'ought'. Having the mother he had also helped.

He thought of her meeting Constance. She would like her. It occurred to him how ridiculous he was being. He'd hardly 'met' her himself. As Pym began talking of Marx, he decided that after the seminar had finished he would go to the library again and if she wasn't there, enquire after her. His father certainly wouldn't like her, women who wished to pursue anything scholarly had 'something wrong with them', he'd once heard him say.

Pym was saying, 'Alright then, forgive what seems my double standards, 'though I would prefer 'strategic hypocrisy'', but we could go back to Socrates if we so wished to find the beginning of dialectical materialism. It is, at base, a discourse between two or more people holding different points of view about a subject but wishing to establish the truth through reasoned arguments.

'In more modern terms, it's a theory which emphasizes the importance of real-world conditions, of the material in terms of class and labour. It doesn't deny ideas, but insists these could only arise as products and effects of material conditions.

'The two people, in effect, are the two classes then,' ventured Rupert.

'Simplistically, yes.'

The seminar leader then continued talking of thesis, antithesis, synthesis, while Rupert's thoughts again turned to the girl on the steps with the books.

The seminar over, he picked up the few notes he'd taken, put them in his jacket pocket and made his way to the library. As he went towards the seat he had previously occupied, he saw Eric at a table with a book.

'You're actually reading a book then,' said Rupert as he sat down next to him.

'Yes, I can even recognise some of the words and, with great effort, understand a few of them.'

'Whatcha reading?'

'A thing on the Auden Group: Day-Lewis, MacNeice, Spender et al. What have you been up to?'

'Seminar thing, structural theory and stuff; getting into Karl baby now.'

'Should think that will suit you.'

'It will.'

Rupert looked around him to the lane of bookshelves where he'd first seen her.

'What you looking for?'

'A girl.'

'I was going to say, 'Aren't we all,' but I've got mine.'

'As you often say. Methinks he doth protest too much?'

'No. She's… mine.'

'Goody for you. This one works here. There's something… I don't quite know.'

'She renders you inarticulate?'

'Just a moment.'

He had seen the librarian standing at the end of a row, went to him and asked him if he knew where the girl who worked there was.

'Do you mean Constance Lange?'

'That's her.'

'She should be in this afternoon.'

Rupert thanked him and returned to Eric.

'Sorry, just wanted to know where she was. How's whatsis-name, Bertrand Flavin?'

'Just as theatrical. He mentioned Shakespeare in his lecture this morning and instantly played bits of the characters' parts.'

'To illustrate a point?'

'Under the guise of that, but showing off really.'

'What's he like in seminars?'

'Treats us as if we were in the front row of the stalls, but he knows his subject.'

'So does mine, I think he may, unusually for this place, be a bit of a Lef-leaning pedagogue. I could be wrong.

'Is that good?

'As far as I'm concerned.'

'A socialist then.'

'Not sure. The Labour Party's a centre-left party, really, an alliance of democrats, socialists and trade unionists. Don't know how far Left it *can* go. Perhaps we'll see after the slump's over, if it ever is.'

'It'll finish. My dad says so.'

'It'll have to for the system to survive.'

'It will always survive. How was the ceremony then? You haven't said anything about it.'

'Missed it, actually, was late, but Hatton Phelps cut the ribbon, made speeches and things. A lot of people there, I saw father. It was big day for him; he's worked hard for it. I suppose I did, too, when in the office.'

'You're here now.'

'And more hard work.'

Out of the corner of his eye Rupert saw some steps being quietly moved. He noticed the stockings before the smock. He wasn't sure whether or not she had noticed him. She was looking upwards, placing books on a top shelf.

'That's her,' he said quietly to Eric.

'Mmm, interesting. D'you want me to leave you?'

'Well... '

With a, 'See you later somewhere or the other,' Eric got up and left.

Rupert walked towards her.

'Hello, step lady.'

'Hello, Aristotle,' she replied without looking away from her shelves.

'I haven't seen you for a few days. Are you okay?'

She looked down at him.

'Yes, thanks. I needed to be home.'

'I see.'

'You don't really, but my mother is an invalid and she was feeling bad so I... you know.'

'Hope she's feeling better.'

'I wouldn't be here if she wasn't.'

'Glad to be back?'

'In a way. I like being surrounded by books, I suppose, and I can take home what I like.'

'Perks of the job. The man said your name was Lange. It's rather unusual.'

'Not if you're German it isn't.'

He wasn't quite sure how to reply to this.

She stopped what she was doing and said, 'I was born there, lived there for a little while before my father left and my mother, who's English, returned here. I am British now, of course.'

He asked her where they'd met.

'She was on a skiing holiday in the Alps with friends, in Wertach, he was an instructor, a skilehrer, and what was, supposedly, a holiday romance, became serious. They tired of each other, according to my mother. She rarely mentions him. It doesn't matter, it happened a long time ago.' She continued with her books.

He wasn't quite sure what to say to her. He knew it was a shyness, one he was aware he had with women, although he hadn't felt like this when he'd first met her.

'What do you think of Adolf Hitler being Chancellor then? Sorry, I'm saying that as if you *should* be interested in the country.'

'You're saying that as if you're a little shy. For 'shy' read 'frightened,' that's what shyness is, actually, fear. What are you scared of?'

'I put my hands up.' He made a brief gesture of doing that. 'You're right, but I find it interesting, anyway.'

'It's more scary than interesting. He's Führer now, and the way he got there; with his parades, posters everywhere, meetings, speeches, special editions of Nazi newspapers, even kissing babies.'

'And?'

'The country was, is, in the grip of the Depression with a population suffering misery, poverty, uncertainty. This was the long-awaited opportunity to let loose his talents. He had a willing audience.'

'You sound as if you were there.'

'My mother had a German friend who visited her here occasionally and brought newspapers et cetera and told her the things that were happening. I speak German, incidentally. Language gets into you when you're very young. What he offered them was encouragement, heaps of vague promises and avoiding the details. Did you know that at one time he had Nazi paramilitary surrounding the Reichstag and told parliament, 'It is for you, gentlemen of the Reichstag, to decide between war and peace.' Long gone is the Charlie Chaplin image of him as the laughable fanatic. The beer hall revolutionary's been replaced by the skilled manipulator of the masses.'

She was both stimulated and annoyed when speaking, her calm eyes almost sparking.

'You look so different when you're angry.'

'Not 'beautiful'? That's the cliché.'

'That, too.'

'Thank you.'

She looked towards the main desk.

'I'm allowed a short break. I can usually go when I want as long as it's only once a shift. There's a kind of miniature refectory in the basement for staff, sometimes I'm the only one there. I could do with a scone.'

'I'm with you,' he said, picking up his book and moving towards her. She climbed down and, pushing her trolley against the shelves, said. 'Follow me.'

They went down the main stairs to a half-concealed door leading to an empty room with a middle-aged woman standing behind a small counter.

'Ah, some business at last,' she said. 'What can I do you for?'

They carried their scones and tea to a small table.

'What she just said, incidentally, is a current catchphrase on the wireless,' he explained to her.

'What would your sociology call her? Working class?'

'There are clues; her job of course, but mostly her accent.'

'Wonder where she lives; probably in the city and pining to get out of it.'

'There's little wrong with this city,' said Rupert, 'though it's a little different in the Capital.'.

'Manual workers more aspirational?'

'Probably.'

127

'For what?'

'A house in suburbia, I guess.'

'Urban sprawl.'

'I suppose it could be, but not the sort of place I was in recently.'

'All privet hedges and evergreens?'

'That's a worker's perception of the middle classes. It comes from lots of surces: films, newspapers, their next-door neighbour telling them of a visit to an affluent relative, et cetera.'

'Not from what they've read then?' she asked.

'Not so much; the poorer wouldn't read a lot.'

'And they would have been brought up by parents who didn't read much.'

He watched her eating, tidily, hardly opening her mouth, lips firmly closed as she chewed.

'Why are we talking about this?'

'Not sure.'

'It's so… comfortable being with you at this moment.'

'Not shy now?'

'Not intellectually, no. I rarely am. I wish you were in my seminar group.'

'So do I.'

'You must feel awfully frustrated not reading for something at a university somewhere.'

'Of course.'

'I'm glad you're not.'

'That's unkind.'

'No. It's just that I wouldn't be talking to you now if you were. We wouldn't have met.'

'Have we met?'

'Yes, we have now.'

'Is that good?'

'It is for me.'

The woman behind the counter asked them if they wanted anything else.

'I'm alright, are you?'' he asked Constance.

'Actually, I should get back.'

They returned upstairs in silence, where she went straight to her steps again.

'I need to concentrate a little now,' she said, looking down on him once more. 'Do continue reading.'

He did for a while, but couldn't concentrate in her presence, though didn't want to move away from it.

I'll see you tomorrow, I hope,' he said, looking at her from the bottom of the steps.

'Alright,' she said, looking closely at a book title. 'Cheerio.'

He left her there wondering why he hadn't asked her what she did in the evenings or when she wasn't working, or where she was living.

He went back to his room feeling pleased that he would see her again the next day. After reading for an hour or two he left for the refectory and on his way saw Eric going in the same direction.

'Hello, amorous man, how's the flaxen-haired lady?' he asked.

'Flaxen. I shall see her again.'

'I must say, she does have something about her, the brief glimpse I got of her.'

'Bright, too.'

'What you having,' Eric asked as they seated themselves, 'more disguised food I suppose?'

The times we're living in. There's some decent stuff, though.'

'Like the pig in a blanket that I'm having,' said Rupert.

'Which you'll follow, I'm sure, with cherry jubilee and sweet potato-marshmallow surprises, Eric said as he ordered a casserole, and mushrooms.

When they'd finished their meals, speaking little, Eric generously wiped his lips with a napkin and announced that Fiona was coming up to see him at the weekend.

'She's never been to Oxford before, so we decided she would come here rather than me going home to see her.'

'Jolly good, I hope to meet her.'

'You shall.'

After attending two consecutive lectures, tone of them given by Pym, the other by a junior lecturer who had recently been teaching at London University, Rupert went to see if Constance could spare time for another chat.

He couldn't find her. She had, according to the librarian, just finished her shift. He was a little disappointed that he'd missed her.

The following day he got to the library early, but again she wasn't there, the librarian telling him, with a frown of curiosity that she was on the afternoon schedule. There were two lectures given by a colleague of Pym that he had insisted his group attend, and another seminar that afternoon. She wasn't at work when he looked for her. The following day was what Eric had called, 'Fiona Day.' He was to meet her at the station mid-day and then see Rupert in the early evening at a restaurant in the city.

It was in Ship Street, with cloth-covered square tables each with a cubed lampshade set in their centres. It was three-quarters full and, towards its end, there was Eric and his girl. She was facing him, and her rather sweet, pert face and fair, wavy hair immediately registered Eric's description. As Rupert came nearer she looked away from her partner and smiled at him.

'Hello, Mister Rupert,' she said, standing and offering her hand. Rupert briefly squeezed it, said hello to both of them and sat next to his friend.

'It's rather nice to meet you,' he said to her, making himself comfortable.

'Only rather'?'

'Figure of speech.'

'We *are* English you know,' said Eric in mock admonishment to her.

'And I am glad of it.'

She was wearing a blouse that Rupert thought may have had banjo sleeves, he had seen his mother in them, but whatever she'd worn would not, he thought, have diminished her personality.

He asked about her journey.

'Easy Peasy, and such a nice place, the little I've seen of it,' she said, briefly reaching across the table and squeezing Eric's arm. She smiled. 'We are not saying you're late, Mister Rupert, but we have been here a little while and are getting rather hungry.' She passed a menu to him.

'Of course.'

As he looked through the dishes, Eric was saying to her, 'Have you noticed that restaurants these days seem to be attracting a new type of customer, I call them neophytes, who seem uncomfortable yet rather excited by unfamiliar dishes and menu language. I noticed a couple as we came in that fitted the type. One of them asked for a croissant and made it sound as if he was ordering an angry insect.'

'It's simultaneously daunting and attractive to them,' said Fiona, standing and telling them she was off to the lady's room. 'Behave yourselves while I'm away, Ricey.'

Rupert asked Eric who or what 'Ricey' was. '

A kind of anagram of my name.'

'Incidentally,' said Rupert, if you were referring to the aspirational middle class just then, I think that's acceptable, the upper working class are becoming so, so why shouldn't the routine white collar worker, also?'

'Aren't they working class?'

'Not really, no.'

'Whatever, they couldn't do your subject. You ask them what the difference between ignorance and apathy is and they'll tell you they don't know and don't care.'

'Not bad, for you.'

'So, what d'you think of her then?'

'More than your description. A bit like someone out of an Ivor Novello musical.

He heard a whispered voice immediately behind him. It was Fiona.

'I heard that. On the contrary, art imitating nature. I came before his musicals.'

'Are you saying then,' replied Rupert as she went around the table and sat again, 'that the way you look, the way you talk, your personality even, are natural?'

'As nature intended, darling.'

'No, as your upbringing intended. You internalize the social world around you, it makes you.' He paused. 'Though I do agree there are some pretty fine natural things about you.'

She looked at Eric.

'Is he always like this?'

'Not always, sometimes he can be human.'

'I'm sure he can, he wouldn't be your friend otherwise.'

Eric beckoned the waiter and they ordered sole meuniere, cas-sooulet, boeuf bourguignon, and a bottle of white wine.

'Here's to us,' said Eric and, clinking his raised glass, added, 'and to my love.'

She smiled sweetly and took a large sip.

'I feel rather honoured to be here,' said Rupert. 'but let us spare a thought for those whom this slump has acted miserably upon.'

'A little depressing, old chum,' said Eric.'

'Nice play on words there,' said Fiona, taking another sip.

'I mean it,' said Rupert. 'We're doing well, our families are also. I do hope I can include yours, Fiona.'

'You can. Whether shares are bought or sold, Daddy's broker-ing firm gets lots and lots of commission. All jolly good.'

'This bottle isn't going to last long,' said Eric, beckoning to the waiter again and ordering another. It came almost immediate-ly as did their meals.

'Have you a female friend, Rupert?' asked Fiona after a while.

'No.'

'Don't you get lonely?'

'At the moment I'm too full of what I'm doing here, and I've got your dearest to occasionally keep me company.'

'That's good; I think he needs you to cheer him up when I'm not in his thoughts.'

'That's never,' said Eric promptly.

'He talks of you often, Fiona', ventured Rupert. 'I feel I almost know you.'

'As long as they're good things.''

'Oh, they are.'

After each had ordered and eaten crème brûlée they drank the last of their wine.

'Boarding school, Rupert?' asked Fiona.

'Why did you ask that?

'Just wondered.'

'Does it show?'

'Don't know. What is it that's supposed to show? Girton girl myself.'

'Well… it does involve control of behaviour regarding several aspects of life including what is appropriate and, or, acceptable behaviour, attitudes and values.'

'Did you read that somewhere?'

'No. And unless they're careful, parents of the governing classes virtually lose any intimate touch with their children from about the age of eight, and, it could be argued, any attempts on their parts to insinuate home feeling into school life are resented.'

'Rupert thinks I'm of the governing class, dear,' said Eric. 'But, thinking back, I didn't like mother mothering me, as it were, at home. Such different worlds,'

'Eric told me,' said Fiona, 'what your father does. Doing a big thing at the moment, apparently, but I don't think he mentioned your mother.'

'She's in the theatre.'

'Fiona's just got a little part on stage locally. Haven't you, my dear,' said Eric.

'A tiny thing. And your mother?'

'Coward at the moment.'

Eric began to quietly sing, 'But don't you think her bust is too developed for her age? Don't put your daughter on the stage Mrs Worthington, Don't put your daughter on the stage.'

'Are you making references to *my* bust?'

'You know I'm not. it's perfect.'

'As are you, sweetie. Would I have heard of your mother?' She asked Rupert.

'Possibly not, she's not always in the West End. Rep at the moment.'

He told her his mother's name.

'You know, it does ring a little bell I think. Tell this lump here what she's in and he'll keep me up-to-date.' She looked at her partner. 'Don't you think we should be going?'

'I suppose we should. Tempus fugit and all that.'

'How can you tell that a clock is hungry? It goes back for seconds,' said Fiona.

'Enough of your silly clock jokes, precious, they're a waste of time.'

'Ha ha'

Rupert asked them where they were staying.

'A nice little B&B near Paddington station; be easier for Fiona tomorrow. Mind you, I would love to smuggle her past the Proctor into my room.'

'I bet you would.'

He and Fiona stood. Rupert suggested he accompany them to the station.

'We'll get a cab, old boy.'

'I'll share it with you then it can take me back.'

On the way out Eric paid and they went to a taxi rank where a cab had just pulled in.

They sat in the back, Fiona between them. It was pleasant for Rupert to be sitting next to a woman again, other than his mother. At the station he went down to the platform with them, waited a short while for the train and waved them goodbye, Fiona blowing a kiss towards him.

'See you on Monday,' shouted Eric, leaning out of a carriage window, Rupert barely understanding what he was saying for the hiss of steam.

He felt a little lonely on the way back and knew he would think at some length of the library girl again as soon as he was in his room.

He lay on his bed and did so, unhampered by thoughts of his course, his first essay, or his parents. He would, however, begin serious work with pen and paper tomorrow and look for her again the next day. She'd be back at work then, wouldn't she?

13

He was in north London looking at the houses as he walked past them - 'shapes against the sky' as he would occasionally refer them to himself - and 'though finding some interest in the larger, detached ones in the Victorian estate, with their Arts and Crafts scrolling and the occasional fluted column, he couldn't really appreciate them aesthetically for they were the same period as the environment of his early and recent life.

George was taking a lunch break from decorating some rooms in a four-bedroom home he had been working on for a few days, his governor seemingly branching out into decorating jobs of late. He had put his employee on a few before when there'd been a drop in sign work, but this time there were an increasing number of them. He had, of course, learnt the rudiments at tech college and had decorated his own house, anyway, so it was no bother for him, 'though he preferred the signwriting.

He turned a corner and there was a Noth London version of that environment: a long, gardenless street, not a 'road' as he lived in now, and not a bush or flower to be seen, 'though there was one house he passed that had shrivelled, unwatered flowers struggling in a half-hearted window box. He wondered if the residents talked of neighbours living a few 'doors' away, not 'houses'.

Such musings inevitably pushed his thoughts to what was at home for him when he returned to it later; quite a bit later, for he intended to work overtime, there were no occupants in the place. It wasn't really the extra money, 'though it would be handy, but he didn't want to return to a kind of ghost existence: the occasional glimpses of her white, strained face as she moved soundlessly about the house, the seemingly permanent odours of her cooking and the ever-present silence. There were no words between them now except for necessary communication.

He'd told Reg about it at last. He'd been very surprised, but not as shocked as George thought he would be.

'I had wondered why you hadn't asked me around for quite a while. I've seen the garden, that's about all really,' he'd said.

'Well, you'll have to come round and see the mural I told you about, and the butterfly pics. I didn't tell you 'cos I didn't want to give the game away.'

'Some bloody game,' his mate had said.

He couldn't bring himself to tell him the reason why he had accepted her living with him. It was too.... awful. And not only for her. He couldn't tell him of the guilt he would feel if he could bring himself to tell her to go. He would also be on his own, but he could live with that, as long as she didn't threaten to do what she said she would do if he didn't want her.

He'd tried to convince himself that as this was a while ago now she may have... he couldn't quite formulate it; grown up, got more mature, more solid, and didn't need him so much. He knew these things needed to be talked about with her. He felt frightened to.

He went back, finished his cucumber sandwiches and his thermos flask of tea and carried on hanging the white with red polka dot wallpaper in the loft. It wasn't easy, barely a flat, vertical surface there, all corners and angles; he had to gently tear the edges of the paper, feather-edge it to match the dots. It took time, but at least it stopped him thinking of home, the home that sometimes seemed to be losing its shine, becoming deadened, even the murals seemed as aged as the age they depicted, the garden a rather ordinary piece of drab green, and the butterflies may as well have had pins stuck through them.

He purposely finished late, he could have left earlier and still claimed overtime, he was a fast worker, thus justifying the claim, but he didn't bother, and if he had thought at all of why he hadn't, it would perhaps have dawned on him that it was the consequence of his mother's God-fearing honesty she had tried to bring him up with. It was dark when he returned. 'You're home then are you. There's some food that needs warming up. It's up to you.'

At least she'd spoken. His lack of appetite being no incentive to bother with any sort of **cooking**, he made himself a sandwich.

'There's tea in the pot'.

That'll probably be it for the evening he thought, she'll be sitting in front of the wireless for the rest of it.

She looked older these days, her lean face pinched-looking, her lips appearing thinner, to him they seemed bitter. He could see why she'd be miserable, but, all in all, why did she look *that* bitter? She had space, could move about freely in it, not like the flat in the block she'd lived **in** with her parents; he had given her room, scope. Why should she be? Perhaps she really did love him, but he didn't… didn't **love** her. He just couldn't.

'What you thinking of, George?' she asked from the kitchen. 'Are you wondering what's happened, why it's like this?'

'You've done this before; you seem to know what I'm thinking. But it's not really that, just that… I don't know what to do'.

'We have that in common at **least.**'

'We just move about in here, and that's it, somehow. We just don't do anything, talk about anything. Nothing happens. I don't know why I'm **doing** it.'

'Doing what?'

'Living with you, with a stranger. That's what you are.'

'Another thing we have in common. But I don't have to be, you could try to get to know me.'

He was silent.

'You don't want to, or don't **know** how to?'

He said nothing.

'Cat got your tongue? D'you know what it's like here? It's like living in a kind of tomb dressed up as a museum. What do you want me to do, George?'

'It was you who - '

'I know, but it doesn't seem to bother you. You just go to your bedroom every night as if was supposed to be like that. As if it's somehow natural. The way it always was.'

'Well, it was before you came **along.**'

'But I *did* come along, I'm here now. Look at me. It's bothering me, what do we do? How long do we keep this up for?

What's going to happen? Don't you think of these things? Any of these questions?'

''Course I do, but I don't know the answers.'

'You're still not *really* looking at me are you. Do you see me? Do you?'

''Course I do; I can tell you the details of what you're wearing.'

'Close your eyes and tell me then.'

He did.

'You've got those puffy sleeves on your blouse that I don't like. The other girls on the switchboard probably think you're trying to look posh. You've got a flared skirt on. I used to like your short one when we went to dances.'

'So you could see the top of my legs. You **couldn't** care less now, though.'

'Like I just said, you're the one who - '

'Do you often notice what I wear?'

'Well, I'm quite visual so I suppose I do.'

'Okay then,' she said, undoing the top buttons of her blouse, I'll take this off, you haven't seen my top part for a while have you.'

She finished freeing the last of the buttons and held the garment at the end of an outstretched arm and let it drop.

'Olé,' she said rather dramatically.

'Do you want me to be a charging bull or something?' he asked

'I doubt whether you could charge anything, except perhaps too much for your bloody signwriting. How about this then?'

Swaying slightly, she almost rhythmically removed her belt, held it high above her head and let it drop to her shoulder before it fell to the floor.

'Incidentally, dearest, you think the bra's sexy?'

He didn't respond.

'You wouldn't know, would you. **Voilà,**' she then said and pulled her skirt down.

She stepped neatly out of it as it lay on the floor and stood facing him, fists on her hips.

'You like?'

'Who d'you think you are? Nita Naldi?'

'Well, you're no Valentino.'

He gave her a mock bow.

'I'm merely a humble husband.'

'You're not even that.'

'Doris, you - '

'You've actually used my name,' she said in mock surprise.

'Look, why don't you get dressed.'

'I'm hardly naked am I.'

'Alright, so you've got your petticoat on.'

'Oh, I'd forgotten that,' she said in more fake surprise, and proceeded to remove it.

'This is all very well, but - '

''Very nice', I think you mean. You sound like an old man. What's the 'but' for? We're living together like husband and wife and this is somehow rude'? That's what your puritanical mind was thinking.'

'That's a big word.'

'Oh, I know lots of others, like frustrated, lonely, depressed. They may not be that long, but they're bloody true.' She had begun to shout now.

She walked to the sofa and sat down, briefly holding her head in her hands. She looked up at him. 'You're so.. still, static, so - '

'Are we playing words starting with the same letter now?' He paused. 'Look, I'm sorry, that's cheap sarcasm. I don't know what to do. It's as simple as that.'

'Simple?'

'No, it's not, 'course not. But we can't keep on like this.'

She sat back on the settee and spread her legs.

'I know what you *could* do, if you had a mind to, though you'd need more than your mind.'

He turned away from her.

'This is so… so - '

'Unlike me? It is for the woman you think you know, but this is me, too. Look at me, George.'

She stretched her arms and rested them on the back of the seat.

'This is for you; it's all yours.'

He turned to look at her. For a second he wanted to. But it wasn't right. He knew that when it was over he still wouldn't want her there, perhaps even less so.

He went towards the door. She tore off her brassiere and hurled it away from her.

'Look what I've done, George,' she shouted. 'I've torn it off. I remember when you used to love unclipping it yourself. That's because I've got a good memory, I'd have to have, wouldn't I. Like an elephant's.'

She almost screamed, 'I can't stand this any more, George.'

He went quickly into the hall and to the front door.

'You haven't the courage to tell me to leave, have you. You haven't the courage to do anything. Anything.'

He pulled open the door, not shutting it behind him.

'I'm not going to be here, George,' he heard her yell.

He turned along the road towards the roundabout. He hurried along not knowing why he was there, outside, in the dark, almost running, in a kind of no-man's land.

Just before the roundabout was a 253 bus drawing into the stop for Rumford. He jumped on the tailboard, paid the driver and went upstairs. He was the only one there. It felt appropriate. He watched the lit shops of The Broadway glide past then the main road and Upper Renham Road and towards its destination. He wasn't sure why he'd got on this bus, he had no real wish to go where it was going; he didn't want to go anywhere, just out.. He saw a pub near the next stop. He rang the bell, alighted and went into it.

He'd been to this one with Reg some time before; he remembered its anaglypta ceiling, the large, ugly chandeliers hanging from it, and the embossed wallpaper. He got himself a brown ale and sat down at a corner table. He looked at his glass and thought of a day excursion to Southend-on-Sea he'd been taken on as a child by his parents, and on the pier train looking up to see a bi-plane with a 'Guinness Is Good For You' banner trailing from it. He couldn't read the first word, his father having to tell him what it was. It was one of the few memories he had of him.

He swallowed half his glass and glanced around; the barmaid was quietly whistling 'Knees Up, Mother Brown.' He thought of the lyrics, 'Under the table you must go... if I catch you bending I'll saw your leg right off.' It was cruel, but then so was 'Goosey, Goosey Gander,' someone throwing an old man down the stairs, and Jack and Jill, and others. He didn't bother to ask himself why, and reluctantly let his head fill with images of what had just happened at home.

It had scared him. He had never known her like this. It didn't seem to *be* her. He finished his glass. A customer came in and told someone leaning against the end of the bar that he'd been for a ball of chalk and that this was the first drink he'd had this week 'cos he was boracic. George got himself another glass, wondering why people used **rhyming slang.** Reg sometimes bought a pair of 'almond rocks' and he'd refer to stairs as 'the apples.' But this was occupying, roughly, one-hundredth part of his mind; the rest was being flooded with pictures of Doris on the couch with just knickers and bra, shouting, hissing at him.

The image was formidable, but it was just... Doris; this girl he'd known - or hadn't known - for a while now, living with him but not sleeping with him, literally and in the other sense. She was ordinary, too ordinary. He tried to face this concept. It meant that she had never really attracted him, not at any depth. What he was attempting to face, he was aware, was whether he was just... superficial.

His idea of a woman was someone glamorous, feminine special; somebody like Myrna Loy or Garbo. She had to have a perfect figure. There, he'd said it, 'perfect.' It was an ideal, something to possess. But he knew he couldn't; by definition an ideal can't be attained because it *is* an ideal. Another concept: possession. He wanted to possess a woman. Was he really that shallow? Did it come from childhood? A child wanting a perfect mummy? He finished his glass, got up and bought himself another.

He didn't want to go home; well, not that one, he just wanted to go back to his bedroom, the one he'd occupied for nearly all of his life and where, when he'd begun going to work, his mum would wake him each morning at half past six saying, as she placed a cup of tea on his bedside chest of drawers, 'Time to get up, and don't spill yer tea.'

He couldn't bother her now though, could he? Perhaps he should go to Reg's, but he still lived with his parents, he couldn't really go there and stay the night. He emptied most of his glass and put it down. He knew he was being a baby, but was unsure whether he should care. He drained the rest of his glass. No, he didn't care; he wanted to go back to his mum's place then go back home tomorrow. He felt as if he was confusing homes a little. Yes, he'd face Doris tomorrow after work.

Taking a deep breath, he got himself up and bought another pint. He drank it and moved a little unsteadily towards the door. After opening it, which took a little effort, he crossed the road, having to move pretty quickly to miss a horse-drawn cart, wondering what it was doing out at this time of night, and waited at a bus stop, not wanting to walk to a station just a few streets away.

He at first waited impatiently then began to tire and by the time the vehicle arrived he was almost asleep leaning on the bus stop post. To keep himself awake, he purposely looked out of the window trying to see details of the buildings and wondering what they were used for, until the bus halted at the station. He didn't have long to wait for a train and when it arrived, prevented himself dozing by doing what he'd done on the bus, though there was less illumination.

His mother opened the door for him without saying a word, as if she expected him to be there on the step. He went along the passage through to the dining room.

'D'you want to sit in the parlour?' she asked. 'It's more comfortable. You look as if you could do with some comfort.'

He turned back and flopped on the parlour couch.

'I'll get you a cuppa, though you look as if you could do with something stronger'

He almost dozed again before she tapped him on the shoulder and handed him his tea with a warning not to spill it.

She looked at him silently for a while before saying, 'You've got yourself bloody drunk, haven't you.'

He felt a little ashamed, a boy again being told off by mum, and nodded in confirmation.

'That's not going to get you anywhere. Come into the kitchen. Come on.'

She helped him up and led him there, then gently held his had under the sink taps until a brief stream of cold water roused him. He moved quickly backwards, shaking his head.

'Dry yourself with this,' she said, handing him a towel.

They returned to the front room.

'Feel a bit better now?' she asked, as he sat upright on the settee.

She looked at him firmly.

'It's home, isn't it.'

He nodded.

'I've been expecting this. It's gone wrong hasn't it.'

He was silent.

'Perhaps it never was right, eh?'

He remained silent.

'She's had a go at you, hasn't she. She's told you some home truths.'

'She… She went a bit kind of mad, mum,'

'She's frustrated isn't she.'

'What is it with you women? Sorry mum, I didn't mean it like that.'

'You're a bit worse for wear, aren't you. We have needs too, you know.'

'Suppose so.'

'Perhaps you don't find her attractive any more. Is that it? It's really nothing to do with me, I suppose, but did you ever really *love* her?'

He looked away from her, saying nothing.

'What you going to do about it?'

'Don't know.'

'It's no good running away from it; you've got to face it some time.'

'I know.'

'Drink your tea, I'll make you another.'

He did so, she briefly leaving the room and returning with a full cup.

He gulped it down and stood.

'At least you can stand straight. But you've got to do something about this, George, you've got to decide, and only you can do that. Do you hear me?'

'Yes, mum,' he said impatiently, I want to go to bed now.'

'Alright, you know where it is.' What time d'you want to get up. Usual?'

'Yeah, half six.'

'I'll bring your tea up, then when you get home from work you'll need to sort it out. And when you do, you can't go back on it; you've got to decide for yourself. Only you can do that. Goodnight.'

He made his way up the stairs to the spare bedroom, removed his jacket and fell into bed. He had to do something. Decide.

He was in a seminar, with Pym, the topic was Deviancy.

'It is,' he began, 'behaviour which somehow departs from what a group expects to be done or that it considers the desirable way of doing things. All pretty obvious, really. Society, as we know, is a system of dominant and central values, a consensual framework, a set of shared expectations of what is 'normal' behaviour.' Deviance, then, are acts which don't follow the accepted norms of groups. That is, they break social rules; they violate apparently taken-for-granted strictures.'

'It's not always illegal though,' someone interjected.

'Quite, there's legal and illegal deviancy. Anyone care to give examples?'

Between them they quickly offered suicides, nude bathers - 'though the latter, it was pointed out, depended on context - and bank robbers before someone said 'tomboys' as an example of legal deviancy.

'Yes, they are to an extent, deviant. Interesting that whilst 'sissy', i.e. a boy acting like a girl is pejorative, tomboy' is almost a laudatory label.'

While they came to the conclusion that that was because the world was male-dominated, Rupert thought of Constance and that the 'something about her' was, partly a certain tomboyishness. He could even imagine her playing football. He wondered why he'd thought of that particular sport, maybe because it involved her legs occasionally high kicking. He had got up a little later than intended and hadn't time before his seminar to see if she was in the library.

'Alright, what's the general reaction to our topic then?'

The response was again swift: fear suspicion, disgust, hostility.

'Why is that?'

'It disturbs our picture of reality, of what behaviour *should* be?' Rupert ventured.

'Indeed, it upsets our feeling of everyday security, our shared expectations that give us a picture of a stable society, an understandable social world. Perhaps we are born with a need for order, we search for it; society provides it. Deviance upsets this. Imagine a married man in Tunbridge Wells leaving his suburban home one morning and his wife says to him, 'Don't forget your gun.' Imagine his picture of reality then.

'If we call them 'deviants,' it emphasises order,' said a fellow student.

'Quite, it's behaviour outside the norm, thus reaffirming what the norms, the uncodified laws are; a world then is still understandable. It's also culturally and historically relative. What is deviant in one country may not be in another, and what was deviant may not be now and vice versa. An example is the circle formed by the tips of the forefinger and thumb meaning 'okay', coming of course from the American 'orl korrect' saying, but do the gesture in Japan and, apparently, you'll be in trouble.'

'I think it suggests the anus, doesn't it?' enquired a student.

'It probably does.'

The same student said, 'in France, men sometimes kiss men on the cheek I think, if they did so here they would be called sissies.'

'Even queers,' said the lad next to him.

'Yes, that's a pretty good example,' said Pym.

'Before we have more of them, let's be clear that there is no behaviour that is deviant as such, there is no absolute, it can only be defined by a social group and is relevant to a particular standard. What did Shakespeare say? 'There is no such thing as good or bad, but thinking makes it so.'

'Homosexuality is an illegal deviancy,' said someone.

'Cottaging,' said a student who hadn't spoken before.

'Which is?' asked Pym.

'It means anonymous sex between two men which happens in public toilets. It's called that because public toilets can look a bit like cottages.'

'I assume some of you purchase 'Health and Efficiency' - and not because you overtly wish to be efficient - but would that not be classified as illegal deviancy?' asked their seminar leader.

'Wouldn't that depend on the age and sex of whoever's reading it?' asked another student. 'And aren't the behaviours we've been talking about, be, to a large extent, natural?'

'It has to be learned behaviour,' said Rupert, 'or perhaps scientists could find little genes in our bodies that have a microscopic, 'little boys pinch green apples,' printed on them.'

The comment raised a few smiles, but Rupert wasn't really as interested as he would normally have been in what was going on around him, he wanted to see Constance.

'Women putting make-up on in trams and trains,' was another suggestion for legal deviancy, as was sexual relations between black and white people.

'Give me an example of deviancy in ideological terms.' asked their lecturer.

'If you're on the side of a terrorist, then he's a freedom fighter,' was one of the answers.

'Yes, and definitions of some behaviour as deviant may depend on the ability of some groups to impose their definitions of 'normal,' behaviour and manufacture an apparent agreement about what is 'proper' and 'improper' conduct.'

'Again,' said Rupert, 'it's largely about power definitions.'

Pym agreed, and continued. 'There are, of course, psychological and physiological explanations, but we need to spend little time on those, you can give them your critical attention when you do your essays. You'll read of so-called 'common sense' notions like, 'born that way, not his fault', et cetera.'

'There's the idea that deviants are throwbacks to primitive man, that is criminality is somehow 'inborn'. There is, of course, no evidence for this. And there's the hereditary argument that, though not causal, states that there's a link.'

'Social class hasn't been mentioned yet', Rupert interjected.

'Yes, it's the working class who commit most illegal deviancy.'

'But there's probably more money stolen, embezzled, in white-collar crime,' said Rupert.

'Almost certainly true,' replied Pym. 'And incidentally, unlike criminology, we attempt not to make value judgements and say that what is considered crime is 'wrong'. Of course, child-beating, rape, et cetera we can agree upon are morally wrong and criminal offences, however, let's say this: biological theories, as our friend,' he pointed to Rupert, 'intimated, cannot isolate the genes that cause specific behaviour.'

'Briefly, sociology looks at ways the social structure and cultural factors create crime; criminal behaviour is learned behaviour. With that in mind, here are your essay questions, three and a half thousand words minimum.'

He handed them out, told them he was needed elsewhere and that he would see them in a week's time.

Leaving the group slowly moving towards the door, talking among themselves, Rupert hurried to the library. Not seeing Constance on the way to his usual table, he sat and looked around. He saw her at the end of a row of books with her trolley but no steps this time.

He went towards her.

'You're not looking down at me now without your steps.'

'Oh, hello,' she smiled. 'I can't imagine you tolerating anyone looking down at you.'

'Metaphorically, no. But physically I'm happy for you to, although it's nice to see you safely on terra firma.'

'Do I appear taller or shorter now?'

'Neither.'

'Would you talk to me if I was appreciably taller or shorter than you?'

'Yes, but perhaps not quite in the same way. How's your mother?'

'She's alright now, it'll happen again though. What have you been up to?'

'I've just come from a seminar.'

She asked him what the topic was.

He told her.

'We're all deviant sometime or other. It's relative isn't it? I used to play conkers with the boys as a child. That would be deviant I suppose, and if *you* didn't that would be, too.'

She moved in front of her trolley, raised her arms, fluttered her hands, made shrill, birdlike and animal sounds and said, 'Would that be deviant?'

'Not if you were a clown in a circus or a comedian in variety it wouldn't be, but as the only woman in the building, except the cleaners and tea lady, you are a deviant. And your strange sounds seem to have bothered a reader over there.'

She smiled at a student looking curiously at her from his table and continued placing books on shelves.

'Anyway, we're all deviants and we've all broken the law.' She said.

He stood watching her; there was a natural competence about her, and a kind of understated femininity. She looked at him

'You're watching me again.'

'Do you wish me to stop?'

'Not really.' She frowned. 'Is war deviant?'

'Not if you're in it. Conscientious objectors, 'conchies' would be. In war, acts like killing would be called murder or man-slaughter in peace time. War is a state of anomie where a kind of normlessness is the norm, I suppose'.

'What deviant acts did you commit when younger, or perhaps are committing now?'

'Getting caught not paying a full train fare, having to go up before a magistrate and ordered to pay a fine and costs. I asked why I had to pay for the cost when I didn't want to be there any-way. They doubled the costs. I broke a window or two playing cricket in the road. Father wasn't best pleased; a child of an army major just doesn't do that sort of thing. Oh, and keeping a shop-keeper engaged in conversation while a pal pinched a couple of Wizards and Rovers from the rack. The Wolf of Kabul, Nosey Parker and the rest. Can't remember much else.'

'Doesn't sound as if you lived a very exciting life.'

'It wasn't, more of a privileged one'.

'You recognise that do you?'

'We travelled a bit: New York, I fell in love with Manhattan, the moustached Mexicans serving in the delis, the Chrysler, which had just been built, the Flatiron building, people going around saying 'Gee whiz'. What did *you* read?'

'Cindy, Vicky, Lucy and a few others.'

'And your naughties?'

'Not as many as I'd have liked there to have been. At least, I can't remember them. I was pretty good at soccer, better than some of the boys, but of course not allowed to take part.'

'I have pictured you playing football. It's a nice image.'

'Did you play?'

'Very little. Rugby and all that.'

'A game for hooligans played by gentlemen.'

'Apparently. Why did you mention war?'

'Probably because a little while ago Hitler and Mussolini sent planes to fly Franco's troops from Morocco to Spain. I don't like the pairing, it will lead to bad things.'.

'What is it with you and Adolf?'

'I learnt a bit about him when younger; my mother would talk of him with her friends. 'Crazy little man' they referred to him as, but my mother didn't. I have a feeling that label won't stick forever. He's got Goebbels organizing thousands of meetings, torchlight marches, using simple catchphrases over and over. People believe him.'

'People *want* to believe him. People need a god, that's why they construct them; collectively, if they feel neglected and angry, they create a messiah.'

'Whatever. I heard someone say that some of last year's graduates have gone out to Spain to fight for the Republicans. Maybe some of this year's graduates will, too.'

'I can't imagine any first-years doing so.'

'Would you?'

'When? Now?'

'At any time.'

'If you mean for a just cause, that would depend on what 'just' means and who or what defines it as such.'

She was holding a book in each hand now, doing nothing with them.

'You would intellectualise the criteria to be fought for then?'

'It would need to have a solid base.'

'What about what you *felt*?'

'That would come from the former.'

'Things like logic?'

'Things like unfairness, lies, the powerful using their power, spreading a distorted message, instilling a surge of dutiful patriotism in the working masses and convincing them that they can fight their way through to a sunlit vista of glorious victory.'

'All war is class war, eh?'

'You've read Marx?'

'You seem surprised. There are a lot of books here, you know.'

'I'm pleasantly surprised. At the moment I'm working for a degree. Maybe I'm being rather insular, but I've heard little and read even less about what's happening in Espana.'

'You're forgiven. We'll have to see where it leads.'

'You're a bit of a pessimist sometimes aren't you. I quite like it, it's realistic.'

'An optimist thinks we live in the best of all possible worlds; a pessimist agrees with him,' she said, resuming her book-placing.

'D'you fancy going to the pictures?'

'When?'

'Whenever suits you.'

'Tomorrow.'

'Alright, I'll work on an essay throughout the night. I'm exaggerating. What do you want to see?'

'What's on?'

'Mr. Deeds Goes To Town's on in the cinema in George street. Want to see it?'

'It's about a poet, isn't it?'

'A greetings card poet.'

'That's it, a nice man from a small town who finds out he's the heir to an immense fortune. He goes to New York to live the high life and finds he hates being rich, and when he tries giving the money away to the poor he finds himself on trial for insanity.'

'Oh, thanks, it's hardly worth going now.'

'I happened to remember a review. D'you want to see the film now that you know the story, or be with me?'

'Both, with emphasis on the latter.'

'Money makes the world go around, root of all evil et cetera.'

'You going to define money now?'

'Any item or verifiable record that is generally accepted as payment and repayment of debts, such as taxes, in a particular country or socio-economic context.'

'I try to remember things while I'm working.'

'Because you're bored? You could do so much more couldn't you. At this moment   I feel like dressing you up as a man and smuggling you into college.'

'That's deviant, and naughty.'

'I don't mean for frolics, but - '

'To write your essays for you?'

'For your sake, for you to be a student here, instead of rearranging pieces of recycled dead trees.'

'Thanks, but I do get to read a lot doing this.'

'You know, I'd sooner us go for a meal, get to know you better.'

'The 'us' has arrived rather quickly.'

'Look, let's just go, and we can argue about it afterwards. Maybe over dinner.'

'Fair enough, opinions on films can be revealing.'

'So could our views on Marx, you've probably read more of him than I have.'

'Gee whiz, that really is the way to a girl's heart. Such sweet talk.'

'Point is, his ideas could soon become the thing here. The thing to do, as it were.'

'A kind of fashion?'

'I hope not, I'd like them to have a deeper credibility than that; his technological determinism, his class analysis.'

'I agree with him on those two, amongst others.'

'I guess we are almost part of the bourgeoisie, eh?' said Rupert.

'We can't pretend otherwise, but our thinking can be more - '

'Déclassé?'

'I was going to say 'detached', but that'll do. It has to be, I suppose, in your subject.'

'Indeed.'

'Does it suit you?'

'Does what?'

'That kind of thinking.'

'Mentally, yes, but not emotionally.'

He looked at her, again with books in hands, stationary, look-ing at him. She seemed for a moment to fill the library. How could he detach emotionally?

'I'm going to do some work now. Have a seminar paper to do and found an essay question in my pigeon hole. I should start on one of them.'

'The main picture nearly always begins at eight. Do I see you outside?' she asked.

He told her he would be there, and went back to his room to do some serious reading.

The next day he saw Eric in the refectory for a short lunch, then after both attending lectures, they met again for a short chat in Eric's room, Rupert not mentioning who he was going to meet that evening, before he returned to his own room to settle down to some work.

'Standing room only in the sixpennies and ninepennies,' called the man in the red coat, peaked cap and white gloves, as he care-fully counted and ushered the line through the door of the picture palace. The queue shuffled patiently forward as a barrel organ kept them company. Rupert had been surprised there'd been such a long file of people. He'd joined it a few minutes before she came to him.

She had dressed up a little. It pleased him; a tailored jacket on top of a blouse and pencil skirt.

He quite enjoyed the film, occasionally watching her profile suggest she was, also. It seemed, for most of it, pretty much on the side of the big townees, with the newspapers In scathing ex-posés of the hero's small-town behaviour, declaring Gary Cooper's character a backwater dope.

'So, in true Hollywood fashion, Deeds and the girl get together in the end, and the big city dwellers get to look nasty,' said Ru-pert as they left.

'One up for Joe Soap, I guess. I like Cooper.'

'The strong, silent type, but with a poetic soul?'

'That's it.'

'I think I meet one of those criteria.'

'Poetic?'

'Just about.' Roses are red, violets are blue, I'm a schizophrenic and so am I.'

'That's rather cruel.'

'Are you hungry?'

'Yes, but have to get back, told mother I would, she's not a hundred percent.'

'Pity. **'What about some potato-marshmallow surprises, and black bottom pie tomorrow then?'**

'If she's **okay'.**

'Are you working?'

'Yes, I'll see you in - '

'The usual place?'

'I suppose it is. I'll let you know then.'

Before a bus pulled in and she hurried across the road to it, she gave him a hasty kiss on his cheek.

She turned and waved from the tailboard. Feeling energised after that brief physical contact he walked back to his lodgings with the image of her smiling and waving at him pleasantly lodged in the front of his memory.

15

Passing his old school again after a hurried but satisfying breakfast supplied by his mother, with a tram, two cart and horses, and a knife grinder hurriedly pushing his barrow moving past him, more unbidden childhood images came. On Monday mornings at Pretoria Road school it was hymns and prayers for the first half hour before classes were formed in the main hall with small boys in the front, taller ones at the back. The teachers, with their backs to the classrooms, would stand to attention waiting for the headmaster to come down from his study and take up his customary position at the side of a big, shiny table

A lady teacher from the nearby girls school would sit at a piano and the words of the first hymn to be sung would be rolled down from high on the wall by Mister Letts who laid his long pointer on the piano beneath it. They would then hear, 'Good morning, boys', as the headmaster strode to the table and stood by it, complete silence reigning as he held up this hands and asked the boys to sing as loudly as they could. The teacher would pick up the pointer, nod to the pianist and indicate the first line of the hymn. They did their best, but it was rarely to the headmaster's liking. 'Wait. Stop, stop,' he would shout. 'You boys at the back, I can't hear you at all. Sing up, sing up.'

At a nod from Mister Letts, the piano lady would try again and again, as did about three hundred boys, short and tall, fat and thin, while Mister Lind's face would become darker and darker, especially when the headmaster snatched his pointer and despairingly pointed at the first line of All Things Bright And Beautiful.

George recalled fretting, on a particular Monday morning, about whether the medicine cabinet he was making for his mother would be ready in time for her birthday. Half an hour later and his class would be climbing the iron staircase and going into a classroom for a woodwork lesson with the tools in racks at the end of benches. He was making the cabinet out of plywood, occasionally hearing Mister Barnes insisting, 'Don't forget, line on the left, saw on the right.'

The memories fad arisen from the need to deflect the decision he had to make and the significant question of whether Doris would actually harm herself if he told her he didn't want her.

He purposely made himself conjure up other pictures from his past. He wanted to wallow in them, wanted to be there in a time when he had no responsibilities, unlike now where he felt he had a responsibility for her.

But there had been no sacred oaths, no promises made in wedlock, nothing sanctified or legal. He felt, nevertheless, that he had a duty. He wondered where it came from; because he was a man and she a woman, he supposed. The fair sex, the weaker one. She didn't appear to be weak when he had last seen her. He didn't want to think of her like that again.

After passing the school he saw some boys dribbling a tennis ball around a lamp post, like he often used to. Back came images of the Boleyn ground on match days when queues formed in Castle Street and bicycles were stored in people's passageways and crowded onto the pavements outside. It was a bonus if it had been raining, for as the wooden doors rumbled aside and turnstiles clicked and the queue edged forward, some of its members wore raincoats that were long enough for the boys, bent double with knees on the ground and head tucked in, to crawl beneath them and scramble in among the boots and shoes. In the gloom and dust, they would straighten and run up the concrete steps and be lost amid the grown-ups.

Nearing the station and walking along a terraced street, he noticed women in adjoining houses sitting on the outside of bedroom window sills, the upper sashes pulled firmly down on their thighs, cleaning the glass and chatting to each other as they did so. His mother used to do it with her next-door neighbour. Nothing seemed to change in this part of the city.

He got to work a little late. There was one more room to paper, eight rolls of a broader, French paper which he competed by five o'clock with only a short break for a sandwich and a thermos of tea his mother had given him. This was, unusually, a décor he liked. Birds, but light in colour and rather pleasing. He didn't usually like wallpaper; stripes, patterns, shapes... too bitty. The work had helped push the act of returning home away a little.

He'd have liked to have had a meal in the room before returning. But things had to be faced. He cleared up quickly and walked firmly to the station and caught a train.

He opened the sunray gate he'd painted black and jade green and briefly thought of his interior colour scheme, a case of, 'You can have any colour you like as long as it's white, green, magnolia or pale grey eggshell.' He could show off his knick-knacks against the simple plainness of these backgrounds: his lamps, sideboard, bookcase and, his latest acquisition, one he could hardly afford, a walnut tallboy.

He walked to his front door, its diagonal glazing bars giving him pleasure. But not as much as they used to, for it opened into a space he wasn't happy in, didn't feel he actually owned as much as he had before, as if, somehow, it wasn't quite his.

Halting, he stood on the step, turned around and looked up and down the road. There was nobody in it. Lights were on in front rooms, curtains closed, street lamps flickering on. He didn't want to be just standing there, but felt there was nowhere else for him to go. He was there, he knew, because he hadn't made a decision. This was his home, and she couldn't force him to love her. She wasn't going to entice him into making love to her, into... penetrating her. She wasn't going to frighten him into it either.

He thought of her actions the last time he had been in the house. They weren't the actions a of a woman who was going to throw herself under a tram or go to the top floor of the building she worked in, climb onto the roof and throw herself off it. Were they? He then remembered her last words to him; that she wouldn't be there. Did that mean that she was going to leave? That she *had* left?

There was light showing at the side of the window curtain near the door. She was in. He put his key in the lock and went into the hall. There didn't seem to be a light on in the house except behind the nearest door of the through-lounge. He hesitated then opened it.

There were piles of her things on the floor: clothes - he irrelevantly noticed her bolero jacket on top of one pile - brown paper bags, one had split and he could see some saucers, there was a pillow, one her mother had given her, a dining room chair that she had bought that looked nothing like those he had, and that she'd insisted upon sitting on at meal times.

And there she was, standing behind the small stacks holding her coat over a shoulder as if to put it on at some sort of given signal.

'You're home then,' she said, 'Bet you stayed with mummy, didn't you. When you going to grow up? It's up to you what I do. I'm ready to go, George. My dad's sitting in a café not far away that has a phone. I've arranged to call him to pick me up. If I don't call him in the next hour, he'll go back home again.'

She looked challengingly at him. She looked tired and strained.

The scene felt hostile, as if any choice, any decision he made could never be undone, it would be for ever. He pictured the room cleared of her belongings, of her, and felt, confusingly, a loneliness.

'It has to be as it was. We sleep together as a couple.' She was briefly silent. 'And dad thinks that the house should be in my name as well. It's only fair. We're living together as man and wife. He knows about the law, does dad.'

This scared him. Surely, as he was paying the mortgage and had paid the deposit, she couldn't do this?

He felt for a brief second he was almost fighting for his existence. But she wasn't going to blackmail him.

'No. You go then. Take everything, Doris. All of your stuff.'

She was quiet for a few seconds.

'Don't want anything to remind you of me then? Convenient, eh? I've made it easy for you, haven't I. *You* haven't had to make the decision. *I* have.'

She put on her coat.

'You haven't the courage have you, I've made the choice for you. You can stay and rot here among your paintings and your... things, and your silly little pond. I've been loyal to you, God knows why; any other woman would have left you long ago. But then, perhaps you would have wanted them to, perhaps you shouldn't be living with a woman. Maybe you can't live with anyone else except mummy.'

She was standing quite still, leaning towards him a little.

'To love someone you've got to love yourself, and you don't, do you. You love things, bits of... this and that, your Egyptians, your coloured moths; that's what they look like. And your fountain, it's a wonder when you switch it on it doesn't play Beethoven or something.'

She bent and picked up two piles of clothes, took them out of the room and dumped them in the hall. She went out of the front door, not closing it, he assuming she would go to the phone box on the corner of the road. He went out and watched he hurry towards it. She wasn't in there for long and walked back quickly and purposely. He returned to the room, which she entered soon afterwards.

She came into the room again. What are you doing, standing there? Going to wave me off through the window?'

She picked up another pile of clothes.

'Bet you'd love to help me wouldn't you, but that'd make what you want too obvious, wouldn't it.' She looked at him intently. 'Say something George - anything. You're not going to see me again. Do you like those words? Are they what you've been waiting to hear? For how long? A long while? How do they make you feel? Remember feelings, George? They're inside you, they make you real. Are *you* real?' She looked him up and down quickly. 'Have you been nailed to the floor? Going to stand there for ever?'

Her face looked like it had the evening before; angry and distorted.

'Going to say hello to my dad then? He never did like you, you know. Did you know that?'

'I... hardly know him, he rarely spoke to me.'

'You can speak then. Good.'

'I really am going George, this isn't some sort of bloody dream, an illusion. He'll be here any minute now and I'll be off. I'm leaving you. Do...you...understand?'

Just then there was a rapid tapping on the front door.

'I'm here Doris, are you ready? It's me.'

She looked at her partner once more, sneered then spat on the carpet. She went out to the hall, opened the front door and asked her father to help her pick up her belongings. It took less than a minute with her parent not looking at him once. The door slammed shut, and George found himself hurrying up the stairs, then into the front bedroom and across to the window. He moved the net curtain aside and looked down.

Under the street lamp her father was throwing things into the boot of a car. He was a rather small, straggly-haired, balding man, whose first name George had forgotten. He got into the car, started it and, just before it moved away his daughter, sitting beside him, turned her face to take a quick look at the house she had once lived in, then firmly faced the direction in which the vehicle was moving.

He remained standing, then looked at the walls, they seemed.... better somehow, almost cleaner, welcoming. He looked around him again, the last months had suddenly seemed to have been stripped from him. He was now the man who had just moved in, the new occupier, the first one, the only one.

He went upstairs, wandered about the rooms, the box room, the two bedrooms, the bathroom. He could hear his mother saying, 'It's only bricks and mortar, son,' and, 'It's not where you live, but how you live that counts.' But they were *his* bricks and mortar.

He went to the bathroom again. It was as it should be: the black vitrolite tiles, their white background, a couple of small ferns. The bedrooms were fine too, 'though on the floor of the wardrobe of the main one, was a dark, rather tatty scarf he didn't recognise, but it must have been hers. He picked it up, went downstairs into the kitchen, dropped the scarf into the bin and went back to the through-lounge. There seemed to be no sign of her at all, no evidence she'd even been there. It was as if she'd borrowed the space for a while and had then returned it to him.

He walked around again; nothing. But there was something missing. It was a feeling about the house. Somehow, now, he couldn't quite feel the same about his home as he had done when he'd first made it his. He reminded himself that it was, in fact, only a kind of psychological ownership for he had years left to pay for it, but the feeling he had then wasn't quite the same now.

Of course, it was partly because he'd been there some time and had done plenty of work on it, but most of that time she had been here with him. Perhaps it would take some getting used to, being here on his own. He sat on the bed in the main bedroom, the one she had slept in without him. He looked about him again and saw a folded blouse in the corner of the room against the skirting. She'd obviously dropped it without noticing. He picked it up and hung it loosely over the wardrobe rail. He wouldn't put it in the bin; he'd keep it, not being sure why. After removing his own clothes from the makeshift wardrobe in the smaller bedroom he'd been using, he hung them there, too. It would feel a little strange sleeping on a different bed.

He thought about her, but for a second not able to picture her clearly. He didn't want to remember her as she had behaved the day before. If, for some reason, he missed her, then he would purposely picture her like that. Her old threat didn't trouble him now, she surely couldn't love him any more, and she would feel safe again with her parents. He went downstairs to the lounge and looked out at the road. He couldn't quite define how he felt.

Putting on his jacket, he went into the street and began walking. He went towards Rumford; he wasn't going for drinks again, that would be pointless, he'd just walk, maybe amble around the market, he'd occasionally wondered what it would be like with the stalls gone.

A bus travelling to his destination halted at a nearby stop so he boarded it, paid the conductor and went upstairs to an empty upper deck and sat on the front seat. There were a few vehicles, horse and carts too, but not many of the latter at this time of the evening.

He liked watching the world go by from a bus or tram, even in the dark, he had as a child; before doing so, surreptitiously taking a little money from the tin on the dining room mantelpiece and, unknown to his mother, buying a half-fare on a tram for a mile-or-two's ride up the road then walking, part running, home again. His favourite walk had been along the path at the top of the Northern Outfall, known by all and sundry as 'the sewer'. His mother would occasionally apply her open hand painfully on his buttocks when he'd got home late. He hadn't known much about girls then; he felt he still didn't.

Most of the stalls had gone when he arrived at the market; those that were left were devoid of their wares. There seemed no-one else there; it felt like a wasteland, as if something awful had happened, even some of the lamp standards appeared not to be working. It was a kind of analogy of himself at this moment, he thought: empty, dark, his mind, emotions, badly lit and, in the darkness, not quite knowing what to do.

16

It had become almost a regular meeting place now, albeit he did genuinely need a book for some essay research and he would sooner sit here in the library than in his room. He didn't need an excuse to be here anyway, he wanted to see her. He went towards his usual table; but there was someone else sitting there, talking to her. She was nodding her head in agreement with what he was saying and smiling at him. He felt a twinge of jealousy as if a proprietary right had been taken away from him.

She looked up at him, said something to the student and came across to him.

'Hello again. Good news, eh?'

'What is?' he asked.

'Equal pay for women at last. It's been voted through Parliament. It's been a long time coming.'

'You got equal pay a few years ago.'

'For some. If you were a certain age and had property or married to a man who had. But now…'

She looked at him with a broad grin.

'I met Pippa and Ray Strachey once, my mum knew them a little. She was all for women's rights, too.'

'Is that why you are?'

'You make it sound as if one has to be influenced by family or friends to be so. I am for them because we should have them. D'you not agree?'

''Course I do.'

'You're not just saying that?'

'Why would I?'

'To curry favour with me?'

'As tempting as it is to do that, no. It's genuine.'

'I believe you, thousands wouldn't.'

'I've heard of those two.'

'I don't remember them much, I was pretty young, but they've done a lot for The Women's Movement.'

'You don't hear that much about it these days.'

'This Depression has, I think, emphasised the rights of women more. Unemployment, you could argue, has strengthened support for equal pay, at least within the Labour movement.'

'You're a lovely blue stocking gal.'

She smiled; a slightly faraway look in her eyes.

'My mother was a sort of secretary for Pippa. It's no good me asking her now, I doubt whether she would remember. She used to say that her and Ray had very different demeanours, but neither of them cared a jot about the away they dressed. Pippa, apparently, would allow her stockings to fall in rolls around her ankles while Ray once went out to dinner wearing her dress inside-out and backwards. They were indifferent.'

'Ray's a woman?'

'Yes, they called her that, her name was Rachel. She was the extrovert, quick and positive; the other was sort of wary and slow. They seem to have won, though.

She turned suddenly towards the bookshelves.

'I've work to do.'

'Fancy celebrating their victory then?'

'When?'

'This evening?'

'Make it tomorrow; I need to care for my mother this evening.'

He felt a little disappointed, but now had something other than a lecture later in the day to look forward to.

She went, with her trolley, towards the other end of the building, while he, after watching her until she was out of sight, began his reading. He read and made notes for two hours then, after looking unsuccessfully for her, had lunch on his own, guessing that Eric was either working in his room or at a seminar, and went to a lecture on sociology's founding fathers.

There was little said about Comte, although as the young lecturer, who Rupert hadn't seen before, mentioned, it could be said that he invented the subject as a scientific discipline, which was then reinforced by Durkheim, then came Weber with his emphasis on people's meanings, and Marx, who Rupert thought was given short shrift, the speaker stating that he emphasised the idea that the rich controlled the economy, the poor didn't, and that the economic system split people into two groups, saying little more than that. Rupert didn't learn much

He spent some time in his room doing some more reading then wrote a short letter to his mother before knocking on Eric's door for a short but interesting chat on the works of Aldous Huxley and William Faulkner, of which Eric knew appreciably more than his friend, then returned to his room and to bed.

'Many 'common sense' notions about 'natural' differences in society do not stand up to scrutiny. The more we know about other cultures and historical periods the more we know that women can be active or passive, argumentative or conciliatory, sexually voracious or sexually timid dependant on the society and their position in it.

'And the psychological determinants,' said someone.

'We can talk about that later,' said Pym.

Rupert, with others in his Year, was sitting around the seminar table next day as Pym introduced the topic of Sexual Divisions, apparently a whole new subject for the University, especially under the generic title of Philosophy.

'I suppose it's really the nature-nurture debate isn't it,' said one of the students sitting around the table.

'Of course,' responded Pym, 'but the idea of much, or most, human behaviour being learned is, I suppose, a relatively new thing, especially in terms of male and female behaviour.'

'Surely,' said the same student, 'patriarchy is natural; all societies, all tribes are male-dominated.'

Another said, 'Initially, at least, because males are, generally, physically stronger than females.'

'Well, anthropologically, there are tribes where pregnant women are seen as merely 'carriers' of a man's child, whilst in others the men are seen as merely entering their bodies for a brief period and from then on they are defunct, of no use, as the baby is theirs, they grow it, carry it.'

'If dominant ideologies, 'truths', are created by the dominant, then some tribes must be kind of matriarchal then,' said Rupert.

Most of the others, even the usually quiet ones, then said, almost as if orchestrated, that the pregnant women example was surely a very singular tribe, at most a very small minority one.

'Indeed, it appears to be so.' said their seminar leader. 'But let's get to some important points about sex differences: the difference between sex and gender. The former refers to the basic biological differences between men and women - males and females - such as genitalia and reproductive capacities, which are universal, gender refers to culturally specific patterns of behaviour, actual or normative, which may be attached to the sexes. That is, what is perceived as 'masculine' and 'feminine', thus culturally determined and variable. Any examples?

'I went to Paris when younger,' said Rupert, 'and noticed that at least half the men seemed to be carrying what looked like handbags, even tough-looking stevedores. If men carried them here they would be seen as peculiar.'

'They'd be called 'pansies'', someone said.

'They'd go to places called 'pansy clubs'' said another lad.

'A good example,' said Pym. He continued.

'These differences then are probably seen by most people as natural. We see behaviours as appropriate to the biological differences.'

'Social constructs again,' someone remarked.

'Quite,' said Pym, 'If femininity' was biologically determined then much of the process of socialization would be superfluous.'

'Are ways of having sex sort of different in different cultures?' asked one of the quieter seminar members.

'Different norms. Yes, there may be some evidence of this,' said Pym.

'May I ask a question?' said a student sitting at the other end of the table to Pym.

'You may.'

'Well, I read that in the sex act an individual's personality just... goes, at least during part of the act, it disappears.'

'Your point being?'

'Well, assuming personality, 'though I'm not sure how that's defined, is largely created by socialization, then if it's no longer there you're back to the primal, to nature, so how can there be any difference in sexual acts in different cultures?'

'It's a question,' answered Pym. 'of what is seen as the 'true' sexual act, some ancient art shows the missionary position - and I'm sure you know what that is - as being less popular than woman-on-top positions in Greece, Peru, India, and China, but Kagaba natives in Colombia apparently prefer missionary because of the stability it offers; believing that if the woman moved during intercourse, the earth would slip off the shoulders of the four giants who held it up above the waters. Some tribes believe the male-on-top position is the only way to conceive warriors'

A student sitting next to Pym said, 'Chimpanzees do it standing up.'

'As a general caution, there are problems with extrapolating human behaviour from animal behaviour. We have an 'I' and a 'me', we have a spoken and written language, consciousness - 'though let's not go into that last concept, I doubt whether its mystery can ever be solved. How did we get onto this subject, anyway?

'To resume: sexual divisions cannot, of course, be subsumed under a question of gender differences. Whilst what is perceived as masculinity varies - we were given an example earlier - in most societies males have more power and authority than women and power over women. In short, the relations are of subordination and domination.

'So, cutting this short, there are some seminar paper questions for you for the next few weeks on the desk next to the door. Pick up one each.' As they did so, he said, 'Incidentally, I would prefer it if you didn't talk about some of what has been said today; it may reach the wrong ears. We are at Oxford, gentlemen. I bid you good day.'

Rupert returned to his room, looked at a few books and decided to find more relevant reading. He sat at his library table, feeling rather proprietary about it and resumed his observations of Constance who was, again, nearby. He felt that even if he'd never seen this woman's face, there was something about the way she stood, leaning slightly forward, that had a presence, a kind of casual authority.

As if sensing he was there she turned towards him.

'Hello, yet again. We gotta stop meeting like this,' she said in a convincing American accent.

'Putting on his Cockney, Rupert said, 'Oh no we ain't.'

She asked him what he had been doing since they'd last spoken.

'Bit of reading, bit of seminar stuff.'

She came towards him and asked what the subject was.

'Something called sexual divisions; it's a pretty new one I think.'

'Women as adjuncts to men?'

'In most societies, perhaps all, that would appear to be the general perception.'

'It'll change, *is* changing.'

'I'm glad.'

'Are you really?'

'Yes, I think I feel genuinely about it.'

'You only think?'

'No, I do.'

'It's taking a long time to change.'

'But you're getting more formal and legal equality now'

'We can enter public office and the professions and we can own and administer property. It's slowly coming.'

'On the subject of gender - '

'Can you sit down. It's cosier.'

'You know I can't do that. Anyway, I looked at some children's books the other day, 'though I'm not sure what they're doing in this library, but there were stories about Julie and James, and going to the seaside and so forth with their parents. They seemed to be mostly about brainwashing the children into accepting their future roles in life.

'James was nearly always in the lead in the illustrations, whether it was buying an ice cream on a beach or putting up a tent. He helped daddy do the men's jobs, 'Here is James helping daddy put the spare wheel on the car', while Julie was shown 'helping mummy wash up', et cetera. And James was given a model railway or a set of toy bricks to build a house with, while the girl was inevitably given a doll and little pram to play with.'

'It's called 'anticipatory role socialization'.'

'Call it what you will, it's unconsciously arrogant; the names of some books, like Little Goody Two-Shoes, and the children's roles were clearly sex-divided in The Swiss Family Robinson.'

'Have you ever thought,' asked Rupert, that if, once a baby is born, it was immediately given to the father to be fed and cared for, would it, as it grew, still have this so-called 'bond' with the mother?'

'Interesting. I read somewhere, also, that some families were asked to bring up their children - for a little while only of course - in reverse, as it were. That is, to give the boys dolls, and the girls toy guns and things.'

'Did they?'

'Not quite. Parents were quite willing to give the girls 'boys'' toys, but not 'girls'' toys to the boys.'

'Quite. 'Sissy' bad, 'tomboy' good. I would have thought that would be more applicable to working class parents.'

'You're interested in class, aren't you.'

'Despite prep school, this university, and a pretty rich father, yes.'

'You can detach from that then.'

'Yes, not just intellectually but, to an extent, emotionally.'

'You can identify with them?'

"Empathise' would be more apt. I don't like the chasms between peoples, between groups, classes. As a child and beyond I'd occasionally be taken by my father to one of his developments, or something he was building for someone else, and watched the building go up and the people who put it up and who worked hard, sometimes in harsh conditions, laying bricks, roofing, working with concrete, loading cranes, falling off high l adders.'

'You saw all this?'

'Not all, some, but enough, and my father forbade them joining a union. I remember once when a painter, painting a flag pole sticking out horizontally from the sixth floor of a City office building, fell off it and was killed. I didn't see it happen, but he didn't have a safety harness because my father, apparently, re-fused to pay for one. I don't know how true that last bit is, but...'

She looked at him silently for a while with her head held slightly to the side.

'You seem to be a nice man.'

'Thanks, but I don't think 'nice' should be a word, it says very little.'

'Want me to think of other adjectives?'

'No, but do you still want to go out this evening? You haven't mentioned it.'

'I was waiting for you to. If you still want dinner, Moncktons in the High Street is supposed to be good.'

'What time suits you.'

'Seven.'

He was about to say that he'd call for her but thought better of it.

'See you there then.'

'Alright, maybe you should book. Cheerio.'

She turned away from him, replaced more books, walked quickly to the end of the aisle and pushed her trolley to the next one out of sight of his admiring gaze.

He tried to read but couldn't concentrate, so went to the phone across the quad and rang the restaurant.

It looked a little like a train carriage but wider, with a series of circular mirrors on its pale-green walls instead of windows, and marquetry tables and chairs. He arrived a few minutes before her. She was almost in silhouette against the evening light as she en-tered, in a blouse and a pair of slacks with high-heeled shoes.

'Somebody told me that, in this Depression, people are dress-ing according to their social status. I couldn't tell yours, but you look great,' he said.

'Thank you,' she said, sitting down. 'If what you say is correct, perhaps you should be wearing a suit and a trilby instead of a casual sports jacket.'

'Maybe. I've looked at the menu; more 'disguised' food'.

'I like it; pigs in blankets especially, hot dogs in croissant dough.'

'Quite. And bunny salad made from a canned pear-half. American influence again, I guess.'

'So is 'I guess''.

'Want to order now?'

'Yes please.'

He watched her with the menu, there was something about her that seemed so quietly and innocently sure of itself. They ordered; he a chicken divan casserole, she the pastry-wrapped sausage and sweet potato marshmallow.

'I was thinking I'd have liked to have picked you up at your place, but I don't know where it is, and you didn't ask me to, anyway.'

'It's a bed-sitter in Colne street, not far from the library.'

'I suppose I thought you lived with your mother.'

'Mum doesn't like me living with her; she doesn't feel she needs looking after, although ,of course, she does. But I can see her regularly. If she got worse I would move in with her.'

'No blue stockings this evening, then?'

'I don't need to make a statement to you.'

'S'pose you could argue that you're saying that because you're wearing trousers you wish to be perceived as good as…. sorry, I meant 'equal to' a man.'

'Wouldn't it imply that I'm a free woman who is, possibly, superior to a man?'

'I' go for the last bit.'

'Thank you, kind sir.'

'A pleasure. It's not just women that need some sort of equality, social class arguably cuts right across it all.'

'It does. When people talk of women's rights et cetera, there's still a middle-class emphasis, and what we've gained so far hasn't helped women workers in factories and domestic servitude.'

He spotted the waiter coming towards them.

'Here come your warm canines, Constance Lange. Enjoy,'

'I shall.'

She did, silently; their food seemed a little too good to interrupt the satisfying of taste buds by talking, though he would have gladly listened to her and been given permission not to reply. After a while she said, 'Sometimes, politicians use the phrase 'more equal,' which implies that a tangible level of equality already exists. Are you aware that nought-point-six percent of the population owns half of all rural land in England and Wales? A third of this land is still owned by rural gentry and aristocrats.'

'Apparently, the top ten British land owners own six million acres among them in a country of sixty million acres.'

'And the ubiquitous 'the economy,' which is a hazy euphemism for profits being made by a relative few, of course.'

She looked at him with a slight frown and her head at an angle.

'Your father was a Major, and not a landowner, right?'

'Thought I'd said, he's a builder and developer now; just opened an estate in Essex. A large one, but I wouldn't call him a landowner as such, and certainly not an aristocrat, though he would like to mingle with them I'm sure. Eric's almost aristocracy; or maybe thinks he is.'

She asked who he was. He told her.

Their dessert came. They both had cherries jubilee followed by a bottle of Chianti.

While holding a glass to her lips she looked at him steadily.

He asked her what she was thinking of.

'Your... well, I won't say empathy, though there seems some there of course, but your interest in the working class.'

'Their education has trained them to distrust their own thoughts and to rely on those of their 'betters'.'

'And a better life is 'not for the likes of them', eh? On the way here - you may have noticed it yourself at some time - there's a church-like building with a sign in its porch that says something like, 'The Shaftsbury Society's Charitable Union of the Gospel Lighthouse Mission for the guidance of ragged children in matters of cleanliness, appearance and manners.' After which it said something like, 'Thus enabling them to take up a military career no matter how short.' It's the last bit that seems strange.'

'Not if you're preparing the ragged to be cannon fodder. 'All war is class war' as Mister Marx says.'

'Doubt whether many people have heard of him and if they have it'll be a negative judgement.'

'They will have about anyone who goes against the system. I recall talking to a few of dad's workers once, they were pretty poor, probably worse now 'cos of the Slump. My father didn't pay them any less than other building bosses, but I tried to convince them that their being hard up was nothing to do with foreign labour, machines or overpopulation, but capitalism itself.'

'They acquiesce in their own exploitation?'

'Exactly.'

She smiled at him. 'I don't think this is the sort of conversation you were expecting or, perhaps, hoping for?'

'I have an urge to dress you up as a chap and smuggle you into lectures, the seminars also if I could get away with it, although I don't think anything could make you look like a man.'

'I could talk with you all evening, but I promised mum I'd call in before she goes to bed.'

'Disappointing, but I'll walk to the stop with you.'

He paid the bill and they left.

As the bus stop was virtually outside the restaurant and a bus was pulling in, there wasn't time to say anything of significance. He did manage to say, as she mounted the tailboard, 'I hope some of the conversation takes a different turn next time.'

He wanted to tell her that her legs would start aching tomorrow as they'd be running through his dreams all night. But he was sure that she swayed her hips a little provocatively as she turned and waved to him.

17

He didn't get a bus back, he walked; they'd probably stopped running now, anyway. He wasn't sure why, but he didn't think it was because he was putting off entering an empty house knowing that she had gone. It was more the reeling that, although it was empty, he did have it all to himself again and was looking forward to it and wanting to delay the pleasure he was at least half-expecting to feel. It would feel a bit like starting afresh, having a new relationship with his home.

He could also see more of Reg now, too, 'though as far as he knew, he spent quite a bit of time with his girl friend. George didn't want a girl friend. Not another one. Well, not at the moment, anyway.

It was gone midnight when he got back. He went quickly around the rooms again. There was not a trace of her, except perhaps the smell of the perfume she sometimes wore. He opened all the windows until it got cold then closed them. He made a cup of cocoa, drank it and went to bed.

When he awoke, he couldn't quite remember for a second what significant occurrence had recently taken place. Then he did. He felt that, 'though it wasn't something to leap out of bed and joyously punch the air for, he did recognise an inner smile as well as a healthy hunger for breakfast. He ate it quickly and made his way to work. It was a Saturday, he'd knock off at midday.

He worked without a tea break, finished the paper-hanging then, after a last tidy-up, left early, deciding to have a meal at a café near Ash Park station and to wander around to see what roads and what buildings on the estate had been completed.

He went along The Broadway towards the park, which was still being transformed from the old farm's pastureland, and went towards the newly finished Assembly Hall which, apparently, was to be opened that evening by a female pilot who, not long ago, had broken Amy Johnson's record flight from England to Australia. It seemed that she had already arrived as, surrounded by a crowd of spectators outside the hall, a woman with dark hair and rather glamorous poise, smiled at all around her. She was, according to Doris, 'the Garbo of the skies'. He liked glamour. He liked beautiful things, and didn't want to think of Doris, didn't want his day to be interrupted by her.

He walked on and crossed the road to the almost completed church. He didn't believe in God, really, 'though, as a child, sitting next to his mother in their local church where she would call him a 'fidget arse' and tell him to keep still, he supposed there remained some kind of belief still there. He remembered the opening of the new one, with a small procession led by white and black clad choirboys moving towards it along the Avenue and scouts just behind them holding aloft a banner proclaiming, 'St. Nicholas Church, Ash Park'

Pushing its main door open, he went in. Although it had a lot of arches, they were made of painted wood and the relatively bare space didn't really feel like a church. He came out and continued to the park land. The old farm buildings were disappearing, but there were still the remains of an old manor house. He hoped it would be retained as a reminder of the area's agricultural past.

He had come here in the summer as a break from her complaining that he was always spending his free time working in the garden instead of keeping her company. There, he had thought of her again.

At the time he'd walked quite a way through the fields, losing his way in fact, and hearing a sound to his left, had seen a train gathering speed and travelling west and had decided to follow the railway lines. As he neared them he could see a high mesh fence running along their side. He went towards it and began walking alongside it intending to walk to the next station at Dagenhamm. He had little interest in looking around that borough, as far as he knew it had the largest amount of social housing west of the Soviet Union.

He didn't like council houses. His mother had always tended to look down on them and their tenants. He'd heard that the whole area had been referred to, probably by its councillors, as a 'neo-Georgian ' estate. He thought it mildly ridiculous, but then it was surely a good thing to house those who, unlike himself, a skilled craftsman, couldn't afford to buy their own homes.

Following the fence until it disappeared into a thick wedge of trees which virtually blocked his way, he'd turned towards a field of barley. The grass along its edge was too long and tangled for a comfortable walk so he'd walked between the rows of cereal.

He was doing this when he'd heard gun shots. As he'd walked further, the sound of the shots had become more sporadic and louder. After another hundred yards or so he'd come across twenty dead woodpigeons laid out neatly at the corner of another barley field. Fifty yards away was a van with a man standing at the back of the vehicle throwing dead birds into it.

George had approached him. The driver was foreign and in heavily-accented broken English answered the question of why he was doing what he was by telling his questioner that the farmer had hired him to get rid of the birds as they were capable of devouring a large proportion of his crop. George hadn't liked the idea of creatures being killed in order to maintain profits, but understood. At least they weren't being killed in the name of 'sport'.

The man had told him what direction to go to get back to the estate and it wasn't long before he caught sight of houses again and made his way back towards his own. He hadn't bothered to relate his little adventure to Doris. He had told her little about anything, really. She lacked empathy; that was the word. He couldn't tell her anything that was… deeply personal, anything about feelings. She'd just say something like, 'Well, why don't you… ' or 'You should …'

Another memory he had of the summer was when walking with her on the south side of the station and she'd decided to return home. She wasn't going to walk 'through loads of rough fields,' she'd said. He didn't try to dissuade her.

A large farmhouse had once stood by the side of the railway which was surrounded by an orchard of apple, pear and cherry trees. When it was pulled down the trees had been handed over to the Residents Association so they could allocate trees to the people who wanted them. He wasn't a member but had been given a raffle ticket by someone who was and, along with quite a few other people, had gone to the orchard to locate trees with their numbers on. His was a cherry tree. He'd taken a spade and, with a little help, had dug it up and, using a barrow, had wheeled it home. It had been an interesting sight to see people from all over the estate struggling along with trees on top of vans and barrows, including the local coalman with his horse and cart.

He recalled Easter Civic Week where various events and activities had been held: The Broadway and the Assembly Hall were decorated with bunting and the latter floodlit at night and where various trophies, paintings and drawings by local kids were shown. There were also shop window displays where the winners were judged on the comments made by the local populace. No doubt the shopkeepers learned more about the psychology of shopping. The bigger shops and stores that were coming to the area were also showcasing their wares on stalls in the Hall.

He'd watched, with Reg, a mannequin parade using professional models where local women could see and order the latest accessories and fashions. Reg had mumbled to him, 'To be a successful model you've got to be tall, skinny, look miserable and learn to walk as if you're half-pissed.'

As well as a dance competition, there was one which, cunningly, Mister Colls had made open only to non-residents. In the five show houses each had one item incorrectly fitted - a soap dish placed upside down, for example. Competitors had to thoroughly check the houses and list the deliberate mistakes in order of convenience.

George had only known of this because Doris had been annoyed that she couldn't take part. He'd shown her the Ash Park Pictorial, the estate newspaper containing many adverts for the houses including one for the type he had bought. She'd cut the piece out and kept it in one of the fitted kitchen cabinets as if it was proof that the room she was working in really was as grand as it was supposed to be.

It promised that their 'woman-designed Arcadia kitchen, this scientific headquarters of housekeeping has fitted storage cabinets supplementing a large larder, and a porcelain sink with coronation taps (hot and cold) pleasantly placed under the side window. Beneath its draining board is a modern copper for easy boiling on wash days and a domestic boiler is neatly installed beside a commodious brush cupboard... ' It went on. He remembered it only because he thought she'd been quite enthused by it. There hadn't appeared to be much that had excited her.

There'd been an open tennis competition and, for football fans, a match between the recently formed Ash Park team and a Hornchurch one on the latter's ground, then one against the Gaslight and Coke Company at a ground in Ilford. He'd gone to neither.

One of the week's evenings had ended with 'stars of stage screen and radio', including Evelyn Laye, and there was a decorated pram competition which Doris had insisted he attend with her; he having not one iota of interest and was filled with a consistent feeling of mild apprehension. Most of the events he hadn't gone to, including the fancy dress competition which had provided the grand finale, but had watched some of the fireworks display in the Hall's large garden whilst standing on his own.

Now, for a bit of escapism, he wouldn't have minded going to the pictures. The proposed cinema on the estate wasn't going to materialise, but the one at nearby Hornchurch had been open for a while and he was tempted to head back there, but the last programme would have started by now. He'd only been there once with her, but Reg had come with him a couple of times.

Apparently, when it had first opened, a huge crowd had flocked there with hundreds turned away; a film had been taken of them and shown on the following week's programme. Someone who'd been present had told him that the feature films and newsreel had been followed by an orchestra and singers, the evening ending with a dance in its opulent ballroom.

There was something about the outside of it he liked: its façade set alight by red and green neon lighting, its name, the Capitol, in huge letters towards the top and down the sides.

He thought of the films he'd seen and the women in them. It was the glamour; it thrilled him. But should he have expected Doris to have it? He stopped walking, sat on a nearby garden wall and thought about it. It was... adolescent to expect a woman who he was supposed to have a relationship with to create that effect upon him, surely. He thought hard. He wasn't sure what affect a woman was supposed to have in a relationship, and he, of course, would have an influence on her, that was the idea of a relationship, wasn't it? He could hear his mother saying, 'You've got to care for each other, son, that's the important thing.'

But he never had. Without it, glamour - he couldn't think of a replacement for that word - there had been, a kind of dulling blanket over him most of the time when with her. He raised himself from the wall and continued walking into the night.

They hadn't had much fun really. She had shared some things with him of course, but he couldn't remember any at this moment, it was as if she'd just happened to have been with him. Okay, the holiday hadn't been so bad and there were times when it had been alright in bed, but she had rarely excited him, rarely made him really desire her. Perhaps she hadn't really enjoyed him. He hadn't thought about it before. So he wasn't Clark Gable, but *he* wasn't in movies, he was signwriter and decorator who lived in a garden city in Essex, and he needed to love someone before he could give himself. He recognised that he had never given himself to her. But she'd never made him feel that kind of giving.

She had gone, and he'd begun his walk to escape the... experience of her, of thinking about her, yet he seemed to have thought of little else. He would think of her for some while, whether he wanted to or not; and he didn't want to. He felt quite empty and, strangely, a kind of painful embarrassment. Perhaps it was about growing up, 'though he wasn't sure what it really meant and whether he was capable of it anyway. But he supposed he had to, somehow.

It had happened, and there was a large, empty space in front of him now.

18

'I have had one or two suggestions that I'm being too specific in my attention to the subject of sociology. It's obviously a particular way of seeing the world, but is within the parameters of our subject - if it has parameters, one could argue that everything is subsumed within philosophy. For those of you who wish for a more traditional approach, I'm not, as previously mentioned, going back to the Ancient Greeks.'

Rupert was finding it a little difficult to concentrate on Pym's opening remarks. He hadn't seen Constance for almost a week. The day after she'd last been with him, she was too busy to speak to him at work and he couldn't see her when she had finished her shift as he'd had a late seminar. He guessed that she was looking after her mother, but not knowing where either her or her parent lived, or having a telephone number, couldn't contact her.

He had filled the time partly by completing an essay, reading, having some refectory lunches with Eric, where they had chatted to Alex and Edward who both seemed to be doing well - 'though neither had seen anything of Thomas - writing a letter to his own mother and, once, telephoning Andrew.

He had also gone for brief walks on his own around the University grounds and further afield into the city. He'd walked along the canal to Iffley Lock, wandered around the outside of Magdalen College and admired the exterior of the Sheldonian Theatre, wishing his mother was appearing there and hoping that one day she would be.

'However,' Pym was saying, 'to make sure you have grasped its fundamental premise, let me stress what should be obvious by now and that, like it's big daddy, philosophy, to an extent it attempts to look behind the scenes of everyday occurrences we take for granted. In short, what we almost unthinkingly feel is 'natural'; behaviour isn't. We've briefly mentioned examples before, but a student told me recently that love and marriage is 'the most natural thing in the world'.'

'He is not alone in thinking that. In Western societies it's assumed that when men and women marry it's because they are in love. There's a broadly-based popular mythology that it strikes where it will, a mystery that is the goal of most young people and often of the not-so-young as well. However, as soon as we investigate which people actually marry each other, we find that the lightning shaft of Cupid strikes within very definite channels of class, income, education, social and religious background.

'If we look a little further into the behaviour engaged in prior to their union under the euphemism of 'courtship', we find channels of interaction that are often rigid to the point of ritual. So, it could be said that it's not so much the emotion of love that creates a certain kind of relationship but that carefully predefined and often planned relationships eventually generate the desired emotions.'

'Are you saying then.' asked a student, 'that when certain conditions have been met, or constructed, people kind of allow themselves to 'fall in love'?'

'You could say that. There's a complex web of motives related in many ways to the institutional structure within which an individual lives his life – class, career, aspirations of power, prestige et cetera'. Pym looked around him. 'The miracle of love now seems somewhat synthetic doesn't it.'

'Are you saying that love, or rather the romantic interpretation of it, is an illusion then?' asked the same student.

'No, but once more, and this is the point of all this, sociology will look beyond the immediately given and publicly approved interpretations.'

'Marriage isn't 'natural' at all,' said Rupert, 'it was originally created, with religious backing, by the rich so that property could be handed down to their children.'

'We can come to that later', said their teacher.

A student who was generally quiet said, rather fawningly, Rupert thought, 'When you explain things like you do, sir, it makes us think of why we didn't think of it before. You make it kind of obvious.'

'A function of the subject, dear boy,' said Pym.

'Marx certainly looks beyond them,' ventured Rupert. 'For virtually any socio-economic phenomenon his first question seems to be, 'Who benefits?''

'He certainly does. Talking of which, our next topic is social class. Anyone wish to define it?'

'Well, there are people like carpenters and roofers and then there are classical composers,' was one lad's answer.

'I didn't ask for examples. Class is a division of society based on social and economic status. In other words, it is a status allocation dependant on an individual's position in the process of production. Status can come from education, consumption patterns, lifestyles, typical beliefs and social behaviour. Weber talks of prestige, not just economic position, but of course prestige generally comes from the former. Can anyone give me an example of where it doesn't?'

'A Bishop has more status than a bookmaker but earns far less,' was another pupil's answer. Rupert didn't know his name but had been told that his father was one of the top clergy.

'Yes, and there are others, but as said, mainly it's about income.'

'What about education?' asked someone, 'Wouldn't that be a criterion for class membership?' asked a student.

'It is the individual's class position that largely determines the education they receive.'

'The plumbers go to elementary schools and we come here,' said Rupert.

'What about leisure pursuits?' asked someone.

'You mean darts, soccer, et cetera for the lower classes and horse racing, bridge, hunting and shooting for the upper,' offered the young man sitting next to the seminar leader.

'Darts is archery for the lower classes,' grinned another group member.

'These activities don't signify class, they are a result of it, but let's look at some occupations.'

'Lower' is a bit of a value judgement isn't it?' remarked Rupert.

'Well, they are', the undergrad that had used the term said.

'I thought in this sort of sociology we didn't make value judgements.'

''Labouring class',' someone else suggested.

'Prefer 'working'', said Rupert.

'All classes work.'

'Not the upper class'

'We are, as implied,' interjected Pym, 'interested in those who work and derive incomes from that work. Alright then, the middle class. Start with higher professionals. Suggestions?'

Various, mostly accurate suggestions were put forward, as were those for the intermediate and skilled non-manual brackets.

'There are some rather odd categorisations I have to admit. For example, both draughtsmen and shop assistants are in the same skilled non-manual group', continued Pym.

Rupert, ignoring this, said, 'It's head knowledge over hand knowledge, really.'

'It is.'

'But how can you have an objective measurement of knowledge'? It has to be what *sort* of knowledge it is that counts as somehow 'superior.' The same goes for skill'. Who, or what, says that mending a complex problem in a car requires less, or 'inferior' knowledge, than, say, brain surgery?'

'You have to use an ordinary drill to get inside the skull,' said another student. 'My father's a brain surgeon.'

'And can 'skill' be measured?' asked Rupert. 'It's pretty arbitrary isn't it.'

Pym resumed. 'So, the distinction, then, in terms of 'MC' and 'WC' - let's refer to the classes like that, it's easier - is between non-manual and manual. Rather simplistic, as has been pointed out, and there are divisions within the WC also: skilled, semi-skilled and unskilled manual. These occupations are designated by the Registrar General.'

His request for naming some of these occupations was answered by the class reasonably in line with the official list, but there were some differences.

'How is it that a barber is in the same category as an electrician?' was one question.

'Interesting as this is,' said Rupert, 'we're missing the point. Definitions are *power* definitions, really. Those who have the power define things to suit themselves.'

'Example?' Pym asked.

'It's a country's leaders, along with the press, that create and confirm the definitions.'

There were murmurs of what seemed like agreement, but rather reluctant ones, Rupert thought.

'Lets talk of social mobility', said Pym.

'Can't be much of that now in this slump,' said the surgeon's son.

'People should think themselves lucky if they have a job,' said somebody.

'You could argue that they're unlucky if they haven't got a job. Workers are not responsible for the economic situation', replied Rupert. 'And with, or without it, there's very little mobility anyway.'

As if Rupert hadn't spoken, Pym began with, 'There are several key variables, most empirical studies of social mobility have been based on some kind of occupational index. For a variety of reasons it's correlated with factors which determine social status like income as well as consumption patterns, typical beliefs, attitudes and behaviour.'

Rupert felt, suddenly, a little annoyed. He wanted to share some ideological ideas and beliefs with someone, with, at that moment, the man who was droning on - 'droning' was unfair, he realised - about class movement, when there was very little happening. There never really had been, he must have realised that. Of course, he had to be as objective as he could, but Rupert would have liked him to have been more aware of the taken-for-granted social position of the students and, for most of them, their unawareness of the labouring class.

Did they *see* them? Did they even notice the road sweeper, the window cleaner, the dustman? Did they even exist in their universe? Perhaps, unthinkingly, they saw the world as organised just for them, a serving, obedient world perhaps working solely for their benefit.

He could hear Pym. 'Occupational prestige doesn't take into account the social distance between types of jobs. There can be occupational mobility, but not social mobility, what of the learning of new norms?'

Pym was an academic, a teacher, not a proselytizer, but...

'Doesn't this approach concentrate on only one dimension of stratification: status?

'Does it not ignore power?' Rupert asked.

Pym flicked a glance at him.

"Power' seems to interest you quite a bit, Mister Colls. Why d'you think that is?'

It was quite a leading question, one Rupert couldn't immediately answer. It demanded, he supposed, a psychologically-based answer. Did he feel that his father exercised too much power over him as a child, power that he resented, that frightened him, and was now perhaps projecting it onto the class his father belonged to, or almost did, and had come to represent?

Maybe a larger part of himself than he had thought identified with the told-what-to-do, the obey-or-sanctions-will-be-imposed sector of the populace. But he had been to boarding school and all that it had entailed; it had provided him with admission, concreted the idea of what class he belonged to.

But he was personalising it. Whatever his reasons for feeling what he did about the iniquities of a system of commerce that was becoming stronger and more accepted, as if there was no possible chance of any other system replacing it, it didn't mean that what he felt, what he believed, was simply a matter of childhood experiences.

Pym was speaking.

'So, although, generally, prestige and status differ between occupational groups, some anomalies of which have been pointed out, class definitions have to be, in a sense, rather basic.'

'But there is, undeniably, class', said Rupert, 'a system wherein, you could argue, workers of all sorts of knowledge and specialisms are exploited, especially the physical workers. Profits are made from them, they are also often alienated in both production and in their consumption. If - '

185

'Been reading Marx have you then?' Pym asked, a trifle sarcastically, Rupert thought.

'If there were no employers, no factories, farms, coalmines et cetera there'd be no jobs would there,' was an opinion rather loudly put forward by the student at Pym's side.

'And you need an elite to run a country, your labourers and chimney sweeps are not going to do it are they,' ventured the young man next to him.

There were a few tittering sounds at this point.

'Excuse me,' said the surgeon's son, and standing and moving away from the table, held an imaginary glass in his hand, placed his legs apart rhythmically flexed his calves and with an exaggerated cockney accent, said, 'Ere darlin', gi's 'alf o' stout will yer.' Amid the laughter he sat again.

Rupert was showing his annoyance now.

'If there were no workers there'd be no profits. What would your factory and mine owners do then? And, incidentally, politicians don't run countries, the system does.'

'This is a seminar, Mister Colls,' said Pym, 'we are not at Hyde Park Corner.'

'Does the setting invalidate what I've said then?'

'No, but you mentioned alienation and it's difficult to have an empirical study of it, it's rather a woolly concept.'

'I think he means,' said another class member, 'that the WCs get bored with their jobs; I mean, it doesn't take much brain to sweep roads does it.'

'What if these jobs weren't done,' asked Rupert.

'I suppose, God forbid, we would have to do them ourselves,' said someone.

'Oh, Lord, no,' was almost a chorus of disapproval from some of the others.

Pym continued with some more complexities of social mobility, not mentioning the actual chances of manual workers 'making it' as he put it, then stopped and announced that seminar papers would be read at the next session by those who had finished them and that he hoped they all had.

Still feeling rather irked by some of his colleagues, Rupert was the first to leave the room and made is way, via the quad, towards his room.

As he crossed it he saw Constance perambulating slowly and casually around the edge of it. He blinked, not sure if he was actually seeing her. She saw him and, with an impudent smile, waved. He went across to her.

'What are you doing here?' he asked. 'You know you're not allowed.'

'A men's only club. I am aware.'

'Its really nice to see you, but...'

'I wanted to walk across the grass and also to see if, by any chance, you would be around .'

'Here I am. Makes a change from me looking for you. I've been trying to find you.'

'I guessed that.'

'How's mother?'

'She seemed a little better this morning so I've come to work. This is my little break.'

'Good. Want to do something this evening?'

'Yes.'

'Dinner? Film?'

'Film. Show Boat s on at the Alhambra. D'you want to meet me at my place? We can go from there.

'Of course.'

She quickly wrote down the address, handed it to him with that impudent smile again and walked, quicker this time, to the end of the quad and towards her workplace.

It was an ordinary Victorian house in a side road and, knowing it was ridiculous, nevertheless he felt it too ordinary for her. She came to the door wearing a long, lilac dress and high heels and saying, ''Come into the parlour, said the spider to the fly'.'

'Are you going to trap me?'

'No, not at this moment. In fact, stay there.'

She turned and ran up the stairs, moving down them again putting a jacket on.

She shut the door behind her, went down the steps with him then suggested, as it wasn't far, that they walk to the picture palace.

'Winter's a coming, you need a coat,' he told her.

'I don't feel the cold.'

'Perhaps you're an ice maiden.'

'I hope not.'

'How's school?' she asked.

'It felt like one today, sniggering school kids.'

'Seminar?'

'Yes, they don't realise how privileged they are.'

'What was the subject?'

'Class.'

'Right up your street then.'

'I sometimes I feel I'm the only one in the street.'

'I'll play in the road with you.'

'Thanks.'

'Incidentally , Paul Robeson's in this film.'

'He visited the Soviet Union a couple of years ago, he's all for Leftie Trade Unions. He'll get blacklisted eventually. '

'He's a bit of a hero to my mum, she loves his voice.'

She told him more about her mother whose memory was fading and also seemed to be losing the concepts of shopping and cooking.

'I don't wish to look after her on my own. I need to keep my job.'

'Maybe it won't come to that.'

She changed the subject, they talked of various popular songs for a while and soon they were at the cinema.

They both enjoyed what they saw, with Rupert again intermittently gazing at her profile and, leaving the cinema, they had a rather ordinary conversation about what they'd seen, especially Irene Dunne's performance, and Robeson's singing. Their talking then, for Rupert, took an unordinary turn when she suggested they go back to her room.

This pleased him; it meant he would have her company for longer. A bus pulled in right beside them.

'Let's get it, it goes past the flat,' she said, and they hurried on. They went upstairs, looked out at the streetlights and shops and then they were there.

Rupert, rather gently treading the hall carpet, followed her in.

'It's alright, there's no need to be quiet, Marjie's away for the weekend; she's the girl I share with. We can do as we wish.'

She smiled at him and did a little twirl.

'Do you like my air of gay abandon?' she asked.

'Indeed. More please, more.'

'Come on,' she said, hurrying up the stairs, I think I may have some wine.'

'No gin and it?'

'No.'

They went across the landing to a door which she pushed open, beckoning him in.

'Do take off your jacket' she said, crossing the room to a gramophone in a corner by the bay window. She put a record on then left the room to, he assumed, get drinks from the kitchen or somewhere. It was a soft, pleasant, crooning lullaby that came from the machine and which helped him to relax whilst he waited for her to return.

The room was as mundane as the house's exterior: panelled doors, brown curtains, dark floral-pattern carpet hiding most of the unvarnished floorboards, a drab sofa, small table and two chairs and the record player. He assumed that none of this was her choice. She entered with bottle and glasses.

'Forgive the paucity of character-full objects; I'm sure your family home is nothing like this.'

'No, but it hasn't got you in it.'

Ignoring his comment, she put what she was carrying onto the table, poured a drink and handed it to him.

'You can sit down, you know.'

He sat on the sofa, she with drink in hand, joining him.

He told her that it was probably the first time they had sat next to each other, it was usually on opposite sides of tables with cups of tea between them, or shelves of books.

They clinked glasses.

'Here's to... what?' she asked, looking at him with casual enquiry.

'Charlie Marx and the workers. That'll do for now.'

'What does your father think of your views?'

'I'm not sure he really knows them, but what he does know of them he doesn't like. If I was to tell him that the man thought all property was theft, he wouldn't understand the concept. He'd agree with Galsworthy's, 'Beauty is a rose that a fair wind blows, but property sticks, and property grows.'

'What of 'An Englishman's home is his castle?''

'Are you suggesting it's somehow 'natural' to wish to own property?'

'I'm not sure, but maybe you oppose it because you don't really like your father and he owns property. Also, I think you're taking your secure upbringing in a family-owned home for granted.'

'Is there, perhaps, a personal thing here? You're hinting at a gap between ideology and an individual's reality, I think.'

'My mother and I have always lived in rented accommodation, and I'm hinting that you finish your drink and I'll pour you another.'

She did and poured one for herself.

'Here's to the proletariat,' she said raising her glass.

He looked at her.

'You're a mixture of duchess and peasant.'

He didn't put the glass to his lips, he placed it on the floor, gently removed hers from her hand, placed it next to his, turned his face to her and kissed her on the mouth. He pressed more firmly then slowly pulled away. There had been no response. She looked at him almost without expression then kissed him back, and with her arm around his shoulder, pulled him towards her.

He laid on her, kissing her just above her breast.

'Come with me,' she said quietly, and moving away from under him, took his hand, led him through a door and into a bedroom. He almost pushed her against a wall as he pulled down the zip at the back of her dress. He then removed a pink brassiere while she rapidly undid the buttons on his shirt. He took it off, bent to remove his socks and kicked away his shoes while she removed her knickers. She took his hand again and led him to the bed.

They lay facing each other.

'Are you nervous?' she asked him with a smile.

'Yes,'

'First time?'

'No, I've been nervous before,'

They both laughed, relieving a shared tension. They made love.

Afterwards, as they lay on their backs looking contentedly at the ceiling, it felt, for him, as if it was the first time he'd ever had sex. He told her so.

'Me too, 'though I wasn't a virgin,' she said.

They then said, together, 'There's only been one before.'

They paused then laughed. He turned to her and held her tightly. He wasn't sure why, but he had never felt so at one with anyone than at this moment. His intellect switched on for a second as he wondered whether this was a learned or natural emotion. Although not having experienced it before it felt entirely natural; joyously so. Love an 'illusion'? A socially created emotion? He didn't care. It mattered not.

19

The signwriting work seemed to have dried up; he was now working on a painting job with several other painters, only two of whom he'd met before on the firm. He had been there a few weeks as foreman. It was a large new building in Holborn, his boss was subcontracting. He hadn't been in charge of a gang before but had soon settled into it, not really wanting authority, but much preferring to tell others what to do than being told. He knew his trades, and after a few rather hesitant days it had become easier, the lads, all older than himself, seemingly respecting his abilities.

They worked well; soon he was occasionally knocking of half an hour earlier on the pretence that they'd had only half an hour for lunch instead of the usual hour. But he was making money for his firm. Occasionally he'd get the more skilled 'toshers' amongst them to skip a coat of distemper and do some walls in one coats instead of the prescribed specified two, dependent on the colour. Few could have spotted the difference. He had noticed that the supervisor for the main contractor appeared a little naïve, so when he'd asked for extra things to be done, George had sometimes slipped onto his daywork sheet a few 'extras' more than they'd been required to do. Sometimes he thought he could have written, '2 coats on 12 new radiators on 10th floor: 11 hours. Applied one coat plaster primer on new wall on 8th floor: 1 hour. Fried egg and two slices: 3 hours', and he would have signed for it.

He also worked himself, picking the choicer jobs: doors, sashes and, of course, if there was any lettering to be done. On the train going to the site he'd work out in his head who to put on what tasks. Things went smoothly.

They were smooth at home also. Sometimes it was as if she'd never lived with him, there was no evidence now that she had ever been in the house, really, 'though he did find a brown beret under the bed which he'd thrown away.

Although things were going well; it seemed that the larger project wasn't. There was talk of safety concerns on the outside scaffolding and of there not being enough scaffold boards available, meaning that there were gaps which, obviously, could cause some nasty accidents. There were also suggestions that the main contractors were demanding that their concreters and bricklayers do extra hours for the same flat rate of pay.

He'd been told these things by the foreman brickie who he'd immediately recognised as a classmate at building school. In their first year there they had been taught the basics of decorating, carpentry, plumbing and brickwork, Phil having taken to the latter as readily as George had the more artistic elements of the former. They'd both been pretty good in the art class though and George remembered spending two hours the evening before an exam in that subject copying a minutely detailed sketch of Tower Bridge and then transcribing every line and dot of it in the test. He'd got top marks, confessed to Phil and been forgiven, 'though his classmate had jokingly referred to him intermittently as 'Cheat Man' for a while afterwards.

He had greeted him thus when the two had first seen each other on the site a few days before. It had got more serious when he told George of the scaffolding situation.

'It's not just the lack of boards, but the poles are crap, they're old and rusty.

George was thinking that work on the outside of the building had little to do with him, when he realised that when the contractors had finished installing all the windows he and his gang would be working on them. He felt a little embarrassed about forgetting, so concentrated had he been on the interior work.

After lunch in the local café - where half the lads seems to have had beans on toast, or 'babies on a raft' as they referred to it, their return to work signalled by his, 'Okay lads, let's do some' - he stepped out through am eighth-floor window he'd been painting onto the scaffold. He walked along the boards for a while and they appeared fine until he saw some 'traps' where the boards hadn't been overlaid at their ends by other boards resting on poles. These could be worse than the empty space of a gap; a workman could tread on them and, with nothing underneath, hurtle down with the boards. George knew that no self-respecting scaffolder would lay boards like this. He guessed that cheap, inexperienced labour was being used. The situation wasn't satisfactory.

He looked along High Holborn to St. Paul's, it looked so solid, as if it had always been there, the city built around it, as if it could never be destroyed, would remain for ever. He went back inside via the window wondering if the workers were unionised. He was pretty sure the brickies were, and the electricians and plumbers, although perhaps not in the same union, but he wasn't and he doubted if his painters were.

He hadn't really thought about it, but there was surely a union representing his trade somewhere. He went down the stairs a few floors, the lifts not ready to carry anything yet, and had a look at how his men were doing. There were two of them on trestles working on the ceiling, two others on the walls; it would be the same on the floor below, the other three members of the bunch working on the foyer. He asked them if they belonged to a union.

'Never 'eard o' one for painters, mate,' was the answer from one and which seemed to sum up the experience of the others, also. One of them, the oldest, winked at his foreman and, to the tune of The Red Flag, sang, 'The working class can kiss my arse, I've got the foreman's job at last.'

George explained to them the current concerns of some of the workers on the site and suggested that most of them would be in one union or another and that perhaps they should join one, too.

'What if there ain't one?' was one question.

'Well... I s'pose we could start one,' George suggested.

'As long as we get a fair day's pay for a fair day's work, I don't mind,' said one of the lads brushing the ceiling.

'Is that what you think you're getting?' George asked him.

'I think so, but I could always do with a bit more.'

George went down a floor and mentioned the subject to the others. They seemed keener to join one, but, again, they didn't think they'd heard of one for their trade.

While working on his window, he thought about whether it was possible to start a local union - there must surely be unions in various parts of the country - how he would do it and where meetings could be held if enough men were interested. There were a few new sites near this one, and there were plenty of painters working on re-decs in the City and West End, though not as many as there had been before the downturn. There had to be decent bargaining positions of course, but with there still being an increase in unemployment and the usual winter reduction in jobs - 'God bless the painters when the leaves begin to fall' - it was hard to see where any leverage would come from, except on, perhaps, large jobs. He knew he didn't have the know-how, or the ability, to start a new union, anyway, what he did was hardly as important as coal mining, he could hardly imagine a National Federation of Painters and Decorators. But perhaps there was one, he had been working mainly on his own in his working life, rarely meeting or knowing any other people in his trades, so perhaps one did exist.

He knocked the men off early and went to a pub they passed daily on the way to the café. He got himself half of brown ale and sat in a corner. He thought about the site and wondered if anyone had had a word with the scaffolding foreman, and whether the site supervisor was aware of the problems. Should *he* have a word with the latter? The man seemed naïve enough to let anything get past him.

He glanced around at what appeared to be a poor attempt at modernising an old pub by placing a rather badly-executed painting of some dancing flappers with their cute, short hairstyles, their open hands across immobile looking knock-knees, and a few Art Deco style geometric shapes in wood hanging from the ceiling. He took a sheet of paper from his pocket which he usually used for work-related notes, and aimlessly began sketching a distemper brush. There were few customers and a bored-looking barmaid, wiping her hands down her apron, came across to him.

'You look as bored as I am,' she said in an accent which he couldn't quite place.

'No, not bored, just... '

'Bored?'

He grinned. 'Suppose so.'

He looked up at her. She had a pale face with eyes almost as dark as her waved hair. He asked her where she was from.

'Leytonstone.'

'I think you know what I mean.'

'Cymru.'

'Only the Welsh could pronounce Cymru as 'Coomree'.'

'We do it to annoy the English.'

'You succeed.'

'Am I annoying you?'

'Far from it, you have a lilting Welsh accent.'

'Thanks.'

'I'm guessing you've lived here for a while.'

'You wouldn't like it if I was *obviously* Welsh?'

'I don't like any extreme accent, especially Belfast.'

'I'm with you there. What do you know about my country?'

'Er, it's often used as a measurement, as in, 'A bush fire the size of Wales,' and you're all either teachers or rugby players.'

'Our image of the English is that you have little talent, and are modest about it.'

'Nice one. Have you heard the rumour that the Grand Canyon was started by a Scotsman who lost a coin in a ditch?'

'What has an IQ of a hundred? Ten Irishmen.'

'We're playing stereotypes. Don't suppose you can sit down?'

'No, I'd be seen as cavorting with the customers.'

'What customers?'

She looked around her. 'Yes, there's very few.'

She asked him where he was from.

'West Ham, nevertheless, I can say 'Llanfairpwllgwyngyllgo-gerychwyrndrobwll-llantysiliogogogoch. 'I practised it for a long while.'

'I an, too, just.'

She bent over him to see what he was drawing.

'Why a six-inch flat?'

'How do you know it's called that?'

''Cos my dad's a decorator.'

'So am I.'Where's he working?'

'In London somewhere.'

She asked him if he liked what he did and where he was doing it.

'Sometimes, and 'just around the corner', in that order.'

'Not in the big building up the road?'

'That's the one.'

'It's a big job. My dad works on houses mostly. He's good at paperhanging, he can hang twelve rolls a day, he says.'

'No 'When father papered the parlour,' then. He's faster than me. In a union is he?'

'No idea. Bet I know what you're thinking; 'There must be a dirty joke there somewhere. 'She was only a painter's daughter but she... '

'I wasn't, but there is one like that.'

'Many.'

'How about, 'She was only a petrol pump assistant's daughter but she knew the smell of Benzole.' Oh, sorry, I shouldn't have said that.'

'I've heard them all in this place.'

'It's just that - '

'You see me as one of the lads?'

'You're joking, you couldn't look less like one, it's just that you're so.... easy to talk to.'

'So, what bits do you like then?'

'Of you, or my job?''

'The job.'

'The arty bits I s'pose. At college I painted murals, learnt lettering, graining and marbling, and the first day of my apprenticeship found myself washing whitewash off a ceiling in an old factory.'

'Disappointing, eh?'

'And you?'

'Not sure, sort of drifted into this work, had to do something. I can't draw but - '

'You can hang wallpaper?'

'No, but I liked language. I worked in an ad agency for a little while when I left school as a trainee copywriter. They used to give me all sorts of things to write about: klaxons, men's trousers, even a brand of toilet roll, sometimes they'd put the objects on my desk. A barmaid friend told me her job was fun and then they had a vacancy so I joined her, not here, at another pub.'

'You're worth more than this.'

She smiled. 'Maybe.'

She looked behind her; some customers had come in.

'Must go,' she said and returned behind the bar.

He watched her. There was little that could be defined as glamorous about her: an ordinary-looking blouse, almost flat shoes, and the apron, but she gave them a certain... style. He was aware that he'd asked whether her father was unionised because he wanted to be offered the relevant information instead of finding it out for himself. He watched her pulling pints, the occasional smile as she moved speedily to serve the drinkers. She was efficient. He could imagine virtually everything she did having the feel of efficiency about it, a friendly, easy practicality.

She smiled across at him, but remained behind the bar. He got up and walked over to her and leaned against the counter.

'Hello, smiley.'

'Not always genuine when I'm working, I'm afraid. D'you want another drink?'

'No. More of you.'

'Really,' she asked, raising an eyebrow.

'Yeah.'

'What have I done to deserve this?'

'You're being sarcastic.'

'Only a little.'

'Sarcasm doesn't suit you, somehow.'

He took a breath and asked if she had a boyfriend.

'Not at the moment.'

'I thought you were going to glare at me and say, 'Of course'.'

'Which implies it's natural and obvious that I *should* have one.'

'Suppose so.'

She smiled at him; it was a luscious one.

'What's the Welsh for, 'Fancy a drink one evening?' he asked her.

'Ffansi diod um noson?' But it's hardly appropriate given what I do here all day.'

'Well, do something... whatever.'

'I like coffee and walking.'

'I suppose you're used to the valleys and such.'

'I am, but I like the city, too.'

'Me, too. I kind of escape into it I think; the buildings, the - '

'They have a kind of atmosphere don't they.'

'Yeah, you can sort of fantasise about them somehow.'

Just then they heard, 'Are you gonna serve me then, or you gonna carry on chattin' all day?'

It was someone who'd just come in. George immediately wanted to grab him by his collar and reduce the size of his Adam's apple; at least, to tell him not to be so bloody rude.

She turned to the man, asking him what he required then serving him and looking back at George..

'It's okay, you can get worse, usually when they're under the 'fluence. What were we saying?'

He didn't answer; he was still watching the man taking his drink to a table.

She laid her hand gently on his arm for a second.

'It's okay. Really.'

He took another deep breath and calmed himself. What was it about her that seemed to necessitate him inhaling air more than normally?

'I'll get you a drink, on the house,' she offered. 'There's some wine left. Want it?'

'Don't think I've ever drunk it.'

'No?' She retrieved a bottle and poured a little into a glass for him. He tasted it; it seemed like a strong, soft drink.

Pouring more into his glass, she asked him if he liked it.

He gulped it down. 'Think I do.'

'You're supposed to sip it.'

'I'm not that sophisticated.'

'That word initially meant 'the art of misleading'. It also came to mean 'deceptive'. I don't think those things apply to you.'

'I hope not. What's your name, by the way?

'Enid Morgan.'

As the door swung open and a group of people entered, he told her his.

'You better return to your duties', he advised her.

'Yes, sir. Are you leaving?'

'No, I shall sit at the same table and look at you.'

He did, watching he for a while. He then tried to concentrate on whether he really should, if one didn't already exist, start a union. He would have to have a name for it, a place to hold meetings and, above all, advertise its presence somehow. He wondered if it would be too much for him. Then he noticed that one of the group that had just been served and were congregating at the far end of the bar, was wearing a paint-splattered bib and brace. George went over to him.

'Excuse me, do you know anything of a painters union? There's got to be one somewhere, I should think.'

'Yes mate, matter of fact, I do. It's The Amalgamated Society of Painters and Decorators. I'm not in it meself. Why d'you wanna know?'

'I'm a painter myself and was thinking of starting one, or rather, now knowing there is one, a branch, maybe.'

'Surprised you ain't 'eard of it, but I don't think there's any branches in the City or West End, 'though their 'ead office could be o' course, I don't know.'

George thanked him for the information and returned to his seat. It then occurred to him that he still hadn't told his mother about Doris. When he had seen her they'd talked of other things. He knew she would be hurt that he'd kept it from her; he shouldn't have done. Perhaps he should go to see her now, go straight there and get it over with. He was a big boy now; there was no need for her to worry about him.

He would like to have waited for Enid to finish her shift then walk with her to the bus or train, whatever. But he wouldn't push it, hurry it along, make it look too obvious, 'though he'd have liked to.

He went across to the bar where she had just handed a customer a glass. She came towards him.

'Er, look, Enid, I have to go now, but I'll come again tomorrow and see you. Perhaps we could chat again, I'd like that.'

'Yes, so would I.'

She picked up a towel and began wiping a glass.

'See you then,' she smiled.

As he left, he realised he had actually been flirting with her. He'd never been much good at that, really, but he felt he'd done okay. He liked her. She was… he couldn't quite describe her to himself. But he would see her again.

20

On the face of it, they were contrasting entities, almost contra-dictory states of experience. There was the supposedly emotion-ally detached world of philosophical thought, and then there was the exciting, tranquil, calm, thrilling world of Constance Lange. He had told Eric about her a fortnight after they had slept togeth-er, but although he wasn't sure why, he had not told Andrew.

They had been sitting in a cocktail bar near the College when he'd told him.

'Well, that was quick work, old man. Yes, she's quite some-thing, although only had a quick look, as you know. Yes, I sup-pose there is a certain quality. Well, for you now of course, more than that, a rare one, a lovely one. I shouldn't think love is men-tioned, or indeed, a valid word in the lexicon of your subject, alt-hough it does drive a lot of the world.'

'It's an abstract concept that we reify, it *seems* real and tangi-ble.'

'Still, I suppose you can step away from the classroom when you're with her and talk of love and rainbows, 'though I should think they're as mythical to social science as unicorns. I wonder how natural the feeling of love is to humans?'

'My immediate response is, of course it is, but I wonder if it was to homo sapiens when we first crawled out of the swamp.'

'They weren't homo sapiens then.'

'You know what I mean.'

'You could argue that the idea of romantic love is a creation, a construct as you would call it, and what of falling in love with love?'

Rupert was silent.

'Dear boy, are we intellectualizing this away into the nether regions and bypassing the true value of the word? Let us try not to.'

'I miss her so much when she's looking after her mother. She has to, of course, but I want her with me. I suppose it's selfish.'

'You're not jealous of mum are you?' asked Eric with a rather surprised look.

'Of course not, how can I be jealous of a daughter's relationship with a parent?'

'I'm sure it exists in some relationships. Anyway, she needs caring for. Can you do anything to help?'

'Don't know. I should ask Constance, I suppose.'

'Do so, old boy, there may be something.'

'How's Fiona?'

'Lovely as ever. So what have you and your Connie been doing?'

'Some dinners; more flapjacks, jellied veal and Chicken à la King, tomato juice, tea biscuits and such. Also saw some films, 'Anthony Adverse', 'Romeo And Juliet', 'Things To Come'.

'You've certainly been enjoying yourselves.'

'At the expense of an essay or two, I'm afraid, but am catching up.'

'An eclectic programme. What was on the newsreels.'

'Franco seems to be giving up his plans for taking Madrid. It seems so chaotic there.'

'He may well do in the end. It'll be a long and expensive war.'

'Constance thinks Franco is as fanatical as Hitler and that they both have silly moustaches.'

'It's a serious business, Roopy.'

'I wish I could shorten your name as easily.'

'Ricey's already been taken.'

'I know. Pathé showed someone being executed; De Rivera I think, his father was a a Falangist.'

'He founded the movement, they're anti-communist, anti-liberal, anti-democratic and all for a hierarchy. Nationalism, in a word.'

'With a bit of dictatorship and violence thrown in.'

'It's a complicated business.'

'Wars often are,' said Rupert. 'Emotionally, it's reduced to them and us, right and wrong.'

'Good and bad.'

'Fascism and Nationalism are bad. I think people have to feel a kind of simplicity of emotions to fight, which is helped, of course by the reasons they're given to do so.'

'Don't do much of this in class, do we,' Eric pointed out.

'The lecturers may not be talking much about it, but more of the students seem to be; especially now after the trouble in the East End, they're calling it 'The Battle of Cable Street' You can guess what side I'm on.'

'I can. I'm not really sure of mine, but I'm for the Church and the State.'

'And the military.'

'Of course.'

'Even if they fight against a freely-elected government?'

'We must have order.'

'Whose order? Who gains most from it?'

'Don't we all gain from order in the end?'

'We search for order, certainly, it's a very valid model of man, we almost unconsciously search for it, society provides it most of the time, but, sometimes, at what cost?'

'Let us not have contretemps, dear boy,' suggested Eric, 'How's Pater?'

'I'm growing father and father away from him.'

'Not a bad pun. You don't see eye to eye then?'

'Let's say he doesn't see me, he sees somebody's son, it's *his* son, but could be anybody's I think. He plays the role of father, and I, the son.'

'A house full of the dramaturgical metaphor.'

'It is. When mother's not playing her roles outside the house, she's playing them inside, or one of them.'

'The dutiful wife.'

'Something like that.'

''Tis a pity. From that little theatre poster you showed me t'other day, she's rather special.'

'She is, certainly to me.'

'And perhaps to thousands of theatregoers, also.'

'It's a nice thought.'

'Who is she playing currently?'

'Not sure, don't know where she is. I was hoping to get a letter from her.'

'She'd like Constance.'

'I believe she would.'

'Oh, to be a strolling vagabond, to stride the stage with eyes cast upon me, to bow low before standing ovations.'

'I can imagine you in tights, legs like matchsticks with the wood shaved off.'

'But withal, a noble bearing.'

'Indeed.'

'I love using the trapdoor in a theatre.'

'It's a stage you're going through.'

'Desist, old chap, let's have a Mai-Tie; love the fruit on top.'

They had more cocktails between them until Eric decided to return to his room.

'You too, old boy; seminar, whatever, tomorrow.'

'Only a couple more before the festivities.'

'What do you call an old snowman? Water.'

'Why did Santa stop smoking?'

'Because it was bad for his elf. I shall be with Fiona, of course. And you?'

'Don't know what's happening, I want to see Constance, obviously.'

'I'm sure you shall. Let us depart.'

They took a bus back to their rooms. In Rupert's was a letter from his mother awaiting him, It was postmarked 'London W'.

She was about to begin rehearsals for a play at the Piccadilly Theatre and wondered if he could come down to see her. She could, she had written, 'have returned home in the evenings but have decided to find lodgings nearby so that I can spend more time rehearsing and do so more intensely after the theatre rehearsals'. That was her usual style, he recalled. He also had a suspicion that she felt it would be better for her to be away from his father for a few evenings; she had, in fact, stayed in the same lodgings before with an actress who was in the same show.

He worked late to finish an essay the evening before he went to see her, he could, apparently, stay overnight in a room at the house. Maybe he should visit Andrew the next day.

It was an old house in Vernon Street, and with its drab wallpaper, high, narrow staircase, faded floral-patterned carpets, an almost quintessential boarding house. He'd wanted to take her for a meal, but they had both eaten, he on the train and she at a little café virtually next door.

'What's it about? Where's it set?' he asked her as she handed him a script in the dusty-looking room.

'All sorts of things,' she said, 'It takes place in Glencliff Manor in rural Cheshire.'

'A change from your usual stage settings. Anyway, what's happened to the play you're in? Surely it hasn't folded.'

'No, the theatre's being refurbished, we're hoping we'll continue with it when it's done. But back to this show. I play Elowen Penhaligan from Cornwall, a maid - I also play Anabelle West later on, there's quite a few double parts for the cast - and you, Robert Crosby, lawyer and owner of the house. Okay, it's about eleven-thirty at night in the library.'

'Manor house plays always seem to be set in the library.'

'You begin.'

'A little more light, Elowen,' said Rupert in am exaggeratedly drawling, posh accent. 'That's better. Well, the old place looks just the same.'

'That it be, nothin''s changed 'ere in twenty year,' said his mother in a strong West Country burr.

'That's very convincing, mother. Right. 'You've been faithful to your trust, Elowen.'

'I has, I stuck right 'ere guardin' the old place the whole time.'

'Have you been lonely living here by yourself?' asked Rupert.

'No, I got me friends.'

'Friends?'

'Aye, my friends from the spirit world.'

'Oh, you believe in spirits, eh?'

'I don't believe. I know. They be with me all the time.'

'You never really saw one did you, Elowen.'

'Aye, sir. I see 'em and they do warn me there be an evil spirit working around this house.'

'Ever see it?'

'No, sir, but I felt It pass me in the dark on the stairs.'

'Nonsense, your nerves are upset. It's with living alone here all the time.'

'No sir!'

'Never mind, cheer up! In a few minutes the house will be full of people and all your spooks will vanish.'

'Again, pitch-perfect, mother. A change from your usual home counties speech- pattern parts, which, of course, is what you speak, anyway.'

'That's why I like it, but I also play Annabelle West, the love interest. That's more like me.'

'Who are the people coming in?'

'Crosby's heirs. Elowen has to decide whether she wants to stay on with the selected one. Have you spoken to Andrew lately?'

'I wanted to, but didn't.'

'I think you should, he may be wondering what's happening, whether you've rather forgotten him. That would hurt him.'

It was, Rupert thought, typical of her to care about his friends, especially one he had known for so long. He would contact him, but he was in a different environment now, beginning a new life: studying, debating, writing, proselytizing in the world of academe. It was different from the days when he worked in the office and they'd meet up and go to the theatre, watch films and occasionally cycle through the countryside. They had shared things, had some fun.

They had met at a business conference Rupert's father, against his wife's wishes, had taken hm. He had only just finished boarding school and assumed that, although nothing had been said, his father wished to indoctrinate him into the feel of a wider business ethos, a preparation for things to come. He felt he was the youngest person there until he had seen a boy of his own age. They'd nodded to each other in common recognition of their shared youth.

After the speeches, which he had little interest in and whose often jargon-filled content seemed to go on for hours, he'd sat silently by his father in the hotel bar trying not to listen as his parent and others continued with the business theme.

He saw his age-compatriot looking just as disinterested as himself. Rupert had summoned the courage and excused himself to his father and gone across to him. They had casually introduced themselves, exchanged opinions of what they'd been forced to listen to and had gone to the end of the bar and ordered tea.

Andrew enquired if he had been with his father. Rupert told him he had, to which Andrew had asked him if it was a case of a boss calling one of his employees into the office and saying, 'Charles, you've been with the company for a year now. You started off in the mail room, were promoted to a sales position, a month after that you became manager of the sales department then four months later you were promoted to vice-president. I'm now retiring and want you to take over the company. What do you say to that?' 'Thanks, dad,' said Charles."

Rupert had smiled and said, 'It may come to something like that, but I doubt it. And you?'

'I think it will come to that, but I shan't mind. I have an idea you would want other things.'

Rupert had told him that he didn't really want to follow his father and they had talked of other things and arranged to meet the following week where they realised they had a shared interest in French films, compiling crosswords, and novels by Huxley. They sat in cafés and told each other jokes, indulged in youthful hyperbole and occasionally went to the theatre, especially if Rupert's mother was on stage.

There were also the Windmill Reviews on Saturday mornings. They would get up early and join the queue to gaze at the motionless nudes. At the end of the first show there would be a clattering scramble of people jumping over seats to see if they could find empty ones in the front row from which to watch the next. Neither of them had told their parents where they were going.

No, he hadn't forgotten Andrew, but his friend seemed to be somewhat receding from what was gradually becoming a collection of past experiences, or, perhaps, merely adolescent ones. Thinking this, he mused on whether his internal phrasing was debasing their relationship. But it was becoming more than that, he was feeling increasingly at home at Oxford. And there *was* Constance.

'I would like to continue,' his mother was saying. 'Let's finish the library scene; it'll be the end of Act One then.'

They did so, with his speech exaggeratedly home counties and his parent's increasingly Cornish.

He went to bed thinking that he should visit his friend the next day, it was only fair, but it would be a Sunday service for the trains and if he did make it he couldn't have stayed with him long, he'd have to be back by the next morning.

His mother woke him. They had a rather paltry breakfast served by a rather grim- looking woman appearing to be playing the role of a stereotypical landlady, then accompanied him to the station. She asked him if he was going to telephone his friend and, after goodbyes, he tried to make himself comfortable in the station telephone kiosk.

His call was immediately answered by Andrew, almost, Rupert felt, as if he had been waiting for it.

'Andrew. Hello.'

'That sounds a little formal doesn't it? 'Andrew. Hello'?' as if I haven't heard from you for several years.'

'Does it feel like that?'

There was a slight hesitation.

'I suppose so.'

'How's things?'

'Well, father's on the warpath against everything, this slump mostly, although he is of course, holding his balding cranium above water. Some of his colleagues aren't, though. It's a fraught time financially, but I expect your pater's doing fine, and yourself, one assumes.'

'S'pose so, it's hard work at times, essays and things.'

'Getting top marks?'

'Have had a couple, yes.'

'Good-oh.'

'What have you been doing with yourself?'

'This and that. You know, this is beginning to sound like a rather ordinary exchange of words between two very ordinary people '

'And that we're not.'

'Well, you're certainly not in that category, Oxford an' all. How is it, anyway?' Again the hesitation before continuing with, 'Made any friends?'

'Er… yes. Eric.'

'Same subject?'

'No, Literature and such woolly stuff.'

'Been doing things with him?'

'Restaurants a couple of times, met his girl friend.'

'And you? Girl friend?'

'As a matter of fact, Andrew, yes.'

'There's that 'Andrew' again. What's she like?'

'Very nice.'

'I feel that you mean more than that.'

'Well, yes I do, actually.'

'That nice, eh?'

This time it was Rupert who hesitated.

'She means a lot to me.'

'At least you didn't say 'Andrew' then.'

'How about you? Any members of the opposite -'

'No. You might have guessed that, anyway.'

'Not really. You have more time now for leisure pursuits.'

'Not as much as you it would seem. This is *your* time isn't it?'

'Sort of.'

'Lucky old you.'

'You sound a little miffed, Andy.'

"Andy' now, is it? You've relaxed a little. You've seemed tense from the word 'go' as if there was something you didn't want to tell me. You just have.'

'I suppose I thought you'd be - '

'Pleased?'

'Something like that.'

'Does it sound it?'

Rupert didn't quite know what to say.

'I suppose not. Why?'

'To be honest, Rupert, I haven't heard from you all this time and when I do you indirectly tell me why I haven't: new friends, new girl, new life, a move away physically and emotionally from your past existence.'

Rupert was silent for a while before replying.

'I suppose it is.'

'A longer silence this time before he heard, 'We may not have had wonderful adventures, Rupert, we didn't scale a mountain peak together, sailed an ocean or run a desert marathon, but…. '

The line went dead.

Rupert didn't wonder why it had; he could almost see Andrew slamming the phone down. He remained in the kiosk for a few minutes trying both to understand his friend's action and not to feel the sudden hollowness he himself was experiencing.

On the train back to Oxford, part of him wanted to return and see his friend, tell him that they could still be friends, that what he was doing was perfectly normal and that… He could feel Andrew's sudden anger, his loneliness, as if he had been deserted. He supposed that, in a way, he had been.

He looked out of the carriage window at the telegraph poles flashing by, they seemed to be saying, 'Constance…' 'Constance…   '

21

'Hello, er, George.'

He was a little disappointed at her greeting. He'd gone to the pub after finishing work, where he had briefly discussed with the men whether they'd be in favour of joining a branch of a painters' union, most of them favouring a meeting place close to where they were currently working, others places nearer their homes. He'd waited until she had finished serving some customers before approaching her.

'Sorry, I've been pretty busy,' She told him, 'what have you been doing?'

'Getting the lads to knock out some lids.'

'Painting ceilings, yes?'

'Correct.'

'There's quite a bit of jargon isn't there. My dad once told a new painter to 'Bring that pipe down.' He meant - '

'Paint the down-pipe.'

'Yes, at the back of a house. He began to dismantle it.'

'Yeah, I s'pose there is, we talk about 'boats', meaning the cradles on the outside of buildings, 'cutting in sashes' for painting windows, 'making good', 'sheeting up,' et cetera.'

She asked him what he was drinking.

'Brown ale, as usual.'

'The good old working man's drink.'

'What does dad drink?'

'The same.'

'And you?'

'A pink lady.'

'Sounds sophisticated.'

'I am.'

She raised her eyebrows and gave him a rather mock, haughty smile.

'I expect you think I have as much chance of being sophisticated as you have of getting into Cambridge.'

'The odds are far smaller for you.'

She gave him his ale, saying, 'I remembered an old one today. 'Three was a young barmaid from Sale, on her breasts were the prices of ale, on her behind, for the sake of the blind, was the same information in Braille.'

'Like it. A change from some of the usual filth you hear, I suppose.' Must get you down at times.'

'Get used to it.'

'Must go, another pint, another fourpence,' she said as a rather loud, obvious regular entered with his 'Pint o' mild, Enid, please.'

George sat down by the door and briefly looked about him, wondering why it was called 'Public' bar and not 'The Public' as The Saloon bar and The Private bar were. Perhaps, he thought, it was to do with its inferior status. He knew that, beyond the wooden partition, there would be plants and padded seats in those areas. What interested him more, was whether there would be a room upstairs, he would need it on occasions if his idea for a union was to be implemented.

She'd finished serving the man and was giving George the hint of a smile. He went towards her.

'Enid - '

'That's me.'

'You do have a room upstairs don't you?'

'D'you want to take me up to it?'

'No.... I - '

'No?'

'I'd like to, but… ' He felt himself blushing. 'I just wondered if you had one, most pubs do.'

'Yes, we have.'

Attempting to push away the image of what taking her upstairs could mean, he asked her if it could be booked and, if so, could he speak to her governor.

'What d'you want it for?'

'Tell you when I've made my mind up. Not sure yet. Can I see him?'

Asking him to wait a moment, she left the bar and went up the stairs. He looked at the bar; the shelves reflecting themselves against mirrors, the rows of bottles and glasses, the stacked matches and Woodbine packets. His gaze circled to see a notice against betting fixed to the smoke-discoloured wallpaper, and by the door a sign he'd seen in other pubs, a square of black glass that had a clock face painted on it and the letters, 'No Tick' across it. He briefly wondered how the phrase had come to mean 'No Credit'.

Then a short, fat man was standing in front of him saying, 'You wanted me? I'm Mister Pickwick.'

For a brief second, George almost believed him; the man had a balding head, mutton chop sideburns and was wearing a bow tie. He grinned at George.

'You wanted to book the room?'

George hesitated. I think so, but don't know when. I suppose, really, I just wanted to know the cost.'

'What's it for?'

'Well, I was thinking of booking it for meetings of a working-men's union.'

The man asked him what sort of union it would be.

'A trade union: painters and decorators.'

'Well, if it's for moral reasons, as it were, to benefit from it, a collective spirit, if you will, then I'm all for it. You do know, of course, that strikes, even sympathy ones, are illegal'

'I wasn't aware.'

'Since 'Twenty Seven, I would brush up on your knowledge of these matters before starting it if were you. But it's all in a good cause, I'll reduce the price for you, you'll be able to afford it, young man. Enjoy your drink.'

With an almost supplicant nod of his head the man went back upstairs.

George moved towards the counter where Enid was beckoning to him.

'He'll let you have it, won't he?'

'Yeah, sure, he seems a nice man.'

'He is, and a religious one. May seem strange 'cos he owns a pub, but he is.'

'Are you?

'Not really.'

'Aren't most Welsh people believers?'

'Probably.'

'Wales, where women are scarce and the sheep are nervous. Christ, I've done it again. Sorry.'

'I forgive you. But no more.'

'Mister Pickwick' then appeared behind the bar.

'I assume you are a painter then,' he said to George.

George told him he was.

'I've been meaning to do something with that room for a while, it's a bit shabby. Give me a reasonable price for doing it up and you can have it free for a while.'

George thought quickly. He worked until midday on Saturdays, he could do it in the afternoons and all day Sundays, except, of course, when it was being used, if necessary he could get one of the lads to help him. It'd be a chance to see more of Enid, too.

'Okay, I'll take a look at it.'

After giving Enid a wink, he followed the man upstairs. Turning on the stairs and shaking George's hand he told him his name was Bishop. It wasn't a large room: three windows, a cornice, picture and dado rails, a ceiling rose and two panelled doors. He would do it on his own.

After Bishop telling him the colours he wanted and that he happened to have some trestles and a scaffold board in the basement - if he hadn't, George imagined himself carrying a pair along High Holborn continuously excusing himself to people scurrying out of his way - it didn't take him long to work out a price. It was readily accepted, as was the times it would be worked on. After George telling him he could start next day, the landlord went back to his own room while his new workman returned to the bar. Leaning on the counter he told Enid his plan.

'Sounds fine, but you won't see me here on Sundays, I have it off.'

'Sod it. Never mind, we can do something in the evening, maybe.'

The raised eyebrow again. 'How do you know that I'm free?'

'I don't, I'm hoping.'

'You're in luck, I am.'

'What d'you fancy doing?'

'Don't know. You?'

'I like walking, but it'll be dark.'

'Can still soak up the atmosphere.'

'Okay, let's walk around here then.'

He suggested he meet her in the pub.

'You want me to come back here on my day off?'

'I'd like you to.'

She placed a finger between her lips, looked skyward and pretended to consider his request.

'Alright, I will.'

He suggested a time, to which she agreed, before he left for home.

Next day, he left his job before midday and went to a decorators' merchants in Tottenham Court Road to buy some of the paint and materials he would need. He got a bus to the pub, where Bishop told him he had some dust sheets he could use to add to those George had bought from the site. Enid was too busy to be able to talk to him.

He carried the trestles, board and dust sheets up from the basement, covered the floor, poured the oil-bound distemper into a bucket provided by Bishop and, using a six-inch brush, put a coat on the ceiling. He applied it thickly but carefully and covered the old paint in one coat. The walls were in eggshell where, after filling the cracks, he used a four-inch brush then a stippler; he would, apply two coats to these. He did the window wall, washed his brushes in the adjoining toilet and was about to take off his bib and brace when Enid looked in at the door.

'So there you are; the Ragged Trousered Philanthropist.'

'Have you read it?'

'My dad has, I haven't.'

'Nor me.'

'The ceiling looks good.' She gave him a quick up-and-down scrutiny. You don't look so bad either.'

'You like a bit of rough?'

'Maybe. Can *you* be rough?'

'Suppose so, when the occasion demands.'

'Must go, can't leave the bar unattended. See you tomorrow. 'Bye.'

After she left he removed his overalls and departed.

The following day he got in just as early as if he were on the site, completed a first coat on the walls and went downstairs waiting for her to arrive. He didn't have to wait long. As soon as she came in the door he went towards her. She was wearing a long, dark coat, high-heeled shoes and a ribbon in her hair.

They walked down Charing Cross Road and into Leicester Square and onwards. She appeared to be in a light, fresh mood.

'It has a sort of magic about it at night, doesn't it,' she said, looking around her.

'It has during the day, too, at least some of London does.'

It was the light, not just created by those outside picture palaces and theatres, but those of shops and the street lights. There was one of the latter opposite his house which would throw its light through the suntrap window, the shadows of its long, thin glazing bars splaying across the chimney breast of his through-lounge. As they were passing the Adelphi he glanced at her. There was something about the shape of her cheekbones and the shine in her eyes when the light struck them.

'It's the little things, isn't it,' she said, smiling, 'like the sun shining on trees, maybe a privet hedge, even chocolate-box roses around a front door.'

'Yeah, and the sun playing on leaves, bricks, glistening on window panes.'

They walked on, he enthusiastically talking of Italianate towers, scrolled balconies, black-and-white tiled paths, and she looking up at him, smiling and telling him he was a poet.

'I used to like it at school, but not the rhyming stuff, it seemed too forced, too kind of dramatic.'

'What about, 'There was a girl named Sally who used to love to dally, she once sat on the lap of a well-endowed chap and cried, 'Oh, you're right up my alley.'

'You *are* one of the lads, aren't you.'

'I can be, I suppose.'

'You know, sometimes when I'm walking and looking around, I feel that I want to become a roof and look down on porticoes and clicking gates, on gardens, and trees higher than me and, say, an unexpected park with a kind of watercolour lake.'

'You don't sound like a painter and decorator now,' she said and then laughed and shook her head.

'The sun is a magical orb isn't it,' he said. 'On a Georgian window, old London bricks, even on a length of guttering.'

'On almost anything, really. I was in Camden recently and watched the sun suddenly illuminate the bridge and the train crossing over the canal. I stopped and just stood and watched it.'

'And the smaller bits, like, you know, the odd castellation on top of a Victorian house, a pediment above Edwardian keystones or the set-back top of modern block. It's almost spiritual'

'Yes, perhaps that's the right word.'

'And the sun hitting a revolving chimney cowl.'

'I went back to Swansea in the summer to visit relations and while I was at Paddington Station I looked up at the sun coming through the station's roof struts on to the columns. Something about it, it made the whole station look for a second almost Romanesque.'

'I like that word. When I'm working in the City or West End on my own I enjoy myself looking at some Georgian frontages, or a Regency town house and early Victorian buildings which, although sometimes tucked away in side streets, are nearly always grand.'

'Where do you get your interest in architecture from?'

'At Building School.'

'People who go to Building School don't talk about the sun glistening on Georgian windows and flashing off chimney cowls,' she said with a grin.

'This one does.'

He put his arm around her shoulder. She halted for the briefest moment then put her arm around his waist. They walked on in silence, both feeling the import of their actions, and continued with the theme as they walked past the stone cherubs and leaning gravestones of a small churchyard.

After a while, he asked her if she fancied a quick drink.

'Why a 'quick' one?'

'Well, I'm not sure how long it'll take you to get home, and I have further to go than you and I'm not sure when the trains will be. I'll be the 'same old, same old' for you, but at least it'll be you that's getting served.'

'Think I'll get a bus, don't fancy a train after our walking. You haven't told me where you live yet.'

He told her. 'I have a house there.'

'You do? Not bad for a working lad.'

'I've got a mortgage; it'll take a long time to pay it off.'

They walked for a while in comfortable silence, he hardly noticing that this woman, whose arm was now settled in his, he had known for such a short time.

She suddenly halted and told him that this was where she should get her bus. She leaned against the pole. He rested the palm of his hand on it a little above her head and looked for the bus's lights, occasionally glancing at her hair with its ribbon neatly tied above attractively shaped eyebrows. They didn't have long to wait.

She smiled at him before stepping onto the tailboard.

'Perhaps I'll see you tomorrow,' she said, briefly placing a forefinger on top of her forehead as if touching a forelock.

'You shall', he said and gave her a wave. She walked to the front of the vehicle before sitting down and disappearing from his view.

Walking towards a station, he was thinking how pleasant the walk had been, and also that he hadn't mentioned Doris to her yet. He hadn't thought about it. Or of her.

22

'When you think of it though, Africans are stupid really, aren't they. You would think that with all the natural resources they have - '

'That have been plundered and controlled by other countries.'

'The good old colonialists.'

'And they're not stupid. When the powerful countries leave, including us, they'll be robbed and exploited again by their own dictators. In short, they don't have a capitalistic mind.'

'America will lead the world in the future, anyway.'

'Arguably, they do now, and its inhabitants speak the same tongue.'

'Britain and The States: two nations divided by a common language.'

'Africa doesn't have that, it's a continent of fifty two countries and over fifteen hundred languages, how can they unite as an economic force?' And don't,' continued Rupert, 'say that you're all for colonisation, it's a euphemism for exploitation.'

Rupert and Eric, after meeting at the end of separate seminars, were having coffee in a restaurant which was a converted room in the gatehouse of the local cemetery. Eric had suggested it because he liked the cakes there. It had narrow, latticed windows with elaborated stone arches, and paintings on the walls of poppy fields, one depicting a fleet of Sopwith Camel aircraft flying over them. The red-and-black scrolled chairs and the single, imitation poppies in small vases on the mahogany tables added to a quasi-religious atmosphere of a chapel of remembrance.

'And don't tell me you're for Empire either.'

'We give as well as take, look at the Indian Railways,' said Eric.

'We, or rather this country's ruling class, sent an army to protect the East India Company's interests, and... better not carry on, Eric, we'll fall out, I've probably already lost a friend, I don't want to lose another.'

'Who?'

'Forget it.'

'Not Constance?'

'You looked almost shocked when you said that. Of course not. And she's more than a friend.'

'I know. Let's talk of shoes and ships and sealing-wax and cabbages and kings, or the whole world even.'

'Whatever that may be. As Wittgenstein says, 'The world is everything that is the case.''

'What does that mean exactly? How can you get a case big enough to hold the whole world? Surely the world wouldn't be in the case because the case itself is part of the world.'

'Maybe you really should be doing philosophy, Eric.'

'Descartes invites a woman out for a meal at a luxurious res-taurant. She chooses the most expensive thing on the menu. 'I think not,' he says indignantly, and 'Poof', he vanishes.'

'Yes, that's definitely the subject for you.'

'Seen much of your gal?'

'No. As said, like to see more of her.'

'Is that a double entendre? Actually, I don't feel philosophical, I feel light, floaty.'

'Why?'

''Cos I have Fiona, my Fiona. We had a meal last evening and before our sweet she said, 'Let's dance,' and pulled me up still eating my duck à l'orange. There were only a few others present, so we did. Not exactly the light fantastic, but a merry, old-fashioned waltz. And then halfway through our little fandango I popped it.'

''Popped' what?'

'The question. *The* question.'

'You mean... ?'

'Yep.'

'And the answer?'

'Don't joke, dear boy, you know the answer.'

'Congrats my friend, to both of you, bet you felt like levitat-ing.'

'I did. I didn't plan it, it just happened, 'though I have been thinking of doing it for a while. I had visions of kneeling before her dressed as a knight, laying my sword before her and dramatically lifting my visor so she would see my beseeching eyes. Or, perhaps, laying out my Eng. Lit. books on the floor to spell the letters of 'Will you marry me?''

'You'd have needed a lot of books, and it wasn't a very good idea. When's the big day?'

'Not sure yet, but it won't be in term time, of course.'

'You know what they say: A man isn't complete until he's married, and after that he's finished. Only kidding.'

'Say what you will; it's her and me for ever.'

'Where do you plan to honeymoon? The Bahamas?'

'We were thinking of hiring the Queen Mary and going on a round-the-world cruise.'

'Can I come?'

'No. Actually, I haven't thought that far yet. I think Daddy will be pleased, perhaps he will help me out. The Orient Express appeals to me, with a first night in a canal-side hotel in Venice then a leisurely gondola trip and, perhaps, swinging from underneath a few bridges as we smooth along.'

'And then dropping down into the arms of your beloved.'

'Yes, then back to the choo-choo and onwards.'

'To Istanbul?'

'Who knows? And what about being my best man?'

'Your best man?'

'Yes. I have other friends obviously, but you.... represent my current life, the 'me' I am now. You'll accept?'

'Well, of course. Yes.'

'Goodo, chum.'

'I expect you'll need a speech from me then.'

'Of course; urbane, witty, sincere and full of hope'

'Not unlike yourself then. May it include literary references?'

'Only if they're appropriate, but no jokes.'

'Not even corny ones?'

'Especially those. Why do we say 'corny'?'

'It refers to the inhabitants of the corn belt in the good ol' U S of A.'

'I suppose that's similar to 'rednecks' with the sun beating on their backs as they work in the fields.'

'This is so much trivia compared with your news.'

'Indeed. Anything we talk about now is bound to be an anti-climax.'

'Like it was, I assume, for Franco in Madrid.'

'You seem to be increasingly interested in things 'Español'. What's actually happening there?'

'I don't suppose anyone knows it all, but it seems that their Foreign Minister has complained to The League of Nations about the political and economic isolation of the Republic by the democratic nations.'

'Including us?'

'Sadly, yes. There's apparently going to be a new government formed in Aragon - it'll have a majority of anarchists, apparently - where some areas and villages will begin reorganising public life under anarchist ideals. They're going to establish communes and begin self-organising factories and farms. Some of the villages will replace money with coupons handed out by local authorities.'

'A people's revolution.'

'Certainly a reformulation of public life.'

'You're not an anarchist, are you?'

Rupert was silent for a few seconds.

'I don't know, Eric, I don't know.'

Eric appeared to take a deep breath before he said, 'The Popular Front government is a coalition of republicans supported by anarchists, Soviet Union and communist parties, socialists and volunteers who fight in the international brigades whilst the Nationalists are supported by conservative groups, nationalists, religious conservative groups and the fascist Falangists.'

Rupert looked at him with surprise.

'You *are* interested then?'

'Not really, I learnt it to impress you.'

'You almost have. But... back to the event, what sort of 'do' will it be, or is it going to be a surprise?'

'Ostentatious, vulgar, loud and full of plebs.'

'And the bride's dress?' A secret, I know, but... '

'A diamond-encrusted tiara, a gold necklace and a silk dress trailing seventy feet behind her.'

'And the pageboys?'

'We will drag them from the slums of the East End, dress them in short, gold lamé trousers, patent leather shoes with silver Blakey's and emerald-tipped laces, and the bridesmaids will be carrying so many flowers their orange taffeta dresses will be barely visible.'

'So, nothing special then. What do the parents think of it?'

'Haven't told them yet, will do so this evening, but Mummy will be pleased, perhaps father will also, although I think, maybe, he was hoping I'd marry into the aristocracy.'

'Realising his own wish-fulfilment, perhaps. What kind? Hereditary titles, political and military elites?'

'The former, I should think. Actually, I wouldn't mind it being in a registry office, but, you know, family and all that.'

'I think there's a part of you that loves the spectacle; Perhaps a flypast of the Graf Zeppelin and a flying circus, at least a plane with a banner proclaiming 'Best Wishes'.'

'It would be nice to outdo father though, I've seen photos of his and mater's wedding; in fact, a couple of paintings of the ceremony he had done. Mummy looked rather lovely and, I must admit, papa appeared his usual handsome self, almost dashing. He did once tell me where they honeymooned, I think his bride wished to go to The City of Light - she can speak fluent French, by the way - but they went to St. Tropez. When a child, I asked her what they did there and she told me they sat outside chic cafes along the harbour and watched people. They also hired a yacht and sailed around in that, apparently.'

'The Queen Mary beats that.'

'You haven't told me yet what your friend Marx thinks of marriage'

'That it's the result of capitalism and designed to perpetuate it.'

'And religion is the opiate of the masses, eh.'

'Yep. But let's not introduce a note of cynicism. I expect Fiona is excited.'

'She is.'

'A little unusual to have a married student in this place.'

'I'm a mature one.'

'Marriage reminds me of a syllogism.'

'Two premises and a conclusion, correct?'

'Whilst wedlock is two promises and a confusion.'

'You weren't going to be cynical.'

'Sorry. Another coffee?'

'A café cornetto.'

'I'll have an Espresso, I like listening to the machine.'

They were silent for a while as they sipped.

'Anything bothering you, old chap?' asked Eric.

'Well…. I suppose most things are going well.'

'I should say they are.'

'Mother's rehearsing a new play, Constance and I are great really, when I see her that is, am getting some good marks for essays, and I think even Pym appreciated my last seminar paper, but… '

"But' what?'

'I don't really know, it's just … not satisfying.'

'What isn't? Life at Oxford?' Not what you expected?'

'I'm not sure what I expected, but I don't seem to be satisfying my, if you like, intellectual ambitions, though these, also, I'm not sure of, never have been really, come to think of it. It's just that I want to… express my intelligence, my perceptions, insights, if you like, but I'm not doing that as much as I could, or should, I suppose.'

'Well, start doing so then, what's stopping you?'

Rupert thought awhile.

'There doesn't seem a good enough reason for them, somehow.'

'Getting good marks isn't enough? Actually, you're in a bit of a minority methinks, people don't really come here for those, it's the life. But, for you, expressing yourself, using your analytical abilities, putting them on paper and getting recognised should be enough, really.'

'Somehow, it isn't.'

'Let us talk of other things.'

'How's Mister Flavin?'

'Posturing and preening. Sometimes when he's giving his lectures I'm sure I see him occasionally sliding an eye up to imaginary theatre boxes filled with royalty and the great and the good.

He's a tough taskmaster though, has given me quite average marks to date for the work I've done for him.'

'Is that a function of him or you?'

Eric, looking a little morose for a second, said reluctantly, 'Both of us, I suppose. I get impatient with research, I shall try harder. Ne'er mind, the festive season is almost upon us.'

'For many it won't be that festive. It's hotting up in Spain again. Thousands of nationalist volunteers have landed in Cadiz, it's a Nationalist port, and thousands of souls will have to spend Christmas Day in the trenches on the front, and many refugees have nowhere to go and will have to stay in refugee camps and subway stations.'

'It sounds rather awful, but, again, let us speak of other things.'

'But not footwear, boats, wax, vegetables and monarchs.'

'I shall keep clear of such topics. But what of the crazy man in Berlin? What will he do?'

'Get crazier, perhaps.'

'Did he really borrow that moustache from Chaplin?'

'Probably. He seems to have rejected the terms of The Versailles Treaty, and we know what he used the Olympics for don't we.'

'To promote his government and the ideals of racial supremacy and anti-Semitism.'

'Indeed.'

'And what are *you* doing over the Hols? I assume you'd like to take her to meet the parents.'

'I would,' agreed Rupert,' I've offered my help it if would be of any use to her mother but I don't see what I could do, and it seems from what her daughter tells me that she has dementia coming on.'

'Which means you'd see even less of your sweetheart. Ne'er mind, it'll come out all right in the end, for both of you, I hope.'

'I'll drink to that,' said Rupert as they drained their coffees, smacked their lips and stood before getting their overcoats and Eric paying for their repast. They shared a companionable silence as they walked to a taxi rank and waited, Rupert assuming that Eric was thinking pleasantly exciting thoughts about his future event, and he looking forward to seeing Constance. After their taxi had deposited them at the College, they said goodnight and went to their rooms.

Rupert lay on his bed looking at the darkened ceiling and thinking that he had never quite articulated to himself, or anyone, what he felt about his current life, but, other than Constance, there had to be more, although he wasn't sure what it was or what he had to do to obtain it. But then, perhaps this feeling would pass; as Eric had intimated, he had a lot to be satisfied with.

He hoped to see his mother fairly soon in her play, and Constance would be at work in the library tomorrow and, maybe, he, too, would work harder at his academic tasks, though the political objectivity that he was required to have in doing them seemed to be wearing a little thin.

23

He was painting a red 'Fire Exit' in Roman san serif across a door on the ground floor of the building after checking that his gang were working on their various jobs, mostly applying primer to recently plastered walls and ceilings. He had another two doors to do. He was also wondering when he would hold a union meeting at the Holborn Tavern and how to advertise it. It would take another three days to finish the room, though this could be cut down if he worked a few evenings.

Although the blokes had said they would attend meetings - they could walk to the pub, so it wouldn't entail them paying bus or train fares - George fleetingly wondered whether their apparent keenness was because of where they would be held and that it was partly an excuse for a drink and a laugh; they could tell their wives that it was serious business and thus be approved.

He had just telephoned the Union headquarters where he was told that documents would be sent to him to be completed and that evidence of his identity as well as the name of his employer would be required. The official also told him that not only were strikes illegal but that sympathetic strikes and mass picketing were also outlawed by government. 'What power do we have then?' George had asked, but the man hadn't given him an answer except to state, 'that the objective of trade unions was to improve the terms and conditions of employment, which meant that members were supposed to continually review them and, where possible, to provide alternative conditions of service through suggestions.' This last part George had thought sounded rather weak.

He had also seen Enid the evening after their walk, but they had exchanged few words because, as she'd said, briskly wiping the bar counter, the place was pretty busy for a Monday evening.

After completing the other doors, going for lunch and returning, he began work on the sashes again, enjoying cutting in their neo-Georgian shapes and looking through them to a bright winter sun. After undercoating three of them, and before calling the lads for the tea break, he again climbed out of one of them and sat on its sill. He looked about him and saw, fifty yards away and on the same level as himself, a brickie pointing some of the exterior brickwork.

The man was casually but carefully smoothing the mortar between the bricks when suddenly he went down, falling very quickly, the other end of the scaffold board he had been standing on smashing against a short, horizontal pole above it. George saw him grab the near-end of the now-vertical board fo before both he and the board continued their fall.

It didn't seem quite real. For a second he wondered if he had seen the man at all. There was now a long gap in the boards resting on the metal tubes, and now no one was there. There seemed to be a deep silence in the world, except for the drone of vehicles and the clatter of horses and carts eight floors below.

He stood there, not moving, wanting to shout, 'It didn't happen, it didn't happen.' Then he went inside again and ran to the stairs. He was the only one on the floor. He heard his footsteps echo as he ran across it. He almost jumped down to each platform of the staircase until he reached the ground floor where two brickies he knew slightly were pushing open the rear fire exit doors, a palm of one of them smudging George's work as he pushed them open. George followed them as they ran across the brick-and-rubble-strewn ground towards the scaffold at its far end.

The body was almost in a sitting position, resting against a cement-stained wheelbarrow, a leg at an impossible angle under the barrow, an arm hanging half torn from a shoulder and the face bloody and bruised. Somewhat detachedly he guessed that the man had hit more boards and poles on his way down, though he hadn't heard the noise it must have made.

The younger of the two bricklayers put his hands over his face and stood motionless. The older man moved towards him and put an arm around his shoulder.

Turning to George he said, 'What happened? It was a simple job he was doing.'

George took a while to answer.

'I saw it. I was watching him and… it was the board, it hadn't been overlaid, he must have been standing on a double then moved to another whose end wasn't resting on a pole. I noticed some like it the other day; others had seen them, too. I think the site agent knew, I don't know. He should have, your foreman does.'

'I know, he told me he reported it to the site agent.'

Just then several other workers arrived, one of them moving the wheelbarrow and placing a small tarpaulin over the body.

The site supervisor, a large, portly man in waistcoat and tie came, panting, up to them.

'Oh, Jesus Christ, what happened?'

'He fell,' Mister Roberts,' said somebody from behind George, 'from a bloody great height. It's the scaffolders, ain' it, they've not been doin' their job have they, and you know it.' It was one of the carpenters.

'I know nothing of the sort, and it's not the time for blaming anyone, it's happened, the poor sod. Has anyone called for an ambulance? Don't stand there. Do it. There's a phone in my office. Use it. Go!'

As one of the men ran back and through the fire doors, the carpenter said, 'I've already done it, I used the phone box outside,'

There was a pause in which nobody spoke. The wailing of an ambulance in the near distance was heard and became louder. George felt a quick trace of guilt at not informing the site agent himself about the boards, but it seemed obvious that it was, ultimately, the agent's responsibility to know what was happening on his site. But what of the scaffolding foreman? George didn't know. It was a mess.

The workers gathered around the tarpaulin shroud were quietly talking among themselves, almost whispering as three ambulance men ran across and asked them to move away. They pulled off the body's covering and gently lifted the bricklie onto a stretcher before throwing a red blanket over it and carrying it to the rear doors of the building. As they closed behind them some of the men sat down, not in any particular formation, not even facing each other, but at random, attempting to accept, to make sense of what they had just seen.

Not being sure of what to do, George slowly turned away and went back into the building. Coming down the stairs were two of his lads. They asked him what had happened, was it true that someone had fallen from a scaffold and had been killed. George told them it was.

'Did you see the body?' asked one of them, a young painter not long out of his apprenticeship.

'I did. I don't ever want to see another one.'

'Blimey, I dunno what to say.'

'I don't at this moment,' said their foreman, 'but it's no good us just standing here, let's get back to work, do something, try not to think about it if we can.'

'Easier said than done,' said the older man.

'I know, but let's get back upstairs. Come on.'

The two went back to what they had been doing and George returned to his window, aware that he was running away from what he'd seen. He looked at the paint kettle on the floor below it, the worn inch brush, or 'dog's cock' as those in the game knew it, resting across it, reminding him that he'd expected to be outside of the window for only a minute or so. He picked the brush up, the paint on its bristles slightly hardened. He dipped it into the paint, tapped it on the inside of the kettle and began finishing the sash, trying not to look out at the scaffold again where he'd seen the man fall.

The foreman chippie came across to him.

'You know what just happened I presume?'

'I do. I saw it.'

'You saw it?'

'Yeah, I did.'

'Christ, Must have shaken you, mate. How did it happen?' The man hesitated. 'If it's too early for you to describe it, that's okay, but we do wanna know.'

'Who's 'we'?'

'Well, the other foremen, and the blokes, really. I mean, was it his fault d'you reckon, or maybe the scaffold, or something?'

'The scaffold. We all knew about it really, didn't we; maybe we should have made the agent do something.'

'Look, let's go to the site office now and you can explain what you saw. I know it's hard, but I should think almost certainly you're the only one who saw it all.'

'Shouldn't we all be there? '

'Let's collect the other charge hands on the way.'

George followed the chippie down flights of stairs, calling in on each floor where there were various trades working or standing around talking to each other, some looking shocked, a few, thought George, showing anger. It was obvious the subject of the conversation was the dead worker. He stood at the entrances to the floors watching the carpenter, who seemed to know most of the men, talking to them and asking where their foremen were. Eventually they were found and corralled into a group on the ground floor to stand outside the agent's office.

As the chippie told the men that the accident had been witnessed by 'this man', and pointing to George, the site agent, a tall, emaciated-looking man, appeared behind them and asked what was going on.

'I believe you know about the bricklayer,' began the carpenter.

''Course I do, I should think everybody on the site knows about it by now. I was going to call you all together, anyway, and express my sadness about it. I suppose,' he said, looking around him, 'that that's why you're here, to hear what I have to say.'

'Something like that,' said one of the men. 'Perhaps the painter should tell us what he saw.'

The agent turned to George.

'Did you see it then?'

'I did, I happened to be watching him when... when he fell.'

'What actually did occur then? Speak up.'

George told them what he'd seen in as much detail as he could remember which, as it had only just happened, was a lot; including the expression on the man's face as he'd briefly clung to the end of the falling board. He forced himself to do it, hating it, reliving it all with every word.

The silence afterwards was broken by a loud, 'it's the bloody scaffolders ain' it, some of 'em don't know what they're doin', there's cheap labour there, I betcha.'

'Is there anyone 'ere who's been workin' on it? 'Who's in charge of 'em?'

George thought it was one of the glaziers who'd asked this. He looked around. There was no response.

'If it was workers on the cheap, then it's not really his fault is it, he has to work with the blokes he's been given,' came from someone.

'But he must know if they're any good or not,' was another comment.

George then said, 'Let's find him; he's got to have something to say.'

'I think I know where he'll be,' said the plastering foreman, 'he had a few men taking down the scaffold on that end bit of the building, that part where there's no windows. Perhaps he don't know about it yet.'

'Stay there, we'll get him,' one of the bricklayers said, and he and a few others went quickly towards a gap where doors were to be fitted.

'Look, I'm going to have to make a report on this,' said the agent, 'I'm going into my office. I'll contact the developers.'

As he went in one of the men said to him, 'You're ultimately responsible though, aren't you.'

'I suppose I am,' the agent said quietly, closing his door.

Two men went towards George.

'Must have been awful for you, to have seen that, very upsetting.'

Another, squeezing the top of George's arm, said, 'You did well, I don't envy you seeing what you saw.'

There was a silence amongst them for a while until the agent came out of his office and said to them all, 'Nobody is to work on the scaffolds until further notice. Perhaps some of you can go out and see if anyone is. If they are, tell them to get off.'

A few workers left. Some seconds afterwards, from the opposite direction, the bricklayer and the men who had gone with him returned with a man, George assumed, was the scaffolding foreman.

He looked a little irate. He and his companions stopped in front of the men that were left outside the office. 'Like I've just told these,' he said, glancing at the men who had brought him here, 'I wasn't there, I've been working on two other jobs, I've only just heard about it, I can't be in three places at once can I.'

'Is this what you usually do?' asked the agent.

'No, but I have since we've been taken over by this other firm. We used to have a charge hand on every job.'

I'm going to contact your firm; I assume it's the same number. This isn't good enough.' He frowned. 'They are qualified though, aren't they? Whether you're present or not they have enough know-how to carry on without you, surely.'

'Well, most of 'em have.'

"Most of them'?'

'Well... not all of 'em are as good as my own men.'

'Your *own* men?'

'The regulars I usually have with me. The new guv'nor sent me a few new ones. They work hard enough, but, maybe, they're not quite up to the standard of the others. Can we talk about this in the office?'

'No. Continue.'

'Well, three of 'em are Polish, and there's a bloke from Turkey. Nice enough fellas, but it's difficult to understand 'em sometimes.'

'But can they understand *you*?'

There was a hesitation. 'They 'seem' to. They're workin' with experienced men, they're being taught, they - '

'Should they be on a job this big if they're learning? It's not as if they're apprentices; it wouldn't matter if they were painters or French polishers, but they've got big responsibilities, men's safety depends on them.'

'D'you think I'm not aware of that?'

'It's not enough though, Mister Staines, is it. Have you said anything to your new bosses?'

'Well, no. I'm an employee; I do what I'm told, just as the men do what I tell them to.'

'But, do they? They apparently haven't or this dreadful accident wouldn't, perhaps, have occurred. I want you to speak with... Woods is it?' he enquired, looking at George.

'Correct.'

'Both of you go into my office and you, Staines, listen. I'm sorry you have to go through this again, Woods, but it's important.'

They went into the room followed by the agent who closed the door and sat behind his desk as George stood and told his story again, reliving it once more, but in trying to remember the words he'd used previously, creating a slight, but welcome, emotional distance.

'Bloody hell,' said his listener, 'I've told 'em about this before. I thought I'd made sure they understood. Oh, shit!'

He banged a fist against this forehead.

'I think you should round up your men and find exactly who was responsible for that part of the boarding and when it was laid. I shouldn't think there's any need for Woods to hold your hand and show you to the spot where the man fell from, it should be self-evident.'

'No need for the sarcasm is there, and I've only a couple of men here now, we haven't started taking this lot down yet, so they're on other jobs, but I'll get 'em.'

He left the room.

'You'd better go, too.' he said to George, 'Sorry you've had to go through that again, but needs must. You'd better go back to your painters; maybe you can find some solace.'

He did so. His men, with two plumbers who often sat with them in the café at lunchtime, were talking among themselves until one spotted George.

'Howd'it go?' he asked him.

'Sounds as if some of the scaffolders were at fault; maybe the foreman as well. But that's not official. Let's get back to our jobs, doesn't help anyone just standing around.'

They slowly dispersed to their different floors, leaving George to decide whether to complete the window he'd been working on and look across at that fatal gap amongst the boards and metal poles, or cross the floor and begin the sashes on the other side of it. He chose the former; they had to be finished sometime.

He felt justified in knocking his men off early and went to the pub. He wanted to tell Enid about what had happened, but part of him, the little boy part, he suspected, desired to mainly so she could comfort him. He realised it was probably selfish, it wouldn't be a pleasant experience for her to hear the fatal details. He left as the place got busier; neither of them had spoken of their recent walk, the pub and her pint-pulling weren't very conducive.

Two days later - he had seen her, again very briefly, the evening before - he was painting the narrow moulding around a door panel before doing the panel itself then repeating the process on the other three before the top, lock and bottom rails, finishing with the two stiles. It was painting by numbers and he was doing it very slowly. For the amount he was doing, he may as well have been in the pub working on the room.

They were on a go-slow strike; all the trades were, including the engineers who were completing the girder'd structure of the last section on the site which had started late. Apparently, they and the roofers had operatives who were being paid below union-recognised rates. It appeared there were more than two firms involved in these areas of work: sub-contracting firms who were paying less. When George had first heard this news it had annoyed him, and it was soon apparent that he was not the only one as the rumour went around that a strike of some sort was being organised.

'We can't join 'em,' one of his gang had remarked, 'we're not in any of the unions.' 'We can,' George had said, 'and we will.'

'What's old Symonds gonna say?' another had asked.

'He may own our firm, but he'll have to understand what's happening and why we have to join in.'

A few of the lads had looked apprehensive. He knew they feared the sack.

He hadn't been completely sure of his ground, but had felt determined to ally with the other workers. He knew that his job was, essentially, to make money for old Symonds, but he also had a moral duty to the men he was telling what to do, didn't he?' He guessed that the discovery of the unequal pay had been triggered by the accident and that others in a similar situation to the foreign scaffolders had, perhaps, approached workers in the other trades and had cajoled them, in their broken English, to empathise with them.

Someone had been killed by a lack of experience, skill and, maybe, of care. Perhaps he shouldn't blame the particular scaffolders, however, but the hiring of them to save money. He tried to define, formalise the situation. It was an expression of a need for some kind of deserved economic parity, and implicit in it was a warning of the grave consequences that could occur if not, justifiably, granted.

He had an impulse to send his men out as messengers of the righteous to gather the whole site together with himself standing on the spot where the wheelbarrow had been and making an impassioned speech. It would be on the wrongs of making money at all costs, the worshipping of the god of profit, then, as he was cheered, asking them to follow him and, leading them in a phalanx, marching military-style westward to Trafalgar Square with applauding crowds lining the streets and women blowing kisses at him as the marchers raised banners on which he'd painted in block capitals, 'Justice Against Greed'.

As he imagined this scene in the Square, he stopped himself.

His men, in effect, were working on ceilings, walls, dados, cornices in a kind of organised slow-motion as a protest at a loss of life. He felt it wasn't enough, that it was, perhaps, a little pathetic. He felt almost cowardly. But didn't know what else he could do.

24

He was, seemingly, going to see more of Constance but in a manner which he hadn't foreseen and one which he, selfishly, he thought, didn't really want. Despite his offer to call upon him if she thought he could be of any assistance to her mother, it was only now that he had spent time with her.

He had been in the library when he'd mentioned her parent again, and it seemed to be on a whim that she had suggested that he accompany her that evening to her parent. He, frustratingly, hadn't seen her outside of her workplace for a week.

It was a medium-sized semi-detached house on the edge of the city and whilst on a bus there she told him that she would soon have to arrange for a carer. He thought for a while and was about to ask whether she could afford one and, if not, whether she would accept any financial help from him, when she gave him a glance which instantly suggested that she'd guessed what he was about to say and that any offer would be rejected.

Her mother, a full-bodied woman with a bush of grey hair, lined face and eyes similar to her daughter's except for their slightly unsure look, was lying on a couch in the parlour with a dressing gown pulled up to her waist. Her daughter gently lifted her bare legs and pulled it down to her feet.

'Mum, do you want to sit up?' she asked, 'This is the man I was telling you about, he's come to see you.'

The woman looked at her daughter and frowned, and blinked in a way that implied that she wasn't quite sure who she was looking at.

'Mother, this is Rupert.'

'Pleased to meet you… Robert.'

'No, mother, it's Rupert.'

The older woman looked at him, frowning.

'Where do you live?'

He told her.

'A university is a place, isn't it,' she said, showing interest.

'It's very near here,' said Constance.

'I'm near here. I'm here,' said the woman on the couch.

'It seems a nice house', said Rupert.

'Do you live in a house?'

'It's a room.'

'I want my breakfast, but don't know where it is.'

'You've had it, mother, it's time for another meal now.'

'Can I have that stuff that I like?'

'You mean cornflakes. You can't have them for every meal, you know that.'

She glanced at Rupert.

'She would if she could.'

'Is… that man going to eat?'

'I've told you his name, try to remember, and I think you should sit up now.'

Her daughter gently raised her to a sitting position.

'Come on, let's make you decent.'

Constance slowly eased her parent out of the room.

Rupert felt a little hollow. He realised that he would have to share his girl with, and she would be tied down by, the needs of an ageing, sick woman. He told himself not to be so selfish and possessive, words he didn't like but realised that they applied to him.

Constance returned to the room with her mother minus the dressing gown and wearing a jumper and long skirt. Her hair had also been brushed; he wondered if she had done it herself.

'She's gone from early to moderate now.'

"Moderate' what?'

'Alzheimer's. It's a form of dementia.'

'I don't think I've heard the word before.'

'You have now. Come on, mother, let's have a cup of tea.'

She ushered her into the hall, beckoning him to follow, then into a smaller room and sat her down at a table. 'Do you want something?' she asked him.

'Whatever you have. Tea and a scone would be fine.'

'I guessed you'd say that. I'm going to the kitchen. Talk to Rupert, mother.'

She left them together.

He glanced around the room; there were several framed drawings and water colours above the mantelpiece. One was of a child
holding a red balloon and looking up at it, another depicted some
sort of sea monster with a small boy riding it. Another was of an
attractive woman in flappers' clothes, yet another of a tall, dark-
suited man. He guessed they were constance's work, done as a
child. They pleased him. Underneath what he sometimes referred
to as her 'matter-of-factness' there was an innocent creativeness
which both attracted and intrigued him.

'Who are you?' the older woman asked him.

He told her.

'Connie's friend?'

'Yes.' He was tempted to say, 'Well done.'

'She's got a job with books.'

'In the library, I know.'

'Do you read the… things?'

'Books? Yes. Lots of them.'

'Hitler reads books.'

'I expect he does.'

'Do you know Connie?'

'Of course, that's why I'm here, to meet you.'

'That's nice. I'm here.'

The subject of their conversation returned to the room with tea
pot, cosy, cups and scones. As she began pouring the tea, her
mother stood and left the room.

'Probably gone to the bathroom, she can manage that,' was the
response to his quizzical look.

'Like the artwork. They are yours, I assume.'

She gave them a quick look.

'Yep. Was about twelve or thirteen when I did them.'

'Who's the man?'

'Dad, or rather an imagined idea of him. The lady is mother, of
course.'

'And the little boy, a wished-for brother?'

'I thought philosophy was your subject, not psychology.'

'I have an eclectic intellect.'

'I hope mother's not causing you any stress.'

'Of course not, but I'm sure she does you at times.'

'An increasing amount of them, I'm afraid.'

'You spoke about a carer.'

'What's she doing in there?'

She left the room. He heard knocking on a door.

'You alright in there, mother?'

There was no answer. The knocking continued then the sound of a door opening.

'Ah, there you are, lying on your bed again. Come on, get up.'

There were some shuffling noises and her mother appeared, with her daughter easing her gently into the room.

'Sit down and finish your tea.'

She sat again. 'Who are *you* then?' she asked him.

'I've just told you, it's... I'm a friend of your daughter's, of Connie.'

'A friend?'

'Yes, I've come to see you. That bun looks nice, are you going to eat it?'

'Oh, is it a bun? I'm hungry.' She picked it up and took a bite. 'Mmm, that's nice, have you got the thing? You know, where the trees are.'

'Rupert looked at Constance.

'It's okay mother, just drink your tea and eat up.'

Constance went out of the room again. He followed her into the kitchen.

'I'm not sure how or if I can help, I feel rather useless.'

'Well, you got her to eat a bun. Thing is, she's not only getting confused, but losing her vocabulary. Perhaps the two go in tandem.'

'Maybe. Shouldn't think you'd want to analyse it, though.'

'Sometimes it takes my mind off it.

'Of feeling it?'

'Suppose so. She's losing herself. She's not her.'

'I guess it's like being with another person, a stranger. Sorry if that's painful.'

'But it's true though, it *is* like that.'

'Come here,' Rupert said, and hugged her.

She pulled away from him and wiped her eyes.

'It's no use me wallowing in it, it won't help.'

'You're not. Let it come out.'

'I'm holding it in for a reason; if I'm to look after her I need to keep a clear head.'

'To decide about a carer?'

She was silent for a while.

'Perhaps.'

'Can you afford one?'

Mother's got some savings, I could draw on them. I don't know how she would react to one, though. It would stop her wanderings, but to do that it would, I suppose, need a full-time one.'

'Does she do that?'

'She went to see a friend in the next street recently and went there in only a dressing gown and odd shoes. It upset her friend. She felt, I think, that I should be looking after her all the time. And then... Oh, It doesn't matter.'

'What doesn't?'

She hesitated before saying, 'The next day she left the house after I'd gone and walked to that new block of flats across the park. She walked into an open front door and laid on a settee in someone's front room. A woman came in and told her to go. Mummy didn't reply and the woman called the police.'

'What did they do?'

'Took her to the local hospital. I knew something was wrong because she wasn't home when I came and she's always in at that time. I phoned the police and they told me to call the hospital. She had no identification with her but she'd told them her name. I should, really, go and apologise to the woman.'

He hugged her again. She eased away.

'It's alright, I have to accept it.'

She gave him a strained smile and said, 'What would your Mister Marx say to all this, eh?'

'Don't know. Perhaps what she has is genetically distributed, but there's little doubt that the middle class tend to get less illnesses and live longer than thir manual counterparts. An upper middle class woman can expect to live some fifteen years longer than a male labourer.'

'I can't see that applying to my mother'. She looked at him. 'It can kill, you know.' She took a deep breath. 'Let's go for a walk shall we? There's still some light left,   mother can come. Let's go towards town.'

She went into the dining room and asked her mother if she'd had enough to eat.

'I'm not hungry how. Who's that behind you?'

'My friend. We'll have a walk now; I'll get your warm coat.'

She left the room.

'D'you like walking?' her mother asked him.

'Yes, I don't do as much as I should, too busy reading and writing.'

'I used to read books but... the thing gets in the way'

Constance appeared with a thick, fur coat and told her mother to stand. After her coat was put on, done up and, when her daughter had put on a jacket, the three of them went to the front door and out of the house.

They walked along, Constance placing her mother's arm in her own and Rupert walking on the outside of them. He asked the older woman her name.

'It's Cissy.'

'It's Cecilia, but people often call her Cissy. Don't they mother,' Constance said, giving her a kiss on the cheek.

'What do you like looking at best when you're walking?' he asked her.

'Those things,' she said, pointing to the homes opposite.

'What else?'

'The green things.'

'Trees? So do I, especially when there's leaves on them,'

'Where have the leaves gone?'

'It's winter now. They'll be back.'

He looked about him; the last light of a weak sun had gone and street lights were coming on, throwing the houses and trees into silhouette. He walked a pace behind the two of them, looked at their backs, noticed again the firm yet feminine walk of Constance - somehow he couldn't quite refer to her as 'Connie' to himself - how upright she was, occasionally looking down at her mother working hard to keep up with her, sometimes frowning, sometimes smiling.

The streetlight rather strangely reminded him of Paris. Not so much the Rococo, Napoleonic, the Place de l'Opera, but a Lavirotte building, the Coulée Verte, the Métro entrances, while across a narrow street a lamp on the corner of a building perhaps illuminated an embracing couple. He looked at his girl again. He would like to have been in Paris embracing her or, at this moment, doing so in the middle of the Sahara or an Arctic tundra.

He heard Cecilia suddenly ask her daughter where her father was.

'He's not here, mummy, he died a long while ago.'

'Died?'

'Afraid so. But we're here, you're here, so that's good isn't it.'

'Who was he?'

'Your husband.'

'What was he like?'

'I'm afraid I don't really remember, but he was a nice man. He must have been, he wouldn't have been my daddy otherwise.'

'Where's that man?'

'What man?'

'Your... friend thing.'

'The one who's walking with us?'

She glanced across at Rupert.

'I'm here, Cissy. Hello, enjoying your walk?'

'We're walking now, aren't we?'

'We are.'

'Are you hungry, mother?' her daughter asked, 'If so, we can go to the place on the corner. Come on, it may make you feel more like eating.'

She held her mother's hand, crossed the road and the three of them went into a café. It was almost empty. They sat by the window, each having Welsh rarebit, Constance cutting up her mother's into small portions and leaving just one on her plate

'If she sees the whole slice she'd say it was too much for her, this way I can feed her separate pieces.'

Rupert pondered briefly and said quietly, 'It does seem that she needs a carer. I know little about this sort of thing, but it looks as if someone needs to be with her most of the time. I may be wrong, but - '

'You're not wrong. I have contacted one, she's from a care home not far away, I'm seeing her tomorrow.' We'll see what happens. It sounds cruel but I don't want to give up my job, such as it is, it's an income.'

They ate their food and walked the short distance back to the woman's home, where he said goodbye to them both, kissing Constance and whispering, 'I miss you.'

He looked back at the house where she was waving from behind the front window, and returned to his room. He sporadically read and took some notes until he felt tired enough to sleep. Before doing so he thought of Constance and the effect on her of her breaking parent, one whose mind seemed to be separating from her personality and the things it had learned dropping from her and blowing away into a place from which it would never return. Lovemaking now seemed a thing apart, sex a forbidden land.

25

He was in the pub getting ready for his first union meeting. He and Bishop had put two dozen chairs in rows, not that George was expecting that many to be sat on, and 'though the room wasn't finished, it was, of course, useable. He had been talking to Enid downstairs, who he still hadn't told about the site fatality. He'd asked his men to tell all the painters they knew about the gathering and had placed hand-written notes around the site in case other workers knew any decorators themselves. He'd also fastened a small notice on the door of the public bar informing anyone who cared to read it of what would be happening in the events room.

The go-slow had lasted only two days, probably, he thought, because the men had been bored, they could have done the work they had in half a day and, preferably, spent the rest of the time at home. There had been reluctance about their movements as if they hadn't really cared whether their tasks were done well or, perhaps, not at all. 'If a job's worth doing it's worth doing badly,' he'd heard one of the chippies say. There had been talk of holding some subcontractors to account, but, as far as he knew, no action had been taken

He wasn't feeling very inspired, but had broadly rehearsed what he intended to say. Most of the painters on the site had come in together, one of whom he knew would be missing, and there were a few other people climbing the stairs to the room. He had told them not to buy drinks until the meeting had finished.

There were a few more than he'd expected, and after they'd put their names and addresses on the sheet of paper that he'd placed just inside the door and had taken their seats, he began.

'Er, good evening. Welcome to the first get-together of the Holborn branch of the Painters and Decorators Union.' He looked around him. 'Actually, we were only officially validated this morning when I received the appropriate documents from Head Office. Thing is, as individual operatives we don't have much power or control on the job, we're pretty much on our own, but on a site we have each other.'

He looked in the direction of those he hadn't seen before just in case they may have been feeling left out.

'If you're working for a small contractor you may not be earning as much as for a bigger one, I don't know, but perhaps you have a sense of loyalty to them. If you're with a larger firm, maybe it's more impersonal and unless the money's good you're less satisfied. Whatever the situation, you find out by a kind of bush telegraph what others are earning on what firms and on what sites.

'I can't make you feel you're getting enough or otherwise, or if your conditions are crappy or not, I just want to let you know that we're in it together. It's a kind of moral thing I s'pose, a sort of gathering of people who share the same means of making a living.' He looked around him. 'Look, what I mean, really, is that we can come here once a month or so and have our moans and complaints, and if we can talk about them, maybe we can... do something about them.'

Surprisingly there were a few 'Hear, hears'.

'Thanks. Are there any particular concerns, any complaints, any... perceived unfairness on any of your jobs?'

Stan, the eldest of George's gang, said, 'Well, we know about our own site, but things seem back to normal now, 'though we ain't forgettin' what happened.'

One of the decorators who came from other jobs asked what was being referred to. He was told.

'Cheap labour, there's more of it about, it can be dangerous.'

'It was,' said Stan.

'As you know, we're keeping an eye on the situation,' George said. He looked around him. 'Doesn't seem as if there's much more to say really, at least we know we've got somewhere to come, official-like as it were, if we've got any grievances,'

'As George knows,' Stan said, 'we don't carry much weight, but I s'pose the ounces, when put together, can add up to a few pounds.'

'You've got a point,' said the ex-apprentice, 'but the guv'nors have the hundredweights.'

'We know that,' Stan said, 'but let's go downstairs for a bevvy.' He looked at George. 'Alright with you?'

'Sure. Meeting over then. Let's meet again next month, ll let you know. Thanks for coming.'

They made their way out of the room with George following them downstairs to the bar where Enid busied herself serving them. He watched her, noting how quickly and competently she did her job, how she smiled when handing out a glass or packet of crisps. He felt almost jealous, wanting her to smile at him. She did so and tacitly pointed to the end of the counter. While the others sat themselves around a table, he went to where she'd indicated. She came to him.

'I was behind the door and listened to your little speech,' she whispered. It was good, I was quite impressed.'

'You're not just saying that?'

'Well, it was hardly - '

'Fist-punching-the-air stuff'

'No, but it was sensible. What else could you have said? You were hardly about to start a revolution, were you. Incidentally, my dad was going to come, he wanted to help you if you needed it. I told him not to.'

'Nice of him, I'd like to have met him.'

The thought came that perhaps she hadn't wanted her father to meet him.

As if again, guessing his thoughts, she said, 'It's alright, I'd be quite happy for him to meet you.' She gave an almost provocative smile. 'In fact, I think I'd like him to.'

She gave his hand a quick squeeze. 'I can see you in a little while if you're staying, Bishop's letting me go early; he does that sometimes.'

She went to the other end of the counter to serve a customer.

George joined the others.

'D'you know the barmaid then?' asked one of his gang.

'A little bit.'

'How come then? It ain't you that's doin' up that room, is it?'

'Well, actually… That was a good guess, if it had been a bigger one, or needed to be done quicker, I'd have asked for help.'

'It's okay mate, we've got trouble-and-strifes to think of, we can't work all the time. You're on yer own, your time's yours, when it ain't Symonds' o' course. It's alright.'

Stan, holding up his glass, then said, 'Anyway, 'ere's to our little union.'

'To the Holborn Tavern,' they said with raised voices as if it had been rehearsed.

'Ere,' said Stan, ''eard the one about the painter who refused to charge for the paint after he'd done the outside of a bloke's home? It's on the 'ouse' he said.'

There were a few groans.

Another of them said, 'What about the blokes who were paintin' a church and didn't have enough paint, so they thinned it with water. A thunderstorm came and washed it all away. A voice boomed down from the clouds, 'Repaint and thin no more.''

There were some louder groans.

A few more jokes were told and some more drinks ordered. George occasionally laughed but his attention was again on Enid. After a snack or two had been ordered. Enid brought them over with a smile, retaining it a little stoically after a 'You're a right little darlin'', and 'Watcha yer doin' later, luv?'

Although knowing it was typical workers' ribaldry he felt immediately on guard and protective. She gave him a wink as she left their table as if saying, 'It's okay, it means nothing.' She bent briefly towards him and whispered, 'I'll be ready in half an hour.'

The new union members began leaving, with George telling them he was staying, responded to by a knowing grin from Stan. He went upstairs, taking the chairs back from where they came and rubbing down some filling on the skirting boards; he didn't need his overalls on for that. He returned downstairs and sat by the exit for a while until she came towards him.

He stood. 'You don't look like a barmaid when you're not wearing your apron.'

'What do I look like then?'

'A pretty girl… woman.'

'Thank you, kind sir. Shall we go?'

'I'll come back with you if you like, at least part of the way to keep you company.'

'Feeling protective?'

'Not really, more a wish to be with you - is it reciprocated?'

'Yes. Let's walk this way, she said, pointing westwards. They went towards Cambridge Circus.

'We could go to Trafalgar Square, I like seeing Nelson's column for some reason, and the National Gallery all lit up.'

'Don't fancy Charing Cross Road, though,' he said.

'Why?'

'All the stuff in the surgical shops: the trusses for hernias, the artificial limbs and such.'

'Not very sexy, eh?'

'Something like that.'

'Well, we're all bones and organs and blood and flesh and so forth.'

'A bit more than that.'

They turned into Shaftesbury Avenue then into Charing Cross Road.

'I'll shut my eyes now,' George said, 'so I don't see those shops.'

'You won't be able to see the lights if you do. It's so different walking in the dark. I walk along a street during the day and the same street at night could be a different land.'

'Sometimes, when I walk past a particular building or house, say in the Victorian style, and somebody comes out of it, if they're not wearing a high collar, bow tie, waistcoat and frock coat, I feel disappointed.'

'For a little while, part of you is actually living in that period.'

'That's what it feels like. I want to rush up to him and say, 'Get back indoors again, you have no right living in this house.'

'A bit harsh, that. Going back to what we mentioned, I read somewhere that we're little more than stimulus-response mechanisms. What d'you think?'

'As said, we're more than that, and what about human consciousness? Perhaps there's no answer.'

'Did you notice those theatre entrances? There's something about them, isn't there,' she said, halting a moment. 'The way they're lit, the bare bulbs dotted in the ceilings.'

'And in the foyer was Charles Boyer.'

'And Clark Gable acts as well as he is able.'

'Yes, the lights enticing us in, an escape from the world of grey London skies, of the clacking of horses hooves, of the iron rumbling of trams, of the newsboys shouting "Star', 'News', 'Standard' as they hand out the papers.'

'You're a poet, George.'

'Hardly. I can see your Column now against the evening sky.'

They turned along the front of the Art Gallery. Stopping outside of it he told her that he'd seen Goya's La Maja desnuda there once with a friend and that it was the first time he had been to an art gallery.

'I don't know what it means, though.'

'The naked goddess of springtime, warmth and increase, a sort of mother.

'Clever you.'

'I just happen to know it, that's all.' She looked at her watch. 'I think I'd better be getting off home now.'

'Already? I'll come to your station with you.'

They went to the station at the corner of the Square, changed trains a few stops later and were on their way to East London. Other than making references to occasional art gallery visits when young with her father - recalling a painting with 'lots of strange people and animals', which she thought was a Bruegel - they were comfortably silent.

Their destination reached, she said, 'Well, I'll see you tomorrow, or whenever you're finishing the room.'

'I'd like to come and see where you live, if that's okay. I won't get a ladder and peer in through the bedroom window one night. Honest.'

After a brief silence she said, 'Alright, if you want to, don't know what my dad'll say, though, if he sees you.'

'Not 'Who's that fine-looking fellow you're with?''

'Perhaps not, he can be rather strict.'

'You never mention your mother.'

'She's long gone; she died when I was a child in Wales. You don't talk about your father.'

'Same really, he was killed in the last war.'

'I'm sorry.'

'It's okay.'

The street wasn't far away. It was not unlike the one he was brought up in, nor was the house with its narrow bay window, small front garden and arched porch.

She let herself in with a, 'Hello, dad.'

George quickly noted the hall's floral-patterned wallpaper, small chandelier, the gloss on the doors then a stocky, broad-shouldered, man who appeared from the front room.

'Hello, and who's this then?'

'A friend - George. He's the one I told you about, from the pub. He's doing the room there.'

He held his hand out for the visitor to shake.

'You're the painter, eh? Me too, as Enid's probably told you. Want tea or a nightcap?'

'The latter, if may.'

'You may. Make yourself comfortable.'

He beckoned George into the room and went over to a cocktail cabinet. 'Whisky?'

'Small one, please.'

'I'll make myself a cocoa,' said Enid, walking to the end of the passage.

George, now in an armchair, was given his drink and asked where he was working.

'Nearby, eh? So that's how you met Enid. She mentioned a union. Is that correct?'

'Yes. I've just started one, not many of us there, but one or two from other jobs.

'Why did you want to start it?'

George told him of the accident on the suite, its apparent cause and the resulting action that had been taken.

'Bit horrible for you, eh? You're not going to get much out of a go-slow, though.'

'I'm aware of that'.

'All the men for it? Foreman, too?'

'I am the foreman.'

'You're pretty young.'

'It's my first time in charge, I do the signwriting mostly.'

'Gill Sans, Roman eight point, et cetera?'

'And more.'

'What did you discuss at your meeting? Incidentally, don't forget to ask for their dues, it's easy to forget 'em.'

'Not much; just laid out the reasons for a union, really.'

'Yeah, a fair day's pay and so forth. It's a get-together, but on a national scale we hope for some sort of solidarity, don't we. But toshing's a nomadic sort of life, which doesn't really make for togetherness and a fight against greed.'

'Some bosses are greedier than others.'

'Of course, but it's still a good rake-off for 'em.'

'Be no jobs without them, I guess.'

'Doesn't *have* to be like that, and they need us as much as we need them.'

'Almost. But it makes me mad, this cheap labour thing.'

'We're nearly all cheap labour.'

'Maybe, but there's 'cheap' and 'cheap.''

'If you're making money for someone, arguably, by definition, you're cheap.'

'I make money for old Symonds, he's my guv'nor, I cut corners; two coats instead of the three specified, et cetera, you know, the usual thing, but the work looks good and I'm pretty fast. Other than the 'writing, I've done quite a few jobs for him and made money over and above, but never asked for a bonus and he's never given me one, except a drink at Christmas.'

'Feeling unappreciated?' It was Enid standing just inside the door with a cup of steaming cocoa in her hand.

'Could be.'

'*I* appreciate you.'

'Thanks.' He turned to her father again. 'Anyway, short of a revolution, it looks like it's going to stay the same.'

'That's the way it appears, but a socialist government could get some things done, like strikes being legal again, more social security, pensions, perhaps even some sort of State health scheme. Anyway, all these things will have their origin in Marx, I suppose.'

'I know only the broad brush stokes of him, really.'

'An apt phrase, coming from you. But most of the changes that are good for the masses will, perhaps, in the end, have been inspired by his ideas. Though, maybe, as he thought that history was a result of material conditions rather than ideas, he would have said that his notions sprang from those. He's everywhere, though, isn't he, Jesuit schools are taught about him, South American generals speak of him, priests are accused of being among his followers, et cetera. Fancy another?'

George lifted his glass. 'Thanks, but this is enough for me.'

The man looked across at his daughter.

'She's heard all this before and she probably wants to get to bed. Anyway, I've to be up early, I'm working over the other side of London.'

Moving towards George, he said, 'Don't bother to stand,' shook his hand and told him to finish his glass before he went. 'Goodnight.'

As he left the room George heard him say to his daughter, 'Don't be long.'

She sat down opposite George.

'Couple of little hints there.'

'I know. I should be going.'

'He was trying to impress you.'

'He did.'

She looked at him. 'I may be wrong but when I left the room I thought I heard you say something about an accident you witnessed.'

'Er... yes, I did.'

'Why didn't you tell me about it?'

'I didn't want to upset you, it wasn't very pleasant.'

'That's hardly sharing is it?'

'No, I should have told you. I wanted to.'

'Anyway, it's time for my bed now. Nighty-night.'

As he went by her to the front door he kissed her cheek and told her he would see her the next day.

Turning into the darkened street he made his way back to the station. He thought of what he'd done that evening. It wasn't bad. Perhaps he was growing up a little. He thought also of her using the word 'sharing'. He liked it. His step became a little lighter.

26

It felt almost natural that he should shop at Harrods to buy Christmas gifts. Of course it wasn't, it was a progression from John Lewis in his teens and then, as his father's development company grew larger and more successful, to here, although he certainly wasn't a regular customer.

There were neon tubes that lit twinkling Christmas trees, men's suits, women's dresses and lingerie, Dutch cheeses, German sausages, French and Mediterranean dishes, and fresh salmon glistened. There were children's clothes, pedal cars, Shirley Temple dolls, pea shooters, board games, toy guns and yachts. Tiny papier mâché elves seemed to be dotted everywhere; standing on the confectionery counter, on the shoulders of suits and even on the heads of some of the mannequins in the window displays.

He hadn't bothered much about what to get his father, it would be the usual Havana cigars, but he wanted his mother to have something special. He would get something here for Constance, but was putting off the present for his mother, it had to be appropriate and also have meaning. She was opening in her new play the day after Boxing Day and he was hoping to see her, though wasn't sure whether his father would be there.

Moving towards the jewellery counter he saw a silver bracelet. It reminded him of one she often wore when he was a child. The memory produced a good feeling. He would buy it, at least, for him, it would be special.

He had arrived here early and instead of waiting outside for Eric, had gone inside. After his purchase, he returned to the entrance to see if his friend had arrived. He had, wearing a blue-striped blazer, cravat and brogues.

'You look even posher than usual today,' said Rupert.

'Roopy, what's in there? Wonderful things? Glorious glitz to put the masses in a state of delirium?'

'Hardly the masses here, old chap, and many have their opiate, anyway.'

'Talking of religion, are you going to church in the hols?'

'Non.'

'Think I'll have to, pater will insist. I want something for my baby, I've got her a wedding present - me - but not yet a festive one. Shall we go in?'

He gave a little skip and they went through the revolving door.

'Ah, the wonders, 'tis just the same, this was probably my first Christmas experience. I was brought here as a tot, by nanny I suppose, apparently daddy was going to make a bid for this place at the time. Imagine that, I could have lived here amongst the lead soldiers, rocking horses, the Meccano.' He spread his arms and spun around. 'All this. I could have chosen any present; a toy car - '

'A real one.'

'Could have had all the trees and put them in my bedroom, sat on Santa's knee and asked for - '

'Demanded.'

'Yes, anything. I could have *been* Santa.'

'You could have had little boys sitting on your knee.'

'I prefer big girls. Let's start on the top floor.'

They went into the lift.

'Who are you here for, Roop? Family? And surely, Constance.'

'Have just bought something for mum, and it's Cubans for him.'

'Show me what you bought mumsy.'

He was shown.

'Sweet. She'll like it I'm sure. I want something exotic for my love.'

They got out at the top floor and walked around looking at miscellaneous but interesting objects then went to the men's designer collection, Eric leading.

'Surely you have your own tailor?' asked Rupert.

'Of course, he's making my wedding suit, but I need another suit, anyway.'

After a brief look, he said, 'That's a rather nice thing, looks like a Panama regular, it'd look dandy with a blue tie and pale-grey waistcoat.'

He beckoned an assistant to him who quickly granted the request to try the suit on. It fitted well, and after a brief look at waistcoats and ties, Eric seemed to have got what he wanted.

'That was quick.'

'I know what I want when I see it.'

'Is that how you obtained Fiona.'

'More or less, but I had to woo her.'

'You've never told me how you met her.'

'I was walking the dog one day and it barked at her as she was passing. It was a rather large beast and it frightened her. I happened to see her a week later at precisely the same spot. We chatted and I managed to persuade her to meet up the next day. She lived, as she still does, some way from the family home, but she'd happened to be visiting an auntie. I persuaded her to give me her address and began writing to her, with no reply. I wrote again and she answered. It was sort of at my insistence that we began corresponding regularly and also, occasionally, meeting. It went from there. A rather ordinary tale, but she is my extraordinary gal.'

'She is. Are you going to buy those items now?'

'Yes, papa has an account here. I'll have them sent to my rooms. Let's wander down.'

They descended via the stairs a couple of floors and looked at club chairs, Chesterfield sofas, black mahogany wardrobes, tables and drinks display cabinets.

'I'm becoming domesticated, old boy,' said Eric.

'Happens to us all I suppose.'

'And mine is happening in the New Year. How's the speech coming?'

'I'll get around to it, don't worry.'

After disinterestedly glancing at lawnmowers, shears and other gardening tools, they went down a floor.

'How's Constance?'

'Struggling.'

'Why?'

'Her mother's ill, she's beginning to need constant care.'

'Is that a play on 'Constance'?'

'No, the subject doesn't warrant levity I'm afraid.'

'Sorry.'

'Until there's some care available, she may have to give up her job.'

''The Bodleian won't be the same without her. Let us bolt into the Arcade for some tea and on the way there'll be a whole pot-pourri of female fancies, fetishes and fads some of which I shall purchase.'

Rupert agreed and they went down to the second floor where his friend bought a Valentino Voce gift set of perfumes. There were scents, hair dyes, lotions, shiny brushes laid out on counters and stacked high at their sides; they seemed to appeal greatly to Eric.

'I sometimes think I would like to be a member of the fair sex for a little while, all their goodies, the odours, their... things.'

He walked away from a counter, turned to Rupert and swayed calculatingly towards him, saying as he did so, 'Don't you think I'd make the most gorgeous model?'

'You were very convincing, you girl-boy, you. I'll buy you a pair of high-heels and a little black number and you can parade in front of your pa.'

'Oh, Lordy, he would erupt, Vesuvius would look like a damp squib in comparison.'

'You have brought bountiful gifts.'

'I want something more for her.'

Rupert asked him if Fiona would spend Christmas at his parents' home.

'Yes, she came for the first time two years ago, last year I went to Neasden. This time it's special, though.

''Cos you'll be nuptial'd soon after.'

'Indeed.'

'Would it interrupt your festive frolics if I were to ask you to come to see mother's play? It's at the Royal Adelphi the day after Boxing Day, I'm sure she can get the tickets.'

'Connie going?'

'I hope so. It's 'The Cat and the Canary'.'

'Fiona will have heard of it, she'll certainly want to go. Ah, here's the tea room.'

They went through a leaf-decorated opening into a spacious but crowded dining room and sat at the remaining vacant table.

'She loves the Cleopatra play, you know,' said Eric. He widened his eyes. 'I could get her a Cleo dress, could I not, a shimmering white thing with a diamond-encrusted tiara, although I don't think pater would sanction that, 'though I could get some gold-coloured paper chains and make one out of those.'

'Or perhaps you could get the regal collection milk chocolate coin for her stocking.'

Rupert glanced around him at the multi-paned windows which were framed by holly, a silver-coloured sled full of colourfully-wrapped gift boxes, a wooden reindeer with a bejewelled collar, and the coiffeur'd waitresses whose aprons were embroidered with a nativity scene. There was a tall man dressed in a dark suit with a large clump of holly in his buttonhole who may have been the manager and who was moving slowly around quietly smiling at everyone.

Rupert was about to tell his companion how pleasant he thought the place was and how tasty the recently-arrived scones were, when he noticed that he was looking down at his untouched tea with a rather serious expression.

Rupert asked him if anything was amiss.

Eric promptly looked up.

'Er… nothing.'

'Yes there is. What is it?'

There was a hesitation, then 'Fiona,' he said quietly, 'she's pregnant.'

'Your Fiona?'

'Yes.'

'Is that not good then?'

'I suppose it is, 'though not right now, I'd have preferred to have waited a while. She'd only just found out and was going to tell me the evening I suggested we get hitched.'

''Insisted'?'

'Suppose so.'

'Quite a coincidence.'

'Precisely, but who's going to believe it? The parents will think we feel we *have* to get married. They won't like that, especially the old man, I haven't told him we're getting married yet.'

'They like her don't they?'

'They seem to, but conception out of wedlock and all that, and the idea of 'having' to wed, they're the big ones.'

'You'll have to tell them, and the longer you leave it the worse it will be. You've explained it to me simply enough, tell him to look up the word 'coincidence.''

'It still means we shouldn't have done it though, he can be a little religious, pater. All these 'shoulds' and 'should nots.' Can't get an 'is' from an 'ought' can we.'

'Like I've said, you should be doing philosophy.'

'Can't talk this away, though it's a pity you can't have a word with my sire and explain that they're not rules set in stone.'

'Merely uncodified laws that we nearly all live by. Anyway, you'll have two babies; think of all that love you can give. Next year you can buy a toy reindeer, and a real one for Fiona.'

'Perhaps she can ride it and pull me into paradise on a sled.' He paused again. 'I don't think he'll believe me. It'll be the shame of it, thinking that other people will assume that we feel we have to wed.'

'You don't need to tell people she's preggers yet.'

'No, but when it's born, people will work it out, it's simple maths.'

'It's not as if it's happening to him though, it's his son.'

'That will be almost as bad.'

'Well, worse things happen at sea.'

'Must be a nasty place, the sea.'

'Drink your tea, eat your scone.'

'Then I must be going.'

'To tell pa?'

'Afraid so.'

Eric finished his food in silence, wiped his mouth with a napkin, got up and went out of the room with Rupert following him. They walked down the stairs and out through the revolving doors where they briefly shook hands with Rupert wishing his friend luck as the latter climbed into a taxi. He looked at Rupert through its window and gave a shrug and the gesture of a wave.

Realising that neither of them had paid for their snack, Rupert returned to the tea room and did so. He then, unlike Eric who had returned to the family home, headed for Knightsbridge station on the way back to his rooms. He thought briefly of Andrew but decided not to attempt to visit him; there had been no contact since their last telephone conversation. It was thoughts of Constance that were more pleasing, he had bought presents for her in Oxford, he had gone to the store mainly to see his friend.

At Paddington, the locomotive was ready to leave and after finding a window seat and watching metropolis turn to country, he wondered how he would feel If the same thing happened to Constance. He wasn't sure.

He wanted her, wanted her with him at Oxford, wanted her life to be unhampered by her mother's difficulties, and there was little chance, anyway, of her having the freedom, the time to conceive. And how would *she* feel about such an event? He pushed away the thought that she wouldn't want it and tried to bury the sudden feeling of hurt. He was, he thought, being rather childish. He allowed his pedantry to correct himself; only children could be childish, he was being 'childlike.'

It was late when he arrived at his room and it was getting cold. He had started undressing when there was a tap on the door; it was a student from a few rooms away who had picked up the ringing telephone in the quad.

'It's for you, it's a woman.'

Rupert moved quickly into the quad. It was Constance.

'Just to see if you were in and to say hello,' she said.

He asked her where she was speaking from.

'The phone box near the house, I've pointed it out to you. I'll give you the number and we can arrange when to call each other. I got the one near your room from the librarian.'

'You won't be seeing him much.'

'No, and you know why. I'll work when I can.'

'How is she?'

'A little worse if anything, she's not eating, though it could change tomorrow, she may want to go out for a walk and I could take her to the café.'

She asked him what he had been doing. He told her.

'Harrods, eh? You're living the life.'

'Hardly. I could with you, though.'

'That'd be nice, but… '

'I know.'

'How's your friend?'

'He had some news, I'll tell you later.'

'Top secret?'

'Not really. Is the Library paying you?'

'So far, 'though I don't think there's provision for caring for a relative.'

'They won't sack you.'

'I could be.'

'It's not as if it's a money-making institution and you're draining their profits.'

'It's not a charity, either. What did Eric buy? The whole store?'

'I think he wanted to.'

He asked her what she was doing at Christmas.

'What do you think?'

'Mum, of course. And you?'

'Parents' place. I want to see you.'

'Ditto.'

'I can see you the day before, but not for long because - '

'The trains finish early.'

'Should have learned to drive, couldn't be bothered; wished I had.'

'It's only a few days away, come to see me then, I shall almost certainly be here.'

He told her of his mother's play and asked if there was any way she could go with him.

'There's a neighbour, a midwife, she's volunteered to stay overnight if I ever needed her to.'

'Ask her then.'

'I don't like to, but I shall.'

'Good.'

'I'm going now, Rupert, I'll see you some time on Christmas Eve then, I'll also try to ring you. Goodnight.'

As he replaced the phone he had the feeling that, somehow, *she* was the invalid, that he was almost… caring for her, from a distance, beginning to will her to get through the day after being frustrated and hurt that she appeared increasingly unknown to her mother, as if she wasn't her daughter.

It was good to speak with her, to hear her voice, a familiar one, yet there nearly always seemed to be something new in it, a slight lifting or falling, a different cadence he couldn't recall hearing before. He hoped it would always be thus.

27

'Oh, blimey, George. For good?'

'Yes.'

'I can't say I'm really surprised. I think I saw it coming, but wouldn't admit it to myself.'

She looked at him with a sideways turn of her head.

'I've asked you this before, you did what you were supposed to do in the bedroom, didn't you?'

'Oh, please, mum.'

He had summoned the courage to tell his mother that Doris had left him. They were sitting in her parlour.

He mused on what she meant by 'supposed to'. It was as if it was a ritual, a rigidly- defined process that allowed for little variety of mood; of feeling, or actions. He wondered briefly what his father had done, or perhaps not done, in the boudoir and how it had affected his wife, whether it was 'Wham-bang-thank-you-ma'am', and whether she had expected no more. He decided to stop dwelling on the subject.

'Took long enough to tell me, didn't it?'

'I'm sorry, I should have said earlier.'

'Well, it's out now. You'd have thought she'd have dropped me a line, though, wouldn't you, I thought we got on okay. I suppose she wanted it all over with, put behind her. Anyway, how are you faring?'

'Okay, I haven't done much, but there's plenty going on at work.'

'Well, you wanted to buy that house and you've got it all to yourself now. How does it feel?'

'Alright. It felt a bit big at first, lots of space, but it's okay now.'

'Well, it's quite a big house.'

'Not as big as some of the houses I've done up.'

'Perhaps you'll invite me over more often now, eh? I can get lonely too, you know.'

''Course.'

'There's plenty more fish in the sea, as they say.'

'I'm not a fisherman, mum, but if I saw one swimming by… '

'Funny. Still doing your signwriting?'

'No, I'm in charge of a job in the West End now.'

'Good for you. Perhaps you'll get a big tip, you need the cash coming in for your mortgage.'

'Don't get tips on sites, mum.'

'Another cuppa?'

'Yeah, ta.'

She went to make it. Telling her hadn't been as bad as he thought it would be. She returned, handed him his tea and said, 'You wouldn't have heard what happened to Mrs. Fox would you, she had the brokers in. They came in with their suits on, opened a window and threw out all her bits and pieces onto the road. The old girl came out, gathered up her things, sat on the doorstep and tried to sell them. I think a couple of her neighbours bought a bit. She had enough, I think, to pay the brokers when they came back so she could stay there a little longer. I hope so, anyway. If she has more trouble I'll offer to take her in for a few days, poor old thing.

'I remember, as a kid, that happening to someone next door to us and the men that came wore top hats and tails. People used do a moonlight flit if they couldn't pay their rent. I thought those days were over, but now we're in this bloody slump.'

'It seems so unfair doesn't it, people rich enough to buy houses letting to people with, in places like Stepney and Bethnal Green, eight in a room, kids, no bathroom, nor even a tin bath and just a tap in the back garden.'

'While the owners live in mansions, I suppose. It was even worse when I was a kid. Your granny used to boil the milk so it wouldn't go sour, there were no 'fridges so we often had con-densed milk, a bit like now, really. Some people - we were a bit lucky 'cos dad was a tally man in the docks, as you know - could hardly afford a penn'orth of bread or ha'p'orth of jam. Five kids to a bed sometimes, couldn't have been healthy for 'em, poor lit-tle sods.

'It was easier if you lived near the Lanes, Petticoat and Brick Lanes, like I did, you could nick things from the stalls, I never did, of course. At Spitalfields Market there was always stuff lying around that they were throwing away 'cos they couldn't sell it. And the houses, they called them 'gardens' but there was hardly any grass in most of 'em. I remember when I was a kid, seeing little Sylvie across the road looking at a tree over the park - granny used to take me over there quite often - sort of stroking it and looking a bit surprised, I don't think she'd been near one before.'

'It's getting like it again in places, there's more people unemployed now than there's ever been, I think.'

'What goes round comes round, but there's always the UIAB, they look after the workers who've used up their insurance benefits don't they?'

'They're still **means-tested**, and it certainly doesn't help everyone. There's riots in Manchester, Dublin, on Merseyside, in Wales and other places; people don't protest for nothing. The National Unemployed Workers Union organised some of them, justified too.'

'Aren't they them 'communists' or something?'

'So what?' And does there have to be this much unfairness?'

'Depends what you call 'fairness' I s'pose.'

'Okay, so you can't have complete fairness, but it doesn't have to be *that* unfair.'

'What can be done about it?'

'Not much, maybe, but... something. I can imagine the landowners - I think there's only about ten people who own all the land in this county - riding to hounds in their jodhpurs and letting their dogs loose to tear out animals' guts then shooting birds for the fun of it and, while they're enjoying themselves, not giving a toss for the people in their properties, like those you've just talked about, and just raking in taken-for-granted cash.'

'What's got into you, George?'

'Just that it makes my blood boil at it all.'

'Sometimes I think you should be at Speakers' Corner on a soapbox.

'Maybe one day, got a bit of learning to do first, though.'

'You're not as backward at coming forward these days are you?'

'Probably not.'

'Actually, I've seen worse than I've told you. During the war, a lot of shops with German-sounding names, and there were quite a few in the East End, were raided by looters who were not really against the Germans but were simply out to get anything they could; I suppose if you're hungry, stealing's not such a terrible thing to do. They used to get a boy, give him a brick and say 'Throw it through that window,' and as soon as the glass was broken, the mob used to move in. I remember little Billy, Mrs. Green's boy, he had to throw a brick once, too scared not to, I suppose. They'd clear the premises, whatever they were, butchers or bakers, whatever.'

'It might seem like mob rule, mum, but if you're hungry, you're hungry.'

'You remind me of your father sometimes, you know. He'd go on about the rich, the 'ruling class' he called them.'

'You've said this before. Wish I'd known him for longer.'

'I know you do, son.'

'I've started a little union branch at work, don't know how it'll go, but it's something.'

'He'd have been proud of you.'

'Doubt it, but … anyway. Was thinking the other day that, really, it was a good thing that we didn't know how dad died. I think you told me at the time that he'd gone away and couldn't come back, so I wouldn't see him again.'

"Reported Missing', yes.'

'Better than knowing the gory details.'

His mother was silent for moment then said, 'I want to show you something,' and went out of the room..

He heard her, briefly, overhead in her bedroom before she came down the stairs and into the room again. She handed him a sheet of paper from an exercise book

'He wrote this to me and gave it to another soldier who managed to survive the war and who gave it to me. 'Cos I was out, staying at Aunt Jessie's at Southend - you just may remember her - he put it through the door with a note explaining about it. It was at one of the battles of Wipers that he went missing.

'Ypres', it's in Belgium, I think.'

'Never mind, read it.'

He began reading it aloud. 'Dear Ethel. Don't know whether this will get to you, but there's another battle starting and we're in it again. I think of you a lot, and George, of course. I probably won't recognise him when I do see him again. I'll recognise you though, my darling. All my love. Albert x.'

He looked up. 'Why didn't you show me this before?'

'I don't know, I didn't want to show it you when you were little, it was painful, and you'd have asked me what a 'battle' was and things like that. I should have let you see it before this, though. I'm sorry.

He put his arm around her shoulders. 'It's okay mum. I'm glad you've shown me it, it must mean a lot to you.'

''Course it does.'

As he moved away from her he thought he saw tears in her eyes.

'You know, I wish you could find someone you could love,' she said. 'I'd be jealous of her, maybe, but I'd like to see you get somebody.'

'Who knows? Some day, maybe, perhaps sooner rather than later.'

'What's that supposed to mean?'

'Nothing, mum. What we having Friday? Turkey? Goose?'

'What do we always have for Christmas?'

'Turkey.'

'That's right.'

'I promise I'll eat my sprouts.'

'You'd better. How you going to get here?'

'There's a special coach from Stepney, it's stopping at all the stations to Ash Park then back again..'

'Good idea. I'm going to the toilet, back in a minute.'

As he sat again, the room felt a little empty. He thought of Doris. He didn't want that again; her face peering at him through the kitchen window as he dug the hole for his pool's concrete to go in, the disdainful glances as he put the fountain in position, and insisting on sitting in the house when it was first switched on and not sharing his minor triumph with him. And the sarcastic comments as he was doing the Egyptian artwork, saying that he may as well paint Wilson and Keppel doing their Egyptian sand dance in a panto. He couldn't, at the time, understand why she was so negative. She was hurt, he gave her very little at the end, but, somehow, he wasn't able to give more. He thought of the word 'incapable'. Perhaps that was how she had seen him.

'George?'

His mother was in the room again.

'Er, sorry.'

'You were looking at the fireplace as if you were a thousand miles away.'

'Not that far. I'll get off and let you listen to the wireless in peace.'

'Work tomorrow?'

'Yep. Another day, another dollar, as they say. I'll see you Friday and bring you a prezzy. 'Night.'

He gave her a kiss, walked to the station and caught a train home. It was an Enid Walk day tomorrow.

She was just pulling her last pint when he entered the pub, Bishop employed the occasional part-time bar girl and it was she who was taking over for the rest of the day. Enid gestured for him to sit. He did so for a brief while until she appeared, pulling on her coat, and they left. It was a cold, bright afternoon and he suggested they walk by the river. They went down Kingsway into Aldwych, crossed the Strand then to the Embankment.

She talked of her father's family, his brothers and sisters, and of his farming and sheep-owning ancestors. He told her he would refrain from telling her jokes about sexual relations between such farmers and their herds.

'Sensible,' she said, 'I don't like gags about stereotypes.'

'We wouldn't understand them otherwise.'

'People say to me, 'You miss Wales?' I say 'No, I look nothing like her, she has long, auburn hair and wears a sash.' She looked at the sky. 'It doesn't rain here as much as it does in my home country.'

'This is your home now.'

'I know. The Bible says that God made it rain for forty days and nights.'

269

'Not a bad summer for Wales then.'

She smiled. 'Okay, I'll accept that one.'

After a lone cloud passed over the sun it brightened the river again, glistening the water and lighting barges and tugboats as well as a pleasure steamer

'I take London for granted,' he said, as he looked along the river, 'but it's kind of in my blood, I feel sometimes I have almost a psychological ownership of it.'

'Why?'

'I was born and raised in it, played in it, worked in it, waked in it, walked around the places where the houses and buildings are that I've worked on.'

'*Your* city.'

'And yours now.'

'Well, Leytonstone is, perhaps.'

'Sooner own the Welsh Hills?'

'Maybe.'

'The more walks we have the more the city will be part of you.'

He glanced backward.

'Look at St. Paul's, I feel that as long as that's still there the world's okay, it can't end.'

'I'm afraid I don't feel that about Cardiff Castle.'

'We'll make a Londoner of you yet, 'though I rarely like songs about London, cockneys sing 'em it in pubs and at knees-ups.'

'You didn't want to be associated with them?'

'No, I'm a bit of a snob, my mum used to call me a 'posh cockney'. I've met some good ones though, blokes at work and that.'

'There's so much good in the worst of us and so much bad in the best of us that it ill beholds any of us to criticise the rest of us.'

'You sound almost biblical today.'

'I think dad believes I still say my prayers every night.'

'Mum used to teach me to say mine, too. Why do people need to believe in a deity? Is it because we don't understand why the universe is here?'

'Why there is something rather than nothing?'

'Yes, or is it because they want some sort of... a master, an order so they don't feel so lost?'

'Who knows?'

'And why are we taught so firmly about God, as if we *have* to believe?'

'And who organises it? There's so many questions.'

'Hark at us, eh?' he grinned, 'like a couple of intellectuals.'

'Do you think of your dad much?' she asked.

'Why did you ask that?'

'Dunno. Just did.'

'That's quite a coincidence. The answer's 'no' I suppose, but my mum showed me a letter from him yesterday that he wrote to her in the war. Last thing she heard from him. Perhaps you've got extrasensory perception.'

'Intuition maybe.'

'Perhaps you're linked to my mind.'

'Perhaps we're all linked to each other.'

'I prefer you to be linked to me.'

'I'll link my arm.'

She put her arm in his and they continued walking. He pointed to a large house just off the Embankment.

'Georgy, my favourite period, 'though I like a lot of what's being put up now, of course, I think the French call it Art Décoratif. But there's the Vicky, Eddie, Reggie – '

'Yes, I know, you've said.' She smiled. 'It's alright, I like them too. I think you know this.'

He squeezed her arm into his side.

'Good.'

'There's so much around us that's interesting isn't there.'

'Such as this kind of ultramarine dusk and the pink reflections on the water.'

They stopped for a while and looked across and down the river.

'Where would you like to go for a romantic evening?' she asked him.

'A pie and mash shop, jellied eels and all.'

She laughed. 'I doubt if there's any around here.'

'So do I.'

He asked her what she was doing on Christmas Day.

'Same as usual, with my dad. He's a pretty good cook, but I make the pudding. I don't work Christmas Day. You?'

'Mum's. Any chance of seeing you?'

She thought a while.

'I think he's going to see one of his friends in the afternoon. I usually go with him but don't have to.'

'I'll have a word with mum and you can come after dinner - how's that? I mean, I've met your dad, you can meet my mother.'

'That sounds a little formal.'

'Didn't mean it like that.'

'I know.'

'Thing is, how you going to get to Plaistow?'

'He has a motorbike combination, he could bring me in that.'

'A bike and sidecar?' Okay, done. I'll ask her, she'll say yes.'

He squeezed her arm again, and when the pink reflections turned into the grey-cream splashes of embankment lamps, they crossed the road and caught a bus towards St. Paul's. He went back with her on the train. She was quiet. He looked at her, she seemed quite at ease. Glancing around him, he noticed none of the passengers in the carriage were talking, even those obviously with each other. He wondered whether it was a British thing.

'You are part of the UK aren't you?' he asked.

'Of course. Why?'

'Nothing,' he said with a grin, and loosely held her hand until they reached her station where, after snapping his heels together and semi-bowing to her, he caught a bus home.

He was glad he'd got away from work early to see her, as a foreman he felt justified in giving himself a little perk now and then. The next day, Christmas Eve, he let the men go early also; they were in front with the job, anyway. He wished them a good time and went to the pub. He didn't stop for a drink; he just wanted to ask her, if he would see her the next day. She'd spoken to her parent who had agreed to bring her. George gave her his address, surreptitiously squeezed her hand and went off to the borough of his birth.

'A barmaid?'

It was his mother's reply to his asking her if it was okay for

Enid to join them for a while after Christmas dinner.

'Not that sort of barmaid, mum.'

'What sort's that then?'

'The sort you're thinking of, all lipstick, bosom and enjoying being chatted up by the lads. She's nice, I've met her dad, he's a decorator, too.'

'Well, you've got something in common with him, then. What's she like?'

'Well... clever, funny, likes the things I do, I suppose. I like her, mum.'

'So she's coming round then?'

'Yes, I thought you'd be okay about it, so I asked her. Her dad's gonna bring her on his motorbike. And I'm off home now to wrap some prezzies.'

He went back to his house, busied himself with paper and string, ''vac'd' through', as his mother would call it, and went to sleep looking forward to seeing his girl again.

'Merry Christmas, and I'm pleased to meet you,' his mother said as Enid, with her father wearing gloves and goggles and standing some way behind her, arrived at the front door.

'Me too.'

'I'm not going to stay, Mrs. Woods,' called her parent, 'I'm late as it is, but enjoy yourselves and say hello to your son. Goodbye.'

He returned quickly to his bike and with an increasing roar it sped away.

'Do come in, dear, and have a cup of tea.'

'I don't mind if I do. Thanks.'

She looked at George coming down the stairs and smiled at him.

'You got here then, and you've met my mum.'

'I have.'

'Come into the parlour,' said his mother, 'it's nice and warm in here, we got the fire going nice and early.'

'Just so I could open my stocking which contained an apple, two oranges, a new penny and a fountain pen, my mother believes in tradition. What did you get?'

Sitting down, she told him her father had given her money for a new dress. 'And here's yours,' she said, handing him a small, wrapped box.

'A new dress?'

''Course not, silly.'

I t was chocolates. He thanked her.

'It's not much, I'm not good at presents, I know what my dad wants, I give it to him every year, a bottle of Cointreau.'

He gave her a small package he'd been holding behind him.

'While mum's in the kitchen, take this.'

She removed the wrapping and revealed a pair of red woollen gloves.

'Not very romantic, but I've noticed that you don't wear them, and I can tell your hands are cold sometimes. Perhaps I should hold them more.'

She smiled. Thanks, George, they'll come in handy.'

'Ugh.'

She got up quickly, gave him a brief kiss on the cheek and sat again.

His mother appeared.

'Here you are, dear,' she said, handing her a cup. 'He bought me a frilly pink pinafore, it's ever so pretty.'

'That's nice.'

'Let's see what's on the wireless shall we?' said George, going across to it.

'There's Sherlock Holmes on soon, you used to like that,' his mother said.

'What, no variety show on? Let's have some music.' He turned to Enid. 'Alright with you?'

'Of course, it's your house.'

'Not mine, but... '

'You haven't seen his house, have you,' his mother said to Enid, 'he's done some smashin' work on it.'

'No, I haven't.'

'You will,' he said, switching the set on, 'and perhaps I'll get a television for the occasion. Was thinking of getting one, actually, think I can just about afford it now.'

'They're good, aren't they,' said his mother, 'I watched it at

Mrs. Bell's the other afternoon, a few of us in the street were there. It's really nice.' She looked at Enid and asked if she was hungry.

'No, thank you, I feel fat and bloated after dad's cooking.'

'You don't look it, you look slim and pretty, dear.'

'Thank you.'

George then went to a small cupboard in the corner, took out a bottle and two glasses and, pouring a small quantity of Martini in each, handed one to Enid, raised his and said, 'I second that.'

'Hear, hear,' said his mother with some exuberance.

'Gonna join in then?' he asked her.

'I've had my glass of mild, that'll do me.'

There was some Latin-American music playing. He turned up the volume.

Gently removing Enid's glass he eased her from her chair, put an arm loosely around her back and began slowly swaying with her. She smiled compliantly.

'You move well together, you're making me feel envious.'

'I'll dance with you tomorrow, mum.'

The music changed and he attempted a foxtrot until Enid gently suggested he resume moving as he had been. His mother left the room again.

'I have an inkling that you know how to dance properly,' he told her.

'Yes,' I learnt to at school.'

'So did I, sort of.'

'We had a headmistress who was insistent that we all had to get a man and a good way to do that was at dances.'

'Where the lads stand around trying to look manly and they're trembling inside.'

His mother returned with some mince pies and more tea.

After they'd finished listening to the music, he dancing with her again and, at her insistence, also with his mother, the latter began telling her guest about her son's house.

'He's got a lovely garden with a pool and rockery and things, and done these murals, they're Egyptian, and painted these butterflies on the staircase and I think there's one in the bedroom, you'd like them.' She paused. 'Oh, I didn't mean that you should see his bedroom or anything like that, just that they're so nice.' She glanced at her son. 'Well, you know what I mean. Doris didn't like them though did she.'

There was a brief silence.

Enid looked at both of them.

"Doris'?'

'Er, somebody he knew, she's not there now,' explained his mother.

Enid looked quizzically at her boyfriend.

'Whoever she was, she came to your house then?'

'Yeah, but as mum said, not any more.'

He saw Enid give an almost imperceptible nod, as if she may have understood something.

'Anyway, there's another variety show on in a minute,' George said rather loudly, 'let's listen to that.'

They did so, speaking little except to laugh and make comments, although Enid, he noticed, was doing little of the former.

George offered her another drink which she refused, before asking her how she would get home.

'Dad's picking me up 'before midnight' she said. 'I hope that's not too late for you, Mrs. Woods.'

'No, dear, that's alright. What are you going to do, George? You can stay here, the bed's made up in the spare room.'

'I dunno, I was thinking of, maybe, walking back.'

'It's miles away, you silly sod, but up to you son, you know your own 'no'.'

He felt that she was a little hurt that he would rather walk back than stay with her.

'Perhaps I should stay then.'

The sound of a motorbike abruptly stopping outside the house was heard.

'That'll be dad,' said Enid, 'I'd better go.'

'Of course,' said her hostess, going to the front door.

'Who's this 'Doris' then?' Enid almost whispered to him, 'is there something I should know?'

'No, it's… nothing really, I'll tell you another time.' He said it as casually as he could.

'Goodnight, George.' she said firmly and went into the hall

where her father, standing on the doorstep and still wearing his goggles, was talking to George's mother.

'Hello love,' he said, spotting his daughter, 'Enjoy yourself?'

'It was very pleasant. And thank you, Mrs. Woods.'

'The pleasure's mine, I'm sure.'

Enid's father had seen George come out of the front room.

'D'you want a lift to your place, son? Ash Park isn't it?'

Forgetting for a second that he said he would stay, he said 'Yes, if you would. Ta.'

He asked his mother if it was okay with her.

'Seems it'll have to be. Have a safe journey, I'll see you soon, I hope.'

The three of them went out to the bike where Enid clambered into the sidecar and her father handed George a pair of goggles.

'Here, put these on, sit on the pillion and hold me tightly around the waist, boyo. I know you'd prefer to do it to her, but…'

As George did as he asked, he smelt the alcohol on the man's breath. He looked down and tapped on the inside of the sidecar. There was no response from within.

'Here we go then,' said the rider enthusiastically and the combination sped away.

It was a noisy, swerving ride back to George's home, with the pillion passenger having to shout directions into the man's ear, not always sure that he was being understood. Accelerating along Rainham Road into Ash park was almost exciting, 'though he wasn't sorry when the journey ended.

He thanked the rider, dismounted and looked into the sidecar's window where Enid was gazing silently in front of her.

He raised his voice. 'I'll see you soon, I assume you'll be working tomorrow,'

She didn't answer or alter her expression as her parent rode off.

Once inside the house, he slumped into an armchair. Feeling restless, he went upstairs. He had hung most of his butterfly paintings on the staircase; the one on the landing was a Red Admiral. He looked at its veined wings. Red was for danger, a warning; this particular shade felt like a threat. He went to the bathroom then returned to his seat.

Why did his mother have to mention her? He would go to the pub tomorrow in the afternoon, perhaps Enid wasn't working in the evening; he had no idea.

28

He had been trying to work on an essay he'd been given to complete when term began again after the festive holiday. It was entitled, 'How different can different conceptual schemes be?' He'd been wanting to do it as soon as he'd seen the question, they had been dealing with conceptual systems since he'd begun his subject.

He'd wanted to discuss the theories he'd learnt and the concepts they contained, but wasn't sure of the actual answer to the question. That is, until he was in a near-empty refectory the day after he'd received the question with two of the younger lecturers sitting immediately behind him discussing the very subject.

'Of course,' one was saying, 'You talk of conceptual systems, but all have to end in formal logic, surely, where else?' They had then talked of other things, but Rupert had his answer. He was toying with the idea of finishing with, 'There are necessary truths linking different conceptual schemes. No conceptual scheme can contain within it a denial of the law of contradiction. No conceptual scheme can be *that* different.'

Feeling quite satisfied with himself, all he had to do now was to read up on a few more philosophical theories he knew little of and, along with those he knew, delineate their main concepts and, as cockneys seemed to say, 'Bob's yer uncle'. Rupert was in his room, and began to get himself ready to see Constance before travelling to his parental home for Christmas. He should have left earlier; he would be able to spend even less time with her now.

She looked rather downcast when she opened the door to him.

'Happy Christmas' he said, briefly kissing her.

'Oh, to be able to have one, I'll try though,' she said without conviction. She beckoned him inside.

'Mother has no idea of what it all means. I managed to get a little tree from the market and she kept asking what it was. I put a few little lights on it which seemed to please her though.'

He held out a small, gift-wrapped package.

'I hope this cheers you up somewhat.'

As she opened it he said, 'I've noticed you've had your ears pierced, so I got you these.'

Her eyes widened.

'They're lovely. Just the right shape, thanks very much.'

Her grin was so broad he realised he hadn't really noticed how straight and white her teeth were.

She looked a little contrite for a moment.

'I'm afraid I haven't got you much, Roop.'

'Not so much of the 'Roop'.'

'I'm teasing. Eric calls you that, I know. Come through to see her.'

She was lying on the sofa again, gazing at the ceiling. She saw him.

'I'mCelia.'

'Hello, Celia', he said gently, standing over her.

'Is that me?'

'Of course.'

'Who are you?'

'It's alright, mum, it's my friend who came to see you the other day.'

'Did he? That's nice.' She pointed at the tree. 'Do you like those little things there?' They go on and off.'

She rested her head again and closed her eyes.

'Come with me,' Constance said, 'I'll make us a coffee.'

He followed her into the kitchen.

'I wonder how she really feels,' he said as she put the kettle on the hob, 'because it is the 'she', the 'self' that's damaged. Perhaps she's not in that much distress, the self isn't aware of its own condition.'

She didn't answer him.

'I expect that sounds rather cruel, as if I'm minimizing it, at least unnecessarily analytic, but... just wondering.'

He leaned against the inside of the door, watching her, appreciating her; the way she moved, the shape of her arms under her roll-neck jumper, the back of her slim waist.

'How's your work coming along?' she asked.

'Alright, I find myself reading more Marx than may be required.'

'Why?'

'Because he's so right in so many things; stratification - '

'Class?'

'Indeed, and in his theory. How can I put it? That our political and cultural systems, indeed our consciousness, are determined by the ways in which the physical world is technologically transmutated.'

'Our reality as well?'

'I suppose so.'

'That's big thinking.'

'He's a big thinker.'

'What do you see when you look at me? Steam mills? Railways? Television? A camera? Am I made up of all these things?'

'I see you, and I think you know this, as fair and pale, and soft and... '

'Your articulacy is failing you.'

'It's your fault.'

She gave him his coffee. He drank it silently. 'Poor mum, eh?'

'Let's go back to her.'

They returned to the front room. He stood over her again.

'Hello, Celia.'

'Hello, do I know you? Do you come here from the west?' she asked. 'Do you take them up? Why would you do that? I didn't see you in the red ones, they were no better and I missed it. At least now that you've got things to do, that's all of the things I want to. If I help others along you may remember what to do. You say this sort of thing. Where is it? Do you know?'

He couldn't hear all that she said. She reached for her dressing gown and pulled it over her. He told her she looked like Red Riding Hood.

'Come here,' she said, tapping her fingers on the space alongside her.

He sat down where she had indicated. She turned her head and closed her eyes again.

He got up. 'Cheerio, Celia.'

'Sorry about the gibberish,' said Constance.

'It may not be gibberish to her.'

'I know.'

'Anyway, it's time I got back to the Queen of the Boroughs.'

'What's that?'

'Ealing.'

'The parental home, eh?'

''Tis indeed.'

'Your mother will be there?'

'Think so, but not Boxing Day, has to be off for a dress re-hearsal. You're definitely coming for the opening night?'

'Yes, as I said, she's being looked after.'

They went into the hall. At the front door he turned.

'Look, er... there are spare bedrooms at home. I'm not sure how father would feel about it, he's such a damn puritan, 'though I'm not even sure he'll be at the theatre, It's always business for him, he's planning another development somewhere, I believe.'

'And if he's not there?'

'We could go somewhere else.'

'We'll see.'

'Three days time then. Catching the same train?'

'Yes.'

'See you at Padders.'

He gave her a gentle kiss on the lips and made his way to the station.

It was an Edwardian house his father had purchased the year Rupert had been born. It had a large, arched opening above the front door and porch, exaggerated keystones, small panes in the top half of the windows, and even a tower-like element on its corner. Its owner opened the door.

'Hello, son,' his father said, shaking his offspring's hand. This was so typical of him, Rupert wondered if other fathers called their child 'son' rather than their name.

'Must get back to work again,' he said, turning and going upstairs as his wife came out of the parlour and hugged her son.

'Merry Christmas, lovely boy.' She took a step back. 'You're looking well, Oxford agrees with you.'

He put his case down.

'May as well tell you now, mother, I've a girl friend. I didn't want to tell you over the phone.'

She looked pleased. How long?'

'A while now, 'though I didn't tell you before because I wanted to make sure.'

'That she was the one?'

'Yes.'

'I think I guessed you'd be telling me something like this soon, and you've been sure for a while, haven't you.'

'Suppose so. Her name's Constance and she's coming with me to see you on opening night. You've organised the tickets I asked you for?'

'I have.'

'Good, that'll be the four of us going. And dad?'

She gave a resigned smile. 'Things to do in the office.'

'S'pose you're used to that by now.'

'You know I am.'

He glanced up at the ceiling. 'He's got two, really, hasn't he, one on the Broadway, the other upstairs.'

'He spends a lot of time in both.'

'Ne'er mind,' he said, putting an arm around her shoulder, 'I'll be cheering for you.'

'Let's hope the rest of the audience does. What's your favourite tipple these days?'

'Whatever. Gin and It will do.'

They went into the front room where she went to the cocktail cabinet and poured two glasses, saying 'I'll join you.'

'How are the rehearsals going?'

'Well. Harvey Gain's a good Director.'

'Tell me about the play again.'

'It's about the death and inheritance of old Cyrus West, a rich eccentric who felt that his relatives have 'watched my wealth as if they were cats and I, a canary.' He decides his Will be read twenty years after his death, at which point his relatives converge on his old family home, now a spooky, haunted mansion. It's a kind of comic-horror, really. The Will reads that his most distant relative still bearing the name of West be the sole heir, provided they are legally sane. The rest of the night is spent at the house calling into question the sanity of Anabelle West - me, as you know - a woman who is legally the rightful heir. She's meant to be a youngish woman, but we have a good make-up man.'

'He doesn't have to be *that* good.'

Just then her husband came into the room and, making straight for the cabinet and grabbing a bottle of whisky, said 'I heard that. Don't understand 'comic-horror', either it's funny or its scary, can't be both.'

Neither of his listeners replied.

'How's your university work then?' he asked Rupert, pouring his drink and not looking at him.

'It's going pretty well, father.'

'Suppose you're doing a bit of politics, eh?'

'Everything comes into philosophy.'

'Jack-of-all-trades, eh? Not a proper subject though, is it.'

His father snorted and finished pouring his drink.

'Well, must return to a proper job now, a true endeavour. See you later.'

He went out of the room again.

Rupert's mother looked at him and shrugged.

'I know,' her son said then, reaching into his pocket, withdrew a small, wrapped box. 'Happy Christmas. Open it now.'

She did. It was the bracelet he'd bought at Harrods. Looking a bit closely, she read its inscription aloud, 'To my dear mother. Love, Rupert.'

'I have a strong memory of you wearing one when I was a boy, but you don't seem to have worn it for years.'

'Your father gave it to me a long time ago. I shall certainly wear this, though. Thank you.' She kissed him.

They listened to the wireless for a while until his mother chose to retire early as she'd had, as successful as her rehearsals had been, a tiring week. Rupert drank a little more, not really enjoying the large tree with its time-honoured baubles, ribbons but no lights almost dominating the room, before going to bed himself, saying goodnight to his father as he passed his door, thinking of Constance and, as much as he enjoyed being with his mother, wishing she was with him.

The next day over breakfast, his mother told them that they were having pastiera napoletana for lunch, explaining, over her husband's objections, that the normal festive meal would be served later. As soon as they'd finished, his father told him to look under the tree in the parlour. Rupert did so, finding a large envelope with his name on. He returned to the dining room and asked if he could open it.

'Of course, it's for you, son,' said the ex-major. Rupert opened it; it was a bundle of papers. They were shares in his father's firm.

'You're not working there any more, so this'll keep you connected to, and interested in, the firm.'

Rupert immediately wanted to decry the whole business of shares and its capitalistic roots, but he rarely received a gift from his parent, and they were also worth money, that most essential of commodities. He thanked his father who told them that he had to do more work in his office and left them again. Rupert and his mother watched the fashion show Clothes-Line on the television which was half-way though when she reminded him that's she had yet to give him a present. She went upstairs and returned with a colourfully-bound package, his unwrapping of it revealing a white silk shirt. He asked her if he could try it on. It fitted almost perfectly.

'A cast member wears one of these in the play, this is a spare. Too good to waste.'

He kissed her.

'Constance will really like you in that, it's tight in just the right places.'

'Talking of her, there's a train or two running tomorrow, I'd like to see her. Her mother's ill.'

'I know you would, you've been a little bit restless since you've been here, haven't you.'

He told her about her mother's condition.

'Go to see her, Rupert, she'll appreciate It.'

They spent the rest of the day, other than enjoying their late, conventional Christmas meal, talking intermittently of her play, his scholastic work and, his father joining them for a while, playing Scrabble and Monopoly, his male parent, not unexpectedly, winning the latter.

After a quick game of Whist and a nightcap, Rupert bid his father goodnight and told his mother that he would see her soon.

He was up early, disturbing neither of his parents, got to Paddington and from there enjoyed his north-west journey; the rhythmic clickety-clacking of the carriage wheels, the telegraph poles buzzing by, almost whispering her name again. Smiling at himself, he stopped the repetitive sound of the nomenclature and enjoyed the fields, hedges, trees, the occasional barn and herd of cows, until they came into Oxford. He caught a cab outside the station and went to her.

He couldn't quite read her expression when she opened the street door; a blend of momentary disbelief, surprise and, he hoped, pleasure. He stepped towards her, put an arm around her waist and kissed her firmly on the lips.

'I felt like a great film lover then.'

'Valentino?'

'More John Gilbert I think.'

'I thought you'd be with your family,' she said her eyes still wide.

'I was, but couldn't resist. I discovered there was a train, so...'

'Here you are.'

'How is she? Dare I ask?'

'The same. I don't think there'll be anything different now, unfortunately.'

She went in front of him into the parlour where her parent was, as he was now coming to expect, lying on the settee. She seemed asleep.

Her daughter sat down by her and tenderly stroked the back of her hand.

'She's been quite talkative of late, but again not making much sense. She knows what she wants to say but doesn't have the words to say it.'

'I wonder if she does know, in words that make sense if you like, in her *own* words.'

'A kind of private language?'

'Not strictly that, language has to have a consensus, fortuitous it may be, but it's not a language otherwise. Sorry, been reading Wittgenstein. Any leftovers from yesterday? How did it go, anyway?'

'Afraid it was no different from any other day, really. She doesn't get the concept of Christmas, I'm afraid. A friend and a couple of neighbours popped in. They left looking rather sad.' She frowned. 'Why didn't we arrange that I rang you from the phone box?'

'Should have done, I know, but the telephone's in the front room and it may have been difficult to speak to you privately. My mother would have made herself scarce, but not father, I don't want him listening to us. But we're here now.' He pulled her to him and kissed her again. 'It's so good to be with you.'

'Let's get some food for you, and, incidentally, I'm moving back here soon, I shall leave my room, I spend more time here, anyway.'

He followed her into the kitchen and watched her make a turkey sandwich and cut a slice of pudding.

'It doesn't seem fair does it.'

'What doesn't?'

'That your mother is as she is, and mine - '

'Is a beautiful and successful actress?'

'Well... '

'She is, I've seen a picture of her.'

'You'll meet her tomorrow, she's looking forward to it.'

He then told her about the upcoming wedding, Fiona's pregnancy and Eric's apprehension of his father's potential attitude towards the latter. .

'It may be too soon for them, but it's a lovely thing isn't it?' was her reply.

'It seems to be so for them.'

'That's all that matters, really, isn't it?'

'I suppose so. Let's go in there again, take the food with you, I'll bring the tea.'

They returned to the room.

'Oh, it's you,' said Celia, moving her head towards them, 'it's that... thing person. Who are you? Where's the orange one? I think that he couldn't consider the one they couldn't get hold of, you know, but he can't stay though, of course.' She looked up at her daughter, who was stroking the back of her hand again, and said, closing her eyes, 'I like this.'

'I'm glad.' Costance bent and kissed her hand. 'I'll let her sleep. Come into the dining room.'

'Said the spider to the fly.'

'I'm hardly an arachnid, I have no web with which to entrap you.'

'Wouldn't complain if you had.'

It was a smaller room, neat and tidy with table and chairs and a Mucha print above the fireplace. She put his food on the table and watched him eat.

'You eat like a gentleman, Mister Colls.'

'It's because I am one, madam.'

She walked to the window and looked out.

'I feel restless.'

'I'm not surprised, you hardly go out, do you.'

'No, I even miss the books.'

'And me?'

''Course.'

Still looking at the darkness through the window, she asked him if he played chess. He didn't. She offered to teach him.

'Somebody told me,' she said, that he had a chess grandmaster over for dinner. I asked him how it went. He said it was fun, but they had to eat a cold meal. I asked him why. He said he had a checked tablecloth and it took his guest an hour to pass the salt.'

'I liked that one.'

She went back to the other room and returned with a chess-board and pieces and explained the game to him. He wasn't that interested, but it meant that he was, as well as being impressed by her apparent knowledge of the game, in close proximity to her. Her teaching and his attempts at learning took up most of the evening, until he told her he should get back to his rooms. He then summoned the courage to add that if he could stay the night they could go straight to London from here.

'That would be a lovely idea if we could realise it, but not with mother like this.'

'She won't really know will she. I mean... you know what I mean.'

'I do, and you're right, she wouldn't know, she's not aware you're here, she's probably not aware that *I'm* here either. Sometimes, just sometimes, I wonder if I'm beginning to forget what she used to be like.'

He felt a sudden sadness, as if the woman who had fed her, clothed her, taught her had faded, had slipped away, had gone.

He cuddled her. She pressed her head into his shoulder.

'I can't do it, Rupert. I'll meet you at the station tomorrow, the neighbour's coming in the morning.'

They returned to her mother's room.

'Sometimes,' her daughter said, I don't take her to bed, I leave her here all night, it makes little difference.'

She went to the front door with him. He told her the time of the train and where to meet him. He began walking to the bus stop, turned and waved at her.

There was, he was thinking as he waited for her, something rather dramatic about stations: The vaulted roof, wrought iron struts, soaring columns, sunlight glancing through glass canopies, the sharp, long hisses of steam, the grinding of engines pulling away from platforms, the meetings, separations, tears.

Tired of waiting outside the stationers, he began to walk around the concourse. Then he saw her. It was probably the long coat she was wearing, but she looked so slender, her body somehow elongated, she'd waved her hair slightly, too.

'Don't say it. I look like Joan Blondell, my neighbour suggested I do.'

'A little. The train's in, let's go.'

Sharing the carriage with seven other people, they kept their conversation blandly impersonal until they were in the café at their destination. He asked her if she'd told her mother that she was going out for the day.

'No, she probably won't notice I'm not there, anyway. Perhaps we can try not to talk of her for the rest of the time we're together, although it won't stop me thinking of her.'

'Okay. You did tell your neighbour that you wouldn't be back until tomorrow, I assume?'

'I told her that I wasn't sure when I'd be back, but she said that it was alright. She's a sweetie.'

They finished their coffee. Holding her hand, he pulled her up and said. 'Let us depart this plebeian place and transport ourselves to the magic of the theatre.'

'Yes, let's.'

She gave him big smile, an almost joyful one, one he hadn't seen for a while.

They were a little early, so after briefly admiring the theatre's Deco frontage, Rupert suggested they have a coffee in the restaurant opposite.

The first thing he noticed as they entered was Eric sitting at a table with Fiona.

'Come,' Rupert said to his companion and they moved towards the table. Fiona looked up with a surprised smile as Rupert bent towards Eric's back and whispered in his ear, "Nothing is what it seems in Macbeth.' I trust you have completed your essay on this, young man.'

His friend looked around immediately.

'What? Oh, Roop. Fancy. We were going to the Savoy Grill Room, but Fiona doesn't like the coffee there apparently, the discerning creature.'

As he spotted Constance he stood.

'Constance,' he said, turning to her. He took her gloved hand, kissed its finger tips and gave a slight bow.

'You've seen Eric before,' said Rupert, 'and this is Fiona.'

'Hello,' said Constance, stretching a hand out to her.

Eric beckoned them to sit and asked if they had ordered their coffee. Rupert answered in the negative whereupon his friend went to the counter and asked for two espressos.

'As you can see, we're early too,' he said as he returned to the table, 'I'm sure your mother will be splendid tonight, we're looking forward to watching her.'

'And I, we,' said his friend, 'are looking forward to your double event. Congratulations on both, Fiona.'

She smiled a little shyly and thanked him.

After Constance excused herself to go to the cloakroom, Eric said 'Un certain quelque chose, Roop, and don't analyse it, she has it,' He looked at Fiona, 'just like my sweetheart has. We are supermen to have these women.'

'Don't kid yourself, cutie, but you're not so bad.'

'Gee, thanks, ma'am.'

Constance returned and the coffee arrived.

'Don't you think we should go soon? Drink, time's getting on,' said Eric.

Rupert, glancing at his watch, concurred, and they vacated their place of refreshment, crossed the road and went into the foyer, where he obtained their tickets from the box office.

'Mid-stalls,' he told them, 'let's go in.'

They sat down with Rupert and Eric together and the girls on either side of them.

The curtains parted and when Elowen said, 'That it be, nothin's changed 'ere in twenty years,' Rupert hardly recognised his mother, with her flaxen wig, flat shoes making her look shorter, and with a wider waist than she actually had.

After the first few minutes, Rupert began to accept her role and became increasingly interested in the characters and the mood of the piece, and found himself immersed in both the apprehension and laughter they created in the set of the rambling, crumbling old house. As Annabelle delivered the last line of the play and the curtain came down, the audience, quite a few cheering, clapped heartily for some minutes.

'A sublime production,' said Eric to Rupert, and your mother were charming. Ah, Annabelle, she was lovely.'

'You'll make Fiona jealous.'

'I'm not, and I enjoyed it very much,' she replied. 'Did you mention that she played two parts?'

'It's in the programme. I loved the Cornish accent,' he said to Rupert, 'but she should have said ''Ello, moy li'le dove,' that would have made it certain where she was from. And as for the heroine, I loved her skittish smatterings of hysteria.'

As they began getting up from their seats and joined the rest of the audience who were leaving, a uniformed attendant looked across from the aisle at Rupert and said, 'Are you Rupert? I've been given your seat numbers.'

'I am.'

'Your mother wishes to see you and your friends at the stage door for a little while, sir. Could you please wait a few minutes?'

'Of course. Thanks.'

'This is a bit special,' Fiona said, as they sat again.

'It is,' agreed her fiancé. 'You must be proud of her, Roop.'

'I am. Changing the subject, where are you two staying to-night, the Savoy? You don't have to drink their coffee.'

'No, we came in pater's Rolls, Charlie the chauffeur picked us up and he's taking us back, or rather, me, he's dropping Fiona off at her place. I really do think pa doesn't want us to spend the night together.'

'Too late now. How did it go with him when you told him the news? I assume you have.'

'Exactly as expected, it's against his values, or rather what he thinks the values of his colleagues and friends are. Mother was both surprised and pleased, which pleased me, of course.'

The attendant appeared again. 'If you'll follow me, ladies and gentlemen.'

They did so, whereupon just before the exit, Rupert noticed Andrew Combes rising from his seat at the back of the stalls. He seemed to be on his own. People, thought Rupert, didn't go to the theatre on their own, the cinema, yes, but not the theatre, although of course he did know the lead actress and perhaps had a particular interest in watching her perform, he had accompanied his friend to two of her shows before. Rupert wondered if he had someone, a friend; a girlfriend. He looked briefly at his companions; he didn't need Andrew. He felt slightly guilty, but only a little.

They were led to the stage door in the alleyway at the side of the building upon which Rupert knocked. It was almost immediately opened by his mother.

'Hello, all of you. You must be Constance, so nice to meet you. And this is Eric and Fiona. Hello.' She was still dressed as Annabelle.

'Mrs. Colls,' Eric began. Sorry, Mercia Colls, I loved your performance, 'the whole thing really, I'm sure it will have an infinitely long run.'

'Thank you, I hope so, too.' Turning to her son, she said, 'Some of us have interviews to do and afterwards there's a little party for the cast. I'd love you all to stay, but... We have a rather strict Producer.'

'It's okay, mother, we understand, we're just glad it went so well.' He kissed her cheek.

'Goodbye then. Thanks for coming and I hope to see you all again, and I shall see you soon Constance, I hope.' She gave a quick wave and disappeared inside the building.

'Short, and very sweet,' said Eric.

'She is lovely, Rupert,' said Fiona.

'I say, Roop, we've thoroughly enjoyed this evening and thank you for it, but we must go, too, our transport back to the parental residence is awaiting, you may have seen the rather conspicuous vehicle at the front of the theatre. I think we should now enter its combustion-engine powered interior. Thanks again for the evening.' He gave his slight bow to Constance, shook Rupert's hand and said, 'See you at the start of term and both of you very soon afterwards on the momentous day.'

His friends then followed him and Fiona back to the front of the building where car and chauffeur were waiting, the latter doffing his cap to his employer's son as he and his soon-to-be-wife took their seats They drove off, both of them waving through the back window.

'Well, said Rupert, ''tis over, hope you enjoyed it.'

'You know I did, but there's a question.'

'Which is?'

'You asked Eric where they would be staying tonight. I'm asking where *we* are.'

He smiled at her. 'I should have told you before. I've booked a room at a small hotel just around the corner. That okay with you?'

'Of course it is.'

She hugged him, put her arm in his and they began walking.

During the ten minutes of pleasurable silence it took them to get to their destination, he thought of the successful evening, his friends, his life and work at Oxford and, with pleasing anticipation, what was to come with Constance.

He should, he knew, have felt happy, satisfied, perhaps feeling almost a completeness, yet, in another part of him, there was a feeling of a slight and intermittent prodding at the back of it all, telling him that maybe something was… missing.

29

He felt like a little boy uncomfortably waiting to confess something to mummy. Enid was on duty, serving drinks and handing out packets of crisps but not, he thought, smiling at customers quite as much as she usually did. He suspected that it was because she had been thinking about who his mother had inadvertently mentioned. It wasn't so much that he'd had a relationship with another girl, of course, but that she had lived with him, and that it was, as virtually everybody saw it, living sinfully. But even more damagingly, perhaps, was that he hadn't told Enid.

He didn't want to think about it, he wished to whisk her away to walk in the winter sun with him, through parks, around ponds and through suburban avenues. And how, he wondered, would she react when he invited her to his home?

He hadn't brought a drink; he just sat there, watching her while she occasionally, and unenthusiastically, glanced across at him. The phrase 'Dutch courage' came to mind and he went to the bar and asked her for a half of brown ale and what time she would be finished. She didn't answer. She supplied his drink, took his money, put it in the till and turned, expressionlessly, to another customer.

It felt like it did sometimes with Doris, as if he should tell her something, reveal something, apologise for his behaviour or for what he felt, or rather, didn't feel. As if he should apologise to her for not doing things he should have done.

But this wasn't Doris; this was somebody so different, somebody he wanted to be with, without the guilt, without the hiding, the escapes. Just being with her would be enough, wouldn't it?

He began to feel a little ridiculous just sitting there, waiting to be seen by her, to be listened to. He finished his drink and went outside. He'd noticed a café next to the pub and went in. He brought a cheese roll and a tea and sat there, he was the only customer. He then realised that, as he didn't know when she would be off duty, he may miss her. He could see a chair on the pavement outside and sat on it.

The sun was beginning to fade, it was getting cold. He finished his snack while watching two pigeons, their heads bobbing, pecking at any tiny piece of sustenance they could find lying around his feet, the larger one occasionally chasing away the smaller. He threw a small piece of cheese in front of the latter which it picked up and tried to fly away but hampered by its enemy who picked up the morsel of food and flew away, leaving the smaller bird gazing silently up at it.

Survival of the fittest, he thought. Was he among the fittest? He doubted it. Perhaps he was the smaller one being chased away from what he wanted, in this case, perhaps, from *who* he wanted. As he mused on what was doing the chasing, she came out of the pub and began walking across the road. She spotted him and stopped.

'What are you doing here, waiting for me?' she asked, stepping back onto the pavement.

'I'd have thought that was obvious.'

'What do you want t hen?'

'To talk to you.'

'What about?'

He hesitated before saying the name.

'Doris.'

'Ah, the mysterious lady.'

'Hardly that.'

Well, *I* know nothing about her, and I'm not standing here all evening, it's cold.'

'Let's walk then,'

Staying a little apart, they began walking.

He had a glance at the surrounding buildings: some Georgian windows, a Roman pediment, a small, Italianate-style house he hadn't noticed before, but it wasn't the same as when sharing them with her, he saw them in isolation, they appeared cold, like the gap between him and the girl not quite at his side.

She turned her head to him.

'Painted any pretty butterflies lately?'

'Look, I won't lie and say that Doris was, I dunno, a friend of my mum's, say, who didn't like certain things or something, the truth is - '

'You're going to tell the truth?'

'Yes.'

'Because you're frightened I'll find out anyway?'

'No, I - '

'You need to, yes?'

'Are you going to let me tell you?'

'Carry on.'

'She was a girl I used to know.'

'And?'

'It was kind of more than that.'

'How much more?'

'If you'll let me finish.' He could do without the interrupting; he wanted to get it over with.

'She... lived with me.'

She turned her head towards him again.

'*Lived* with you?'

'Yes.'

'For how long?'

'Not sure.'

'I don't know anyone who lived with someone unless they - '

'Were married. I know.' He stopped and touched her arm. 'See, I thought I was in love with her I think, but I wasn't, that's why, I realise now, I did all the work on the place. I was doing it to escape having - '

'A real relationship?'

'I suppose so, but I didn't really want it, not with her.'

'What happened?'

'She left.'

'Let's carry on walking, I don't want to stand in the street arguing.'

'We're not arguing, I'm trying to tell you something.'

'Not very well I'm afraid, perhaps you should have rehearsed it.'

'I did.'

He had rarely felt so inarticulate. He realised that he couldn't even describe what he felt about it all, except the relief that she had gone. He didn't think about her any more. He tried to say this to the girl by his side as honestly as he could.

She turned to him, her face expressionless.

'You seem confused.'

'Except that it's over, I'm not confused about that. Its finished, Enid, I don't think about her and there's nothing left of her in the house. Gone.'

She was silent for a while.

'Well, thanks for telling me. You have, of course, the right to have girl friends, but it's the 'living with' that's wrong.'

'I know, but it's religion again isn't it, and you're not that religious but you still see it as wrong.'

'Because everybody else does.'

'Brain-washing.'

'We have to have standards to live by.'

'Where do they come from, though?'

'You're getting me off the subject.'

'I want to forget it ever happened. Can we?'

"We'?'

'If there wasn't a 'we' you wouldn't be so... angry about it and I wouldn't have been so scared of telling you.'

'I knew you were, I could tell it.'

He stopped and held her hand.

'I know you'd like to ask some questions, I can understand that, but let's forget those for now and enjoy the last of the sun, eh?'

She nodded, not pulling her hand away as they continued towards Oxford Street. He felt relieved, He looked around him.

'I always look up to spot the good bits, the pediment above Victorian keystones, the odd crenellations on top of an Edwardian hotel maybe, the set-back top of a new block of flats, like the one over there,' he pointed at it, 'like the bridge of a liner sailing out of a poster.'

'You haven't lost your artistic appreciation then.'

'No.' He glanced at her then away again. 'And those scrolled capitals and that door under them, it's had about thirty coats of paint over the years, the shine's softer, kind of friendlier.'

'You're dragging me into your little universe again.'

'Am I? Make it *our* little universe. Look, I - '

'You seem to like that word.'

'I want to emphasise something, that's all.'

'Which is?'

'D'you think that… that you could come and see the house. I shouldn't ask you at this moment I know, timing's never been one of my strengths, but I want you to come, if just for a minute or two.'

She didn't reply.

'Shouldn't I have asked?'

'As you say, your timing's not great, but may as well get it over with, I suppose, but certainly not now.'

'No, I didn't mean tonight. Tomorrow, maybe?'

'We'll have to see.'

He asked her what time she was finishing.

'Afternoon.'

'I'll be in there before you leave.'

'Okay, but it's not a promise.'

'I know. I'll take the chance.'

'Up to you. It's time I went home.'

They weren't far from the Underground station and went in. They stood next to each other in a crowded carriage saying nothing. At Mile End, she suggested that he get his train from there, she would continue on. He briefly kissed her cheek and alighted, telling her he would see her the next day.

He'd cleaned the place, mopped the kitchen floor, put cutlery and crockery away, straightened the curtains - each time he drew them he'd thought of his mother's disapproval at him not having 'nets' as she called them - tidied his bed, put a dish of potpourri on the bathroom sill, and was now, again, waiting in the pub for her to finish her shift. He'd got there at three, assuming she would be finished in an hour. He'd asked her with some trepidation if she'd wanted to come back with him. She'd looked at him with a rather firm look before saying that although she wasn't really that keen, she would, but wouldn't stay for long.

Bishop came to him and asked when the next union meeting would be. George told him that no date had been fixed. He tried to remember a few jokes which he thought might amuse her then dropped the idea and patiently waited for her. After a while she came over to him.

'Ready then?'

'For you, always.'

He asked her what her morning had been like.

'Same old, same old. I get fed up with it.' She shrugged. 'I have to make a living, though, can't expect dad to keep me, and things are getting worse, apparently.'

'There are more unemployed now than there's ever been.'

'Well, you're not doing so badly, and you're buying your own house too, lucky you.'

'I've worked for it.'

'I know.'

She smiled at him, but he felt it was a rather reluctant, distant one.

They talked little on the journey except for him trying out a few alternative definitions; 'Logarithm: contraceptive method used by lumberjacks', and 'Overdue: Rabbi.' She appeared mildly amused and as they left Ash Park station he asked if she had been to the area before. She hadn't.

'It's very new isn't it,' she said, looking around her, 'lots of clean-looking shops.' She looked down the hill. 'And some nice-looking houses, too.'

They walked down the hill and turned into his road.

'Wanna guess which one's mine?'

'If you like. Going to tell me what side of the road it's on?'

'This one.'

She slowed her steps.

'They look the same.'

'They're meant to, the same design, the harmony of congruence.'

They went past several houses before she announced, 'It's this one.'

He asked her how she had guessed.

'It's the only one with a green door and no net curtains.'

'Well done. Come in.'

She crossed the small front garden and peered in the window.

'I like it, it has a certain - '

'Class?'

'Maybe. And are they Egyptian things on the wall, they look like it. Very Tutenkahmenish.'

He opened the door and they went inside. She stood in the hall.

'Ah, so there they are, the butterflies. What are their names?'

'Sally, Pauline, Emma, Lily… Kidding. This one's a fritillary and the others up the staircase are a peacock, purple emperor and red admiral.'

'The look so real they could fly.'

'They've got nine-inch wingspans.'

'If they were life-size, silly.' She looked at him. 'And the one in the bedroom?'

'Er, clouded yellow.'

'Going to show me?'

'If you want.'

He went past her and she followed him onto the landing and into the bedroom. It was hanging above the headboard.

'Why did you put this one here and not one of the others?'

'It's kind of softer, it doesn't dominate.'

'You like 'soft'?'

'Depends on who or what we're talking of.'

'Do you think *I* am?'

'In what sense?'

'Not in the head I can assure you.'

'I know, but there's a softness about you sometimes that's hard to explain.'

'You're losing your explanatory power again.'

'Again, it's the effect you have. And that's a new bed, by the way,' he lied, 'I bought it after… you know.'

She didn't respond, except to ask him if he had any coffee.

'Yes, look in here first and I'll make some.'

They had a quick look in the smaller bedroom and the bath-room, the latter impressing her with its oriental painting and black tiles.

'You're clever.'

They returned downstairs where he made her coffee and took it to her as she stood in front of the Egyptian paintings.

'Such detail.'

'Where the devil is. Sit down and partake of your beverage.'

'That's a fluffy sort of phrase.'

'I'm just glad you're here,' he said as they she sat at the table.

'You have a nice home, Mister Woods.'

'Thanks.'

'How long have you had it?'

'About, I dunno, fifteen... eighteen months.

'How long was she here? From the beginning?'

'No.'

'But quite a while?'

'Aren't you going to have any coffee?'

'No, I'm happy to watch you drink yours.'

'You're easily pleased.'

'Not really.'

'Did you think you were in love with her?'

'Suppose so, but... I don't want to talk about it.'

'You don't think I have a right to know?'

'I didn't say that. I suppose you have, really.'

'I haven't, but if there's going to be anything between us then you, we, have to be truthful.'

'Look - '

'That word again.'

'I'm trying to emphasise something.'

'Which is?'

'That there was pressure from her to live with me, but after a while I didn't want her here.'

He'd been looking down at the table while saying this, but now looked up at her.

'Yes, I suppose I thought I was in love with her, but I wasn't. She knew it. That's why she left.'

'Would you have told her to leave if she hadn't?'

'Eventually. I'd have had to. Can we not talk about this any more?' He leaned towards her. 'It's over with. Please believe me.'

She gave him a reluctant smile and said, 'Alright, for now, at least.'

There was a silence.

'I'm going to go home. I assume you'll come to the station with me?'

''Course.'

They went out and turned towards the station.

He asked about her father; if she knew where he was working, how long he'd had his motor bike, had he ever been to her pub. He hardly listened to the answers, As her train arrived he gave her quick kiss on the cheek.

'This is honesty for you, I'm so glad you came.'

She smiled at him, went into the carriage and took her seat.

He returned home, sat on an armchair, restlessly reached under its fitted cushion and pulled out an old newspaper' he put them there because his father had always done the same at home. He flicked though it disinterestedly... a bit more on the Crystal Palace fire, unemployment, a new flying boat service, more on the King's abdication, thousands of Nationalist volunteers landing in Cadiz - what he understood of it he felt sorry for the Republican fighters.

He flung the paper across the floor. He felt lonely. It was ridiculous. She had only been in the house five minutes, she had come, they had talked a little and that was it, really. He missed her. He wanted her here.

30

'Well, here we are at Claridge's, which has housed royalty and its friends and is an opulent hotel where every polished corner tells a story. The tale here, of course, is about the bride and groom.' He looked across at Eric. 'How lucky you are. You'll leave here today with a woman who is warm, loving and caring, and,' he glanced briefly at Fiona, 'how lucky you are also. You'll leave here today having gained a lovely dress and a wonderful bouquet of flowers.' There were a few chuckles. 'No. Marriage is a wonderful institution.' He glanced questioningly around. 'But who wants to go into an institution?'

Rupert was speaking at a reception in the hotel after his friend's wedding in a church near his parental home where he'd worn the suit he had bought at Harrods, while his wife had worn a green satin gown with a delicately embellished sweetheart necklace, halo crown, long veil, ruched sleeves and a waistline that emphasised her almost-petite figure. During the ceremony there had been a pageboy, and six bridesmaids linked by a garland of flowers following her.

It was a week into the new term and he had seen Constance at her mother's place twice, one of them being New Year's Eve, and spoken to her when she had rung him on the phone near his rooms from the call box in her road. He had booked a room for them for the night at the same hotel they had strayed in after the theatre visit. She was smiling at him from her seat, drink in hand and wearing a puffed blouse and fluted skirt with a fashionably high waistline.

'However,' he continued, pulling a scrap of paper from his pocket, 'who do I start with? A rhetorical question, it will be the groom of course.' Looking down at the paper, he said, 'He is handsome, clever, intelligent, has oodles of charm and... ' He frowned and looked up at the man he was describing. 'Sorry Eric, having trouble reading your handwriting, you can tell me the rest later.'

There was some laughter, especially from Fiona who was sitting at the front next to her new husband and nudging him rather vigorously, especially when the speaker said 'If there's anybody here this evening who's feeling nervous, apprehensive and queasy at the thought of what lies ahead, it's probably   because you've just married the   groom.' There was a pause. 'Incidentally, if you can't hear me at the back, the silence from the people at the front should reassure you that you've not missed anything. However, it has been an emotional day, even the cake is in tiers.'

He noticed Constance putting a finger to her lips.

'Well, that's all from me except to wish them all the luck in the world. And incidentally, the management have requested that you do not stand on tables or   chairs for my standing ovation. Thank you.'   Most of the guests clapped and he returned to his chair next to Constance.

His mother had been invited but, as she had a matinee that afternoon and couldn't attend, he had conveyed her apologies. He noticed again the grim-looking man at the back of the room where, as he had done during the wedding, assumed that he was Eric's father. The woman sitting next to him was his wife who Rupert had been introduced to, as well as other family members, at the ceremony. She had appeared to be pleased by the whole thing. Eric had said in an aside to Rupert, 'Family, eh? Aunts, uncles nephews and cousins twice removed, whatever they are, seen mostly at weddings and funerals.'

Eric, now standing, turned to his guests and said, 'Well, I'm not going to attempt to follow that. All I want to say is to thank all of you who attended the ceremony earlier for being here now and for all the lovely gifts you have given us. Now, you may have noticed the gentlemen sitting quietly in the corner of this pleasant room, but they are now going to make a noise, some lovely swinging and jiving sounds. I present,' he again gestured towards them, 'The Ray Peters Band. Let's give them a big welcome.' He and the rest of the room clapped. 'Take your partners and dance,' he requested loudly, pulling Fiona from her chair, putting a hand around the back of her waist and moving with the rhythm as the band picked up their instruments and began playing.

A few people began dancing and when 'Alabama Slide' followed, Eric and his wife slid into a foxtrot, gliding and spinning smoothly around the room. The few couples that were on the floor stepped back to allow them space and joined in the applause. A male vocalist then appeared and sang 'They All Fall In Love,' prompting more couples to get up and dance.

'They're good aren't they,' Rupert remarked to Constance, although there doesn't seem enough of them to be a proper dance band.'

'They're hardly Ambrose.'

'They certainly make up for it though, perhaps the bride and groom got them here, Fiona does a bit of acting, perhaps she knows them.'

'What are we talking for? Let's dance.'

He wasn't really sure how to foxtrot, he certainly couldn't match Eric, but Constance patiently guided him without making it look too obvious and he began to relax and move with the tempo. The Bouncing Ball jitterbug was then announced which he felt more at home with and spun his partner around with almost abandon. He couldn't do it as well as he'd seen it performed in American films, he wasn't as quick and he wasn't sure he could lift his partner over his shoulder in the almost casual way shown in those movies. But she was good, surprisingly agile and her broad grin seemed to light the room.

He felt a little gratified and rather embarrassed when the music ended and Eric and Fiona enthusiastically clapped them. Eric then turned to the band leader and spoke to him who then clicked his fingers and exaggeratedly pointed at his musicians who began playing Love Is Just A Bit Of Heaven, halfway through which the vocalist started singing.

Eric waltzed with his new wife, easily turning and gliding in unison with her, the other couples on the floor, standing, watching them. When the melody had finished there was again applause, which Rupert thought they had thoroughly deserved. His friend came over to him and politely asked if he could have the next one with Constance.

'Of course,' replied Rupert, and they danced away to another waltz, again accompanied by the singer. They danced it well together, Rupert thinking that, although his jiving was passable, he didn't have the - he searched for the word - 'grace' to move like that, knowing that he would probably have been pumping their joined hands up and down instead of the smooth, casual movements of his friend, indeed that of most of the other dancers there, also. Eric thanked her and she returned to Rupert.

'I didn't know you could dance that well,' he said to her.

'Depends who you're dancing with.' She kissed his cheek. 'But he can't jive as well as you.'

'Thanks.'

'I'm going to the cloakroom, try not to miss me.'

'I'll try.'

Eric then came towards him and occupied the vacant seat.

'They're good aren't they, Fiona knows them, they love their jazz, that individualistic self-expression of our class, dear boy.'

'You still haven't told me where you're going to honeymoon,' Rupert said to him.

'Sorrento, dear boy, the cliffs scattered with pastel-coloured houses, piazzas at every turn, the local wine, trips to Amalfi, Positano, Capri.. we may even get to Tuscany. Scalderemo il mare, rendere la terra piu verde... '

'What does that mean?'

'We will warm the sea, make the land greener... '

'I bet Italy can't wait for you to land.'

'Possibly not.'

'I am pleased for you, though.'

'Thank you. We depart on the morrow. And speaking of Italia, Franco's Italian and German friends are helping the Nationalists become dominant it seems, and the French, apparently, are going to stop aid to the Republicans, although they can still buy arms from the Soviet Union. And you can bet there'll be divisions within the anarchist and communist ranks.'

'There'll always be splits and factions in any movement that goes against a dominant value system. Incidentally, have you become political suddenly?'

'You mean, am I on *your* side?'

'I don't think your upbringing allows it.'

'And what of yours?'

'I've reacted against it, I suppose.'

'Reacted against your father, you mean. Talking of the Ruskies, did you hear about the chappie who went to a shop in Moscow and asked, 'Is this the shop that has no meat?' 'No,' was the reply, 'we're the shop that has no bread, the shop that has no meat is across the road.'

'That's a barb created by a system of rampant inequality, and whose leaders, deep down, are probably scared of something similar to what happened in Russia happening here. It wasn't that long ago that near-starvation was one of the triggers for their revolution.'

'Perhaps it still exists.'

'It takes time to create a new system.'

'What are you two talking about?'

It was Fiona, she had Constance by her side.

'We've been in the Ladies Room.'

'I'll get a couple of chairs and bring them over,' suggested Eric, 'It'll be a table for four then.'

When he had done so and they'd quickly made themselves comfortable, he stood, put a hand up towards the band who were preparing to launch into their next number.

'I think it's time for an interval now,' he said, looking at the couples who were on the floor waiting to resume dancing. 'And, dear people, food will be served shortly. Return to your tables and enjoy.'

Waiters then appeared with embroidered tablecloths and swiftly laid them on the tables along with cutlery and requests for drink orders.

Constance asked Eric what was on the menu.

'As it will say, when it is brought any moment now, there'll be navy bean soup, oysters, beef stroganoff, foie gras, white truffle, baked apple pudding and chocolate chip oat cookies amongst other delights. I hope they satisfy our guests.'

'They certainly will me, thank you,' said Constance.

'The pleasure's mine, one doesn't get married every day nor does one have the delight of seeing you tripping the light fantastic.'

'No caviar?' enquired Rupert,'

'He thinks it's overrated,' said Fiona as her partner began singing, 'Caviar comes from the virgin sturgeon, virgin sturgeon's a very fine dish, the virgin sturgeon needs no urgin', that's why caviar's a very fine dish.'

'You should have been the vocalist for the evening,' murmured Rupert.

Fiona asked how his mother was.

'She's well, and sorry she couldn't be here. I think her play will run for quite a while.'

'As I forecast,' said Eric.

Waiters were now busying themselves placing menus and champagne on the tables, the recipients of which, after filling their glasses, raised them briefly to the pivotal couple who nodded in appreciation. Eric filled the glasses of those at his table and they toasted each other.

'Eric Pullis,' said Rupert, 'may you and Fiona have a long, fruitful, fulfilled and happy life.'

'Hear, hear!' joined in Constance.

'They say there's no such thing as happiness, you have to be happy without it, but we'll try.'

He then asked them to state their preferences and he would order them when the head waiter came. 'Billings is his name by the way.' He glanced around quickly then said, 'Talking of 'by the ways', what makes you so interested in politics anyway, Roop?'

'I'd be quite happy to put a ban on its mentioning whilst we're here to celebrate your nuptials. The whole of Neasden should be out on their doorsteps or thronging the streets, standing in trees waving flags to honour you both.'

'You're not exaggerating?'

'Maybe a little.'

'Actually, other than you and, of course, my tutor and the Proctor who've given me special dispensation for the time off, I haven't told anyone at Oxford/ let me ask again what made you so interested in the 'political', anyway? I want to know.'

'I'll give you permission to ask it, but *every*thing's political, anyway. It's not just about elections, coups, assassinations, et cetera, it's about any individual or group having power or potential power over any other individual or group. A father telling his teenage daughter that he wants her home by midnight is a political act.'

'Would he say the same thing to his teenage son?' asked Constance.

'Probably not.'

'Why can't both offspring be treated the same?' asked cFiona.

'Because the father has internalised cultural norms and, as they are the current ones, he could hardly be accused of being old-fashioned. Anyway, it was merely an example of the definition of the political.'

A rather corpulent man then appeared at their table and said to Eric, 'I do hope you enjoyed your dancing, Mister Pullis, I certainly did, you make a handsome couple.'

'Thank you, Billings, we've changed tables, as you can see.'

'D'you wish to order now?'

'I think so.'

They made their minds up quickly and ordered their meals.

'Shall we let the men talk politics then?' said Fiona.

Constance frowned. 'Cannot *we*?'

'The feminist movement?'

'Doesn't have to be.'

Have you read Woolf?'

'Of course, getting on a bit now but still inspirational I think.'

'The movement seems to have gone to sleep a bit.'

'You could always wake it up,' suggested Eric. 'Isn't there The National Society for Women's Service?'

'Depends how one does it.'

'One needs a collective, a gathering, a concerted protest, really,' said Rupert.

'It would make a difference if men were seen supporting it,' volunteered Fiona.

'I doubt it'll happen,' said Rupert, 'men wouldn't gain by it, they like their women in subservient roles, or at least, perceived as such.'

'They are as such, we're here to do men's bidding, the very word "their" women.'

'That's the current and the past worldview, but over time it can be changed.'

'Most women have an identity only within the home,' said Fiona, 'wives and mothers.'

"Mistress' is another,' said Constance.

'I suppose they're all master statuses,' said Rupert.

'And awarded by men,' said the woman at his side.

'My dears,' interjected Eric, 'whilst agreeing on the unfairness of it all, I can see Billings's men holding trays aloft and heading for us. Let us enjoy our food, undoubtedly prepared by a master chef.'

'And not a cook, which could of course, mean a woman,' said Constance.

'Indeed. Here they are, let us enjoy.'

They ate mostly silently, except for a few subtle sounds of smacking lips, 'Mmms' of appreciation and, from Eric, 'Absolutely scrumptious', 'heavenly taste', 'such sensory delight', and other words of appreciation. Their desserts finished, all four having different ones, they wiped lips with napkins and leaned back on their chairs.

'Well, that was, indeed, a most satisfying repast,' said Eric.

'And we thank you for it,' Rupert replied.

The former again looked toward the band, who had been snacking and talking amongst themselves, and held his hand up to them. He then turned to the rest of the diners and said, 'Dear people, I trust you have enjoyed your food and refreshment, and in a short while, you may, if you have the energy, continue cavorting.'

There were a few 'Hear, hears', and the musicians began to ready themselves for more music.

'Let's see you two again, just for me,' Eric urged.

They quietly watched people dance the opening waltz and foxtrot then Rupert and Constance got on the floor for their jive. Eric applauded them when they had finished and said, 'I'm going to ask the band for a quickstep and you can watch *us*.'

He went across to the bandleader who had already raised his hands and began a samba. Several couples danced, Eric not being amongst the most rhythmic of the males, although his partner was certainly the best amongst the females. Rupert and Constance clapped heartily when the tune finished, to which Fiona gave a brief curtsy before coming back to the table.

Rupert asked Eric where he would be staying the night.

'Right here old chap, we have a special honeymoon suite.

'I'm sure you will both enjoy yourself immensely.'

'Of course we shall, and in the morning we're on our blessed way to Croydon and an Imperia flying machine on board which we shall soar into the heavens. Talking of which, I think one more dance for us and then we shall retire for the night.'

He nodded towards the band, whereupon its leader called for attention and said , 'We will now have this last waltz, to be led of course,' he gestured to the table 'by the bride and groom, and once again, congratulations to them,'

There was some clapping before the man continued with, 'If any of you wish to stay for some more drinks and a little light music, please do so.' He turned to his musicians and they began playing a Viennese waltz.

After leaving them alone on the floor for half-a-minute, several couples joined the leading pair, Rupert and Constance watching in appreciation their friends' successful performance. When the dance had finished, Eric thanked them again for attending and that he and his new wife would now leave. There was more applause after which he returned to the table where he thanked his friend for being his best man.

After the goodbyes, Rupert stood and said, 'Let's go now, Constance, our room awaits.' As they left, he caught the eye of his friend's mother and exchanged smiles and brief waves.

They caught a taxi for the short distance to the hotel, went through the foyer and the lift to their room. They entered.

'This has a lovely familiarity about it, doesn't it,' he said, looking about him at the magnolia walls and ceiling, triple mirrors on the dressing table, and walnut wardrobe. 'Good memories, eh?'

'Very. It was a night to remember, but... we're not going to make any this time, I'm afraid.'

'What is that supposed to mean?'

'It's the time of the month, I have my period.'

He hesitated briefly before saying, 'There's more than one way to skin a cat. Sorry, a crude analogy.'

'I'd sooner you just keep your pyjamas on and lie next to me. I'm sorry. Let's just talk, hold hands.'

He turned from her, dropped their bags, delved into his, pulled out pyjamas, quickly removed his clothes, and put them on. He turned back to her.

'This do?' he asked. 'I didn't bring my sophisticated dressing gown.'

'No need for sarcasm. I'm going to the bathroom to change, and it's not into my sexy underwear. I'm sorry, Rupert.'

He kissed her cheek. 'Don't be, it can't be helped.'

He got into bed and waited for her to return, thinking of the old saying that one should never go back to one's favourite restaurant. Maybe, he thought, you shouldn't go back to your favourite hotel room either.

She came out of the en suite wearing a silk crepe kimono, and sat on the edge of the bed.

'That's what you wore last time. You're torturing me.'

'I shouldn't have brought it I know. I didn't think.'

'What do you wish to talk about then? He asked.

'Up to you.'

'Well, we can't talk dirty, that's for sure.'

'Stop it.'

'Okay, are women born or made?'

'Well, I shouldn't think common sense assumptions about 'natural' behaviour would really stand up to scrutiny.'

'There is an argument that it's not just the way girls are brought up that makes them 'feminine' but that femininity is recognised immediately by the parents and is thus encouraged.'

'Still means that women are the product of, what do you call it, 'socialization'?'

'Yep, and it's been shown that if relatives are told that a newborn girl is a boy then there'll be comments such as, 'Ooh, he's just like his dad', and 'He's a handsome lad', and 'Look at those legs, he'll be a rugby player I reckon,' and so forth.'

'The opposite if they're told that a 'he' is a 'she' then?'

''Course. Those eyes, she's gonna break some hearts she is', et cetera, et cetera.'

'Down to patriarchy in the end, is it?'

'Probably.'

'So it's not necessarily natural that to be attractive to men, women should, ideally, be tall and slim?'

'It seems to be generally so in the Western World.'

'But in Africa, does not sexual attraction mean well-rounded females?'

'What we would call, perhaps, 'rotund'?'

'Or an 'African arse'.'

'That's the tomboy in you again, which I like.'

'On that note, perhaps we should go to sleep.'

'Or try to.'

She pulled the sheet down then up over her and lay down, looking at him as if expecting him to do similarly. He reluctantly did so.

'Well, Miss Lange, do you wish for anything from the bar? I can dress again and go down to it or call room service.'

'I don't need anything.'

'Do you *want* something,?'

'No.'

'Not even my close proximity?'

'I want that, but as we are.'

'You and Fiona briefly mentioned the cause earlier.'

'The women's movement. Yes.'

He turned his face to her.

'You know, I'd miss you if you spent a lot of time taking up that cause, as worthy as it is, though, unless your mother's position alters, you won't be able to.'

'What about what you want to do then other than your degree, I probably won't know where you are, even.'

'What does that mean?'

She bent forward then looked back at him.

'Well, I don't think you're as satisfied as you'd like to be in what you're doing at your College. I don't think the degree's enough. I'm not sure, I really don't know, but there's something, something inside you that wants to... fulfil itself, perhaps a thing you feel you have to do. I've felt it from you of late, there's something there that's kind of prodding you.'

He didn't answer her.

'I may be completely wrong, but I doubt it. You may not be able to articulate it, but it's there.'

He wasn't quite sure what to say except, 'I didn't realise you were so empathetic.'

'Verstehen. Anyway, to your relief I suspect, I'm tired and wish to sleep. Is it an early train in the morning?'

'No, you can sleep as long as you want to. Suppose I'll have to content myself with just gazing at you when I awake.'

'Don't be silly. Goodnight.'

Before lying down he kissed her cheek.

'Goodnight, lovely lady. I'll try to sleep.'

He lay with his back to her, wanting her, feeling restless but trying to lie still and not disturb her. He thought about what she'd said, what he couldn't articulate. Was it, then, becoming that obvious?

31

He was looking down at pigeons again, this time there were two that seemed to be either kissing each other or sharing the cake crumbs stuck to a wrapper he'd purposely dropped on the pavement beneath him as he sat, waiting for Enid outside the café again. He was hoping it would become a regular meeting place for them to begin their walks. It was a Saturday afternoon. A few days ago they he'd gone to North London, got off randomly at a station and walked past a nearby block of recently-built flats with pantiled roof, curved bays and herringbone bricks.

She seemed to appreciate the design, the feel of the building, especially the roof's colour, but when they were on the returning train he had wondered whether she really saw them as he did, their relationship to the movies he liked so much, showing the bright, sunlit colours of Los Angeles homes, of New York sky-scrapers with their set-back peaks, the white walls and palm trees of California, 'though he didn't expect to see any of the latter in London.

Although he had, seemingly, opened her eyes to these things, perhaps she had only pretended to share it all with him,
though he was fairly sure there was some genuine interest from her. He wondered if he had had any right to expect her to be like him in this way, in *any* way even, but then he wouldn't want to be with her if she wasn't. Thinking back now, he realised more and more that Doris had shared hardly anything with him.

Enid had worked only the morning shift and had seemed re-laxed and pleased to see him. With the sun breaking through clouds and illuminating the cannon-lip chimney pots of large-garden'd roadside houses, they had wandered through a park and then long, terraced streets with tall pavement trees.

She'd appeared to be in a pleasant mood, but he wasn't quite sure. It had been almost a week since she had been to his home, a period where, because two of the girls at the pub had been off sick, she'd had to work their shifts. He had phoned her place of work but had been able to speak to her for only a minute, which had consisted of her telling him how tired she was and that her boss wouldn't be too pleased at her being on the phone when there were customers to see to.

He'd had no contact with Reg for a while; he'd recently gone to see him but he'd been out on both occasions. Work seemed to be less satisfying, 'though he had earned some extra wages by working a weekend at a nearby office block that needed some names painted on various staff members' doors. Nobody seemed to have heard anything about events, if any, after the accident and whether any action had, or was being taken. He sensed a feeling amongst the workers on the site of some sort of acceptance, an acceptance of a shocking happening about which little could now be done, a fatalistic occurrence that somehow would never happen again.

He tried to avoid thinking of this by ordering another coffee and turning his thoughts to filmic images again, thought not of Hollywood this time, but of him on his way to work.

He saw a straightforward shot of himself leaving his house wearing a grey, black-flecked sports jacket, tie and worsted trousers. The camera tracks towards him as he walks quickly along the street with head bent forward on stooping shoulders then a dramatic close-up, the camera on its trolley twelve inches from his bobbing face, minute particles of sleep in the corner of an eye, an off-white filling in a front tooth, the pallor of his smooth skin.

The houses in the background are in view as the camera move away, travelling faster than he walks. The corner of a road, a blank wall, a dog trotting past, then he appears again, turns quickly and moves from left to right of the screen. A side-view this time as he runs to catch a bus pulling away from a stop then a casual leap onto the platform with an aerial shot that looks almost directly down at him as he swings around the pole with one hand and instantly disappears into the interior.

The blue-grey, acrid air of the crowded top deck, a low shot showing cement-spattered boots, shiny black Oxfords and a pair of brown suede casuals. Stark close-ups of men with a day's growth of beard and the just-shaven ones putting rolled cigarettes between their lips, faces with closed eyes endeavouring to finish off harshly interrupted sleep, faces with eyes narrowed, reading the cartoon pages of their Daily Mirrors or Daily Mails, faces with open mouths panting with the effort of the double exertion of running for the bus and coughing from an early cigarette.

'Sorry I'm late, it couldn't be helped.'

It was Enid interrupting his cinematic jaunt, and wearing a beret, the first the first time he'd seen her in one.

'Er, hello. It suits you, you look particularly Gallic.'

'Merci, monsieur.'

'D'you want a tea or something?'

'No, I've had some. A walk would be nice.'

'There's a church not far away, a Hawksmoor. Let's visit it.'

'Alright then, lead the way.'

He asked her about her work, she about his, and they were there. He suggested they walk in the cemetery. 'A bit of green away from the smoke and bustle.'

It was a rather unkempt one with large trees and wild bushes hanging over blackened, eroded tombs and headstones, and long grass growing over inscribed slabs of granite. They looked at the winged angel monuments, a testimony to Victorian piousness and order, at the names on the mossy headstones, Braithwaite, Dobson, Samuels - junior school images settling in his mind - the long grass, the wilting flowers, and wondered what exactly mourners felt at the moment the coffin moved from a decorated facade to the earth. He had never been to a funeral.

He could imagine that after one, in a bowling pavilion or somewhere, the fake jocularity and superficial memories, ''e liked a good laugh, did Alf,' 'Yeah, 'e once said that if 'e couldn't take it wiv 'im, 'e wouldn't go,' or earnest sadness, asking himself whether any of it hid the reality of their pain; how many there actually felt it, how many a quiet relief.

Coming away from the graves they spotted a horse-drawn hearse followed by several black limousines stopping in front of the church. He wondered aloud who and for what reasons its passengers had been allotted their seats in the church.

'I can imagine,' he said to his companion, "'ere, you sit wiv Glad, she's yer aunt,' or 'You better go in the back wiv yer baby, Joan.'

'Perhaps,' she said, 'it was 'Do sit with me, Charles, we need to talk arrangements and Wills,' or 'Hello Percy, mind if I plonk next to your good self?''

He was rather surprised that a cortège was allowed this far into the city to hold up traffic, perhaps it was someone perceived as important, one of the 'great and the good'. Everyone seemed to be in traditional black; most wearing hats, some men carrying them in their hands as they walked up the wide steps towards the tall, heavy doors. They watched them all enter before the doors closed, their clanging feeling like a prohibition, of something banned.

'Let's go in,' he suggested.

'But we haven't been invited... We don't know who - '

'Doesn't matter, let's hear some music.'

He slowly opened the doors and they sat at the back, the nearest mourners a dozen rows in front. They looked around. It wasn't precious, no Catholic gold and glitz, just white columns, acanthus leaf, rams horns, dulled oak. He imagined a sparrow looking down on the grey heads, black coats, wheelchairs, a corner painting and tomb, hearing a violin in a square nave that had housed hatreds, saccharin cant, that had never seen a flowered 'Grandad' nor crossed hammers in claret and blue roses; and this before the spirit's weakening to the body, the fidgets, coughs, desire for the wine and smoked eels, the toilets...

They listened to the organ for a while until he felt her becoming restless.

'You're right, we don't know anyone, and the music's a bit dirge-like isn't it. Let's quietly leave.'

They silently made their way out of the building and onto the road again where he noticed her smiling and shaking her head a little.

He asked her why she was doing it.

'Because, I dunno, you do things I haven't really seen anyone else do.'

'Such as?'

'Going into a random funeral service.'

'You did, too.'

''Cos I was with you.'

'You didn't have to come.'

'Would you have gone in on your own?'

'Good question.'

'Going to change the subject now?'

'No. I wouldn't have gone in without you.'

'Nor should you have.'

'First time I've done it, though. I've walked around graveyards before. I worked in one once, or rather, in a crematorium. Me and another tosher were painting the room that the back of oven was in. It was hot standing on it and painting the ceiling. I could hear the two men below me talking about taking the gold fillings from the body's teeth and pocketing its wedding ring. Apparently, it's the norm, their perks of the job.'

'How ghoulish.'

'I know, but forget that, there's plenty of green in a church-yard, and it's more interesting than a Corporation park.'

'You sure know how to lure a girl into a world of light and joy.'

'I only - '

'I'm kidding. I actually like the long grass and the quiet my-self.'

'You may have noticed the sun's shining through again, and there's a cemetery near where I live. Let's go there, we have time, I haven't been there before.'

She looked at her watch.

'Dad's going to buy some curtains this afternoon and I prom-ised to go with him, so I'm afraid I'll have to, but there's always tomorrow , if you're not doing anything.'

'We could always go to the flicks.'

'No, I'll come with you.'

They walked to nearby Chancery Lane, caught a train going to her station, he getting off before her to get a train to his, and cheered with the promise of seeing her soon.

The next day they met at his station and decided to walk to the cemetery. It was in the opposite direction to his home on a road which led them though a lane, the tops of trees touching across it making it almost a curving tunnel. They went through the cemetery gates and walked along a path. There wasn't, he felt, quite the same sense of peace here that was to be found in older, unkempt cemeteries, this place was built very recently, probably at roughly the same time as the Estate.

There were low, cream-painted buildings, Palladian-style roofs, a discreet chimney above the crematorium, and a neat symmetry of rose bushes measured along red-brick walls. Sculpted hedges bordered curved paths and small, numbered plaques stated whose ashes were uniformly spaced in the earth with its cropped, tended grass and the occasional paper-wrapped bunch of flowers.

'I can see a tea room,' he said, 'let's visit, they just may have Swiss roll.'

It was nearby, with only one empty table, the rest occupied by darkly-dressed mourners and undertakers' employees in black coat-and-tails.

'Nice roll,' remarked Enid, eating her tea, 'but I think I've had enough of gravestones, however Moderne or intricately carved they are.'

'It's not like this everywhere. Apparently, funerals in New Orleans have processions where people are sad going there and happy coming back, they have swing music and banners.'

She asked him whether he had always walked around places on his own. He thought for a while.

'I s'pose I've always gone out on my own really, like when a child I used to walk for miles along the top of the sewer, I think it's called the Northern Outfall, there's a lot of green there, and you can look down on the back gardens of the houses. Mum used to smack me sometimes when I got home late.'

'Sounds like the making of a loner. When's the next union meeting?'

'Want to sit in on it? You'd be bored silly. Actually, I don't know when. Nobody at work has asked, I'm not sure they're interested. Don't think *I* am, really.'

'But you seemed so keen to hold them.'

'It's too... small, this union, insignificant. What power have we? If we went on strike, the way the law stands they could, and would, sack us and get some other blokes in.'

'But, you'd be doing something.'

'Not enough.'

'Well, your union branch wouldn't alter the world, but it's something, and what's 'enough', anyway?'

'Don't know, but more than a gathering of painters in a room in a pub once a month or so.'

'A lot has been accomplished by a gathering of a few people in a small room.'

'Powerful people, yes.'

'Would you like power?'

'Enough to stop people having it.'

'Dear kettle, Yours, pot.'

'I'm not pushing Communism, arguably currently, the sharing of poverty, but Socialism, the sharing of plenty.'

'In theory.'

'I don't know a great deal about the theory, but it could eventually happen I suppose, though it would have to be a world-wide thing.'

He glanced around him. Noticing the other people there he felt that what he had been saying was inappropriate, he was getting quite enthusiastic about something and around him were people dealing daily with death, and others who had only just buried someone they had loved.

'Finish your tea and we'll go,' said Enid quietly, as if guessing his thoughts.

Once outside, he suggested more walking and they began following a path that wasn't surrounded by so many graves.

'I love the sun on trees, even on chocolate box roses around a cottage door,' he said.

'That's corny. I like it playing on leaves, sort of twinkling.'

'And glistening on windows. '

'Going to tell me a joke, then?

'How d'you know when an accountant's an extrovert? He looks at *your* shoes inst when he's talking to you instead of his own.'

'Not bad.'

Looking around them and enjoying the pale sun, they were silent for few minutes until he said, 'I remember when I went out on my own as a kid walking the streets and could see houses with bits of cemetery and park touching their back gardens, and I'd follow a little stream.'

'In the East End?'

'There are some. There was also a canal with narrowboats on, and I remember gazing up at a factory chimney and a crane. They fascinated me, dunno why.'

'Think I understand.'

'Get your curtains yesterday?'

'Yes, green ones, similar to yours. I was wondering where they were made. Dad went on about 'cheap labour in China'.'

'It's everywhere, and if it wasn't cheap it wouldn't be used.'

'He was going on about the thing in Spain.'

'It's a war really, people vote for a party, it gets into power then people with more power who don't like it, like the Army and Fascists, declare war against it. Well, it looks like that.'

'So much for democracy, eh?'

'Whatever that is, but this was pretty near it. The Catholic Church seems against the Republic as well. Must be horrible to fight for something which involves being against people of your own country, your compatriots, but there it is.'

'Is that what *you* want to do? Fight for something?'

He hesitated before answering.

'Sort of, yes. You're right - for something.'

They were both quiet as they walked towards the gated exit with its large arch and a small flower shop at the side of it.

'Have you heard about the barmaid who - '

'You have a knack of changing the subject when the talk gets near to something l think you feel strongly or deeply about.'

'Do I?'

'Yes. I wouldn't have said so otherwise. What if I were to ask you what you meant by the 'pressure' that Doris put on you?'

He didn't want to answer, didn't want to feel what he had at the time.

'Are you going to run away again?'

He took a breath.

'She... she threatened to kill herself if we didn't live together.'

'You believed her?'

'Yes, I believed her at the time, but I don't know now. I don't know.'

'Perhaps part of you wanted to believe her so you felt justified in her living with you.'

'That's a bit sick.'

She was quiet once more. He wanted to push the silence away.

'Come back with me, it's not far. I want to... fill the house with *you*.'

'You can be persuasive, but I'm in no mood to fill anything.'

'Let's try. Come on.'

He took her limp hand and they walked back to his home talking little except mundanely about their jobs.

He made her a coffee as soon as they were inside then asked her to come into the garden where he explained how he had built the waterfall and pond.

'I can feel that this was for you, not her.'

'I'm glad you said that.'

'You've done a good job. I'm going to powder my nose now.'

She went back into the house while he stood looking down into the pool. Inside again, he felt her presence. It felt good.

She came down the stairs, into the through-lounge and looked at him challengingly.

'I've just seen something in your bedroom.'

'What is it? What were you doing in there?'

'Looking at the view from the window. I saw your wardrobe door was open and I went to shut it and there was a blouse lying on the bottom of it. I couldn't help but notice.'

'A blouse? Hold on a minute. '

He went upstairs and opened the wardrobe. He looked down and saw a thin, almost transparent one part-hidden by a pair of shoes he hardly wore. He picked it up and went downstairs again.

'This it? I've never noticed it. I just get my clothes out, I don't look down.'

'Not even when you get your shoes?'

'I put 'em by the side of the bed, and this thing,' he held it above his head, 'is almost the same colour as the wardrobe floor. That's why I didn't see it.'

'Perhaps you pretended to yourself that you didn't see it.'

'Are you gonna mention another 'part' of me again? What am I, schizoid?'

'What I'm saying is, you may have kept it as a souvenir, you have every right to of course, but you promised me that it was all over, finished and forgotten, but it seems it isn't.'

'But it is. I didn't know it was there, I've told you.'

She narrowed her eyes.

'I wonder.'

He strode over to the fireplace and threw the garment on top of the burning coal.

'That suit you? No more now, it's over. I never really wanted her, you know that. Look... I don't want to be on my own any more, I want *you* with me.'

She said nothing, her face holding the same questioning expression.

'I know this sounds over-romantic, if you like, but I want you to walk with me   and... I dunno, point out flowers under a Victorian window in Hampstead or somewhere, the glint of sun on a canal, the curved windows of a block of flats in Chelsea, maybe a steeple rising above chestnut trees, you know what I mean.'

'Maybe a girl guiding her horse gently over Kensington cobbles. It's the poet in you again.'

'And in you,'

'But that doesn't mean I... trust you. I'm sorry George, but I'm not sure of you. There's something that makes me doubt. I don't want to, I want to believe you, but I can't. I like you, you know that, but I think it should be just as friends.' She looked down briefly and shook her head. 'I don't want to fall in love with you. Just let's be friends. I like walking around with you, being with you, but It's not going to be any more than that.' She paused, looking pained. 'I'm sorry. I really am, but... '

He felt confused.

'Why are you saying this? I've told you the truth.'

'I don't think you understand yourself, you're not... solid, George, you're kind of running around inside, somehow.'

He tried to lighten what she was saying.

'Is that why mum used to call me a flibbertigibbet?'

'Whatever it is, it makes you interesting, attractive, but in a relationship there has to be, I don't know, something more.'

He looked at her. She seemed as tall as he.

She sighed, 'I wish I could explain it better, but I can't.'

He felt something akin to fear.

'What are you saying? You don't want to see me any more?'

'Not really.'

"Not really'? *What* then?'

'Like I said, we could still be friends.'

'I hate that phrase. I thought we'd be more than that, and so did you.'

'But not now, I can't.'

He wanted to grab her shoulders, shake her and demand why she couldn't go any further than - at that moment he hated the word - 'companionship'. Not knowing what to say or do, he said and did nothing.

'I'm going now, George. Don't come to the station with me.'

She moved towards the front door and opened it. He followed her. She turned to him from the porch.

'Don't come to the pub, I'll contact you.'

She walked past the open gate and moved quickly towards the station. She didn't turn her face towards him.

He was about to stand at the gate and watch her walking away, but instead went inside, slamming the door. He looked at the fire. The blouse had disappeared. Why hadn't he noticed it? He was sure that he hadn't, wasn't he? He went to the garden and kicked some loose stones towards the pond. He felt like picking some up and throwing them as far as he could across the back gardens. He went inside, leaned on the draining board and put his head in his hands. Another woman gone. The first one he wanted to go, but not Enid.

He wondered whether she would contact him as she'd said. He had a strong feeling that she wouldn't. He felt empty, deserted.

32

'It was absolute heaven, paradiso, the sea, the sand, the sky, the very air.'

Rupert and Eric were sharing a bench in the quad where the latter was describing his recent honeymoon.

'The arancini, lasagne, saltimbocca, the gelato, the chianti, even the waiters were beautiful.'

'The Fascista?'

'Forget them.'

'Bit of a jolt to come back to Shakespeare, Milton and Thackeray, eh?'

'We haven't touched those yet.'

'If Shakespeare was Norwegian or Japanese we would hardly have known of him.'

'The spread of the English language, Empire.'

'The spread of American-English mote like, their increasing economic power, their films, and they have teachers of their - sorry, I mean 'our' - language in most countries of the world.'

'You may be right. How's Constance?'

'Caring for her mother increasingly low, she's moved in with her, haven't seen much of her.'

'Can't she get carers?'

'No. She refuses my help. She does have a neighbour who provides some relief occasionally, as I did for an hour or so before term began.'

'How's Pym?'

'Alright, but I suspect he's not quite as Left as he perhaps pretends, and he seems to have a weakness for Parsons, an American chap who talks of a whole collective of institutions serving society, but it's teleological, as I pointed out.'

'Which is?'

'A reason for something as a function of its end purpose as opposed to a function of its cause. The effect precedes the cause. We're on the subject of work at the moment, something which, of course, defines an individual's class and market situation and their commanding of specific goods and services, et cetera, et cetera.'

'Sounds mundane.'

'It's stating the obvious, yes, but it's real, and for a lot of workers it's a shitty way of life.'

'Hope you don't include that word in your essay.'

'I'd like to, academicizing sometimes tends to dilute the real world. You could argue, though, that it's not just the industrialisation of Western society that's responsible for the way the basic structure and organisation of work has developed, but capitalism.'

'Guess so.'

'But factory work has been the biggest change, the concentration of labour in factories and workshops, separation of home and work, the disciplining of workers, their subordination and economic dependence, the division of labour and specialisation, increase of unskilled tasks, personal relations with employers lost.'

'And the work process kind of fragmented.'

'Quite. Less intrinsic satisfaction, and increasingly workers are becoming alienated.'

'Which means...?'

'The concept has a long history, theologians use it to describe society's secularity, psychiatrists point to a state of disassociation and - '

'The real world?'

'Okay, imagine working on an assembly line, not just in the States but in Dagenham, and it's not just cars that have them, but the manufacturing of household goods, electrical goods. Mass production is on the increase, or was until the slump, but that will prove temporary. Imagine working on an assembly line where you're consigned to a specific spot, can't move, you stand in the same place for eight hours, six days a week doing the same thing, putting a bulb in a car reflector, or tightening the same nuts on a carburettor, screwing the handle on some container or other. Whatever, it would almost destroy a man's soul.'

'But what if a worker doesn't *feel* like that, that he has no control over what he does and can't do anything about his situation, is estranged from himself, is alienated? *Is* he? And most manual work isn't like that.'

'Perhaps he doesn't expect any more, but he's still exploited though, and we could go on for ever about objective definitions and the subjective experience, but he, or she, is going to feel a sense of... meaninglessness, utter boredom, powerlessness.'

'Perhaps this is really about the mood you're in.'

'That's irelevant, the worker's situation is thus. And when he goes out to buy something, more profit's made out of him.'

'Kind of alienated in both production and consumption then.'

'At least, exploited. You're coming along nicely, Ricey, we've got to get you away from the seductive and sometimes obfuscating prose of Literature.'

'How does all this affect you?'

'Very indirectly, but it's so unfair.'

'Life's unfair.'

'That's a cliché.'

'Most clichés are born of truth. However, I do have some sympathy for these people. But, that's progress.'

'What does that mean? One man's progress is another's poison. What if houses were built on a hillside in the Lake District? It would be progress for those living in them, but for those admiring the beauty of the lakes and hills it would be sacrilege.'

'Alright, you have a point. But what about coming to a party?'

'Whose? Where?'

'Mine, mine and Fiona's, at the flat, we've only just moved in.'

'Your new place? You haven't mentioned it, although it was obvious you weren't going to live at your parents even for a short time.'

'It's in town, not too far from College, it's in a new block of apartments. You'll like it, it's a penthouse flat.'

What's the party for?'

'Nothing in particular except that we're happy and want to celebrate it. It's on Saturday, three days' time. Do come, I'll accept no excuses, and do bring your lady.'

'I hope I can. She's ringing me this evening, pretty soon in fact. Give me the address.'

It was promptly scribbled on a scrap of paper.

'Here you are. I've a lot of work to catch up on and I may well not see you till the party.'

With that, they returned to their rooms.

He didn't have long to wait. He picked up the phone and made his usual enquiry.

'She's the same, or rather, if I'm honest, worse. She defecated on the bathroom floor this morning.'

'Oh, Christ. I wish you'd let me pay for a carer.'

'Thanks again, but she has a little put by as I've told you. If she makes a habit of doing it I'll see what I can do, I need to work again soon.'

She asked him how he was.

'Missing you, but Eric's having a party on Saturday in his new flat. Can you come? Maybe your neighbour will help out again.'

'Yes, I think she'll stay with her for a while.'

'Better not tell her what she did in the bathroom, though.'

'I'm hoping it's a one-off thing, but if she does it again I shall have to tell her, it's only fair.'

'S'pose so.'

'How's your work?'

'A couple of essays, one on sexual divisions, it's a new subject.'

'Should interest you, wish I was doing it.'

'Maybe, one day, you'll be an undergraduate somewhere doing just that.'

There was a brief pause before she said, 'That's mother calling, I'll go to her.'

'If, for any reason, you can't ring me before, I shall call for you on Saturday.'

'"Call for me", a sweet, old-fashioned phrase, What time?'

He told her.

'I'll try to ring you if I can, if not, I hope to see you then. ''Bye, sweetheart.'

She hadn't called him that before. It pleased him.

He saw neither his friend nor heard from his girl for the next two days and was leaving his room to go to her when the alcove phone rang. He went across and picked it up.

'Hello, is Rupert there?' It was Constance.

'The aforesaid is present.'

'I'm sorry, but I can't come, my neighbour's had to do something at the last moment and can't look after her. I told her what she'd done, and she's done it again, but it wasn't that. I'm sorry.'

'So am I.'

'I seem to keep disappointing you lately.'

'Ne'er mind.'

'But I do.'

'Yes., but I'll try to enjoy myself without you, and tell you about it when I see or hear from you again.'

She asked him to say hello to his friend and his wife and, apologising again, rang off.

He had a bus ride to the new flat, feeling a little lonely and, as she had said, disappointed.

It was a new block with green-tiled roof, white-painted render, curved metal windows, and a chrome and chevroned foyer. He felt, somehow, that it was too contemporary for his friend, he imagined him feeling more at home in a house in a Georgian square.

He took a lift to the fifth floor and turned in the direction of the music. The walnut door he knocked on was immediately opened by Fiona. She kissed him on the cheek and asked where Constance was. He briefly explained her situation and that he was to convey her best wishes to her and her husband.

'That's too bad. Come in.'

He entered a large room in which were twenty or so people, mostly women who were, he assumed, Fiona's friends. She had a quick word with Eric, looking smartly casual in a turtleneck sweater, who welcomed him and, with a quick gesture around him, said, 'Well, what d'you think of the place? We've only just begun setting it up.'

'Very nice, very… modern.'

'It's called the Moderne actually, note the Eileen Gray side table, the chrome-plated tubular frame of the sofa and, the pièce de résistance, a Marcel Breuer chair., though I smuggled in my little Regency table I've had for years. We got them delivered yesterday. Do have a drink. I'm sorry that your lady couldn't make an appearance. Come and meet some people.'

The host then introduced him to some guests, amongst them two who were introduced as students from his seminar group, and one who looked rather familiar.

'You'll know this man, ran into him a few days ago.'

He was short, rather skinny and mournful-eyed. Rupert then remembered him from their dorm when he had first arrived at the university, although couldn't recall his name.

'How's things?' he asked him. 'You were going to do History weren't you?'

'No, that was Edward, I'm reading Maths.'

'Maths are *a priori* analytic truths, true by virtue of the meaning of the numbers and tells us nothing about the real world until applied to it.'

'That may be so, but - '

'That two cats plus one cat equals three cats is true regardless of whether the cats exist or not. Sorry, had to share that with you, it's a habit.'

'You're not doing Philosophy by any chance are you?'

'How did you guess?'

Thomas gave, what Rupert remembered, as a rather rare smile.

'I'll leave you two,' said Eric, 'and help yourselves to the drink.'

Thomas got them and asked how his course was progressing. Rupert briefly described it to him and asked if he saw much of Edward.

'He's reading History.'

'The paucity of historicity.'

'If you say so.'

'Well, it does seem that, consciously or otherwise, historians tend to skew facts and their interpretation to what *they* want them to be.'

'It happens.'

'And they'll refer to something like, Queen Victoria's 'strong sexual appetite.' How do they *know*?'

'Well, she did have nine kids in seventeen years. How do positivist philosophers 'know' that there is no God?'

'You can criticise the premises of every discipline.'

'An engineer, chemist, an economist and a philosopher are shipwrecked on a desert island with only a tin of beans. The engineer suggests using a stone as a fulcrum to bend it open, the chemist says, 'Leave it in the sun and the contents will get so gaseous it will explode, while the economist said. 'Assuming we have a tin opener… ' And the philosopher said - '

"*What* tin of beans?"

'Yep.'

'We could go on.'

'Interestingly, yes, but this is supposed to be a party, 'though the music is hardly conducive to a wild one, but I guess that's Eric.'

'He can let himself go when he wants to.'

'I bet he can. D'you see much of him?'

'Went to his wedding. Give me your glass, I'll get you another.'

Rupert filled the glass, came back to him and asked if he saw Alec at all.

'Occasionally, he likes his subject, Architecture, but I don't think he's that happy at the College really, he thinks Cambridge may have been better for him. He said that he wanted to visit Spain to see the Sagrada Familia, but there's a war on over there.'

'Shouldn't think he'd risk life and limb for that. What do you know of the war?'

'Well, since Franco appeared to have given up on his plans for taking Madrid, Julio Álvarez del Vayo has complained about the political and economic isolation of the Republic by Democratic Nations and The Non-Intervention Committee, a new Anarchist government is in Aragon, thousands of Nationalist Italian volunteers have landed in Cádiz, the Nationalist port and the Antifascist militias have... I could go on, but I won't.'

'You have a geek's brain.'

'No, just a retentive memory. It's a strange battle, it's being called a revolution, a counter-revolution, a religious war, a - '

'Class war. All war is class war, anyway.'

'What's that to do with what's happening in Spain?'

'As far as a Democracy is possible, a government was legally elected, the Spanish working class put the Popular Front in power and now it's in danger of being swept away. And to talk of it as a this-or-that kind of war somehow dilutes it, what of the compelling reasons, the needs?'

'D'you think capitalism turns wants into needs?'

'Of course, it's in the interests of the big producers.' He looked a little quizzically at Thomas.

'You seem quite different from when I first met you.'

'It's the effect this place has on me. Life's good at university for you, too, eh?'

'Not sure.'

'Is it enough for you?'

'Why do you ask that? My girlfriend implied something like that recently.

'No reason, just asking.'

At that moment Eric came over to them.

'You remember each other, eh? Not that I'm going to ask you to dance together. Seems ages, doesn't it, that we were in that dorm wondering what it would be like. Well, now we know.'

'I suppose,' said Thomas, 'I expected it to be stricter, more like prep school, I guess.'

'Actually,' said Rupert, looking at Eric, 'I think your lot'd be happier if the Proctor or your tutor was a female. There's nothing the English upper class male would like better than a good telling-off from nanny.'

'And I think, Mister Philosopher,' said Eric, 'that positivists attempts to quantify the qualitative, in order to delude themselves that classification somehow gives them control, will engender an academic and, perhaps, cultural ethos in which creative, intuitive intellectualism is penalised by grey people who think in straight lines and who cannot comprehend any other form of mental activity.'

'That's some reply, you've surpassed yourself.'

'He surpasses himself all the time.'

It was Fiona standing in front of him.

'Are you going to dance with me?'

'Of course. What do we do to this particular tune then?'

'It's a kind of sway number. Do what I do.'

Rupert lightly held the side of her waist and took her hand as they moved a little away from the other two. It felt strange to touch the body of another girl, this one so slim it was almost childlike.

'I'm sorry about Constance's mummy. I read that the loss of bodily functions occurs in the last stage.' She looked suddenly apologetic. 'I'm sorry, that sounded so cold and matter-of-fact.'

'I think the process could already have begun. Nice place you have here.'

'It will be when we've finished it. We'll probably get some prints of surrealist stuff, cubism's getting popular, too. Maybe we can get something original. Eric's father would, perhaps, pay for something as an investment. That's what art is for him, I think.'

They moved rhythmically and slowly along with four or five other couples.

'We should be making merry, really, shouldn't we.'

'You and Eric could.'

She squeezed his hand.

'I wish you and Constance could.'

'So do I.'

'You will do.'

'I'm not so sure.'

She frowned slightly.

'Why not? Is it only because of her mother?'

He hesitated a little.

'I don't know.'

'Other things?'

'Perhaps.'

'Such as...?'

'Just… life I suppose.'

'Is that what philosophers say?'

'Everybody.'

'But it's rather ordinary for you, it's not, how do you say, 'intellectualized."

'I don't wish it to be, that can be an escape.'

'Interesting. And what would you be escaping from?'

'I'm not really sure. But I'm dissatisfied.'

'With what?'

'Just… the University, or at least, my part of it. It doesn't, quite rightly of course, get involved. It talks, lectures, analyses, as is its wont, but doesn't *do* anything. Of course, that's rather silly of me to say it, but I want it to, somehow, get hold of some of the things it lectures about, puts a spotlight on, shake them up, do something about them.'

'Such as… ?'

'Well, we talk of exploitation, the huge economic gaps between social groups, yet nowhere is there a plan, a scheme for trying to right things. By that I mean morally right.' A brief pause. 'Huh, I could hear a voice then saying, 'morals are culturally relative.' That's what I mean by academicizing.'

'It's not the job of Higher Education, surely.'

'No, it's not,. But I want it to be.'

He felt their movements becoming more repetitive, almost mechanistic.

'Maybe you shouldn't be there, perhaps you should be doing something about it yourself, or trying to.'

'What d'you want me to do, lead a Marxist revolution single-handed?' Sorry, I'm being sarcastic.' He looked behind him briefly. '*He* was implying that perhaps I needed something other than my life here.'

"He'?'

'The person I was talking with.'

'You do, don't you. I think we've established that.'

'Are you an Earth Mother to Eric, too?'

The record finished. Neither of them spoke until the host put another on the turntable.

'You're right, I *would* like to do something, but am not sure what.'

The new tune didn't elicit a response from him, they were almost motionless now, they had virtually stopped dancing.

'I'm saying these things to you, yet haven't formulated them to myself yet.'

'I think you don't know what to do, or where the urge, the need perhaps, comes from. You can make jokes about my attempts to psychoanalyse you if you like, but.. there it is.'

'Are you two going to stand there all evening?'

The question was from Eric.

'Er, we were just talking.'

'About enormously significant world events, I trust.'

'Sort of, your wife was seeking clarification.'

'Of what?'

'Me.'

'We made some progress, darling,' said Fiona,' now I think you should dance with me.'

'Excuse me, Roop, my rhythmic nimbleness is required.'

They moved away and began to dance.

'He's pretty good isn't he,' said Thomas.

'He is.'

Rupert felt a little uncomfortable; he couldn't give himself, however casually, to where he was, there were things to think about. He didn't want to talk any more to the man he'd just spoken with, any of them, really, even Eric. He grabbed another drink, swallowed it, and as the music finished went to his friend and told him he thought he should be leaving.

'What's to do, dear boy?'

'Was thinking I should see how Constance is doing.'

It wasn't really true and he disliked lying, but he needed time alone, to think.

'Give her my best wishes, it would have been nice to have seen her.'

'I will.'

'Mine, too,' said her partner.

'Well... goodbye then.' He turned to Thomas. 'And you too, carry on enjoying our illustrious institution .' With a 'See you,' to Eric, he left.

He decided to walk back to his rooms, Moving through the city centre and making his way around the gatherings of people outside a cinema and a theatre, he suddenly had images of Spanish citizens running from uniformed soldiers whose guns were firing bullets above their heads, some shooting into them. There were images of soldiers in different uniforms alongside armed men in civilian clothes in their Christmas trenches standing or kneeling in muddy puddles with bits of holly and mistletoe sticking from the trench sides.

He had little idea of how realistic or otherwise these glimpses were, and wondered why he was thinking of them. It wasn't a random occurrence, something perhaps his unconscious, was conjuring up images, impressions of Spain, a country he'd never been to, knew relatively little about. He had also been thinking of events in Spain on the journey back to Oxford the day after he and Constance's 'misspent' night as he inwardly referred to it, where she had rather morosely looked out of the carriage window, or slept.

He thought of his privileged background, although it had never really impinged strongly upon his consciousness for it was the sort of economic and social cocoon one took for granted. And, inevitably, he thought of Constance. How long would she have to look after her mother? Would there be any time in the future when he would spend more time with her, have her… mind, her humour, her love, or was the last too much to hope for? He wanted to be with her - he knew he was being selfish thinking it - not sharing her with her parent.

As he drew nearer the College he felt a strong desire, a need to do something, but this time, as part of a wild, untettered feeling, he thought of the International Brigade. He knew little about it other than that it used to be known as the Garibaldi Brigade and had been set up by Communists to help the Popular Front Government. He would find out.

He wondered what his mother would think if he took action, if he actually *did* it. She would hate it. His father would be proud of him, of course, if he was going to fight for his country, but not for the 'dagos' as he would call them. Was this partly about 'getting his own back' against his father's political views? He thought of his girl again. What would she think? Would she feel that he was leaving her, running away for some misguided ideological cause? No, she wouldn't think that, and he wanted her to be there for him; come what may.

As he entered his room he realised in a moment of trivial irrelevance that he hadn't referred to the man he'd been speaking to for a good part of the evening by name. He still couldn't remember it.

33

It was the day after he had seen Enid. In the morning, after a sleepless night, he had caught a bus outside the station and went out into the misty estuary. He had alighted at a random stop and now walked towards a Victorian tower rising from the mist. He stood near it, looking upward at its balconies and barely discernible Palladian roof then stopped and gazed at its arching curves, its symmetrical, almost dusk-like loveliness. For a second he yearned to embrace it, to hold on to a sash window, its glass starting to brighten as the sun twitched on glazing bars and window sills. He gazed upward again, wanting to pull it all inside of him, but not knowing why.

He remembered telling Enid that he had a psychological ownership of London. A strange thought occurred to him that perhaps, somehow, he hadn't enough real self and he was filling the space with bits and pieces of the city, impressions, images of it, cluttered, floating; sometimes almost insistent.

After a long wait, he travelled back to his station and caught a train to his mother's house. He had brought her some oranges, which prompted her to relate another childhood story.

'I remember', she was saying, 'we were all standing outside this wharf in the docks and they were loading crates of oranges and 'accidentally on purpose' one of the dockers dropped one of the crates, and I remember the girls filling their knickers with 'em - we wore navy blue ones, fleecy things - and the oranges made 'em treble the size and they wobbled home with all the oranges. The boys, of course, put theirs in their pockets.'

'Let's hope the dockers are still as generous.'

'Saw Reg's mum the other day, she said he hadn't seen you for quite a while.'

'I've tried to see him.'

'I asked her how he was and she said he'd been feeling browned off for a while now and that he felt like joining the army or something. He'd mentioned the International something or other.'

"Brigade'?'

'Well, it wasn't the bleedin' Girl Guides.'

'It's serious, mum, there's some sort of war going on over there, involving all sorts of people, all kinds of factions.'

'Never was any good at them in school.'

'That's fractions.'

'Well, as long as you're not getting involved, don't want yer landin' up like yer dad did.'

'I know, mum.'

'She reckons they have to go to Paris to join this thing. Can you imagine that?'

He couldn't, his friend had never been out the country before, but then, neither had he.

'Dunno whether he's gone, ain't seen his mum for a while, he could have done.'

He was finding this hard to believe. Reg wouldn't be thinking of doing this would he? Why? He was a well-paid chippie, he'd picked the skills up instantly at Tech and had always been employed, now this. Perhaps he, too, had an urge to do something else, to *say* something. He wished he had seen more of his friend in the last year, Reg would have told him about it; they could have talked it through.

He had first met him at school when he was with a group of the lads trying to peer through the curtained windows of the room where the local grammar school girls came once a week for Domestic Science. Girls at Tech were a rare event and without decreasing their efforts to catch glimpses of them, Reg had come over and told him a joke. He had heard it before, but it had been told well, he'd liked him immediately,

It was his occasional sense of the ridiculous, his hyperbole, their shared interest in drawing and for detective novels like Death In The Dusk and the Mrs. Bradley stories. Reg liked him, he once said, because although he played football - George played in his favoured position for this school until, rarely passing the ball to anyone and inevitably losing it, was dropped - he looked as if he wrote poetry as well.

Soon after they'd both started work, George serving his apprenticeship in the City and learning a lot about conventional decorating and also a little of graining, marbling, signwriting and mixing colours 'on the bench', while Reg worked for a local joinery firm, they would go 'up west' mostly to see films, occasionally French ones, although relying completely on subtitles.

Sometimes they had ambled around London at weekends and once walked the eighteen or so miles from Plaistow to Epping, smoking most of the time and stopping at nearly all of the cafés on the way. It took them nine hours. Opposite a bus garage his friend had suddenly leaned heavily against a bus stop and decided he couldn't continue. Some years later they made the same journey and, again clinging to a bus stop, he called George back to tell him that he'd had enough. It was the same bus stop.

They once went on a foray to a nudist colony near Watford, a nearby farmer seeing them and calling them 'dirty little sods', and decided it wasn't really worth the bother just to see occasional flashes of septuagenarian flesh through the trees.

If his pal was actually going, why not go with him? He felt the old relationship stirring again. The two of them. But maybe Reg wouldn't see it like that now; perhaps feeling they had drifted apart.

There had been only a few moments with Reg that he hadn't enjoyed, one being when he had no cash with him and had needed a shilling for his train fare home and, accidentally running into his mate at Mile End station and asking to borrow that amount, had been refused. 'Audrey wouldn't like it,' his friend had said. He had been in a relationship for a few months with a girl who had been rather controlling and it was obvious that his pal was reluctant to go against what he thought her wishes would be. The incident had hurt for a while; George had felt a kind of betrayal.

But was it really about him and his friend? Perhaps it was just that he knew someone of his own age, could have been anyone, who seemed intent on going off to fight for something, something they believed in, 'though he wasn't sure in his friend's case how strong the belief was, even if there *was* one.

'Are you with me, son?'

It was his mother.

'Yeah, of course.'

'You were miles away then.'

342

'I could literally be one day, and pretty soon maybe.'

'What's that supposed to mean?'

'Nothing that need worry you.'

'That means it will worry me, doesn't it.'

He thought it time to tell her about Enid, it was partly the reason he had come to see her.

'Mum, I don't think you'll like this, but Enid and I have parted.'

'You've *what*?'

'Split up.' He forced himself to add, 'It may be for the best.'

'But why? I thought she might be the one.'

'So did I, but we decided it wouldn't really work. But it's okay.'

'But she has such a lovely voice, sort of lilting.'

'I know, but there it is.'

He knew he had disappointed her, he'd done it before. He remembered as a child sulking all through some commemorative thing for his father because he couldn't understand what was going on. People had looked at him and mentioned his 'Daddy', but he wasn't there, only Aunt Rose and Uncle Bert, Aunt Glad and Uncle Jim. Nanny and granddad were also there. His mother had told him to place a bunch of flowers somewhere, he'd merely dropped them.

And when he was the only one in his school who had been chosen to go to Art College and he'd refused to go because his mates weren't going and his mother had found out. 'I don't care how big you are,' she'd said, and smacked him. She told him how proud of him his father would have been.

She looked at him now with some concern.

'You're letting yourself go a bit, you haven't shaved, have you. Look at you, like the Wreck of the bleedin' Hesperus.'

He supposed she was right, he hadn't shaved, probably not even combed his hair.

'I'll be okay, really, I'll have a bath tonight.'

'Old habits die hard don't they. The tin bath hanging on the fence out there and the Friday night bath in it, but you've got your own bathroom now. Cleanliness is next to Godliness remember. Anyway, you've still got yer job, that's something to be grateful for.'

'We shouldn't have to be 'grateful'.'

'Now don't get like your father, he used to go on about people making profits out of him and his mates, 'the workers' as he called them. Things are the way they are for a reason, it can't be helped.'

'They can be helped, it's the system, mum, it's… never mind, doesn't matter.'

'We can't do anything about it, anyway.'

He wanted to tell her that if she believed in fate then there was an inevitability about everything and therefore people wouldn't attempt to change anything because it couldn't be changed, things were almost preordained. He had tried to explain to her before that her belief in God meant that if He had wanted things differently then He could have made them so, the situation was a consequence of *His* will. He felt a familiar annoyance at the thought of people's acceptance of so many things. Religion was like some sort of drug.

And this acceptance of the status quo, was it really partly because she was a woman? Women, he felt, were more conservative then men. Perhaps it was because they bore children, they conserved life, and they would certainly not want to give birth in a world of upheaval and sudden change.

Normally, he would talk about such things with Enid and, before her, with Reg. He seemed to be in contact with neither of them now, but at least he knew where Enid would be. Maybe he could make a plea for them to begin again, for him to be honest with her about everything, and perhaps tell her of his need to do a lot more than go to work every day organising labour and himself to make money for someone else.

He looked at his mother. She seemed sad.

'Sorry if my news disappoints you, mum, but that's life, as they say.' He heard himself say it with an inward groan; it was such a cliché, like 'And the rest is history, as they say'. He wondered why he was caring about clichés when there were more significant things to think about. He wanted to think about them, he also wanted to see Enid.

'Mum, I'm getting along now. Was good to see you and I'll visit again soon.'

He kissed her or on the cheek, a habit he had never comfortably acquitted, and went to the front door. Before closing it behind him, she said, 'keep yer chin up, son, and be careful.'

Working her normal shift, Enid would be there. Based on this assumption he went to the pub.

She looked up as soon as he walked in. She frowned, pursing her lips. There were few drinkers present and he went to her and ordered a beer. She poured it for him.

'Sixpence, please.'

He gave it to her and began with, 'Look, I wanted to see you because - '

'I told you I would contact *you,* remember?'

'I know, but - '

'But me no buts. You shouldn't be here.'

'I was thirsty.'

'There are other pubs.'

'But you're not in them.'

Just then the landlord interrupted them.

'Hello, young man.'

'Hello, Mister Bishop.'

'You two look as if you could do with a bit of time to yourselves. It's pretty quiet, you may leave the bar for a few minutes, Enid. It's okay.'

'Thank you, Mister Bishop,' said his employee and moved from behind the counter and towards the far end of the room. George followed her.

'That was nice of him,' she remarked as they seated themselves at a corner table, 'though I don't see much point.'

'The point is, I want to start again. From now.'

'You can't do that, I ... we ... had a relationship, but - '

'*Have* one.'

'It's not as simple as that, you can't just pretend we've met this second, we have a history, as brief as it is, and you have a history with a woman you lived with and has only just gone out of your life.'

'I don't want it to be like that.'

'There are lots of things we don't want. '

'I'm not implying that we can change what's already happened, but just to forget about it. I don't think of her anymore.'

She looked briefly down at the table then up to the ceiling,
then at him

'I'm sorry, George, you shouldn't be here, I don't want to see
you.'

'But you said you would contact me.'

'If I wanted to, but I don't any more. Perhaps I'm an untrusting
person, perhaps I get it from my dad, 'Don't trust anyone, girl,'
he'd say, perhaps I've picked that up. But that ... thing of hers I
found, It's too strong an image, it's too meaningful.'

'I've explained it.'

'I know, but it's not enough.'

She stood.

'Sit down a minute,' he said, 'I've been wanting to tell you
what I might do. I think I've made up my mind, I don't know, but
if I'm not going to see you again... I probably will.'

'I don't know what you're going to do, but whatever it is,
don't blame me for it.'

He took a deep breath.

'It's like this... I need to do something, but I'm not really sure
what.'

'That sounds carefully thought out.'

'Listen, please. I've got to tell someone.' He paused. 'I was
thinking of joining up.'

'Why? Are you falling apart?'

'I did say, 'please'. I meant going to Spain, I've heard that
people of my age are going as well.'

'The posh boys.'

'I don't think it's just them, and it seems so wrong what's going on over there.'

'D'you want me to say, 'Oh, what a brave soldier! D'you want
me to swoon?'

'Where did that come from?'

'It's the way you make me feel.'

'Look, I'm sorry about ... you-know-who. Let's forget the
whole thing. It's in the past.'

346

'Is it?'

'Yes, and I've told you so. You've pushed her out of me. Look, can't we have a pact to always be honest with each other?'

'I have with you, and you're jumping ahead of yourself, I don't want there to be an 'always'.'

'How many times do I have to say I'm sorry?'

She gave him an indifferent smile.

'Like I said, that's my reaction to you. '

'It's not me that's making you like this.'

'And it's not just me that's making you do what you say you're going to do.'

'This is ridiculous. I wanted to explain, to see if you understood why I feel I should go.'

'Go on then.'

'I don't feel I've *done* anything, just held a meeting with a few toshers, gone on a pointless go-slow, done little more than complain when somebody died falling off a scaffold. That's about it. There's still not many safety standards on sites and in factories, there's not much sick pay, unemployment benefits, and all that stuff. And it all takes so long to get it, if at all. I know you're going to say, 'What's this got to do with Spain? but it kind of comes together in my head, The whole, unfair world, people who have power, money, military power, putting the decent person down, keeping him down.'

'And you want to risk yourself trying to change it?'

'Yes, I think I do.'

She looked at him, shaking her head.

'But whatever happens over there won't change anything here. I don't understand.'

'Perhaps I don't either, but it's what I feel, I thought you'd understand.'

She stood again.

'I'm sorry, George, but you're expecting too much of me, what you do is your business, it's nothing to do with me any more.'

She moved away from the table then turned her head. 'I am sorry, really.'

She walked quickly back behind the bar. She was still wearing her apron.

He got up from his seat, went out of the exit by the table and walked to Holborn station. It had been no use then, she hadn't wanted to know. He thought that she just might have understood what he was trying to say, but then, he wasn't really sure of what it was himself.

But he wanted to do what he'd said and had to find out how. Where would he go to do so? Maybe the Town Hall, or a Police station, they'd know about these things, wouldn't they? It was madness, perhaps, but his dad had done it, 'though that was more understandable - duty, patriotism, his country was at war, but it wasn't now, it had promised not to intervene.

Changing trains at Mile End, he saw a newspaper on a seat. He automatically picked it up. Turning a page he saw something about Hitler's support for the Nationalists then an article talking of the International Brigade's Paris Headquarters. The latter seemed to be more than a coincidence. It felt like some sort of fate, a kind of fate he could believe in. He read the article and felt almost as if the thing was settled, that he knew he would go, that he was supposed to.

He felt a stronger sense of self. He would telephone an operator and she would give him the number of the place where he was supposed to enlist. He went straight to the telephone box outside his station and received the required information.

He then made his first international telephone call. The man with the heavy French accent at the Place du Combat informed him that he would first have to contact his local Communist Party. He was also told not to tell people what he was planning to do. He had no actual plan and felt apprehensive, partly because of the man's accent, and wondered whether he would have to learn another language if he was to live some time in another country.

After a restless night he went to work, where, before approaching a brickie who was rumoured to be a Party member, and after he had told a painter who had informed him that he couldn't prime a wall because the plaster was still damp, to 'blow on it', he asked the bricklayer for the address of a local branch. The nearest, apparently, was in Shoreditch.

After calling them, George went that evening to an ordinary-looking building where he was shown into an office with framed

Hammer and Sickle paintings on the walls where he was quizzed by a bushy-haired man about his Left Wing credentials. George told him that he had started a branch of the painters union and, rather lamely he felt, voted Labour. He thought, perhaps, he should tell him that he read communist literature, but he hadn't and didn't really know of any.

He was a little surprised that he wasn't asked why he wanted to join the Party, and was about to state his wish to go to Spain, when the man said, 'Some of our members have recently gone off to the continent to see what they can do in Spain. If that's your intention, then best keep it quiet outside of these walls, but to get there you need to go to our head office in King Street, they'll tell you what you have to do. You'll also need a passport.' He didn't have and had never had one.

'Incidentally,' the man continued, 'It's only recently that the Party have begun helping people get across to the Continent, before this you and others would have had to make your own way there.'

The man gave him a form to complete containing a few questions relating to his background, job, formal qualifications, age, general health and what the behavioural expectations of being a member would entail. He completed it and returned it to its giver.

The man looked at it briefly then shook George's hand.

'Welcome to the Party.'

George thanked the man and left, wondering if he really was a suitable candidate to join an organisation whose reason to exist was about ideological politics, a subject he knew relatively little about. But it didn't really matter. It was a means to an end.

The following day, determined to get a passport as soon as he was able and telling the lads he was going to buy some paint for a special signwriting job - he surprised himself at how easily he was lying - he went to the passport office in Eccleston Square with as many relevant documents as he could find and obtained a passport.

The next day, a Friday, he knocked the men off early and went to the Party's Covent Garden headquarters. The appointment had been arranged by the man who had previously interviewed him.

The building, 'though larger, looked just as ordinary as the local branch. Inside there were more framed hammer and sickle paintings but, this time, alongside two large wall murals, one depicting a phalanx of people carrying large red banners proclaiming freedom and allegiance to the Party, the other a landscape of wheat fields, farmhouses and tractors in a stylised land of plenty. There were other objects he wanted to peruse but was called into a front office almost immediately by a person who introduced its occupant as Comrade Hexel. Behind a large oak desk sat a bewhiskered, rather militaristic-looking man who waved him to a chair in front of it.

George sat, trying not to look nervous, and for a brief second wondered what he was doing there.

'Well then, Mister Woods,' said the man as he picked up a sheet of paper, 'you wish to join us in Spain then.'

'Yes, I do.'

'According to Mister Lewis you are a Socialist and have started a union branch'

'Yes, and I took part in a recent go-slow strike.'

'Have you attended any protests? Demonstrations?'

'I went to the one against the Means Test in Hyde Park about four years ago.'

He had rehearsed this. He had never been.

'Good. Well, at least good enough.'

He looked up and down at his interviewee.

'You seem a reasonably fit young man. You'll get a medical of course.'

He leaned back on his chair.

'So, why do you want to go?'

'To help free the Spanish people from tryranny.'

As he said it, it felt both too practised and over-ambitious.

'If Franco is successful it will, indeed, be a tyranny.' He leaned forward a little. 'Why else do you want to go?'

'Well, I sincerely want to do something worthwhile, there seems so much unfairness everywhere, and this seems kind of part of it.' He hesitated. 'I do really want to go you know. Honestly.'

'I do believe you do. There are some young fellows however, and this is between you and I, moneyed, educated people mainly, who appear to want to go because it's somewhat expected of them by their peers. They're not all like that of course, there are genuine people wanting to help in this war. I think you're one of them. So, have you had any military experience?'

'No.'

'Cadets?'

'No, but I was on in the cubs once, I was deputy pack leader, but when I joined theI scouts i was just a scout, so I left. But I'm reasonably strong, work with my hands, played football a bit.'

'So, some inculcation of discipline, but no experience with firearms, et cetera'.

'No.'

'Well, I think you may have some potential other than Arkala and 'dib, dib, dab.' I'm joking. I think you may do. If you go, you won't necessarily be with just your own people; but possibly with Italians, French, Spanish obviously, and perhaps, Russians. You know, incidentally, that Hitler and Mussolini are bombing the country. Facism incarnate. What I must say to you, however, being duty-bound to do so, is that if you go, there is a good chance you may not return.'

There was silence for a while.

Comrade Hexel leaned across the desk and shook George's hand, saying as he did so, 'Ring here when you are ready to go and you will be given instructions. And just remember that what you are about to embark upon is, actually, illegal.'

George felt a mixture of emotions: apprehension, a sense of daring, a hollowness which he felt Enid should have occupied; the feeling of a dull panic at the thought of leaving his home, his house, but, above all, a slowly building excitement. He decided to go straight to his mother's and tell her what he had done.

Deciding on the way that he would tell his employer that he was going away with a friend to work for a few months so that he could leave in good grace if he ever wished to be re-employed by him, and that the Holborn job needed fewer men now, anyway, and he could make one of them up to charge hand, he reached his parent's home.

He told her briefly what he had been doing over the last few days.

'Perhaps I'm not completely sure I know what I'm doing, but I have to do it. And I'll be okay. You lost dad, mum, but you won't lose me, I promise.'

She cuddled him, her eyes tearful. He pulled away.

'That's how I feel. I'm sorry, mum.'

'But, what about the house? You've only been paying for it for a while, It'll be yours one day.'

'I know, but I could let it.' He had decided this a few hours earlier. 'I'll arrange that the mortgage is paid through you and you can take the money from the rent. There could be a bit to spare as well, you can have that for your trouble.'

'I'll have a look over the place every time I collect their rent and see everything's kept okay. Trust me.'

'I do.'

'I'll be pleased to do it. Cor, to think that my son'll be a land-lord. Well, I never. And, come to think of it, Mrs. Ball at the end house has a nephew who's getting married soon, he'll be looking for a place. He works over Hornchurch way. I'll tell her about it. I've met them, they seem a nice young couple. But I still don't want you to go.'

'I know, mum, but it all seems ready for me now, I'll ring the mortgage company tomorrow.'

'You'll let me know exactly when you're going, won't you.'

''Course. You know I will.'

He went home thinking of Enid, wanting her with him, but not the Enid of the last time he'd seen her. He wanted the one who he could talk of Italianate towers with, of scrolled balconies, black-and-white tiled paths, she looking up at him, half-smiling as they strolled together. But she had gone now. It was over.

He thought of his home. Soon, someone else would be sitting on the armchair listening to the wireless, reading a newspaper after eating a meal, looking at his paintings, and in the garden watching the fountain play.

It seemed to have happened so quickly, so... efficiently. He could, of course, change his mind, nothing was signed and sealed, it was voluntary. He didn't *have* to do it. But he would telephone the head office soon. He would be on his way.

34

Pym was talking about deviancy once more and, to illustrate a point, again asking the class for personal examples. Rupert was wondering who benefited most from certain acts being defined as deviant, the answer being rather obvious: the richer, more power-ful sections of the population. He decided not to relate any of his own norm-breaking activities although he did momentarily recall an incident as a schoolboy when he'd been bullied by an older boy named Tom Brand - an apt name for a character in a Western movie, he thought - in the changing room after a practice rugby game.

He had hit him back and immediately regretted doing so, de-served as it was, and continually apologised whilst being chased around the room and punched by his assailant. The other boys had obviously thought Rupert's repeated 'sorrys' were an attempt to halt his punishment. But, was bullying a deviant act in schools, any school, or was it a norm? Perhaps, theoretically, it was like the anomic nature of war, anything went, it was anomy, a state of normlessness, or could there be anomic norms? That the norm is that there are no norms?

His mind didn't stay long on the subject in any of its myriad forms, but coalesced on what he was to say to the College Proctor - he had bypassed his tutor; he would have had to see the former anyway - to tell him of his decision to leave the College.

The seminar over, in which he had contributed little, he made his way to the appropriate office.

The Proctor was a large man with dark eyes and hair and wear-ing an even darker cloak, even whilst sitting at his desk.

'Do sit.'

Rupert perched himself on a chair diagonally across from the man.

'You have an appointment to see me. About what, may I ask?'

'It's about going to Spain, sir.'

'For a holiday? There's Barcelona, Madrid, Ibiza.'

'No. The reason - '

'You're thinking of joining the International Brigade? The country is becoming a rather nasty place, a theatre of war, no less. I assume you wish to be involved?'

'I think I do.'

'I like our young men to be sure, to realise what they will be getting themselves into.'

'Obviously I'm not certain of what I'll be facing, but I do want to go there, I feel strongly that I should.'

'You wouldn't be the first student from the University who wishes to go and, indeed, has gone, but you're the first from this College. They're going from Cambridge also, of course. Some people see it as a kind of status race between them and us. I shouldn't, however, think that there will be many of the great unwashed participating.'

'Maybe it's too far away, many manual workers have never travelled outside the country, and it's not as if it's about blind duty, loyalty to the flag, etcetera, as the last war was. In fact, as you know, the government of this country has promised no official intervention.'

'Also, they may not be that aware, ideologically, of what is at stake, partly I suppose, because of their work experience and almost certainly their education. It is well-known that the working classes bring up their children in a domestic background of talking and relating to the concrete and not the abstract; their crowded living conditions also are not exactly conducive to their having a knowledgeable connection to the wider world. Do forgive me; I studied Education before reading Law.'

'However, although you haven't theorized to me yet, I'm wondering if there's a danger of your intellectualizing all this and that the strength of that is, if you like, stronger than, shall we say, your rational self, indeed, your emotional self, that you are being propelled by your intellectual convictions and not by your true self. It does happen.'

'What is my 'true self' then? We could debate this concept for quite a while, I think, Sir.'

'I expect so.'

The Proctor leaned back in his chair.

'So, why do you really want to go?'

'I genuinely feel that I want to contribute. An elected government is in danger of being overthrown by religious dogma, militarism and a kind of blind nationalism.'

'How do you know of these things?'

'I can only deduce from what I read in newspapers, hear on the wireless, the little I've seen on television. The papers are, of course, biased towards one side or the other, nevertheless, my mind is made up now. I need to do something, sir.'

'You have friends you have discussed this with?'

'I haven't as yet.'

'Do you not think you should?'

'Now that I have made up my mind, I shall.'

The man briefly glanced at a sheet of paper on his desk.

'I've checked your academic record, your grades are quite good; it seems a pity that you want to leave the university.'

'I don't really, sir, I enjoy my subject. What I want to know is if I can come back to complete my studies.'

The interviewer thought a while.

'It's a rather unusual request, but in this particular case I think we can say yes. He paused. 'I do think however that you may, perhaps, want to consider your decision for a while.'

'No, I don't think so.'

He looked at Rupert meaningfully.

'I think that your target, Mister Colls, should be *to* come back.'

He stood, holding his hand out for his listener to shake.

Rupert did so, thanked him and exited the room.

He was pleased. He walked back towards his room knowing that the essay he was completing - this one dealing with a critique of Aristotelian philosophy Pym had, asked for - wouldn't be the last he would write at the College. It seemed too early for spring, but the sun, falling on leaves and reflecting on windows, made it feel like it.

As he approached the college, someone nearby was also walking towards it. It was Eric.

Rupert called to him. 'Paying a sentimental visit to your old room?'

'No, I'm supposed to be seeing my tutor, but that can wait. Was wondering where you'd got to. Got time for a coffee?'

''Course.'

At Rupert's suggestion they sat at a table at the back of the refectory.

'This is good coffee,' said Eric, smacking his lips.

'How's the beautiful one?' he was asked.

'Very well and getting the flat together, more prints for the walls, lights for the ceilings, rugs for the floors. And Constance?'

'Haven't seen her much.'

'Her mother?'

'Quite.'

'To state the obvious, It's such a pity about you and her.'

'Worse for her mother.'

'You know what I mean.'

'I do.'

After a short silence, Eric said, 'My darling one mentioned after the party that you had talked with her about inequality and such and that you were dissatisfied with things and wanted to do something, something she felt that would, perhaps, be quite dramatic.'

'I was merely... chatting to her about things.'

'You can't keep a secret from the head that shares the pillow.'

'Well, I shall tell you what it is, but it has to be between you and me for now.'

'What is it?'

'I'm going, if I can, to Spain, to be with the Republicans.'

'Are you serious? You're going to... fight? Actually fight? Fire guns, kill people?'

'I hope I don't have to do the latter.'

'So do *I*. But what if it's them or you?'

Rupert was quiet.

'You haven't really faced it, have you, actually ending someone's life, maybe your own, because that's what you may have to do.'

'But if it's for the greater good? Sometimes it has to be.'

'Easy to say. How are you going to get there?'

'I have to join the Communist Party first.'

'A communist, too? Jesus, Roop, you really have got it bad, haven't you.'

357

'Got what?'

'I dunno, a desire to… throw yourself into something, whatever you have to do to get there. And what will Constance say?'

'I don't know, I don't know what'll happen.'

'She'll think that you're leaving her.'

'I will be, temporarily, not for ever.'

'She may feel you are, though.'

'I hope not.'

'How are you going to get over there?'

'Initially by boat, I suppose, I know no more than you.'

'You'll have to learn so many new things in an army.'

'Of course.'

'You seem to be taking it all so calmly.'

'I don't feel it.'

Eric looked down, briefly shook his head then looked at his friend again.

'This may sound crazy, but if it wasn't for Fiona, I'd be tempted to come with you, if I was more political, more single-minded, more… wholehearted, that is.'

'If it was a cause to stir you.'

'It does, but on a minor level I'm afraid, I don't really feel it.'

Rupert stretched out a hand and squeezed his friend's shoulder.

'I don't expect you to, it's okay.'

'It's not certain yet though, is it, they may turn you down.'

'I should think they'd want everybody they can get.'

'When are you going to tell her,' asked Eric.

'I wasn't sure, but now you've asked, I may as well go now, she'll almost certainly be at home.'

'I think you should. Finish your coffee, I'll come part of the way with you if you like.'

'Thanks, but no need to, I'll prepare myself on the way there.'

They left the refectory with Eric telling his pal to contact him soon.

Rupert decided not to go to his room, but began the walk to see Constance, there was no point waiting until the evening to see whether her mother was sleeping and her daughter free to talk with him, she could fall asleep at any time.

There was no sun at all now; the day was getting greyer, as was his mood as he tried not to silently rehearse what he wished to say to her. He wanted to *feel* what he was saying and, surely, if he could be himself emotionally with anyone it was with her. There was a little warmth, however, in the thought of going to the Continent. What was the saying? 'It's not the arriving, not even the travelling, it's the getting up and going.'

She looked surprised when she opened the door to him.

'Wasn't I going to ring you this evening?' she asked.

'Not sure, but I didn't want to wait.'

'Come in, she's asleep. Come through to the scullery and I'll make us some tea.'

He followed her into the room and sat watching her. She had finished pouring a cup when he said, 'I want to go to Spain and… do my bit.'

She looked up and frowned.

"Your bit'? What does that mean?'

'I want to join the fighting there. I feel I have to go.'

' You're… serious?'

'I am.' He stepped towards her. 'I have to go and I *am* going. I'm sorry.'

She put the tea pot down.

'So am I.'

She was quiet for a moment, then, 'I feel as if it's my fault.'

'How is that?'

'Because… because mother and everything. I can't see you very much. I'm sorry about that, but - '

'No, it's more than that. I want to see more of you, of course, but other than you and, to an extent, Eric, my life here isn't enough for me. I'm not sure what I expected really, but as much as I enjoy theorizing, analysis, debate, it's somehow distant, it's - '

'Not real enough for you?'

'Something like that. You're the realest thing in this place.'

'And I'm distant too, I suppose.' She frowned slightly, 'This is nothing to do with me refusing your help with a carer is it? There's not enough room for a live-in one and that's what she needs. I could work if there was a day carer, but I would have to be here the rest of the time.'

'Whatever arrangements could be made I would still need to go.'

She poured another tea and gave it to him. He took it, still standing in front of her.

'I want to drink *you*, I sound like a cannibal, I know.'

He was aware of his deep intake of breath.

'I want you to wait for me. Will you?'

She hesitated before replying.

'I want to wait for you, but I feel that you're deserting me.'

'No. I'm leaving you for a while. I'm coming back.' He looked at her steadily.' I don't want to leave you ever again.'

'I'd like to believe that.'

'You can.'

'So, there's a future then.'

'For us, yes.'

'You haven't gone yet and you're talking about coming back for ever.'

'But I *am* going.'

'I believe you, Rupert. I can see it in your eyes, you'll go.'

There was a movement behind them; It was her mother. She wore a cardigan, slippers and nothing else, and was frowning at them.

'Keep away,' she said, then louder, 'Don't touch me.'

'It's alright, mother, you remember my friend, he won't hurt you, he's come to see you.'

Her mother glowered at them and turned away.

'I'll see to her,' said her daughter and, briefly looking at Rupert, said, 'You're welcome to stay, but... '

'It's okay, I'll leave, but I'll see you soon and tell you what's happening.'

'Please do so, Rupert.'

He pulled her towards him, holding her firmly.

'I' shall always want you,' he told her, as he made his way out of the house.

On the bus back to College he began mulling over what had just happened.

He hadn't been sure of what her reaction would be, but it could have been worse, he thought. She could have been what his father would have called a 'typical woman' and spat sarcasm at him in the form of, 'So you'd prefer playing soldiers than being with me then?' and become angry, but she had been understanding and he felt that what had been said had concreted what he felt for her. Come what may, he wanted to come back to her.

Using the telephone near his room, he rang the exchange and was told that there was no number listed for a local Communist Party Office and, at his request, informed him that the nearest branch they could find was in Paddington, London. Assuming that it would be open in the late afternoon, he rang. He told the girl who answered what he wanted and was given an appointment for the next day. After a rather restless night, and skipping a morning lecture, he boarded a train for the Capital.

It was a new office block north of the station, shared, apparently, with a trade union. The man who saw him looked as if he could have just given a lecture at the College. Tall, slim and bespectacled, he shook the newcomer's hand, leaned back on a chair at a mahogany table inlaid with a hammer and sickle, and beckoned Rupert to sit on a matching chair, the back of it containing the same emblem.

'Well, the inevitable question, why do you wish to become a member of the Communist Party? Mister - he looked at a piece of paper in front of him - Colls?' A fan of Marx are we? A belief In the sort of world he believed in, each according to his need and that man was born 'good' and made 'bad' by society? He seemed to be saying that, anyway. Unlike Freud, who thought - '

'Man was hedonistic, egoistic, selfish, individualistic and competitive.'

'Quite, man born 'bad' and made 'good' by society. Perhaps a Marxist utopia will never be achieved, certainly not according to what's happening currently in the Soviet Union, despite being recognised by the US and The League of Nations. But, then, there had to be the revolution, people were oppressed, starving.'

'You could argue that they still are I suppose, some of them anyway.'

'That's not the founding theorist's fault though, is it, it's the Executive, those in power. But the preference is for them rather than the rampant capitalism of the West, of indeed most of the world. That is the context some of us in the Party have to come to terms with, I suppose. A decision, I assume, you agree with, otherwise you wouldn't perhaps want to join, 'though I suspect it's a means to an end for you. Am I correct?'

Rupert smiled. 'Yes, you're right, I wish to go to Spain.'

'That's fair enough, although I must admit that with you sort of fellows, young, educated, idealistic, I do hear some fanciful reasons for joining the party and unfortunately, it's also obvious that when they do reach their desired destination they're going to receive a bit of a shock. However, you seem to possess an honest desire to do something positive.'

'You're correct.'

'Incidentally, you may not know until the last minute where you and your companions will be joining the conflict, you may take part in various places in the campaign which, unfortunately, seems to be becoming more widespread. Any military background? Immediate family? Relatives?'

'My father was a Major in the last one.'

'Any of it rub off on you?' I have an idea it didn't.'

'No, he certainly won't like the idea of me joining your Party.'

'*Our* Party. I have some forms for your perusal and signature. Won't take you long.'

He opened a drawer in the table and pulled out two sheets of paper and handed them to Rupert who began reading the first sheet. Becoming bored with the stilted, bureaucratic language, he signed the second piece of paper without reading it.

He handed them back to his interviewer who placed them on the table top and said, 'If you've come here from the University, you could, perhaps, skip your journey to Covent Garden this evening for the office will almost certainly be closed. Just a moment.'

He picked up the telephone from the table and dialled a number. He held the instrument for a while, put it back on its receiver and said, 'As I thought. You may, of course, have arranged to stay the night locally, I don't know, but if not, there's no point in returning to Oxford and travelling all the way back here tomorrow or whenever. I'll inform them that I have interviewed you and send the necessary documents over, it should be okay.' He stood. 'If there is a problem I'll notify you. Have you a number? '

Rupert gave him the number of the phone in the quad.

'It should be alright. If I don't contact you, ring Head Office when you are ready to leave for the fray.'

They shook hands and, after Rupert had left the building, and wanting to finish the telling of his intentions to the people who mattered most to him, decided to see his mother. He caught a bus and went to the theatre in which his mother was performing.

The show had started and there were, apparently, no seats left. He told an attendant who he was, gave him proof of his identity and asked if he would inform his mother that her son would be waiting for her. He waited for half an hour after the audience left until, smiling she entered the foyer. They hugged.

She spoke first.

'If I had known, I would have arranged a ticket.'

'I know, mother, but I was in London, anyway, so I came.'

'What are you here for?'

'Let's go back to your lodgings and I'll tell you.'

In the taxi she asked him how Constance was, how Eric, Fiona and his studies were. When they were in her rooms, she guardedly asked what he wanted to tell her.

He told her what he wanted to do and did his best to articulate why. There was a silence.

'But… you'll be in danger, there'll be - '

'Horrible things. I know, mother, I don't want to talk about this with you, but I need to. I'm sorry.' He cuddled her. 'I'm sorry.'

'It's no use you saying it, you're not as sorry as I am. You're a brave boy, I love you for it, but it's so… real.'

'It's not a scene in a play is it, it's the real world. I think you understand, a little bit, anyway.'

'Your father went, and now you.' She forced a smile. 'I'm not going to say, 'Like father, like son,' of course. Have you told your girl?'

'Yes, obviously she doesn't want me to go, and incidentally, I can continue my studies when I return.'

'I wonder what your father will say. He's in the Midlands, another development project, I don't know how long he'll be there. I haven't got his number, but can find his address, I'll contact the office. If he's not back before you go, you can drop him a line.' she briefly wiped an eye. 'I think I know what he'll say, though, 'Why fight in a second class war when a first class war will be available.' He'll be thinking of Germany, of course. He won't want you to go, he'll worry about you.'

He looked at his watch, told her that he wouldn't be able to make the last train back and asked if he could stay with her.

'Of course. I don't know when you'll be leaving the country and I don't suppose you do, but if this is the last time I'm going to see you for a while, perhaps a long while, I want you to stay.'

It had been a tiring day. His mother made them toast and cocoa and they retired for the night, she to a bed, he to a sofa.

He could see that she was holding back tears when he left next morning, the image of her face staying with him for a good part of the journey back to Oxford. If he hadn't heard anything from the Paddington office by the end of the day, he would ring the Covent Garden number he'd been given and tell them that he was willing and ready to leave as soon as they thought fit.

35

He was sitting in a room at the King Street office in Covent Garden, close to where he had been interviewed six days previously, with several other men of roughly his own age, only a couple were a little older. Above more framed Hammer and Sickle motifs was a large poster of a sun-drenched landscape with 'ALL FOR SPAIN' written across the sky. He had a large suitcase with him as did the others, a few also had rucksacks, all were in casual clothes; this wasn't the sort of occasion that demanded smart ones.

Things seemed to have moved quickly. He'd received a short letter to report to the Party's London headquarters in a few days, the married couple who his mother had suggested may wish to rent his house were going to do so - although he hadn't met them, he trusted his parent - and the mortgage company had had no qualms about the debt being paid through his parent.

None of them seemed to know each other, although one of the older men seemed to want to alter this situation and, reaching his hand out to George, who was sitting next to him, said. 'Hello, I'm Paul.' He then stood and went to the person next to George and said the same thing. He then went around to the others, learning their names, and returned to his chair.

'I wonder what we're all letting ourselves in for,' he said, looking around him.

There was a momentary silence, then Bert - George thought that was his name - said, 'Whatever it is, you gotta do it, ain't yer. Fings are bad over there it seems to me. They need 'elp.'

'A man's gotta do what a man's gotta do?' asked Paul.

'Summink like that, I s'pose.'

One of the others, Allen, joined in with, 'Nationalism's okay if it's for the good of the people of that nation, But not if It's going against the wishes of the majority of the population. That's what it seems to me.'

He sounded rather educated, thought George, but it was good, he quickly decided, to have a mixture of backgrounds joining together.

There were replies of, 'You're right, mate,' 'Never a truer word,' and 'Of course, stands to reason, don't it.'

There seemed to be general agreement.

'I'm all for that,' said one of them, 'that's why I'm here, but 'though I've joined the party, it don't seem to be going so good with the Ruskies does it. I heard that one of them recently bought a car and asked when it would be delivered. 'Next year, June the third' he was told. 'Mornin' or afternoon?' he asked. 'Mornin' 'That's no good,' he said,' I've got a plumber coming in the mornin'.'

There were a few laughs, nervous ones. But then, as George was aware, they were, after all, waiting to leave the country, not knowing what was going to happen to them.

'Let's have your attention, please.'

It was a loud voice and belonged to an upright, officious-looking man with a rather gaunt, lined face and dressed in suit and tie.

'Remain seated, please.' He surveyed his audience, two of whom had begun to stand.

'Now, most of you will have just joined the Party probably as a means to an end. The important thing is, of course, that the 'end' is going to Spain to help fight the Nationalists, Falangists and the rest of the rabble - and whether the Falangismo are ultra-Conservatives or Fascists is a moot point, they're on the side of the Nationalists. As you may, or should know, it was first suggested in September last year that our Party should help the Republicans in Spain. Since then, more and more people have signed up.

'Franco is a fervent defender of Roman Catholicism, and is reversing the secularisation process that has taken place in the country under the Republic. As you know - well, one hopes that you do - Marx argues that in a capitalist society, religion plays a critical role in maintaining an entrenched inequality in which certain groups of people have far more resources and power than other groups. The bourgeoise use religion as a tool to keep the proletariat pacified.about the rich.'

'The opium of the people, sir,' shouted one of his listeners enthusiastically.

'The *opiate*,' corrected the man. He paused then raised his voice. 'Franco desires a Fascistized dictatorship. We must help stop him and his supporters. He now has a rebel army at his command.'

George was listening earnestly, as he had to the comments made before the man had begun speaking. He felt he was learning.

'Some of you,' the man continued, 'may have thought you would see a uniform or two here. There aren't. You will not see one this side of Paris, and possibly none then. That you are here as a first step, as it were, to join the conflict is not something to be shared. You must keep your intention secret.' He looked at them sternly. 'Is that understood?'

There were a few 'Yes, sir's,' coming from his listeners.

'You may be alongside many nationalities, Polish, Americans, Belgians, Canadians, there will be Russians, men from Czechoslovakia, even Cuba and, of course, the State army and citizens of the country you will be fighting in. You were informed by letter that after you reported here you would be taken to France. That is so. You will shortly leave here in a charabanc which will take you to Dover then you'll cross the channel. It's just around the corner, turn left when you leave the building then left again, we don't want people putting two and two together if it's parked right outside, do we.'

'However,' he glanced at the wall clock, 'food is served for those who wish it. Through the door there.' He pointed to it and looked steadily at them for a while. 'Good luck to all of you.' He turned and left the room.

The group, led by Pul, went through the door indicated and sat themselves on a large, rough wooden table. The food, brought to them by two matronly ladies, consisted of corned beef, mashed potatoes and custard-less bread pudding. George wondered whether this was an early indoctrination into army-type food, but, then, he thought, maybe it would prove to be luxury nourishment compared with what he may have to live on in the not-too-distant future.

'Well,' said Paul, who was the first to speak, other than the 'Thank yous' to the women for the food, 'this could well be the last taste of English food we get for a long while.'

'Probably have to get used to that fancy French stuff,' said Bert.

'Mostly frogs' legs annit?' enquired someone else.

'The French do not eat frogs' legs,' said Paul, but they do consume escargot.'

'What's that when it's at 'ome then?'

'Snails,' answered Allen.

'Fink we'd better get this down us and get on the charabanc,' said Bert, speedily pushing food into his mouth.

There was little conversation before Paul, who somehow seemed to have become the leader of the group, stood up, wiped his mouth with a napkin he'd produced from somewhere and, after seeing that those around him had finished eating, said, 'Well, let's collect our luggage and go outside then.'

The diners left the room, collected their belongings, some nodding their goodbyes to a man at a desk just inside the swing doors, and left.

They found the coach, the driver outside leaning against its door. As he saw them he opened it and, after pointing to the rear of the vehicle where the boot had been opened for larger pieces of luggage, returned inside. They stored their bags, took their seats and were driven off.

The immediate feeling for George was one of going on holiday, to Margate perhaps, Clacton, or Canvey Island, where he had his first childhood glimpse of the sea, a disappointing, long, grey line of water. But, of course it wasn't a holiday he was setting off on; he was with strangers who would eventually be with him in another land, a dangerous one.

There weren't enough of them to fill all the seats, most of them sitting separately and quietly, with Paul sitting just behind, and talking to, the driver. George watched through a window as the landscape turned from city to suburbia to country.

After a time, the vehicle slowed and the driver said in a voice that they could all hear, 'I'm not supposed to know this, but I know where you're heading, so we'll have a little stop off at a road house a coupla miles along and you can have your last drinks in England for a while. No gettin' pissed mind yer, though we won't be in there long enough for that.'

The charabanc slowed and turned into a car park behind a new building that looked, to George, with its white walls, black-painted wooden beams and pitched roof as if it was from the Tudor or Elizabethan eras. The style was, he'd noted, becoming popular and he wondered when he would see buildings like this again. He mused on what the architecture would be like in Spain and whether he would see that much of it anyway.

They got off the coach and walked through the pub's garden into the public bar. George noticed Paul and Allen begin to move separately towards the saloon bar before changing their minds and joining the rest of them. While the majority were ordering beer, Paul and Allen requested gin and it and sat at a table behind the others who had collected around one end of the bar.

George got his drink from a barmaid who reminded him a little of Enid. He didn't think of the latter for long as Allen was beckoning to him. He went across to him whereupon his companion asked him to join them. George wondered why he had done so, but wasn't displeased.

'Hello,' said Allen, 'I doubt whether you'll get ale like that where we're going. '

'Maybe you'll develop a taste for something better,' said Paul. 'I'm quite looking forward to a Cointreau. You know my name, and this is Allen.'

'George Woods.'

'What brings you to this merry throng?'

'Perhaps the same reasons as you, to… do something.'

There was laughter at that moment from the rest of the group.

'So, this junior officer gets shot and goes to heaven. At the pearly gates he tells St. Paul that he's not coming in if there are any regimental sergeant majors about. 'We don't have 'em, they go to Hell, he's told. He then sees a man in military uniform pompously striding around. 'Thought you said there's no sergeant majors here,' he says. 'Oh, that's not an sergeant major,' St. Peter says, 'that's God, he only *thinks* he's a sergeant major.'

Bert, with a big grin, and who George thought seemed a typical East Ender continued the theme with, 'Talkin' of sergeant majors, this one 'ad an obsession with cleanliness and insisted that the soldiers wore nuffink when paradin' in front of 'im. He went along the line and came to one who had an extra large 'ampton. He put his baton gently under it and lifted it up. 'I bet that's been in many a nest, soldier.' 'Yes, sir,' was the reply, 'but it's the first time it's been on a perch.'

'They're telling war jokes,' remarked Allen.

'They're telling them,' said Paul, 'to make them sound like war veterans, they're doing so because they're scared of the real thing, of what may happen to them.'

'Like mother-in-law jokes, an escape from stark reality,' offered George.

Allen then said, 'A sergeant major growls at young soldier, 'I didn't see you at camouflage training this morning.' 'Thank you very much, sir,' he replied.' Lord, *I'm* doing it now.'

The coach driver, who was standing at the bar, said. 'It's alright you making them jokes, but I was in the last lot, and I don't want to hear anything disrespectful to the British Tommy.'

'We're not really,' said someone.

'Mind you don't. Anyway, drink up, we're leaving soon, we've got a ferry to catch.'

'Perhaps,' said Allen, swigging his drink, 'it's a good thing we've got to leave, we then don't have to talk about why we're here.'

'There's possibly as many different reasons and motives for being on this journey as there are people on it,' said Paul. 'The main thing is that the collective impetus is strong and that we *are* here.'

George asked if either of them had any military experience.

'No,' answered Paul, 'but I've shot game birds on the estate of a friend's father. You?'

'I've used guns at fairgrounds, had an air rifle once and, when younger, a catapult, but doubt whether those would count.'

'Really are a novice aren't you.'

'I'm on a similar bracket,' said Allen.

'I would think most volunteers are in that position,' remarked Paul, 'but here we are.'

'Let's go then, ain't got all day.' It was the driver, heading for the door.

Quickly finishing their drinks, the group followed him into the car park with George and the other two a little behind, and clambered aboard the vehicle. George returned to his window seat whereupon Allen joined him.

'Alright to sit here?'

''Course.'

George's companion was quiet for a while then asked, 'Are you running to or running away?'

It was an unexpected question.

'Dunno. Bit of both, I suppose.'

'Perhaps you're trying to run away from yourself and are not really aware of it.'

'Could be. I don't want to talk about it, just wanna get there.'

'Like we all do.'

He didn't want to think about it; maybe he *was* running away, partly from his sense of frustration, of loss. He admitted to himself that he still felt these things. But he was on his way now to somewhere new, and certainly to do things he had never done before, 'though he wasn't sure what they would be.

'I wonder what will happen,' Allen said, as if knowing what his companion was thinking.

'I don't know. Are *you* running away from anything?'

'Sort of. Well, to be honest, from a rather dominating sister.'

'You're enlisting to get away from a sister?'

Only partly, she's rather controlling, probably because she's insecure, although you certainly wouldn't think it. We haven't a father and she virtually controls our mother.' He paused. 'I feel a little guilty really, I'm leaving my parent at her mercy, but I had to go.'

'There are other places to escape to, you don't have to go to a war,' he told him.

'I know. Perhaps I'm projecting from a domestic tyranny to a national one, but that's what appears to be happening in Spain.'

'It seems that you can't fight your sister so you've decided to battle against rebel armies.'

Allen smiled.

'Sounds ridiculous, but you don't know my sister. 'Anyway, Franco's made his Pronunciamiento, and that's it. He seems to be getting them from all over now, he's got army battalions, from Morocco at least, and with a little help from his German and Italian friends, I can see France eventually aiding him also.'

'Maybe, to a part of you, Franco's your sister.'

'That sounds rather clever.' He turned to George. 'What d'you do for a living?'

'Decorator.'

'If you can piss, you can paint?'

'There's more to it than that. And you ?'

'This and that. Why *do* people become Nationalists, eh?'

'Maybe something to do with wanting to belong, be part of a gang, and if they have a common enemy, us against them, it gives a stronger sense of belonging. I don't know.'

They were quiet then, both looking out of the window, seeing fields, trees, a farmhouse or two, some large, isolated houses and then the beginnings of a newly- built suburbia before the city streetscapes of Dover.

The vehicle made its way to the docks and to the ferry port where it halted, the driver turning to its occupants and saying, 'As I'm sure you've been told - if you haven't, you are now - this vehicle will not be joining you on the ferry, you'll be going by train from Calais to the capital, so take all your luggage with you and have your passports ready. To remind you, You're not supposed to talk about where you're going, as far as anybody who may be interested knows, you're holiday makers out for a good time in Gay Paree. Out you go then and the best of luck to yer.'

Most of its occupants thanked him as they left the charabanc and made their way to a large shed with 'Customs' writ large above its door.

The process was smooth and uneventful, although George, who was just behind Bert in the line, was surprised when seeing his open passport that its holder was not yet twenty-one. The group made their way to the ferry berthed nearby

'Did you know' - the voice was Allen's who was standing just behind him - 'that we derive our name from the old Germanic word for 'ship'? The earliest French-bound travellers were welcomed on the other side as the 'Brit-folk' or the 'boat people.' We were all 'Britons', from Britannia, the land of boats'. If you wish to know any more useless information, just ask.'

Just then Paul walked to the front of the group, turned to them and raised his hands.

'Look, briefly, if anyone asks where you're travelling to, tell them you're going to Paris, see the Eiffel Tower - '

'The Folies-Bergère,' shouted Bert.

'That sort of thing, you're going to see the sights.'

'Shall we get some balloons and paper hats?' asked someone.

'Let's not go that far, but you've got the point.'

There were some murmurs of agreement and they walked up the gangway and onto the ship.

Holding their belongings, most of them made their way to the prow. The weather was like an early spring day with a late sun lighting up the funnels, the bridge and the water beneath them. The scene reminded George of a poster for the Queen Mary ready for a transatlantic voyage. But he was going in the opposite direction, to a continent where the inhabitants at the end of the larger ship's voyage probably viewed as a collection of warring, feudal states. They wouldn't have been far wrong this time. He remembered the old line that God created wars so that Americans could learn geography.

As the gangplank was rolled away and ropes from the side of the ship dropped onto the dock, there were two loud, whistling hisses of seam and the deck slightly swayed as the vessel left its berth.

Although most of them had never left Britain before, the group seemed to get collectively bored with just looking at the sea and the dwindling Dover cliffs, and as it was beginning to get chilly they went down to one of the ship's lounges, which they had almost to themselves. With a quiet warning from Paul not to imbibe too much, they ordered their drinks and sat themselves down. Somebody asked how long it would take to get to Calais.

'It's only twenty-something miles, less than two hours I should think,' was an instant answer.

'We'll be met there. I assume,' enquired another.

'Of course,' said Allen, 'we're not going to Paris willy-nilly, we'll be taken somewhere for a medical, at least.'

'I think we should consider ourselves fortunate,' said Paul, sitting cross-legged with gin and it in hand, 'initially, volunteers had to make their way to Spain independently, which needed money of course. Our journeys are being paid for by the Comintern, we're fortunate.

'So, we're kinda being paid for getting our heads blown off then,' said a member of the group who then stood, raised a fist and almost shouted, 'Come and get decapitated for free!'

The person in the seat next to him pulled him down.

Someone turned up the volume of the music playing in the lounge, and with some slow, peaceful background sounds they relaxed and chatted amongst themselves, mostly about thing others than those they may be involved in a few days hence.

During the voyage, which took less than two hours, George discovered that Allen had been a draftsman, a trader at the Stock Exchange, and a guide at a large country house in Wiltshire. About Paul, he discovered nothing except that he was single. He knew that these two weren't typical of the group, but as he was feeling tired and a little apprehensive, couldn't be bothered to converse with any of the rest of the men.

They moved to the prow again as the vessel came into Calais, and of the hundred-and-fifty-or-so passengers, were the first to go ashore. They made their way through Customs and as the last of them left the building, a tall man in a trilby and belted raincoat approached the front of the group.

'Hello, my brave boys,' said he said in a heavy French accent. 'There is an omnibus waiting to take you to Calais-Ville station where you will get a train to Fréthun station then another to Paris. You will, however not dine until you have reached your destination. Please stay in your carriage.'

There were a few mumbled comments about 'cloak-and-dagger stuff' before Paul asked him how he knew who they were. He replied that he had been watching them since they had boarded the ferry at Dover. He led them to a stop where a bus was standing which they entered with him. It was a short, silent journey to the station where a train to Féthun was ready to depart.

Again, the Frenchman went with them, standing in the corridor outside the two carriages they occupied. The Paris locomotive had just come in when they arrived and departed shortly after they boarded it.

The carriage George sat in, with Paul and Allan opposite him, was quiet. It was as if they were, partly, still in their home country, still holding on to its familiarity, not feeling free enough to release themselves away from it.

There was an early moon and it was cold. From the carriage window George could see only the silhouettes of trees, bushes, telegraph poles and an occasional house. Some of the occupants seemed to be dozing; Allen and Paul appeared to be fast asleep. Then he heard voices from the adjoining carriage raised in song, young Bert apparently leading them.

'The ragtime volunteers are off to war. All the girls have got the blues since they heard the latest news… ' It was a World War One song that was audible enough for George to make out the words, words he recalled as a child. The sounds continued. 'They're gonna leave today, that's what the papers say, See those ragtime soldiers, left right left right… '

Perhaps he was in the wrong carriage, the wrong train, maybe he shouldn't be on a train at all, at least one to where he was heading. He thought of his house, its design, the style of it, the bricks, the French windows, its architect, its brickies, chippies. He thought of the building site job and the pub, but there were things attached to both that he didn't want to dwell upon any more. No, he was on the right train, and, they would be in Paris fairly soon.

They stopped just the once before the capital, some of the carriage occupants rousing themselves to look out of the windows to see where they were - probably, thought George, few of them any the wiser, he certainly wasn't, having scant geographical knowledge of France and the Continent. Paul began telling those who would listen about his favourite Parisian places, the Moulin Rouge, the Tower, the Boulevard Saint Michel and other attractions. Someone joined in for a little while in praise of all things French then all was quiet again until they slowly clanked into the Gar du Nord.

On leaving the train, George was impressed by the station, especially the height of its roof and looked interestedly about him as they followed the trilby-hatted man through the barrier where he briefly spoke to a member of the station staff in French. The group followed him out of the terminus, along a few streets then, at an intersection of roadss near a canal, towards a rather nondescript building. As he stood at the door ushering them in, he told them that they were in the Headquarters of the Parti communiste français.

They went into a small hall and were told to sit. They did so, spreading their belongings in front of them. They had been there barely a minute when a tall, auburn-haired, simply-dressed woman of about forty appeared on the slightly-raised area in front of them.

'Welcome to La Place du Combat,' she announced. 'My name is Rita, that's all you need to know for the present.' She had, for George, a certain glamour, whatever she wore she would have possessed it. He imagined having a relationship with her and felt instantly immature and rather small.

'You are probably aware that the movement of volunteers into Spain is now illegal. The route currently favoured, or rather forced upon us, is across the Pyrenees which involves a hazardous and exhausting climb of some twelve hours.' She paused. 'Don't look so worried, there is no need for you to undergo this, you will cross the border by a different route.' She paused again, all eyes upon her. 'I am here partly to process you volunteers and also to confiscate your money in order to avert the danger that any of you should get drunk, start brawls or become involved in them, or be lured into the neighbouring brothels.'

She looked around at them once more. 'However, as you are staying here just the one night, I shall not do so, but you will stay in this building. Now, when your names are called I want you to go through the door there,' she pointed to it, 'where you will be given a medical examination and be asked a few questions. When the process is completed you will then go into the kitchen and eat.' She gestured towards another door. She then left the hall.

George was one of the first names called and, upon entering the room, was told by a short, stocky man in a white smock and with a French accent, to strip. He did so and was briefly examined, the use of a stethoscope seemingly the most important part of the process. After he'd finished dressing, he was told to go into the next room, which he did.

A seated man, paper in hand, asked him his name then said, in a London accent, 'Okay, so you want to join the International Brigade and fight for the Popular Front because... it says here, 'to fight against tyranny'. You want to 'help the people's government stay in power,' et cetera, et cetera. Good enough reasons, though, like most of you fellows, you have no military experience. You'll learn. Well,' he gave a rather practised smile, 'that seems to be it then. You'll officially join the Brigade in Spain.' He briefly shook George's hand, followed him out and called the next person's name.

George went straight to the kitchen where he sat with the two others who had been examined and was served sausage, mash and peas by a plump woman with a heavy French accent who said, 'You English and your sausages, eh?'

It was good to be eating something familiar in a country that wasn't, which was more than he could say for a dessert of caramelized butter and chocolate; it was too rich for him. The rest of them came in at short intervals, but although sitting together there wasn't much conversation between them. It was as if they were in limbo between their everyday lives, their normal selves, and what they imagined would happen to them when they reached their destinations.

Just as they finished their meal, the man in the trilby came in and told them to follow him upstairs where he pointed out some shower cubicles then opened the door to a dormitory with thirty close-together beds and told them that they would be awakened in the morning to catch a train to the border.

After most of them had used the showers, there was little more than a few 'Good nights' between them, even Paul said little more, and they slept. For George, and perhaps others, it was a rather fitful rest.

They were woken by the same man, had a croissant and coffee breakfast and were directed to pick up their belongings and walk back to the station. They were hurried on to a train, again found adjoining compartments and travelled south. This time, George was in a carriage without Paul and Allen, with Bert telling them a few jokes and unsuccessfully attempting to create a sing-song. Most of them seemed bereft of ideas, of things to say as the compartment appeared to fill with a silent, fatalistic acceptance.

There were few stops, George having never heard of the stations, but the pleasant, wooded countryside, although lacking, to his mind, an 'Englishness', wasn't far removed, its relative flatness and occasional copse of trees emanating an almost comforting restfulness.

It wasn't a main line station at which they alighted but a smaller, rural one. A covered lorry was waiting for them outside of it. After an uncomfortable thirty-minute journey which ended at the edge of woodland, the trilby man, who had been sitting with the driver, introduced them to a figure that had been leaning against a tree as they'd arrived. He was, they were informed, going to lead them through the woods. No explanation was offered, but the man who had been their constant companion during the last twenty-four hours, doffed his hat and wished them the best of luck.

The terrain became more uneven and the woods denser. Hardly anyone spoke as they followed the man. After two tiring hours the wood suddenly ended at the edge of what appeared to be a deserted plain. The man they had been following then halted, turned, raised his arms and, in an accent George couldn't place, told them that a hundred metres to their right would be a lorry which would take them to station where they would board a train for La Mancha and that they would be told what to do once they were there.

George had heard of the region; it was somewhere in Spain. They had, then, crossed the border. He smiled to himself. They were, at last, in the land of the toreadors.

36

Rupert was gazing out of the window of an aircraft seeing clouds like cotton wool and idly wondering why people never likened cotton wool to clouds. He spotted furry chickens, horses and huge mice in them. He looked down. They were over the cliffs of Dover.

There were other young men in the aircraft, they had taken off from Croydon and had travelled from Covent Garden before proceeding to the airport. He had rung King Street and been told that no further checks were necessary. They had then contacted him by letter to give him, if he was of the same mind, a date and time to be at the office prior to leaving the country on the same day.

It had seemed obvious to him that they were there for the same reasons as himself when he'd first seen them at King Street. Some of them had introduced themselves to each other, but their general conversation had been muted and for some, non-existent. They had been called into a room where they had been sternly warned by a rather short, fat man who was, he said, standing in for someone else, that there was a chance they may not come back from where they were going, and that an anonymous private benefactor, who had expressed a wish to 'get them out there as soon as possible', had paid for the flight. 'For the Oxbridge boys', he had, apparently, said.

He thought back to his calling on Constance two evenings previously, wanting her to at least spend an hour or so with him, preferably the night. This had proved impossible; her neighbour had told her a little while before that she couldn't look after her mother any more, she was too difficult to be with. she was sorry and hoped that she could make other arrangements.

Rupert had stayed with her until near midnight - her parent often randomly wandering into the room - telling her that he was leaving in two days. Constance had asked him what he thought might happen. He'd told her that her guess was as good as his. He hadn't wanted to leave, but had forced himself to, kissing her gently and holding her close for longer than he had ever done.

He had also written to his father telling him what he was going to do and, as best he could, the reasons why. He was unsure whether his parent would quite understand, but felt it only fair that he should say goodbye in some form or other.

He had also left a note for Pym:

'I am leaving the College for a while. I have - although I would have appreciated you, against your positivist grain, of course, to have leaned, politically, a little further away from the Right - enjoyed your lectures and seminars.
Thanks.
Sincerely, Rupert Colls.'

He realised it was a rather unsatisfactory message, but felt it would do.

He had also seen his mother once more in the theatre foyer, after a Saturday matinee, and they had gone to a nearby Italian restaurant where they had enjoyed a classic aperitivo and Margherita pizza. He promised her that they would go back there and have the same meal when he returned from the Continent. He'd walked back to the theatre with her afterwards. She was quiet and there were tears in her eyes before she hugged him outside the stage door and closed it quickly after her. Their parting had been upsetting for her, as it had been for him.

The sea seemed to turn a little greyer as they neared the coast, and then came the land; the hills, valleys, villages and towns of France. He briefly stopped gazing out of the window and watched the other passengers. The person sitting next to him was immersed in a newspaper, few appeared to be talking; they looked serious, as they had done when he'd met them at the airport.

He thought of the country's capital, he had, of course, been there before, with Andrew, when he was seventeen; he felt a trace of sadness thinking of him. He remembered them wandering into the Rive Gauche bookshop on their way to Pont Saint-Michel. As they walked, they'd looked across to the Rive Droite, above which there had been some sort of air display. They'd caught a train from the Gare du Nord's Métro line to Paris Saint-Germain, dropped their bags off at a hotel and almost ran to the Folies Bergère.

He recalled that, en route to Paris, they had got off the coach at Abbeville and had negotiated the language and national currency successfully enough to order some chips, a choc ice and a packet of Gauloises. He also remembered when they had, for some reason, pretended that they were east Londoners, their Chanel-groomed tour guide calling them 'cockney sparrows' in her luscious French cadence.

He thought of being at Pont de la Tournelle and watching the Seine moving quietly and aristocratically beneath it and, hearing jazz music from a café across the street, had gone into it and stayed for three hours.

He mused on the things he had liked about Paris other than its cleanliness and order: tree-lined boulevards, their symmetrical aesthetic, slim women and insistence on salad with everything, the lack of fly-posting, advertising hoardings and the lack of American influence. What he enjoyed most, at a more satisfying level, was the normative protection the country's culture seemed to provide against the rest of the world.

He wasn't sure where this pro-French attitude came from; his mother perhaps, certainly not his father, who would refer to that country's citizens as the 'Fancy French.'

The aircraft gradually descended into Orly Airport, landed smoothly and taxied towards the large customs shed. They disembarked, but before reaching the building, the man who had accompanied them from London briefly gathered his twenty-or-so charges on the tarmac and told them that, before catching the train to Paris, to spread themselves along the platform and get into different carriages.

They showed their passports, left the airport, did as they had been instructed and arrived at Châtelet's Métro Station in Paris. Here they were told to take separate trams to the PCF Headquarters, where they were expected, and to wait in the foyer until the man who was to instruct them would arrive.

Again they did as they were told, their 'boss', as Rupert had heard one of his travelling companions call him, travelling on the second tram. The first few were ushered into a hall and instructed to wait for the others to arrive. When they had, soon afterwards, they were told by their guardian that he would, in the absence of the person who usually welcomed them, make a short speech. He told them that they would be given a medical, eat and be taken by an evening train to the border. He then produced a piece of paper, called out a name, pointed to a door and announced that the named person should go in for his examination and, upon its completion, would leave to allow the others to enter singly.

The group were quickly called for a process that took very little time. When they were seated again, the same man told them that he, and others, had read their reasons for wanting to go where they were going and were quite satisfied that they were genuine volunteers. He then took them into a kitchen where the soupe à l'oignon, cassoulet and chocolate soufflé were hungrily and appreciatively wolfed down.

Rupert was sitting slightly apart from most of the others, and opposite him was a tall, broad-shouldered man whom he'd noticed at Orly. Rupert turned his head and nodded at him.

'Hello,' said the man, picking up a napkin, 'I'm William, it's about time more introductions were made, we've all been pretty quiet haven't we.'

'I suppose so. It's Rupert.'

'Hello, Rupert, he said, shaking hands, 'we're the 'Oxbridge Boys' then.'

'It appears so. Cambridge?'

'Yes.'

'And reading?'

'History.'

'I could argue with you about that, but I won't.'

'Good.'

'It's just that I want, I suppose, some debate to wake me up. Bring me to life again.'

'Is it that bad?'

'History? Yes.'

'Funny. I meant the way you feel.'

'I would think we're all feeling rather strange.'

'It's a strange thing to be embarking on.'

'Especially, I suppose, as we don't *have* to do it.'

'Precisely, although Isuppose most of us feel we have to, including you, I suspect.'

'Indeed.'

'This was a rather jolly meal,' William said, wiping his lips. 'And what's wrong with History, anyway?'

'Well, it often seems based upon historians skewing happenings and ideologies into what they *want* to believe happened, satisfying their own theories. Also, as confident as they seem; how do they *really* know what actually occurred?'

'You're reading Philosophy aren't you. Analytic philosophy is inherently ahistorical, your thinking somehow independent of the past. You can't help yourself. I forgive you.'

They both laughed, Rupert was beginning to like this man.

'What did the student say,' said William, 'when asked if his philosophy degree was useful? He replied, 'I don't know. Was it?''

'No more cheap jokes about my subject, or I'll hit you with a fusillade of History ones,' said Rupert.

'Agreed. A truce. Did you know that it's now illegal to help people like us cross the border?' William asked

'Not until I was recently told.'

'Nor I. Ever fired a gun before?'

'Not a real one. I wonder if we'll have to wear a uniform of some kind.'

'Whose?'

'Good question. Perhaps our uniform will be not having one.'

'A raggedy-arsed army.'

'Something like that.'

'Scared?'

'Another good question. How's Cambridge, what College are you at?'

'King's College of Our Lady and Saint Nicholas, beside the Cam and facing the King's Palace in the centre of the city.'

'You sound like a tourist guide.'

'There are worse jobs.'

'Guess we're rivals, eh?'

'In the boat race, in research and other ways, bur not, one hopes, in the heat of battle.'

'A scary cliché.'

'I wonder how they'll get us across.'

'We'll find out soon enough,' Rupert replied as the 'boss man', as he internally referred to him, appeared at the door and asked them to come out as soon as they had finished their meals.

They left the kitchen, went to the hall again and were told that they would be supplied with train tickets, food packets and some French francs at the entrance desk and return to the **Gare** du Nord on the trams, then emphasised that he wanted no more than four them on any one vehicle. After arrival, he would meet them briefly inside the station's main entrance where they would travel to Canfranc **station** on the border. They would separate out into the coaches, 'ideally, one in each carriage, that way there **should** be no suspicions aroused. It will take quite a few hours to get there. There are no sleeping compartments.'

'Incidentally, Franco has ordered the tunnels on the Spanish side sealed to prevent arms smuggling. However, because of the Franco-Spanish International Convention under which it was built, the station itself remains open.' He continued. 'When you arrive, make yourselves scarce, there are a couple of cafés, don't sit together if possible,then make for the main entrance and, in dribs and drabs, follow me, it will be dark again by then. Off you go.'

They went to the desk, left and took their trams, Rupert and William In the last one. When they arrived, a train was in, the next one due half an hour later. The two went into the same carriage, which they soon had to share with some French men and women. Rather than potentially arouse any suspicion, they spoke little, although both aware that they didn't need to be quite as guarded as they had been instructed. After eating most of their food, they both, along with the others, tried, mostly unsuccessfully, to sleep.

In the early morning, the remains of their food was consumed and the rest of their time was spent by most of them largely reading and looking out of carriage windows although some of those who understood French listened, mostly disinterestedly, to the conversations around them.

Many of the volunteers were both bored, yet apprehensive by the time they drew into the border station where they congregated loosely around the boss man and then, as casually as they could, followed him quietly towards a side entrance and then towards the nearby village of Canfranc.

'You do know that we are now in Spain, don't you,' William remarked casually to Rupert as they neared the village, its street lights just coming on,

'Are you sure?' Rupert asked. 'What about customs, et cetera? This seems like some rather crazy anomaly where you just casually stroll from the station without going through customs. Perhaps there are none, I don't know.'

'There will be, but it appears that we have done it, and he's obviously done it before. Maybe the villagers who use the station use that entrance.'

'Perhaps he didn't tell us we were actually across the border because he wanted us to feel and look innocent or something. The station's an anomaly also.' He turned and looked back at its lit windows. 'Look at the size of it, the design, it should be in Paris. It looks almost Napoleonic somehow.'

'Its main building is elaborate, isn't it, it has three hundred and sixty five windows, a hundred and fifty doors and a length of nearly eight hundred feet.'

'You really *should* have been a guide.'

'I looked it up before we came, I guessed we'd go under the Pyrenees.'

'Well, it wouldn't be the Urals. It did go dark for quite a while, it surprised me that it was such a long tunnel.'

After a while, as they passed a Moderne apartment which had been built on the edge of the village, their leader informed them that a railway line was at the end of the copse of trees which they would walk by to the next station approximately five miles away. He told them to keep in single file. They were unsure why they had to walk to the station, but it seemed obvious that they would catch another train and which would arouse less suspicion than taking one from the main station.

Under the sporadic lights at the side of the track, some of the scattered group turned their heads to others with rather muted 'Things we have to do, eh?' 'What a palaver,' and 'Be glad when we're there and can have a sit-down.' Most of them looked weary, or strained, or both.

On two occasions they had to clamber onto the line as there were tall fences built at right angles from it, but apart from areas of long, tangling grass, it was a reasonably comfortable walk. As they got to the station, crossing to it by a small bridge over the track, the boss man gave them each a train ticket and telling them they were with the 'compliments of the Comintern.'

They strung themselves out along the platform of a rather ordinary-looking station building and awaited the locomotive, their leader standing quietly erect at the end of the platform looking along the line. Again, the timing was appropriate, the train arriving within minutes.

As before, they took separate carriages and compartments, the night journey taking seven hours to reach its end, a time in which most of them, including Rupert, uncomfortably slept. As they alighted, boss man gradually rounded them up and gathered them together at the platform's end. They were alone; the other passengers going into the station, there were no staff in sight.

'Alright then, you are now at Albacete Castilla-La Mancha,' their authoritative guide began, 'which is your last destination with me on board for I shall catch a return train. This is the International Brigade headquarters, or rather the Gran Hotel is, where you will be divided by nationality and language. You, because you're British volunteers will be sent to your base at the nearby village of Madrigueras where you will be given rudimentary military training before joining your comrades on the frontline. You are certainly not the first party I have enabled to arrive here and you will not be the last.'

There was silence. The man, who had throughout worn a rather stern expression, smiled at them then, bowed his head momentarily and wiped a **tear** from the corner of an eye.

'This is the part that upsets me,' he said, briefly looking down again, 'but you need to be told that this is a serious situation you are venturing into. Few of you will, unfortunately, escape unscathed. '

He looked at them steadily and said, 'I wish you well in your good fight.'

He bowed his head briefly and told them that they would be met outside the station and be given further instructions.

'Goodbye again,' he said and moved his hand in a slight wave.

Most of the group thanked him as they left the platform and made their way out of the building.

They immediately knew who it was that was meeting them. For Rupert, the man at the exit appeared the quintessential British sergeant major. Perhaps a little below average height, with a moustache that looked almost waxed, and so upright he was virtually leaning backwards, what was missing was a uniform and a baton in his hand.

'Right then,' he said, 'we are going to the Gran Hotel which is the headquarters of the International Brigade, of which you are now members, or will be when you have signed the appropriate document, and from there you'll be billeted outside a nearby village while you'll get some military training. You're here to learn to look after yourselves and learn to fight.' He turned away from them. 'Step it out and follow me,' he said firmly.

William joined Rupert as they walked at the rear of the others.

'It begins here then, the process of making us men.'

'I was about to ask you how you define 'men', but I can't be bothered, I'm weary.'

'We all are, a billet and a bed is just what's needed.'

Rupert wanted more; he wanted to know if he could handle the training, and that which would follow. Ideologies, debate, argument, the political were things that were far away from his thoughts at this moment.

37

'Right then, here's your uniforms, the Frenchies have supplied them, put them on and try to look the part.'

There were standing in front of a burly Englishman in a uniform similar to those he was handing out but with three stripes on one of its arms. They had just finished breakfast in a roughly assembled canteen on the edge of thee village of Madrigueras adjacent to the headquarters of the International Brigade in a large hotel whose architecture George didn't recognise, but guessed was fairly recently built and in a style which he christened to himself, 'Old-fashioned Spanish'. They had been ushered into it to sign a document stating that they were now part of that organisation. Few of them bothered to read it all.

It had been a long journey. The covered lorry they had travelled in had crossed the border on the flatter, eastern side of the mountains. There had been room for a few of them to lie down to sleep, the rest had slept, or tried to, sitting down. Again, conversation was stilted, they were tired.

For their train journey they had travelled in separate compartments, George sharing one with two French and four Spanish men. On the off-chance that they may have spoken some English, he attempted to speak to them, but they seemed to have as much understanding of his language as he of theirs.

They were told to return to their billet which was one of two large wooden sheds each with thirty rudimentary beds and lockers. He'd had little time to acquaint himself with the shed's poor lighting and small windows before he slept, he had seen   it all in a kind of unfriendly blur.

He took off his jacket and trousers and put on the uniform. Looking at the others, they did, he thought, look something like soldiers; the garment was, after all, fashioned from a rough, khaki-coloured material.

Paul and Allen were at the other end of the billet, as was Bert who had begun to exaggeratedly march along the aisle between the beds until the door opened and the sergeant entered, ushering them out onto the parade ground, a flat, concreted area upon which the billets stood. They were told to 'right dress', to stand in line facing towards him, stretch their right arms, touching the shoulder of the next man then drop their arms to their sides and stand upright, looking straight ahead.

'Right, you lot,' the sergeant announced, 'I want you to learn to march. You won't be doing much of it where you're going, but you should know how to. Right, copy me.'

Standing erect, he turned and, with straightened arms and wrists turned downwards, marched briskly along in front of them. He halted and marched back again.

'Looks easy, doesn't it,' he said. 'Right then, following each other in a line, try it yourselves. Quick march,' he shouted.

Positioned behind each other, they began marching.

'No!' he exclaimed, 'You put your left leg forward and your right arm at the same time, then your right leg and left arm, like you do when you walk, not the same leg and arm. There's always one isn't there.'

George noticed that there was more than one, two of them were doing it, looking rather ridiculous.

They continued to the edge of the concrete, correctly this time, until they were told to turn back. That they didn't do this to the sergeant's satisfaction was made clear when he told them to stand still and he would show them how to 'about-turn', which he did where he was standing.

'Now, get in line next to each other as you've been shown, turn away from me, take two steps and turn back as I've just done. One, two, about-turn.'

They did as ordered, some more adeptly than others. They were asked to repeat the process several times before he was satisfied. He then told them that they could return to the canteen for a short break. This they did, enjoying their croissants and coffee.

George heard Allen ask Paul what he thought of what they were doing so far.

'Much as I expected I suppose, 'though I thought that there would be more of us here .'

Bert then said, 'I 'eard the sergeant talkin' to a bloke in 'ere earlier and I think 'e was sayin' that there'd be some Eyeties comin' in to use the other billet.'

'Interesting,' said Allen, 'that the Italians, well, at least Mussolini, are on the Nationalists side yet we've got some of his fellow countrymen helping fight against them.'

'Forgive my cynicism, but I can see the French helping Franco eventually,' replied Paul, 'although they're helping us now. It's a civil war, there's splits, it's a mess, but as long as *we* know what side we're on, that's what really matters.'

'I s'pose we're sort of an army, us lot, eh?' commented Bert.

'A pretty small one, but there are others like us, perhaps it's growing into a real one.'

'You have to treat the building of an army as a political problem, a question of propaganda, of ideas soaking in,' offered Paul.

'You sound as if you're quoting somebody,' someone said.

'I am. It was said by Tom Wintringham a few months back. He was in Barcelona representing the communist party of Great Britain where he developed the idea of a volunteer international legion to fight on the side of the Republican army, the true army. It started off with about ten lads, a bit like us I suppose, it's now apparently growing larger.'

'I 'ope so,' said Bert, 'or we'll 'ave no chance.'

As he listened, George was thinking that he really should have known more about what was being talked of, read more, listened to the wireless more attentively. But he also knew that it was more than a case of knowing about things, about the situation and what was happening; it was to become a part of it, as he expected himself and the others soon would be.

He considered what he'd just thought about: a part of something. Had he ever been? His signwriting work meant that he had often worked on his own, and his art work at home had been his, not hers, and he had never been part of *her*. Even at work as a foreman, 'though he was part of a gang, he was kind of outside it, an intermediary between the governor and the men. But here - he looked around him - with Posh Pete, Allen, Bert and the others whose names he wasn't quite sure of yet, he was one of them, he had some feeling of belonging. They'd shared little more, really, than some uncomfortable journeys, and a few meals, but the feeling was growing.

The door opened, the sergeant standing there.

'Right, let's have you lot then, things to do.'

They hastily followed him out onto the concrete again where he told them to repeat their last 'about-turn' exercise. They were required to do it several times until their instructor appeared satisfied.

'Now, let's see you march again, and correctly this time.'

As they did so, George felt they were all now getting into the swing of it.

'Okay, stand at ease. I want two volunteers.'

He pointed at George and Bert.

'You two follow me, the rest of you go back to the billet.'

They went back towards the Gran Hotel, past the side of it and to the back of its garden. There was a large shed there, a new one. The sergeant unlocked a padlock and opened its door. As he went in, George took a step forward to see what was inside. He could make out stacks of rifles and some larger guns, there were metal boxes stacked on shelves, 'grenades à main' displayed on two of them, an opened box with what looked like bullets inside, and coils of rope.

The sergeant grabbed two rifles, went to the doorway with them and held them out to his helpers. George took them, whereupon he was handed two more, Bert being given the same number.

Carrying another two, the sergeant told them not to be scared of them. 'You'll soon be used to handling them. And don't call them 'guns', they're rifles.'

The three of them went back to the billet, laid what they were carrying on the first bed where the sergeant told its occupants to take a rifle each.

'You may as well learn to carry them formally and, not that you'll be doing much of it, to 'present arms.''

Out on the concrete, copying their instructor, most had difficulty with the exercise, but after a while, the sergeant seemed to moderately satisfied.

'That'll just about do, but now comes the hard part.' He pointed to George and Bert.

'You two come with me agin, the rest of you carry on practising.'

He gestured to them to follow him back to the shed. This time he brought out the box of cartridges George had spotted and a large box with the word 'Targets' written on the top of it, both of which he gave them.

They returned to the others, still practising tricks with their rifles, and, looking at his watch, the sergeant told them that they were going to be picked up in a few moments when a lorry would take them to where they would learn to use the weapons for their designated purpose.

Bert was the first to see the lorry.

'Oh, not annuver one, is it?' he exclaimed.

George had had enough of covered lorries, but he was sure this one wouldn't need to take them far.

Carrying their weapons they clambered aboard, its driver pulling the canvas down at the back so that nobody could see inside, and drove them away from the village and towards the mountains. After a silent half hour they came to some trees with some rather dense undergrowth where they stopped, the sergeant lifting the back covering and ordering them to get out and follow him.

They walked into the trees where, about fifty yards in, the sergeant told them to stop and for his two helpers to give him what they had been carrying. He took some cardboard roundels with bullseyes from the box and went over to a tree and stuck one of the targets to it with sticky tape. He then took some cartridges out of their box and gave six to each to his men.

He took a rifle from one of them and told the rest to watch him carefully. Opening its breach he inserted a cartridge, walked twenty yards from the target, parted his legs, put one foot in front of the other, lifted the weapon and, securing the butt against his shoulder, fired at the roundel. The shot hit the edge of the bullseye, eliciting a brief round of applause.

'You're not at a fairground now,' was the response and, pulling a sheet of paper from inside his jacket, called out, 'Cummings, stand next to me and do exactly as I did.'

The tallest member of the group came forward and, carefully observed by his instructor, placed a cartridge in the appropriate place, held the weapon in the correct manner and pulled he trigger. The sound was loud, as was the first shot, George wanting to put his hands to his ears, but too embarrassed to do so.

'First time you've done that?' asked their teacher.

'Yes, sarge.'

'I thought so, but at least you've hit the tree, try again.'

He did, this time hitting the edge of the cardboard. The sergeant put another roundel up, called out the rest of the names on his list and told them, in that order, to shoot at the target.

They took their turns, some more successfully than others, Bert almost hitting the bullseye at his second attempt, as did Paul. When it came to George's turn, the weapon seemed, somehow, ugly and felt heavy when he fired it, the sound, more than the recoil, seemingly pushing his shoulder back. He thought he saw the trunk splinter just above the square of cardboard. To the sound of 'Try again,' he shot once more, this time hitting the edge of the outer ring.

Their teacher then instructed them to lay down on their fronts, put their elbows on the ground and fire from that position. This was difficult for all of them, the new piece of cardboard being hit even less, though George surprised himself by making a mark not too far from the centre of the target. They were told to repeat the action twice more, most of them at the second attempt hitting the roundel, two of them, including Bert, the bullseye. They then went back to firing, standing, their ammunition running out after two tries in which two more bullseyes were scored.

George and Bert, as directed, gathered the squares of cardboard and any spent cartridges they could see, put them into the back of the lorry, the trainee riflemen following, and with the sergeant on board and the back of the vehicle covered, they returned to the billet.

Once inside, as they sat on their beds, Paul was the first to speak.

'We'll have to have more of that before we leave here, I'm sure.'

'I seen some bigger guns in the shed,' remarked Bert, 'dunno wevver we're gonna use 'em.'

'They won't be there for decoration,' somebody said.

'I don't know about you chaps,' said Allen, 'but I don't fancy firing hot metal into flesh and blood, I prefer cardboard.'

'We may well have to, it could be a case of you or him,' said Paul.

'But if we don't stop the Fascists, then it could mean more and more people dying.'

'We have to kill to stop the killing?'

'Something like that. I suppose most wars are the same.'

'Dunno about you blokes,' said Bert, but I quite enjoyed it out there.'

'You seemed to be okay at it,' another pointed out.

'Well, me dad bought me an air rifle when I was a kid, 'though I ain't used it fer years. How d'you get on?' he asked, turning to George.

'Well, I suppose I got a little better as it went along, but... I wouldn't have wanted the target to be somebody's head.'

'When we get where we're going, it may well be,' said someone else.

Listening to them, George wasn't sure what he felt. He'd begun learning, learning something new, being educated, in essence, to shoot accurately at something, eventually at people, that was the reasons for the lessons, the end product. While the others talked amongst themselves, he lay on his bed, thinking.

He hadn't expected it to be like this, really. He knew they had to be trained, and there was more to come, but not quite like this, but then he hadn't known what to expect. The sergeant knew what he was doing, he must do. Perhaps some of the others saw it just as shooting practice, nothing more, like a firing range thing, shooting for shooting's sake, that it was an end in itself, not a means to an end. No, they wouldn't have experienced it like that. He wasn't sure. He would have to do the best he could and wait to see what would happen, as would the others.

He wondered briefly if he was being cowardly. He didn't mind staying where he was for a while, though he still felt strange sleeping so close to other people, a thing he hadn't done since he'd gone camping with the school in the summer holidays, but to go on and be embroiled in real fighting, to be in danger... he could hear a boy from his class, after George had said he didn't want to jump from the top of one set of railings to another when they were playing above the sewer near his home, shouting, 'Cowardy, cowardy custard.' But they were kids.

He heard somebody ask what a 'civil war' actually was, upon which Paul answered with 'A violent conflict within a country fought by organized groups that aim to take power at the centre or in a region, or to change government policies.'

'Know-it-all,' somebody said.

'Sounds rather like what we're going to be involved in,' said Allen.

Bert joined in with, 'Anyone fancy some grub then? Fink the canteen's open.'

As they went out to it, George glanced at the other billet and thought he saw the sergeant through one of its windows; he'wondered where he was doing.

He didn't enjoy his gazpacho, garlic was odious to him, though some of the others, particularly Paul, it seemed, did. They remained where they were for some time, talking of what they'd seen of the locale, village, the country - although only one of them had been here before - the weather, which was warmer than it would have been back home. With a few of them talking of personal things; parents, girl friends and, in a few cases, their wives, two of them having children, they kept away from discussing what was currently occurring in the country, not that they knew much of what that was.

Their sergeant appeared at the door and announced that he wanted them to get to bed early as the following day, when they would be wearing their civilian clothes, after more shooting practice, he would be taking them on a march where they would be supplied with backpacks in which, as well as flasks of water, they would put in some stones and small rocks to help them get used to the weight of the things they may have to carry in action.

'I've got a couple of packs of cards for you to keep you occupied before you turn in,' he told them.

He gave them to Bert who had enthusiastically stepped towards him. George played Spades and Gin Rummy without much interest. Later, as he lay trying to get to sleep, he pictured the words, 'into action'. It could mean many things. He saw an explosion, large wads of earth scattering around it, a body... He briefly pushed his face into his pillow and pushed the images away.

The same vehicle picked them up the next morning, their weapons already on board, again the sergeant sitting with his men. Before their practice, he pointed to several places on the ground between the trees where there were stones to put in their packs which the driver had produced from his cab and handed to the sergeant who then distributed them. George filled his pack over halfway before deciding it was heavy enough.

He enjoyed the firing exercise a little more this time, hitting the inner ring twice and actually scoring a bullseye. After they had returned the rifles to the lorry, the sergeant removed the tarpaulin sheet lying behind the cab to reveal a collection of larger, heavier guns. He told them to come to the tailgate whereupon he handed them out.

'This,' he announced, 'is the **Labora Fontbernat** submachine gun. It has a high rate of fire, a thirty six rounds box magazine and an effective range of more than two hundred **yards**. It's **locally made** in Catalonia and also bloody heavy. I want you, after watching me demonstrate its use, to spread yourselves in a semicircle about forty **yards** away from the target.

He lay down, attaching a bipod to the barrel and fired. It was a short burst that almost ripped the target off the tree trunk.

'Take half-a-dozen rounds each from the box, which one of you may well have been sitting on. It'll be a short burst.'

They took the required number, loaded their weapons in the manner shown and spread themselves out, laying with their guns as instructed. The order to fire was given. The noise quite startled George, almost sixty small missiles released simultaneously. It was probably the loudest sound he'd ever heard. He looked at the tree; lumps of its bark had been torn off, the target gone.

'That's gonna do you for now, at least you've fired it, and maybe there'll be other chances to do so. Put them and the bipods back in the lorry, get **your** packs on and, when you're done, follow me.'

They did as ordered and, in a single, straggly line, left the trees and began walking on the flat land, the sergeant, with an obviously light backpack, leading.

George thought he had finished thinking of Enid, apparently he hadn't, almost automatically imagining himself pointing out a distant, lone building, its turrets suggesting to him a religious establishment, a monastery maybe, he wasn't sure. He looked at the distant mountains, he wouldn't have drawn her attention to those, there was little to say; mountains were mountains, they weren't designed and constructed by men.

He was getting used to the feel of his backpack when Bert came up behind him.

''ow did yer get on wiv the big gun,' he asked.

'It's got quite a recoil.'

'S'pose we'll 'ave to get used to it, eh? Lots of uvver fings, too.' He smiled. 'Furthest I've been away from 'ome was Canvey, me mum and dad booked a bungalow there when I was a kid, ain't bin since, bin to **Southend**, o' course.'

'Wherever we go in this country it's not going to be like the Kursaal.'

'No, don't s'pose it **will** be. Why you 'ere, anway?'

'Why are *you*?'

'Me dad left us 'bout three years ago, and me mum's got a boy friend livin' wiv us now. He's **all right** I s'pose, well, 'e would be if 'e 'ad a brain, but I don't get on wi'im really, 'though I felt I couldn't leave me mum, gotta be loyal, 'aven't the cash to move out and get a place, anyway.' He looked briefly around him. 'So, I thought I'd do me bit, as it were, like you I s'pose. It's a kind of proper reason to leave 'ome for, It upset mum, but I told 'er I'd be **alright**. **D'you** fink they've got a post office 'ere? Like to let 'er know 'ow I am.'

'Wondered about that myself. The sergeant'll know.'

'e seems an alright bloke, really, don't 'e.'

'Where are you from? Stepney?'

'Born and bred.'

'I'm George, incidentally.'

'I know. D'yer speak any of the local lingo? I do. No te entiendo, Lo siento, no **habla español**.'

'What's it mean?'

''I don't understand', 'I'm sorry', 'I don't speak Spanish.''

'Impressive. Shame about the accent.'

'Me mum told me to learn it, thought it might come in 'andy.'

He pulled his backpack up a little. 'Fink I'll be quiet **for** a while, I'm feelin' knackered already.'

'I think this is the Iberian Peninsula, good job we're not gonna walk all the way around it.'

'Gimme the Genesis picture 'ouse, the Blind Beggar, and the Royal London any day.'

They walked silently on. After almost an hour their leader halted, turned and said, 'That'll do, march yourselves back again, I'll stay behind you, you shouldn't **get** lost. And incidentally, when we return, You'll be provided with some pesetas, you'll probably need them.'

They made their way back, the few trees acting as landmarks, and there was always the mountain range. Before they got to their billets, Bert asked the sergeant if there was a post office in the village, he was told that there was. Once in **their** billet, half of them pulled sheets of paper from their belongings and began writing. When they had finished, the sergeant appeared with several small cloth bags and gave them out. Don't lose these will you,' he remarked, 'and those of you writing home, I advise you not to mention all you've been doing.'

It was an appropriate time to receive the local currency, the writers then walking to the village and, finding the appropriate store, posted their letters. George had merely told his mother that he was in Spain, was well and had done some basic training, not mentioning the weapons.

After their meal, the sergeant told them that they should have another early night as first thing there would be some exercises to do on the parade ground.

Most of them slept well after their walk and, after breakfast, went outside the billet and, in uniform, did some on-the-spot running and other exercises including several short sprints to the edge of the concrete. George likened it to being back at school doing PT.

As they were finishing, they heard a phone **rang** from inside the other billet, the sergeant going to it immediately. He appeared after a while and told them, with some urgency in his voice, that they were to gather their possessions as quickly as they could for the lorry would be here any moment to take them further into the Peninsula to 'begin doing what you came here for'. George wasn't quite sure what to make of this announcement, but knew that something rather important had occurred.

A short time later, as they climbed aboard the lorry which had just halted in front of them, George saw a group of men **walking** towards the vacated billet. They were carrying cases and rucksacks and were in civilian clothes. They looked rather posh, not like most of the lads he'd been with for the last few days. The timing appeared uncannily accurate, but perhaps, initially, this lot were supposed to occupy the billet the sergeant had used. But the one in which George and the others had stayed in was now empty; they had been called away, **apparently to do** something they had come all this way to do.

38

As they walked around the edge of the village, Rupert and his group saw uniformed men leave what looked like a large shed and climb into the back of a lorry which drew quickly away. For a fleeting second one of them seemed familiar. The officer, who had travelled in the same train, told them to go into the nearest billet and find themselves beds. He went into it and dropped his case on the first bed, William doing the same on the adjacent one. After placing what belongings they could in the lockers, the majority sat on their beds.

'I think the army call them 'pits',' said one, looking down at his bed.

'Well, here we are,' said another. 'What happens now?'

'We're going to get trained, of course' said another, 'we're going to be made men of.'

'Fighting machines,' suggested someone.

'We obviously need to learn something,' said William, 'we're greenhorns, rookies.'

The group were made up of roughly the same number of students from both universities. From what Rupert could ascertain they seemed to have split almost fifty-fifty on beds either side of the aisle. There was some rubbish to clear away, the previous occupants, it would seem, having being called away suddenly.

Their officer entered and suggested they get themselves something to eat in the canteen, pointing out that they must have noticed the rather ugly hut as they walked through the village.

'You must, be pretty hungry,' he suggested in his quietly spoken, mellifluous voice.

He seemed, to Rupert, a rather gentle man, but one who wouldn't gladly suffer fools.

They found their eating place, ate their pizzas and ice cream until replete, although some of them who had visited the country before, had expected something a little more exotic. They played a guessing game of what their basic training would consist of, most of them seeming to think it would be twenty percent firing guns and eighty percent marching.

'That's why it's called 'square-bashing',' said someone. 'Let's go back.'

As they entered the billet, William said, 'Did you hear that at one Army base the annual trip to the rifle range was cancelled for the second year in a row, but the bi-annual physical fitness test was still on as planned. One soldier apparently mused, 'Does it bother anyone else that the Army doesn't seem to care how well we can shoot, but they're very interested in how fast we can run?'

Their officer, Captain Gerrard, who was standing just inside the doorway, spoke.

'I've heard better. Listen up. I'm afraid that no uniforms have been left for you, but you're not here to join the Coldstreams, if their absence makes you feel you're of less value, you're wrong. There'll be all sorts of people alongside you wearing their working clothes. Some of you just may have brought some things to amuse yourselves, but I've put a chess kit and a Monopoly board on one of the lockers and also a few packs of cards so you can play Bridge to your hearts content. In the morning, early, you start learning. Sleep well.' He went out and closed the door.

Most of them played the games, a few of them watching a game of chess between opposing University students, Rupert content with Bridge and Whist. Afterwards, they slept until awakened by their captain calling them for breakfast. There was more local food to be had in the canteen before they assembled outside their temporary home where a lorry was awaiting them. The driver was female.

'Good Lord, what's a woman doing here?' was one comment. 'Perhaps she's just helping out, she won't be put in danger,' was another.

'I think you'll find, Gerrard said, 'that this conflict is, possibly, helping remove the influence of the Catholic church in defining men and women's roles, especially on the Republican's side, *our* side.' He made a brief gesture towards the vehicle. 'I'm sure she would be happy to agree, but I don't think she understands enough English. Let's get into the lorry.'

They did, some of them, Rupert felt, feeling a little insecure with a woman driving. It wasn't long before they halted, helping themselves, as instructed, to the rifles under a tarpaulin in the vehicle.

The lorry had stopped at the edge of some woodland. Rupert looked at the driver as she alighted. She had black hair and shadows under her dark eyes. He hoped that she wouldn't be caught up in the war. He thought of Constance, imagined her behind the wheel casually and competently controlling the vehicle, perhaps smiling at him encouragingly when she saw him. He would write to her and his mother soon.

The shooting practice went rather well for him, he thought; he'd done at least as well as the others. It had felt alien, but he knew that he had to get used to it. Their was no point thinking of the economics of war, of the manufacture of armaments; the large profits that were made, and that small conflicts were used as trials for the effectiveness of military products so more could be sold for larger wars. The armaments existed, they were here, now; he had just used one of them.

'You haven't finished,' the officer said.

He had a box of cartridges in his hands which he held out to them.

'Take five rounds each and fire in the same order as before.'

The way he was holding the box, it could have been full of sweets, thought Rupert. They discharged their bullets; Gerrard replacing the roundels after each of them had fired.

'That was a little better,' he said. 'Incidentally, you're not going to do much marching drill, you can all walk and run and you're not, at the moment, in a formal military organisation.' He paused. 'I want you to know this, however. I am obviously Army, retiring recently from the Royal Engineers, actually.' He looked steadily at them. 'I came out of retirement for this. Also for you.' He paused again to let what he'd said sink in.

'Another thing. I had a call an hour ago that we are going to where the fighting is as of now, or rather, when the lorry picks us up. This message was, apparently, supposed to have been passed on to me by the sergeant in charge of the men you saw leaving when you came here, they had been using your billet, let's not blame anyone.'

'I'm Sorry you've had hardly any preparation, but it can't be helped. Return the weapons to the lorry and when back in the billet gather your belongings and wait there.'

There were some murmurs of understanding and a few 'Yes, sirs' before they turned to climb back into the lorry.

'However,' he continued, halting them, 'there may be a delay as the route could be subject to alterations, I'll get information back in my billet. You may just have time to let your loved ones know you're alright. I did notice an oficina de correos at the near end of the village.'

They returned to the vehicle but not before Rupert noticed the sad-eyed driver. She caught his eye and smiled. He smiled back, briefly feeling a little lighter.

Their officer stayed with them in the lorry again and when their trip ended they went to their beds, gathered their possessions and deposited them outside their billet. They were then told that those who wished to should send their letters and return quickly. He went to the cab and came out with small packets containing pesetas which he gave to them.

Most of them hurried to the post office, some running. Rupert bought stamps and envelopes, he had paper with him. He leaned on a shelf and began:

'My Darling Constance, I miss you, but I'm glad you are not with me, for your good of course, not my own. We have done some training and are now, it seems, going into action. I feel that I should tell you this. But I shall be alright. There is no time to say more, I shall write to you again when I can. I hope your mother is no worse. Much love, my dearest. Rupert.'

The next was for his mother.

'Dear mother,

This has to be a short letter as we are, I believe, off to action. I am aware that this is sudden and a bit of a shock for you, as it is for me, really. But there it is. I am well and we've been training so I'm not as unprepared as you may think. I hope your show is going well. Love, Rupert.'

He was about to write a short note to Eric, but realised that he was the only member of the group let in the shop, the rest making their way back to the billet. Posting his letters, he moved quickly after them.

They stood outside with their bags and cases watching Gerrard looking southward to see if he could spot the lorry. There was a tenseness. William turned to Rupert and said quietly, 'I've never fired a weapon before.'

'Nor I, it's got quite a kick.'

'Shouldn't think it'll be the only one we'll have to use, especially if we land up alongside the Spanish army. We'll need to use all sorts of things, I dare say. There'll be peasants involved in some of the battles I should think, they'll need to be trained up, too.'

'Wonder what that would be like for a woman?'

'There'll be females involved in this war and they'll be using arms.'

'You think so?'

'They can be politically angry, too, especially when it comes to their government being potentially overthrown.'

'Maybe their husbands will influence them.'

'They may have minds of their own, you know.'

Rupert thought of Constance and his mother. Most women weren't like them, but then, other than these, he had known only a few. Was he, almost automatically, thinking like his father and aping his attitudes towards, and opinions of, women? He rejected the thought instantly. His sweetheart and his mother had, he knew, understood the ideological reasons for his being here as well as the emotional ones.

Everything was political; someone once said that water was. Perhaps they meant that it divided continents, countries, states, or, perhaps, that the water we drink is supplied by companies who inevitably do so with the intention of accruing profits.

The captain brought him back to the pragmatism of the present by looking earnestly at is men and telling them, firstly, the obvious, that the lorry hadn't arrived yet, and then stating, 'You should know this, that the Nationalists attempt to dislodge our lines along the Jarama - it's a river to the east of the capital - has failed, no breakthrough was achieved. But before you cheer, the Brigade's fight-back gained nothing either, counter attacks, likewise, failed. There have been heavy casualties on both sides.'

For Rupert, the words had a slightly unreal quality; it was like listening to a news bulletin on the wireless in his room at College about some distant conflict in a foreign land, a place that had nothing to do with him, an irrelevance. But he was becoming part of this news. He felt that he didn't want to be. He shook the feeling from him, he had volunteered to come, had a while ago made up his mind, had decided what he would do and had done it.

Just then the lorry came onto the concrete and stopped. Gerrard went to the driver as she left her cab. She pointed to the nearside wheel. 'Lo sienbto, tuve un puncion.' 'Puncture?' he asked. 'All fixed now? Reperado?

'Si.'

'You have the guns? Pistolas? The food?'

'Si.'

'Good.'

She then leaned towards him, gesticulating earnestly and speaking, from what Rupert could ascertain, for the most part in Spanish. Gerrard nodded understandingly and the driver went back to the cab. He turned to the men again.

'There was a puncture. More importantly, the battle has moved away from Jarama and we are now going to Guadalajara.'

He looked at them silently for a while.

'I'll let that sink in. You can talk about it amongst yourselves, I'll travel in the cab.'

He parted the tarpaulin sheet, dropped the tailgate and they climbed into the vehicle.

They sat quietly, now knowing where they were going, 'though at least they had a name.

'Where the hell is Guadalaraja?' asked Cummings.

'The Central Plateau,' someone replied.

'Where's that?'

'The Iberian Peninsula.'

'We're *in* it. As large as it is, it shouldn't take that long.'

'Why do you think our admirable captain isn't sitting with us?' asked Cummings.

'If you had the choice between being with us or the dark-haired señorita which would you choose?' another asked.

'Depends on your sexuality.'

'Well, the captain's certainly no bum boy.'

'Does this stuff really matter?' asked William. 'In a few hours we may be using weapons we've just learned to use against people we've never seen in a place we've never heard of.'

'That sounds like a rather neat definition of 'war,'' Rupert said.

'This is so much trivia,' said William, 'an escape from what we've got to do.'

'Does it matter? Cummings asked, 'We've still got to do it, we're on our way there now in case you haven't noticed.'

'No need for sarcasm,' pointed out someone, 'we've got to be friends, have to stick together, we're going to need each other.'

'It's true,' said Rupert, 'it's what the captain would want, perhaps why he left us alone, so we'd have this sort of conversation.'

'He's got quite a lot on his hands,' suggested Cummings 'he probably wishes he'd never come out of retirement.'

'I must say,' said another voice, 'that I'm beginning to miss the old alma mater, I shall feel very differently about it when I'm back there.'

'*If* you get back,' murmured William.

There was a momentary silence.

'Sorry, I didn't mean it quite like that.'

'Like what?' Brutal?' someone asked.

'I meant - '

'You meant exactly what you said,' interjected Cummings. 'It's quite rational, we all have to face it, as hard as it is.'

The absence of sound, except that of the vehicle's engine, continued until William asked, 'Did you hear about the Spanish-speaking magician? 'For my next trick, I will disappear on the count of three. Uno, dos - ' But then he vanished without a tres.'

As well as the groans there was some rather high-pitched, nervous-sounding laughter, as if the joke had brought some relief to the darkening atmosphere of the lorry's interior.

'What do you get,' he continued, 'when you sit down in a Spanish field?'

Nobody answered.

'Gracias.'

There were some more groans then Cummings said, 'If you don't **stop** it I'll insist we talk about cardinal numbers, dynamical systems, differential equilibrium and ask you to solve the **Poincaré** conjecture.'

'Don't you just hate maths?' William asked.

There was silence again. It carried on until they stopped.

Gerrard opened the back flap, lowered **the** tailgate and told them to get out, pass the cab in line where they would be given packets of food which they would consume in a nearby copse of **trees.** They were handed out by the driver with what Rupert thought were rather forced smiles. They ate their food which, to him, tasted very Spanish, exaggeratedly so, but something like roast lamb or spotted dick, although comforting, would have been too much a reminder **of** home. As they were returning to their transport he looked ahead and saw that the road had began to climb towards **the** Plateau.

After almost an hour, Rupert thought he heard the sound of guns. It came from the direction they were travelling towards, to the city of their destination

39

The journey that George and the group took meant that they would be amongst the first members of the International Brigade to reach Guadalaraja, or so their sergeant informed them when they were within twenty miles of the city. This made George feel - although he was aware that it was rather ridiculous - a certain responsibility, as if, somehow, after only a few hours training, he and his compatriots should attempt to uphold the Brigade's honour.

They had stopped at a village inn on the way, their boss telling them that the natives were friendly and that their food would probably be provided for free, which it readily was. They had mostly sat on one side of the vehicle, the other occupied by their sheeted weapons.

The sergeant sat with them, his conversation other than telling them that their rifles were their best friends and that he, unfortunately, hadn't had time to teach them to strip and reassemble them, consisting mostly of telling them that they must do exactly as they were told, whether they were orders from an officer or himself.

George wondered whether the things he had felt, the emotions that had propelled him here, were - he couldn't quite articulate it - the real ones, the right ones. Momentarily, he had a feeling of blankness, of being lost. But he was, he reminded himself, now here, and so were those around him, some, he supposed, he knew better than others, but they were now his mates. What did they call them? 'brothers-in-arms'. That's what they were.

When the vehicle stopped, Bert, rifle in hand, was the first to leave it, jumping from it almost before the sergeant had dropped the tailgate. The others followed quickly. They were on the edge of the City, there were some trees and a few streets of houses before the main buildings and office blocks began, there were also other men with weapons. Two were on the balcony of one of the nearest houses and two partly hidden in a nearby tree. One of those on the balcony shouted 'Benvenuta', and in a thick Italian accent, another yelled, 'Spread out, they are in that building.' He pointed towards it.

Their own sergeant told them to take cover where they could find it. They needed no second telling. As George lay down behind the nearest tree, he could see Paul and Allen take cover at the side of a house. Bert, with the sergeant and some others, hid at the side of a car.

George heard the first shots he had experienced other than when the group had been practising. One of them smashed the windscreen of the car; another ricocheted off its bonnet, while another thudded on the ground in front of the tree. George looked up at the building whose third floor windows were open with a trace of smoke across one of them. George almost intuitively pointed his rifle at it. A face appeared. He pulled the trigger. As the weapon recoiled, the side of the man's forehead seemed to disappear, the body dropping to the floor.

He heard, 'Well done that man.' It was the sergeant. 'Let's get inside there,' he shouted. The group, rifles in hands, ran behind the sergeant into the building. George didn't move. He had shot someone, had killed a man.

He tried to explain the situation to himself. 'In the heat of the battle' seemed utterly inappropriate. There had been no heat; he had seen just a face, now part of it had gone. He saw the sergeant who, spotting George, shouted at him to get inside the building.

He didn't want to, not wishing to see the body. The sergeant shouted at him again. George reluctantly ran to the building and went inside. He heard a shot and then Paul's's voice saying, 'That's the other one, there were only two, I think. It's okay now.' George stayed where he was until their sergeant, with Paul and the others, came down the stairs, Bert wiping his mouth and looking as if he'd just vomited.

The sergeant led them outside. The Italian, who had spoken to them before, was now outside the ground floor of the house along with the others who had been in the tree.

'We have a van, we should go further into the centre of this place I think, to help to stop them capturing all of it. Follow.' His accent made it difficult for them to understand.

George assumed 'them' were the enemy.

With the sergeant leading, the group followed the Italians to the corner of a nearby street where a large van was parked.

'It will take all of us. I am Matteo.'

He opened the back doors and beckoned them inside. When they had squeezed in, he said, 'I know you are uncomfortable, but, sergeant, I want you and your men to listen to me. Some divisions of the Corpo Truppe Volontarie have attacked our positions outside of the city. They are now advancing. It is slow, but they will be here soon enough.

'There are tanks coming along the main road into the city, many of them. What we are hoping is that our Italian aircraft will attack them.' He paused. 'Yes, it is a crazy world, Italians attacking Italians, Spanish fighting Spanish, but it is that kind of war.'

They piled into the van. George, trying to assimilate what they had been told and wedged against the doors, could see through their windows ordinary civilians in the suburban streets, though not many. There were a few groups of men, some carrying rifles and pistols, most of the buildings had all their doors and windows closed.

'What are we supposed to do against tanks?' he heard Bert ask.

'Very little,' replied Paul. 'By the way, Mister Woods, you hit a *real* target this time, well done.'

'I'm not proud of it,' said George quietly.

'You could well have saved a life or two, we were sitting ducks.'

'Yes, well done, lad. Good thinking,' said someone.

'Hear! Hear!' said Bert, and gave a little clap. A few of the others briefly joined in.

There was a part of George that wanted to shout at them, 'You're applauding me for blowing part of a man's *face* away?' He didn't, he continued looking out of the windows as they drove on, uncomfortably and in silence. He saw more streets, buildings and less people. The outside world seemed silent.

He found it hard to believe what he had just done. He felt that he had murdered someone and that at any moment police cars would surround the van and he would be dragged out and taken away. The vehicle stopped, it hadn't travelled far. He saw Matteo go towards a small office block and knock loudly on its door. As it opened, the Italian said something to the figure who had stepped out in front of him then turned and gesticulated to the van's driver. 'Out,' he shouted, and as the group vacated their transport, he pointed in front of him and went into the building.

They followed him in; it seemed deserted except for the man who had let them in. They went up the stairs to the top floor where the Italian was talking with their sergeant. The **latter** told them to go to the windows and see if they could spot any armed men.

'Some of the Spanish army, it seems, have turned rebel. We don't know whether they will be wearing their regular uniforms. See what you can see.'

They went to the various windows, George seeing no-one except a woman with a child hurrying into a block of flats, the rest of them reporting nothing As the others turned away from the windows, Bert stayed. It was he who first saw the tanks. There were just the two at first, the leading one on a pavement, the other in the middle of the road.

The other men went to the windows again. It had begun to rain. They saw an unarmed man come out of a doorway, possibly to see what the noise was, but before he could get back inside, the first tank knocked him down and ran over him. It didn't stop.

Then more came around the curve of the road, one of them firing at the building opposite where the group were. A large section of its ground floor fell away, part of the floor above it falling. The sounds added to **George's** turmoil.

He could see more tanks coming, some on the pavements, as if they were attempting to get around those in the road. The building that had been hit suddenly collapsed with a roaring cloud of dust and debris, some of it falling on two of the machines, halting them. More tanks came and had to stop abruptly as their drivers saw the impediment ahead.

He went to one of the other windows where he could see, beyond the curve of the main thoroughfare leading into the city, even more tanks. They seemed to be gradually stopping.

Then they heard the aircraft, the sound becoming louder as they came lower. There was the sound of rapidly firing guns as they flew over the tanks. George saw some of the furthest tanks explode and then the nearer ones as the aircraft gunned and bombed them; smoke beginning to fill the sky.

The noise was shattering; some of the group lay on the floor, their hands over their ears. George kept watching, looking up and seeing the planes veer away, climb higher and then back again, swooping lower. More tanks caught fire, more exploded.

'Get out now' Matteo shouted at them, 'Go to the back of the building.' As they hurriedly descended the stairs, he said, 'If we see any of the tank crews alive, we must shoot them.'

'Come on,' the sergeant yelled, 'move.'

They ran down the stairs, pushed open a fire exit door and went into a deserted car park with trees at the rear of it which the sergeant ushered them towards. Some of them stood behind the tree trunks. The sounds of the aircraft's guns reached a crescendo, and there were further explosions, some near, some further away, as more tanks were destroyed.

A man appeared around the side of the building and ran towards them, the trousers on his left leg on fire. George moved away from his tree to go to him; maybe he could somehow extinguish the flames. He didn't go far, Matteo shooting at the man, who dropped immediately. George turned back, pulled up some of the undergrowth, ran to the body and threw it over the flames, trying to stop an instant cremation. Bert pulled up some of the long grass and part of a bush to help quell the fire.

He looked up at George.

'Why are we doing this?' he asked.

'Just… just seems the right thing to do.'

He knew that, sometimes, bombs and shells didn't always explode on impact and wondered what it would be like if a round from an aircraft pierced a tank and ricocheted forever inside of it. It would reduce its inhabitants to pink spawn. He looked back; the others were still sheltering under the trees with the sergeant. Matteo was now standing at the other side of the car park.

The sound of aircraft receded, and there was little noise from the tanks.

In this relative silence, George began hating war. It felt like a cloak of loathing had been draped over him, sliding inside of him, pulling at his guts. He ran to the side of the building to get into the road, maybe he could help someone. Anyone.

From the corner of the building he saw a tank turn from a side street into the main road, there was little space for it to manoeuvre, the tanks, some of them ablaze, filled the road. This was an errant one that had escaped the bombardment. The turret swivelled and a fierce acceleration of smoke issued from its gun barrel as the booming sound filled the air.

Above him, the edge of the building was smashed away, lumps of concrete scattering over the ground. George felt a jagged pain at the top of an arm. He gripped it, dropping his rifle, felt blood creep over his knuckles. He stood for awhile, then, feeling faint, he fell.

He lay on his back and felt his grip relaxing as he looked at the sky. It was cloudy, but had stopped raining. He turned his head and saw a gaping hole in the side of the next building; saw the debris still settling and heard another shell fired from the tank. He then heard the faint noise of engines becoming louder. He looked at the sky again, saw the aircraft return, they were coming nearer and lower. He thought he saw a salvo of bombs fall from one of them. He wanted to shout, 'I'm on *your* side, don't drop them on *me.'* It all felt so ridiculous, surreal. He started to giggle, 'though unaware of doing so. He felt the blood run down the hand that was squeezing the wound.

Images of Enid floated into his mind: the way she pulled pints, her small hands gripping the wooden lever behind the counter, that look of competence and slight boredom interrupted by a smile as she looked at him across the room. His arm was hurting now, he didn't want to be here any more, he wanted to be with her, in Hampstead, Brakenbury Village, or Edwardes Square, or gazing at a buttress on a Highbury church, noticing a shop awning in Ealing, Putney streets, the Arts and Crafts of Noel Park, a soft-focused, gentle, vivid montage of small excitements and peace along canal towpaths, roads… a trunk load of observations and feeling. What he felt mostly now was the pain; it had spread to his shoulder and down his back.

He tried to push it away and think of his mother and his childhood home; playing street games with his mates, the knife grinder and scissors sharpener who used to knock on the door every few weeks, and the miniature roundabout that came down the road with children, and sometimes an adult, whirling around on it. He saw the Italian man pushing his red-and-white ice cream barrow along the road and children playing eagerly around it and following it until the end of the street gorging cornets and wafers. He could almost taste them. He could taste blood too, it seemed to be filling his mouth.

He thought of his house, his home; he seemed to see the butter-flies he'd painted fluttering in front of the mural as if they were trying to land on the green reeds, of fluttering above the horses pulling a chariot, of trying to settle on the head of the Pharaoh on his throne... he felt something near him and heard his sergeant's voice, 'Get something to put round this for Chrissake'

A little after, he felt, or thought he felt, something being wrapped around his arm and shoulder. His hand felt wet. He looked at it. It was red, covered in red. Then all turned black. Then there was nothing.

40

As Rupert and the group drew nearer the city, the sound of guns gave way to the crackle of rifle fire. Their vehicle stopped. Gerrard instructed the men to get out and to keep to the sides of the road as much as they could. There were trees on the pavements and a bus stop where they had halted. They hurried to the nearside of the road and crouched against a building. They could see a thin cloud of dark smoke hovering ahead of them. Gerrard told them to move nearer it, keeping tight against the buildings. There were no passers-by.

Moving forward around a curve in the road, it was William who first spotted the mounds of metal. He pointed, his mouth silently open. There were flattened tanks, black, scorched ones, jagged bits and pieces of them, twisted lengths of burnt tracks, overturned gun turrets, as well as the occasional limb; a foot, a leg, and scorched corpses, shattered bodies.

Rupert wondered what had done so much damage. It could have been field guns, he supposed, but although there were damaged buildings, surely anti-tank fire would have caused more destruction. He guessed that it had been aircraft that had played the major part in causing such carnage, coming in low to hit their targets accurately. He wasn't sure.

He saw some movement amongst the motionless pieces of metal. There were a few soldiers dressed in khaki with berets pulled down the side of their heads and carrying long-barrelled pistols. Gerrard informed the group that they were the Republican Army. They were, seemingly, picking through the industrial and human debris.

He looked at it all again, it was an aftermath; this particular battle was over, won by the side he was on, or supposed to be on. He wondered why he was here, why he had come all this way to… do what? This was mass murder. He was surrounded by it. He wasn't a military being, a reflex of conditioning, of a training that suppressed any doubts about what one was doing with a weapon in his hand and pulling a trigger.

He felt suddenly like a dispassionate onlooker, a detached observer of a meaningless scene of death. He'd had a desire; it had felt like a commitment to help quell an attack on democracy. Was he, perhaps, intellectualizing the whole thing? What was 'democracy'? There were so many forms of it; delegatory, participatory. It was a kind of abstraction where people were manipulated into who to elect from a choice of limited, flawed options. And what was 'nationalism'? A wish to belong, to be part of another abstract concept, one where a desire for more power for a powerful few had led to what was lying all around him.

He heard their captain's voice; he was talking to one of the soldiers. Rupert was uncertain what language he was speaking, but they obviously understood one another. Gerrard briefly clasped the arm of the man he was talking with and returned to the group.

'We are not needed here,' he said, 'it seems to be over.'

'What's over, sir?' asked one of the group.

'This particular battle.'

'But there are others,' another said, 'What about the capital? we're not far from it.'

'We're not, but it's besieged, man, you should know that.'

'Perhaps we can get into it and do some damage on the way.'

'And then *be* besieged? It seems illogical. We need information. Let us get into one of these buildings; there will be telephones, unless they are cut off.'

He went to a front entrance and thumped his fist against the door repeatedly. There was no response. He turned his rifle around and beat hard at the door with the butt until a panel gave way. He put his hand through the hole and opened the door. He ushered them in and up the stairs to the first floor.

It was an utterly innocuous incident. Rupert happened to be the last of them to reach the first floor, and as William turned to say something to him his arm caught Rupert lightly on the chest just as he was about to place his foot on the floor. It was enough to cause him to lose his balance. He fell backwards heavily, his thigh hitting the edge of a step then rolled down to the landing. It was a small one and didn't halt his fall down the next flight of stairs. Hearing his own shout of pain, he tried to suppress it, an image of his father telling him when he was six to 'be a brave soldier', sliding into his mind.

He came to a stop on the next landing. Most of the others rushed down to him.

'Rupert!' William was shouting as he bent over him. 'I'm sorry if that was my fault. Oh, Christ!'

Rupert couldn't move at all without pain in his hip and down his leg.

'Where does it hurt?' It was Gerrard.

Rupert laboriously pointed to his hip. He could feel his tears.

'To state the obvious, this man is hurt rather badly. He needs a hospital, try to comfort him.'

While William and the rest made attempts to comfort the man who had fallen, Gerrard made his way through a door from which he shortly returned to say that the phones were down.

 He put his hand inside his jacket and produced a map of the city. He spread it out on the floor and after a brief, crouching, perusal, said, 'There's a hospital back along the road we came, let's hope it's been left alone, or our side have it. You're going to have to carry him to the lorry.' He paused a moment. 'Damn, she's probably still there, I should have brought her here. Lift him carefully and take him downstairs' He pointed to Cummings. 'You're in charge.'

He hurried past them as they carried Rupert down the stairs.

As they went towards their transport, they could see Gerrard in the cab talking to the driver, he had an arm around her shoulder, obviously comforting her. She was nodding, apparently saying that she was alright. He climbed into the lorry and joined in the lifting and, after jackets had been placed on its floor, Rupert was laid on them.

He wasn't sure where he was, but it didn't matter, the pain pushed everything else aside. Before they reached the hospital, he fainted. He came to as he was being carried into an emergency department where he briefly saw some Republican soldiers before being put on a stretcher and taken to a white-walled room. He saw a nurse bent over him and passed out again.

He awoke, in somewhat less pain, in a ward. It was empty except for an elderly man on an end bed. The same nurse gave Rupert something to drink, after which a man in shirtsleeves and wearing a green apron, informed him, matter-of-factly and in an English accent, that he had suffered a dislocation of a hip joint which had now been corrected and that there would be no permanent damage. He was also heavily bruised. He had been given something to ease the pain.

'You must rest for a while, you certainly cannot return to what you were doing. Incidentally, I am also a volunteer, I came here to help the hospital.' He paused. 'The tanks could easily have turned their guns on this place. We could see them pass.' He looked out of the window at the side of his patient's bed. 'We were lucky, I suppose. We have,' he said quietly, 'two injured tank crew in another ward, it could well be that they were the only survivors from the machines. Enemy or not, I have to help them. You will be given regular doses of morphine. You will be looked after for the short time you will be here.' He walked away. 'Good day to you.'

Rupert wondered where Gerrard and the group were, they had obviously brought him here; he hoped they were safe.

He would have to return home, he was now, supposedly, not fit for duty. He hadn't even begun to fight for anything or anyone, and was now being retired from active service, or rather, non-active service.

Noticing the ward's only other occupant looking across at him, he drowsily raised a hand. The man energetically pointed to his mouth and ears and vigorously shook his head. Rupert assumed that he was informing him that he was deaf and dumb. He would, he suspected, have no company for the next few days except short visits from a nurse.

He had heard that volunteers did things other than fighting on the front line, they worked in engineering, medical and other capacities, but he wasn't qualified for those things, for anything, really, except some sort of admin work, but then, he couldn't speak Spanish. It would also, he mused, be a rather pointless activity telling anyone who cared to listen to accounts of the various sociological models of the world and the strengths of positivist philosophy. He would rather leave, go back, he was of no use here.

He felt rather a fake, an imposter. He wanted no one, other than the two people he had written to, to know what had happened to him and how it had occurred. If pushed, he would tell them where he had been, but that was all. He had done nothing of any significance, of any real meaning.

He hoped that he would be able to return by train, but it didn't really matter how he got home, he would be with Constance again, and he would see his mother, Eric, the College, Oxford, even Pym. But mostly, he would be with his girl.

For no apparent reason he thought of the man who he had seen as he was about to board the lorry by the billet at the village and who had seemed familiar to him. Then he remembered. He had met him once. He was the man who had bought one of his father's estate houses at Ash Park. He wondered what had happened to him, what he was doing now.

EPILOGUE

George Woods's body was transported home by sea, as were the bodies of many other International Brigade volunteers. He was buried in West Ham church, not far from where he had grown up. His mother never really got over the loss of both her husband and only son in different wars. She was a regular visitor to the latter's grave until she died at 89 years of age. She sold her son's house to the married couple that had initially rented it, the husband eventually distempering over the mural.

After her break-up from George, Doris married an airman who worked at various RAF bases around the county during WW2 until, after several unsuccessful attempts to get him to see if he could arrange to settle at one particular base, she left him. They had no children. She lived on her own, rather unhappily, for the rest of her life. She died at the age of 77.

Enid met and married a Welshman, an elecctricain, who she met when she was visiting her father on one of his decorating jobs. They had two children, both boys. She recalled occasionally the walks she'd had withy George, but not often. Familiarity and security appeared increasingly important to her, and her and her husband, as well as their children, often spoke in their native tongue wit each other. She returned to advertising as a copyrighter for a few years until the birth of her offspring.

Reg hadn't known that his friend had gone to Spain. He had changed his own mind abut going, unsure why he had thought of it at all. When he was told, after accidentally meeting George's mother, that her son had gone, he was rather hurt that he hadn't bothered to tell him. He often wondered why he had gone.

George's group fought in The Battle of Brunete near Madrid. The sergeant, Bert and Allen were the only survivors from the group.

The inquest that was held over the death of the man who fell from the scaffold on the Holborn building site found that it was 'Death by misadventure'. No action was taken against any employer. Safety regulations stayed the same for many years. Nobody bothered to carry on the local branch of the painters and decorators union George had started.

Mister Bishop left the pub in Holborn and became manager of a hotel in Bath where he regularly attended services at the local church.

Rupert didn't send a letter to Constance, knowing he would arrive on his train journeys back to England, before it. He was eager to see her. When he did so, he almost injured himself again when, in their joy at seeing each other, Constance clasped him so firmly they fell on the hall floor. They spent the night together, temporarily locking her mother in her room. Constance eventually did accept Rupert's financial help, reluctantly placing her parent in a care home where she stayed for six years before dying of dementia.

Rupert's old room was available and he resumed his degree. After gaining it he taught at a private school in Oxford before returning to his old College to lecture in Philosophy, later, to his surprise, becoming a professor. There were the occasional ideological spats with Pym, who had grown more conservative as he'd aged, until the latter retired. Bertrand Flavin, the English Literature lecturer continued making the same jokes to new undergrads until he, too, retired.

Rupert and Constance married, living in an Oxford suburb, and had a son, Barry. She worked for the Women's Liberation Movement and for the Women's Employment Federation. She continued to work part-time at the Bodleian Library. Despite her husband's encouragement, and for reasons best known to herself, she never studied for a degree.

Mercia Colls appeared in several more plays in London's West End, her most successful playing Lady Saltburn in 'Present Laughter' and Ruth Condomine in 'Blithe Spirit.' She died at 91, her later years made richer by her relationship with Barry, who later became a Labour MP for Watford North and a member of the Cabinet. Her husband, after developing two more housing estates in Greater London, died several years before her. Although disagreeing with the Republican agenda, he was, although not admitting it to anyone, least of all his son, rather proud of what Rupert had done. His development and building business was sold after he died, the proceeds being shared equally between his wife and son.

Eric and Fiona Pullis bought a tudorbethan house near Rupert and Constance and eventually had twin girls, Cora and Fleur. Rupert was pleased to be their godfather. Eric went to work for his father and took over the business when his parent passed on. Fiona sometimes acted in local amateur theatre productions, watched on one occasion, and to her delight, by Rupert's mother. Cora became a fashion designer, and Fleur the first female assistant editor of The Daily News.

Rupert didn't see Alex, Edward or Thomas again, nor, despite the occasional feeling of disloyalty and missing the good times they'd shared, did he see Andrew who remained in his father's business and became its president when his parent retired. He never married; preferring to spend much of his recreational time entertaining male friends. He never saw William again, who, along with Gerrard and the others, also fought in The Battle of Brunete, only Cummings surviving. Gerrard was awarded a posthumous International Brigades medal for destroying a Nationalist machine gun position single-handedly before he was killed.

The Spanish lorry driver lost her hand when the lorry she was driving for the International Brigade overturned into a roadside ditch. She married an English volunteer and settled in her home town of Toledo. They had no children.

The tanks destroyed by Republican aircraft found in the traffic jam on the main road from Guadalaraja to Madrid were the mechanised spearhead of the Italian voluntary Corpo Trupp Volontarie who were thrown back with casualties in the thousands. It became known as the 'Italian debacle of Guadalajara.' One of its long-lasting effects was that the Italian Army of the Mussolini dictatorship acquired a reputation for incompetence that never left it before the armistice of 1943. Republican forces enjoyed an increase in recruitment as a result of the victory.

Between October, 1936 and the summer of 1938, some 35,000 men and women from around the world made the journey to Spain to join the Brigades, with as many as 2,500 of them coming from Britain and Ireland. Initially, volunteers made their way to Spain independently, but following the decision by the Communist International in 1936 to organise international volunteers, the role of the national Communist Parties - in particular the PCF in Paris- became crucial both in the recruitment of volunteers and getting them to Spain. To many people's surprise, 95 percent of volunteers were manual workers.

Memorials for those who fought the tyranny in Spain still exist in cities in the UK.